The Left Seat

Read aboard United Airlines flights 950 and 951 from Dulles International to Brussels, Belgium on 12 and 15 Oct 03.

Stephen J. Nichols

Books by Robert J. Serling

The Electra Story

The Probable Cause

McDermott's Sky

When The Airlines Went To War

The Presidents Plane Is Missing

She'll Never Get Off The Ground

From The Captain To The Colonel

Only Way To Fly

Something's Alive On The Titanic

Stewardess

Wings

Howard Hughes's Airline

Legend and Legacy

Air Force One Is Haunted

Loud and Clear

The Left Seat

ROBERT J. SERLING

B.D. King Press

Dayton, Ohio

2002

All of the characters in this book are fictitious, and any resemblance
to actual persons, living or dead, is purely coincidental.

*To Captain Rod Coston and
Stewardess Supervisor Clancie Henderson of
American Airlines,
this book is gratefully and
affectionately dedicated.*

The Left Seat

Chapter 1

His name was McDonald McKay and before entering a door marked CHIEF PILOT, he hesitated.

He had the somewhat corny but nevertheless very real feeling he was about to cross more than a literal threshold. Being that rarity in men, a sentimentalist who also was a realist, he acknowledged the corn but refused to shrug off the feeling. After all, on this day of January 5, 1946, he was indeed crossing a threshold. He was about to become, he hoped, an airline pilot.

A pilot he already was, or had been. Up until three months before, it was Captain McDonald McKay, United States Army Air Forces. And at this particular moment in his life, he wished he still had on his uniform. It would have made him feel a little less like a routine job applicant, trying to walk the tightrope of eager sincerity versus the nonchalant indifference of a man who was doing the corporation a favor just by applying.

He had never regarded his Air Force uniform as a "my country owes me a postwar living" symbol. Orphaned in his teens and reared by an uncle in Columbus, Ohio, he had led a prosaic, rather lonely life even through college. His commission and his wings were his first real accomplishment, and the war his first real test of ability under pressure. If he suddenly yearned for the prestige of his twin silver bars, it was merely a grasping for the confidence and pride they had radiated.

Aviation had been his chief interest since boyhood. He had wanted to learn how to fly a plane before he had learned to drive a car, but a flight lesson was eight dollars an hour and his uncle was just slightly to the right of being poor. His parents, killed in an automobile accident, had left him nothing but a legacy of knowing right from wrong. In his junior year in high school he began doing odd jobs around the Columbus airport and wangled a few flight lessons from a sympathetic air taxi operator who took a liking to the eager youngster.

He never really expected to have a pilot's career. By scrimping and saving he managed to squeeze out enough flight time to obtain a private license but the financial obstacles of going on to a commercial or airline ticket were too great. A good student, he earned a scholarship to Ohio State and chose aeronautical engineering not because he particularly relished this phase of aviation but because he reasoned it was the closest he could get to airplanes until he could afford to continue flight training.

He didn't enter college until he was twenty, because he worked in a gas station for two years after graduating from high school to build a modest bank account. He took ROTC at State and when World War II came along in his senior year, he had no trouble picking a branch of service. He joined the Army Air Forces the day after he got a degree in aeronautical engineering—and even at that stage he knew he had no intention of becoming an engineer.

For a while McKay thought he would stay in the service. The notion of airline flying did not occur to him until the war was almost over and he began thinking of a civilian future in more optimistic terms. He liked the responsibility of military flying, but not its formalized discipline, and this is what started him thinking seriously about the airlines. Also, in a negative sense, he was admittedly not very interested in anything but flying—a restless fate common to so many airmen who won their wings before any other kind of career had jelled. He had written Midwest Airlines a couple of months preceding his discharge, receiving in return a noncommittal letter and employment application form. The latter brought back an answer noting his considerable multi-engine experience and suggesting an interview with Personnel at the airline's Washington base.

Midwest sent him a pass for the flight to Washington and on the DC-3 that flew him to the capital, McKay's notion of an airline job had solidified from vague restlessness into practical ambition. A lot of little things had done it. The salute of the ramp agent as the DC-3 rolled away from the gate. The captain's easy, friendly cabin PA announcements en route. Even the stewardess had contributed to a new determination. A trim, tiny brunette mixing no-nonsense efficiency with sex appeal, she had noted his nonrevenue status, had adroitly drawn from the quiet McKay his future hopes, and had whispered a discreet but friendly "Lots of luck" as he got off. In just that brief encounter and on the two-and-a-half-hour flight he had sensed the camaraderie that makes an airline flight crew a breed apart, and a pilot's career a professional way of life instead of just a job.

After the interview he had gone through a platoon of tests that recalled his military examinations mostly by comparison. No Air Force doctor had spent the time on him that Midwest's physicians had as they prodded and poked. The battery of intelligence, aptitude, and psychological tests were almost obscene in their thoroughness. After this gauntlet, the silky-voiced man in Personnel had given him the usual "You'll hear from us, Captain McKay"—a remark which McKay would have interpreted in the same spirit as a "Don't call us, we'll call you" kiss-off, except that he knew he had done well in the interview and tests and he felt confident.

This was not conceit. If anything, he was somewhat oversensitive and sensitivity is not a handmaiden of conceit. But since boyhood McKay had had a kind of dignified self-introspection that seemed both to admit and to analyze his faults without giving him an inferiority complex. In a way, this ability to self-criticize merely added to his confidence when he knew he was in command of a situation. It was mildly exciting but no surprise when the telegram arrived.

CONGRATULATIONS. YOU HAVE BEEN ACCEPTED FOR FIRST
OFFICER TRAINING WITH MIDWEST AIRLINES. CLASS TO
START JANUARY 7 1946 IN WASHINGTON DC. PLEASE RE-
PORT TO CHIEF PILOT JOHN SHEA ROOM 12 HANGAR 6
WASHINGTON NATIONAL AIRPORT 8:30 AM JANUARY 5.
CORDIALLY F J TERHUNE PERSONNEL DIVISION.

Now he was standing before the door of Room 12 in Hangar 6. He was twenty-eight years old, an even six feet, one
hundred and seventy-three well-muscled pounds, had light
brown hair cropped to almost a crewcut, gray eyes, was single,
and wore the gold "ruptured duck" of World War II screwed
into his lapel.

He was handsome in a totally masculine way. He smiled
rarely but when he did his eyes smiled with his mouth and
the recipient always felt bathed in warm sincerity.

McDonald McKay opened the door of Room 12 and
crossed the threshold. It was a sparsely furnished outer office
into which he entered, after glancing at his watch to make
sure it was exactly eight-thirty. For quite a few more years
he was to live by the dictates of a watch, but on this occasion he wanted merely to be punctual.

The only occupant was a woman in her late thirties or
early forties, attractive without being beautiful, her graying
hair carelessly combed. She was typing a letter but looked up
as McKay approached her desk.

"Yes, sir?"

"I'm McDonald McKay. I have an appointment with ah,
Captain Shea."

He had almost said "Mr. Shea" but instinctively assumed
that chief pilots must be captains. As if reading his mind,
the woman smiled.

"I'll tell Captain Shea you're here," she said. "I understand
you're going to join us."

"Yes—ma'am," McKay said. He had wanted to say "Miss"
but he had noticed the gold band on her left finger and decided that his intended little touch of flattery was silly. Be-

sides, a woman her age would resent being called Miss as an assumption that she was an old maid.

She smiled again, got up from her typewriter, and disappeared into an inner office. McKay, being a normal male, watched her and noted that she had trim legs. Invariably it was the first thing he looked for in a woman and he suddenly remembered, with wry nostalgia, that his B-25 squadron mates used to rib him for going steady with an extremely flat-chested English girl who also had lovely limbs.

"Ole Mac's a leg man, not a tit man" was his bombardier's inevitable and eventually wearying crack.

The door of the inner office opened and out came the woman, followed closely by a barrel-chested runt of a man with a shining bald pate and a loud tie that must have been cut out of a surrealist painting.

This, thought McKay, must be Shea. He was frankly surprised, assuming that in addition to holding the title of captain, chief pilots closely resembled Greek gods. Shea looked as if he'd have trouble reaching the rudder pedals on a Piper Cub.

"I'm John Shea," said the little man. His handshake was like a vise. "Have you met Mrs. Gillespie, my secretary?"

"Not formally," said McKay. "I'm glad to know you, Mrs. Gillespie."

"Best goddamned secretary in the airline," Shea proclaimed. "Come on into my office, McKay, and we'll have a talk."

Shea literally disappeared behind his huge desk, emerging in reasonable view only by leaning back in his chair and surveying McKay with frank, sharp blue eyes. He lit an obviously well-smoked briar, puffed contentedly for a good five or six seconds, and started rummaging among papers and folders on his desk.

"I've got your file somewhere around here," he said. "Just wanna go over a few things with you."

McKay glanced around the office. There were a few pictures of Midwest planes around--a DC-3, a DC-4, and a brand-new Constellation. Directly in back of Shea hung a small picture frame surrounding a motto that read: AN AIRPLANE IS A COLLECTION OF SPARE PARTS FLYING IN CLOSE FORMATION. McKay couldn't repress a smile and Shea grinned, too.

"Mrs. Gillespie found it someplace," he explained. "Gave it to me framed for Christmas. More truth in it than poetry. Here's your file."

He opened the brown manila folder and perused the contents, nodding now and then as if in agreement with whatever it contained. "Good war record," he observed. "About four thousand B-25 hours. Like the plane?"

"She's a tough bird. I guess I like tough airplanes. Honest, too."

Shea grinned and McKay liked his grin. Shea's face was the proverbial map of Ireland and his smile was quick and natural, warm and sincere. The chief pilot also had the disconcerting habit of turning it off suddenly like a faucet. He looked seriously at McKay.

"I like pilots who are tough and honest, McKay. Not only honest with the company and me, but with themselves."

McKay wasn't quite sure what to say. He just nodded.

"McDonald McKay. I suppose they call you Mac?"

"Yes sir. I never had any trouble acquiring a nickname with those two handles of mine."

"I don't believe in being formal with my crews," Shea said. "It's Mac to me from now on—including when I'm chewing your ass out. Which may be frequently. I think modesty is a bunch of bullshit so I might as well let you know I'm a better pilot than anyone flying for me. Which, I might add, makes me a good boss."

"I had a tough CO in the squadron," McKay said. "I don't mind a tough boss if he's fair."

"You a good pilot?"

McKay wondered at the motive of the question, but hesitated only a second.

"I'm a good pilot, yes sir. I'm not a great one. I don't think I'm what you'd call a natural-born flyer. I think the best I can offer you is that I'm a careful pilot."

Shea chewed the stub of his pipe. "You love flying, Mac?"

Again McKay wondered if the chief pilot was fishing for answers that might disqualify him at the last minute. But he decided honesty was the best course to take with a man whose face looked so damned honest.

"No sir. I like flying. I like it a lot. But all of it's been in wartime and I don't know anyone who could say he really loved airplanes in the middle of a war. I got scared plenty of times—maybe it was getting scared of being shot at, not being afraid of an airplane, but you asked me if I loved flying and right now I'd have to say no."

"Why the hell do you want to be an airline pilot?"

McKay had the uncomfortable feeling he had said the wrong thing. But Shea turned on the faucet again and chuckled.

"Relax, Mac. You don't have to love the business to be a good airline man. Hell, I've got about nineteen thousand hours and I still sweat out every landing. Controlled crash, like they say. Nope, I honestly want to know why you want in."

"You may think the reasons are a bit screwy," McKay ventured.

"Nothing's screwy coming from a pilot."

McKay at that moment envied Shea the relaxation of his pipe and thought he must take it up. Sort of a crutch to lean on when formulating difficult answers to difficult questions. Puff on it or chew it while your mind is computing and composing the right thing to say.

"I could cite money," McKay said slowly. "I know the salary's good after a few years. But that wouldn't be the whole story. For one thing, flying's about all I know. I've got a degree in aeronautical engineering but I don't think I'd make much of an engineer. I just about scraped through college.

I had my fill of the military as such. I didn't resent discipline but I got damned tired of it."

"About discipline," Shea commented. "You won't be entirely without it in this job."

"I know that. But I think it'll be a kind of self-discipline more than anything else. And that brings me to the biggest reason why I applied. I just hope it doesn't sound phony."

Shea's sharp eyes told him to continue. McKay felt like asking him to hand over his pipe. He lit a cigarette instead.

"Well," he said, "I've always had, well, you might call it a devotion to responsibility. I like being responsible for somebody or something. That's what I liked best about the war. The guys in my crew, they always looked up to me not in the sense that they made me feel I was playing God . . . they just depended on me more than on themselves to get them back. I think knowing that made me a better pilot. Like I said, I couldn't rate with some of the guys in ship handling. I was more mechanical than natural. But I had this thing about being responsible to my crew. It affected my flying. It affected my decisions."

He paused for a moment, both to marshal new words and to watch Shea's face. He didn't want the chief pilot to think he was trying to sound noble or virtuous. As a matter of fact, what he had said surprised himself. He had never put these thoughts into exact words before, even though he had sensed their presence as one senses a religious or philosophical belief.

Shea's simultaneously homely and pleasant face wore a slight smile on the corners of his lips.

"Go ahead, Mac."

McKay won a few more seconds for transforming thoughts into words by leaning forward and snuffing out his scarcely smoked cigarette.

"I guess that's what I figured would be best about the airlines," he said. "Someday I expect to sit in that left seat again. I'll have the same sense of responsibility toward a bunch of trusting passengers as I did toward my crew. Maybe 'sense of responsibility' sounds corny. Maybe I should say 'duty.' Maybe there isn't even a word or words for what I'm trying to say. I guess it's almost intangible, this feeling. Like trying to describe the color red. I know what it looks like but how the hell do you put it into exact words?"

Shea refilled his pipe and looked at McKay's folder without even seeing it. "Something like the father image," he suggested. "No, don't knock the father image." McKay had started to say something in protest. "It's nothing to laugh at. I sure as hell don't deride it. It's a very real thing. It's real with passengers as well as pilots. Most people are scared to death of flying. They put a helluva lot of faith in that guy up front. Whether you call it father image or what, damned if I know. But it's been a part of aviation as long as I've been in it."

"I don't consider myself a father to anyone flying with me," McKay said. "That's almost like thinking you're playing God."

"Mac, what the passengers feel is the father image. When a pilot responds to that, he's admitting that the image has touched him, affected him. Maybe his response is the sense of responsibility you talk about . . . that sense of duty. Whatever it is, for my dough it should be as much a part of an airline captain as his uniform or his ability to handle a plane or read instruments."

"Well," McKay said with an embarrassed laugh, "I didn't expect to undress emotionally in front of you."

"I'm glad you did," Shea said seriously. "Any sonofabitch can be taught to fly a transport. But not every sonofabitch deserves to fly one with passengers on board. Now, any questions? You got a place to live yet?"

"I'm checked in at the Willard," McKay said. "I hadn't thought much beyond that."

"We've got a couple of leads for a temporary apartment," Shea informed him. "You'll have to share it with a couple of other guys in your class. Nothing fancy, but no point in getting too settled."

That sounded ominous, McKay decided.

"After we get through with our talk, wander around for an hour or so. Two more new men are coming in and you can go out with them to look at one of the apartments. Anything on your mind?"

McKay pondered for a moment, then shook his head. "I've got a few hundred questions," he admitted, "but I suppose most of them can wait till classes start. I did want to ask . . . well, skip it. It'll keep."

"Go ahead," Shea urged.

"I've heard I have to join a union—airline pilots' group or something, is that right?"

"Any objections to a union?"

"No, I just never gave it much thought. I don't have anything against unions, I guess I just never figured on joining one. I don't know a damned thing about this pilots' outfit."

"You don't have to join ALPA, but about 90 per cent do. It's your own decision. I belonged when I was flying the line. I'm management now so I shouldn't say this, but the Air Line Pilots Association does a helluva lot of good. It's won a lot for pilots that had to be won. Don't let the union label fool you. ALPA's a professional organization just as much as it's a labor outfit."

"Okay, no anti-union prejudice," McKay said with a grin. He got up to leave but Shea motioned him back in the chair.

"Mac, I'm inactive in ALPA now . . . can't be a union and company man at the same time. So maybe I'm a little off base giving you some advice. But you were talking about a sense of responsibility. Let that govern your union membership as well as your flying. I don't give a damn how wild-eyed you get about salary and maximum monthly hours and all that. Too many pilots figure a union is just that—just fight with management and screw the company. Okay, ALPA does exist to get more benefits for pilots. So a lot of members go to meetings only when they've got a contract renewal coming up and they want ALPA to know they want theirs.

"That's fine. Pilots should be interested in what their union is negotiating for. But if ALPA ever becomes just a labor outfit, pilots are gonna become nothing but goddamned bus drivers. Safety—that's what pilots should be interested in. As long as you're gonna be a member, work with some of ALPA's committees . . . Air Traffic Control . . . accident investigation."

"Accident investigation." McKay repeated the words as if savoring the taste of a rare brandy. Shea looked at him curiously.

"You know something about it?"

"I did some work in the war on it," McKay replied. "Served on a couple of investigative boards. Funny, but until just now I thought there must be something sadistic or perverse about liking that kind of stuff. I wouldn't even admit I was fascinated by it. I didn't know pilots, airline pilots I mean, got involved."

"Up to their asses," Shea said bluntly. "When one of our birds goes down, ALPA's as much a part of the investigation as the airline or the company that made the plane."

"Trying to prove the pilot didn't goof?" McKay asked, and instantly regretted the sarcasm. But Shea merely shook his head.

"Sometimes," he said quietly. "Maybe too many times. But usually trying to find out *why* a pilot goofed."

Both men were silent for a long moment. Shea got to his feet and stuck out his surprisingly large hand. "Didn't mean to deliver a sermon," he said. "Get the hell out of here. I'll talk to you later. Like I said, come back in about an hour and meet some of your new playmates."

Again McKay rose. Shea walked around his desk and slapped McKay on the back as he escorted him to the outer office.

"Come back in an hour," he repeated. "Hi, Barney."

The last was addressed to a tall man in a Midwest pilot's uniform, four gold burnished stripes on the sleeve and dull gold wings on the chest. A real live airline captain, thought McKay. And a veteran, if the crow's feet around his eyes were any indication. The captain had been sitting on the edge of Mrs. Gillespie's desk but unwound almost languorously when McKay and the chief pilot entered the outer office.

"Hi, Johnny," he said in a surprisingly high-pitched voice. "Got something on my mind if you're not busy."

"See you right now," Shea said. "This is McDonald McKay, late of the Army Air Forces. He starts pilot class Wednesday. This is Captain Robert Barnwell, Mac. Lousy pilot, but he makes a helluva good cabin PA announcement."

The old and the new shook hands, somewhat warily, as each man gave the other a brief inspection. As he had with Shea, McKay liked the older man instinctively.

"Welcome aboard, like they say in the Navy," Barnwell said. "Hope you'll be flying with me one of these days."

"I hope so, too," McKay replied. "I know I've got a lot to learn."

"What were you flying in the Army, B-17's?"

"B-25's."

"Good airplane, from what I hear. You shouldn't have any trouble with a DC-3."

"From what I hear, they fly themselves," McKay suggested.

"Not quite," Barnwell chuckled. "Anyway, I'd never admit that to Shea. Always make a chief pilot think you're earning your dough."

"On your way," Shea told McKay. "Come on in, Barney."

"Good luck, McKay," Barnwell said with a smile.

"Thank you, sir."

The "sir," McKay thought, might have sounded like a little bit of brown-nosing but he figured Barnwell wouldn't take it that way. He watched the two men go into Shea's office and he heard Barnwell's high-pitched voice rise almost to a falsetto.

"Goddammit, Johnny, when I tell maintenance a ship

trims lousy, it trims lousy. . . ." The door of Shea's office slammed shut.

McKay grinned and wondered when and if he'd reach the pinnacle of self-assured authority that would prompt similar outbursts. He nodded to Mrs. Gillespie, who was looking at the door to Shea's office with a kind of resigned "Well, here we go again" look on her face.

"See you later," he said, and walked out.

The Midwest offices were on the second floor of Hangar 6. McKay walked down the corridor and glanced curiously at the tiny signs on the doors. PLANNING AND OPERATIONS. PUBLIC RELATIONS. COMMISSARY. STORES. FLIGHT PLANNING —he could hear teletypes through that door.

The other side of the corridor was mostly a series of big windows, overlooking the actual hangar space below. McKay paused to watch mechanics working on a Midwest DC-3, its nose removed to reveal an almost indecent glimpse of wires and tubing. There was something about the intricate innards of an airplane, denuded of shiny metal covering, that instilled in McKay a kind of sadness. Like seeing a supposedly beautiful woman suddenly bereft of makeup and looking unexpectedly, shockingly disheveled.

He observed the mechanics for a few minutes and remembered his own crew chief in England, a happy-go-lucky, pornography-mouthed little Italian with a four-letter vocabulary and a genius for diagnosing the aeronautical ailments of a B-25. Sergeant Lavelli had cheerfully regarded all officers except McKay with an irreverent lack of respect, but he had referred to McKay as "my captain," and had frequently given him such oblique praise as "He ain't like the rest of those chicken-shit pilots."

His flight crew also had obviously liked him, McKay recalled with satisfaction. He had worn the cloak of Command Authority with dignity, firmness, and yet tolerance toward the men who had depended on him. The thought of them suddenly bothered him. He admitted that he would find himself looking up to men like Shea and Barnwell with the same total sense of dependence that his men had shown toward him. He wondered if he ever again could achieve such unquestioning—well, what would you call it—loyalty? Hero worship? Maybe it was that damned father image Shea had talked about.

McKay fought off an almost inexplicable surge of loneliness and maybe a touch of jitters. The same way he had felt on his first night at Officers Candidate School. A tiny needle of fear that maybe he wouldn't cut the mustard. He decided he was being asinine. He had no illusions that what lay ahead wouldn't be a challenge to himself both as a man and as a pilot. But he had made it through the war, for which he would always feel grateful. He had never been particularly religious, but the day he had left for overseas he had said a quiet prayer. Something like "God, if You'll pull me through this, I'll always be what You'd want me to be toward my fellow beings. That's all I ask. And I figure that's all You'd ask."

Still looking down on the stripped DC-3 below, an inanimate symbol of what was to be his new life, unashamed he repeated the prayer and walked away.

At this very moment Shea and Barnwell were discussing him, Barnwell having unloaded a few generalized opinions of Midwest maintenance and some very explicit opinions of a certain Midwest mechanic, none of which would have found their way past the airline's Public Relations office. Shea promised faithfully to relay those opinions to maintenance (he would, too, but slightly censored inasmuch as the chief pilot had an uncanny knack of presenting to other departments pilot complaints with such an air of innocent apology that the recipients felt guilty about turning him down).

Now they were relaxing, with a cup of coffee for Shea, while Barnwell sipped an inevitable Coke. He was one of the few pilots on the line who detested coffee.

"What did you think of our new boy?" Shea asked.

"McKay? Seems like a nice kid. I never make snap judgments, John. Wait till I fly with him a few times."

Shea took a tentative sip at the steaming paper cup and grimaced at the hotness. "It's a funny thing, Barney, but I was more impressed with him than I've been with damned near any new man who's come in."

"Well, you talked to him more than I did. Good record?"

"Reasonably good. He was no outstanding hero, I suppose. Air medal for so many missions—I forgot how many."

"The air medal," Barnwell observed dryly, "was about as exclusive as a GI mess kit. Hell, I got one for ferry flights across the Atlantic. I felt like a shit taking it."

Only two weeks before, Barnwell's wife, Ruth, had confided to Shea at a party that "Barney has that medal framed on our mantelpiece." He also knew exactly why Barnwell had been decorated—for bringing an unarmed B-17 into England safely with his copilot dead and two engines shot up after they were jumped by an ME-109. Shea had never gotten around to telling Barney he knew all about the episode.

"I dunno, Barney, I just got the feeling he's gonna make us one damned fine pilot. I'll bet he'll make a helluva captain, too, someday. There's something about him—well, he's mature. Lot of plain common sense."

"One of the war's few virtues," Barnwell commented, "was its ability to speed up the maturing process."

"Yep, but McKay's the kind of guy I'll bet was mature when he was a kid."

"He married?" Barnwell asked.

"Single according to his application. I never did get around to asking him about his personal life."

"Good-looking kid. I suspect our stews will be flipping."

"Yeh," sighed Shea. "I suppose that's his inevitable fate—marry a stew. Like you did."

"Don't say it with such cynicism, Johnny," laughed Barnwell. "They usually make good wives."

"That I'll buy. But I hope he stays away from matrimony for a while. I gotta hunch he's gonna be more than just a run-of-the-mill pilot. He told me he's interested in accident investigation."

"Unusual," Barnwell said. "We sure as hell could use a few hard workers. I've been trying to get help on the safety committee. You'd think I asked some of the guys to give up sex. Tell you what, Johnny. When he gets through school, assign him to me the first month if the bids work out okay."

"Fair enough," promised Shea. He looked up as Mrs. Gillespie entered.

"Two more new men," she announced. "Culver and O'Brian."

"O'Brian," chuckled Barnwell. "Another bloody Irishman. I hope he's a better mick than you are."

"There is no such thing as a bad Irishman, only Irishmen who vary in degrees of goodness," Shea remarked. "O'Brian, now. Obviously the makings of a fine captain."

"So long, Johnny." Barnwell went out with a wave of his hand, nodded to the two rookie pilots who were too surprised to nod back, and disappeared out the door.

McKay had gone over to the main terminal building where he put a dime in a turnstile and stood outside on the observation platform, watching the arriving and departing flights. Midwest's ramp area was between Eastern and American— Eastern with the rather gaudy "Fly the Great Silver Fleet" emblazoned over its aircrafts' windows, American with its traditional orange peel. McKay looked down the line where a Pennsylvania Central DC-3 was waddling up to its gate. A brand-new United DC-4 pulled out toward a runway, grumbling and belching.

He felt like a kid gaping at a toy-store window. Indeed, it was almost a childish feeling of glee that gripped him. He had seen many airports and even more airplanes, but somehow this all looked new and exciting. The little throb of depression and doubt that had touched him back at the hangar was gone.

McKay looked at his watch. The hour Shea had given

him was almost up. He walked briskly back to Hangar 6, whistling a few bars from "Bless 'Em All," climbed the stairs and re-entered the chief pilot's office. This time it was bustling. Shea was in the outer office with two other men, both obviously virginal trainees like McKay; they were trying to look bravely nonchalant and failing completely at the task.

"McKay," Shea called out genially. "Meet Les Culver and —what the hell was your first name, O'Brian?"

O'Brian was a towering, homely youngster with flaming red hair, huge handlelike ears, and a frame built along the robust lines of a pipe cleaner.

"Parnell," said the redhead. "I prefer Paddy." Shea couldn't repress a grin that was half humor, half pride in his new Irishman.

"I'm McDonald McKay. And I prefer Mac."

Culver sighed as he shook hands.

"My first name's Lester and for Christ's sake call me Les. You guys are lucky—if anyone uses your real names, at least you don't have to feel like explaining how you got them."

Culver was about McKay's height, but more slightly built. He had wavy blond hair that would have looked effeminate except for his face—a bit pock-marked, with a square jaw that looked as if it had been hewed out of solid granite. The new class, McKay thought wryly, was not exactly of the Greek god variety thus far.

"Give me that address, Mrs. Gillespie," Shea said to the secretary.

She handed him a slip of paper.

"Sky Harbor apartments, 1300 Bennett Street in Alexandria," he read. "I know the place. It's a dump but it'll do while you're in training. Cheap, too. About one-fifty a month, furnished, and you don't have to sign a lease. Might as well splurge and take a cab over."

"I've got a car, sir," O'Brian said. "Culver came over with me."

"I don't," said McKay, "and I'd appreciate the ride."

Shea gave his new men a last look. At this moment he

felt warmly paternalistic. A tinge of affection and sympathy for what he knew they were facing. Pilot training was more informal when he joined Midwest back in 1931. He had been hired at 10 A.M. and was sitting in the copilot's seat of a Ford trimotor at three the same afternoon on a Chicago-Pittsburgh trip.

Of course, he had been a barnstormer and an air-mail pilot before that. These kids had plenty of cockpit time but they were babies compared to what he had been the day he was hired. He remembered his own first interview—a Midwest vice president saw the applicants in those days. He had been questioning Shea sharply on navigation procedures when a lushly curved brunette slithered through the room and gave Shea a look that would have raised the blood pressure of a Tibetan monk.

Shea's discourse on navigation sputtered to a sudden halt and his neck virtually swiveled as his eyes followed the vision on her course through the office. He apologized to the interviewer and figured he had blown the job. Years later the VP confessed that when he interviewed pilot applicants, he always had one of his better-looking secretaries take that interview cruise.

"If you hadn't looked at her, you wouldn't have been hired," he had told Shea. "I just had a theory, and a pretty damned accurate one, that a good pilot never concentrates so much on one problem that he doesn't notice anything else that suddenly comes up."

It had sounded crazy to Shea until in actual airline flying he learned that the VP was right. Overconcentration could be a booby trap for a pilot, focusing so much attention on a single task that a spreading, mushrooming emergency got out of hand. Now the Personnel experts were doing the interviewing, sans sexy distractions, but Shea still passed on that philosophy to his own pilots.

He sighed, for no apparent reason to the new men.

"I'll be seeing you," he said—it was almost a barked threat

the way he said it. Then, being John Shea, he softened momentarily and added, "Good luck."

Riding toward Alexandria in O'Brian's battered 1940 Olds, the trio managed to get acquainted on remarkably short notice. All were bachelors and McKay the oldest. Culver was an ex-carrier pilot but also had flown Catalinas on sub patrol—and he was well aware that Midwest was more impressed with the latter assignment than the more glamorous one. O'Brian had been in a B-24 squadron.

"The sonofabitch flew like a bathtub full of water," he recalled happily as he steered adroitly through traffic. He seemed to know his way around and McKay asked him if he was from the Washington area.

"Lived in Baltimore part of my life," Paddy explained. "Went to Maryland U. Baltimore—boy, if they ever give the world an enema, that's where they'll stick the tube. God, how I hated the place."

"Guess you won't want to be based here," McKay said. "Too close to Baltimore?"

"Los Angeles would be too close to Baltimore," O'Brian said firmly.

Culver confided, almost apologetically, that he had spent a year at Harvard. His two new roommates forgave him this unspeakable transgression when he added hastily that he didn't like Harvard and had transferred to Oberlin.

"Well, that's the Harvard of the Middle West," McKay said. "I'm Ohio State."

"Play football?" Paddy asked.

"A little. I was a fourth string end or maybe fifth string. I only got into a couple of games."

They found Bennett Street with no trouble and 1300 turned out to be a rather seedy, large red brick apartment house. The resident manager, who looked far more dapper than his building, was a bit snotty at first.

"We understand you have an apartment available," McKay said.

"Well, now, we *might* have something for you soon. These are extremely popular and an excellent location."

O'Brian, who was suspiciously sniffing the strong, rather feminine aroma of the manager's after-shave lotion, decided to try Influence. "Captain Shea of Midwest sent us. We're, ah, new pilots with Midwest." No harm in stretching the truth a little. The manager warmed up instantly.

"Oh yes—Captain Shea. He sends a lot of Midwest people to us. We have some pilots here and stewardesses, too. Lovely girls. Well, now, it happens that I believe a family is moving out of 201-B—in fact, they've already moved. There's a waiting list but we always try to cooperate with the airlines. You'll sign a lease, of course?"

McKay was glad Shea had tipped him that no lease was necessary.

"I'm sorry, but that's specifically why we were interested in this place. Captain Shea happened to mention that a lease wasn't required."

The manager seemed a little crestfallen. But he noticed the service discharge buttons in the lapels of all three men and clucked approvingly.

"Well, now, we do usually require a lease but we try to stretch a point for you airline folks. And I see you're former servicemen. We want to do something for you boys. I was in the Army myself, you know."

He escorted them to 201-B, walking, or rather mincing, alongside McKay. O'Brian and Culver hung back and Paddy murmured: "*That* was in the Army? How the hell did we win the war?"

"Probably the WACS," whispered Culver.

Apartment 201-B turned out to be cleaner and bigger than they expected, with considerable cracked plaster in the ceiling and on the walls the only real sign of wear and tear. The furniture was old but serviceable—a couch, an uncomfortable-looking easy chair, a coffee table, and some nondescript lamps. The living-room rug reminded McKay of Shea's tie. It was red and green with threads of black and had all the esthetic appeal of a neon sign. The two bedrooms were small and the mattresses apparently were stuffed with frozen straw. But the closet space was surprisingly ample and McKay figured they could do a lot worse.

"Okay with you guys?" he asked.

"Okay with me," Paddy said.

Culver nodded agreement.

"We'll take it," McKay told the manager.

"Well, now, that's fine, gentlemen. The rent is one-fifty a month, payable the first month in advance."

"I'll give him the dough and you guys can pay me back," McKay told his roommates. He had four fifties in his wallet and handed over three of them.

"I'll make you out a receipt and you can pick it up on the way out," After-Shave Lotion beamed. "Will you be moving in right away?"

"As soon as we can," McKay said, "if that's all right with you two."

"It's fine with us, Mac," Culver said. "Our bags are at the Raleigh. We can pick them up and get yours—where are you staying?"

"Willard. Incidentally, if Paddy has the only car I want to pay my share of transportation. When we get through school and know where we'll be based, I guess I'd better buy some wheels."

"Me too," said Culver. "I'll buy the next tank, you can get the next gas and then we'll keep alternating."

"I love fair-minded roommates who are not cheapskates," O'Brian announced.

"That reminds me," McKay said hesitantly. "You two sorta teamed up before I arrived on the scene. If you know anybody else coming in who wanted to room with you, no hard feelings. I seemed to have taken this trio for granted."

"Hell no," Paddy assured him. "What's good enough for Midwest is good enough for me."

"Same here, Mac," Culver said. "I'd rather have two stewardesses but I figure you guys can protect me from that manager."

They took another and more detailed inventory of the apartment. They decided they could use one more reasonably comfortable chair for the living room and a good floor lamp, but agreed with Culver's objection that there was no use spending money on what might be their diggings for only a few weeks.

They picked up the rent receipt on their way out to O'Brian's car for the ride downtown. Getting an apartment that fast was a load off all their chests and feeling rather expansive, they fell in quickly with Culver's suggestion that they splurge on a good steak that night.

"And we've got tomorrow free," O'Brian reminded them. "If you want, I'll take you sightseeing."

Instinctively, almost imperceptively, they had fallen into a comradeship that came easily and naturally. The Olds headed downtown. As they approached Memorial Bridge a DC-4 roared over on final approach.

"Midwest," reported Culver, and he said it in a tone of pride.

McKay voiced what each was thinking. "Good luck to us all," he murmured.

Chapter 2

Apartment 201-B arrived for the first day of school at 8:15 A.M. on Wednesday, after an anxious moment when O'Brian's car wouldn't start. They were having panic-stricken visions of getting washed out before they started training when Paddy, through a combination of profanity and what must have been a surge of last-minute sympathy from the Olds, finally got it to turn over.

"I hope what we fly will be in better shape than this car," Culver said testily.

"So do I," sighed O'Brian.

A total of twenty-two trainees were present by the starting time of eight-thirty. The room itself was only three doors down from Shea's office. The chairs were of the schoolroom variety, with a writing shelf for an armrest. The walls were void of any pictures but the room was brightly lighted and almost cheerful.

The student pilots spent a few minutes introducing themselves as they took their chairs. Apartment 201-B, not wishing to appear either too eager or too blasé, compromised by grabbing three seats in the middle. The class looked curiously at the two men sitting behind a small desk facing the trainees. One was gray-haired, big, and broad-shouldered, dressed in a tweed sports jacket that accentuated his bulk. The other was slightly younger, thin faced with a trim black mustache, and rather handsome in an oily way.

The older man rose and the room stilled dutifully, except for a few nervous coughs.

"Gentlemen," he began, "I'm Bob Bender, otherwise known as the chief instructor. You'll meet other members of our—shall we call them the faculty?—later on as you progress through training.

"The gentleman with me is Bennett Kane, vice president of flight operations. He's my boss, he'll be your boss, and you won't find a better one. He's a former captain himself so he's no desk-chair general. He'll be talking to you after I finish these few remarks.

"First, let me welcome you to Midwest. When you got that telegram, the inclusion of the word 'congratulations' just about sums up the way we feel about you, and we hope the way you'll feel about Midwest and your new profession. You are entering one of the most demanding jobs in the world, one requiring complete dedication and devotion. The training you are about to undergo will be rigid, strict, and even ruthless. Some of you may fall by the wayside. But I expect the majority will achieve the privilege of wearing a Midwest pilot's uniform. You were hand-selected to begin with from more than six hundred applicants.

"Now, a few facts which you already may know but which I'll repeat," continued Bender. "Your training time will be seven weeks. Six weeks of ground school and approximately one week of Link and actual flight instruction. The latter will involve qualification on a DC-3. Later on, when you progress to larger equipment, you'll naturally have to go through additional training.

"This entire class has had military flight experience. This is fine and I don't want to disparage what you've been taught in the Army or Navy. But airline flying you'll find completely different. You may feel like a bunch of college kids being sent back to grammar school. Believe me, we think it's necessary.

"Now, we can't tuck you in every night. We aren't going to run bed checks. So you're on something of an honor system. We advise against drinking—you'll be hitting the books too hard to be hitting the bottle, even just a little. A couple of beers at night, that's okay. But lay off the hard stuff during ground school and lay off anything remotely resembling alcohol during flight training. As they say in the military, that's an order.

"Your salary during the training period will be $190 a month. If you get through school, you'll be on probation for a year. During that time you'll be paid three hundred a month, out of which we'll deduct the cost of your uniform. You won't get rich for a while but after the first year, you'll find Midwest a generous employer. And that reminds me, while it may seem a bit optimistic, at 11 A.M. tomorrow you'll be measured for your uniforms."

The class laughed politely. Later they would regret having uttered even a polite laugh when they learned how much uniforms cost.

"Now," said Bender, "Ben Kane has a few words about the company you're going to work for."

Kane arose and surveyed the trainees for what seemed like

an eternity before speaking. McKay always had harbored an inbred suspicion against men who wore mustaches, but the minute Kane opened his mouth he knew that the Operations VP was one smart, smooth cookie. Kane's voice was a rather low, modulated one, but forceful like a well-tuned engine.

He began by wishing the new pilots good luck and made it sound like a benediction. He went into Midwest's history, which most of the class already knew was more or less like the history of every other airline. In Kane's voice and in Kane's terminology, it more closely resembled the history of the United States complete with Self-Sacrifice, Patriotism, Loyalty, Pioneering Spirit, and Glorious Deeds.

Yet despite themselves—and their military-acquired cynicism—the new pilots became interested and even impressed. They sensed Kane's sincere if flowery pride in the past. They got their first inkling of what an airline can mean to men who have not just watched it grow, but made it grow. They listened in half awe, half amusement as Kane told anecdotes about the early days when Midwest had ordered some of its ground employees to take two flights a week so people visiting airports would think that ordinary citizens really did take plane trips. When Midwest used to carry card advertisements on the cabin walls, like streetcars, because like all carriers it was desperately scrounging for revenue. When Midwest charged extra fare for that luxurious rarity—a nonstop flight. When its pilots once threatened to walk out because the government announced that they would have to qualify for instrument flying—an ultimatum reeking with danger to any self-respecting airman who knew damned well that instrument flying wasn't nearly as safe as sheer instinct.

When the airlines used to run the Air Traffic Control system themselves. When every pilot carried, along with the pistol he was allowed to wear slung from his belt to protect the mail, special forms authorizing passengers to obtain railroad tickets if a flight was grounded or canceled. Which was so frequent, Kane added, that the airlines were among the railroads' best customers.

When a stewardess won her wings after only three hours of training in the back room of a hangar and pilots loaded their mail sacks with bricks because they were paid by the weight of the mail they hauled. When Midwest in a brilliant economy move bought a few thousand cardboard ice-cream containers to use as receptacles for airsickness and then had to throw them all away because someone discovered that each container carried a friendly "Thank you—Come Again." When two Midwest pilots (McKay found out later one of them was Shea) swiped a couple of United uniforms and lurched up to a UAL ticket counter in feigned drunkenness, each carrying an empty whiskey bottle—thereby causing seven passengers to switch hastily to a competing Midwest flight.

"Obviously, no longer do we fight for traffic in this way," Kane was saying. "But you'll find competition just as tough in more, uh, dignified ways. As pilots, you'll find you'll be a part of helping Midwest win or retain its share of business. Through your own skill as airmen. Through your dedication to this airline's motto—Safety, Courtesy, Efficiency. Note that the company motto puts the word 'Safety' ahead of the other goals. All three are important, but without safety, it will do us little good to be courteous and efficient. No one in Midwest, from President Karl J. Mencken on down, will ever challenge a decision you make that is based on sincere devotion to safety."

Kane went on to explain why an airline with the name Midwest had its headquarters in Washington. Originally Midwest's home base was in Chicago but the airline in 1938 had merged with East Coast Airways. It was more of an absorption by Midwest, the larger of the companies, than a merger but East Coast's Washington facilities were regarded as superior to what Midwest had in Chicago. (This made sense to the class, but Kane diplomatically neglected to reveal that the chief reason for the move to Washington was Karl Mencken's intense dislike for Chicago weather.)

Kane spoke for more than an hour before turning the class back to Bender. The vice president smiled, nodded graciously at the applause, and left the room—a departure which, O'Brian observed during the lunch break, had reminded him of a full-rigged frigate sailing out of a harbor.

Bender distributed the approximately twenty pounds of books and manuals to be used in ground school. Meteorology. The DC-3's various systems—hydraulic, electrical, power plants, flaps, landing gear, steering, and lighting. Navigation. Radio communications. Routes. Air Traffic Control. Company regulations. The CAR's—Civil Air Regulations. And, to their surprise, a rather lengthy history of Midwest which Bender informed them was the first subject on the curriculum.

"What you heard this morning was just a brief outline," he said. "We're going over it again this afternoon and there'll be a test on it tomorrow morning. There will be a test on each subject covered and a final examination at the end of ground school. The passing grade, I might add, is a minimum of 85 on each test up to the final—and on the final you've got to pull down at least a 90."

At that last bit of information, two pilots whistled.

"I know it's rough," Bender conceded, "but there's no such animal in Midwest as a fair pilot. Our minimum standard is good and we prefer to rate every man flying for us as very good or excellent. Now, let's take a coffee break for fifteen minutes. There's a machine right down the hall to your right."

The class broke up, chattering like school kids. Apartment 201-B joined the line in front of the coffee dispenser. Just ahead of them was a tall, crewcut youngster with pale blue eyes and rosy cheeks who gave the impression he was one of those blessed who didn't have to shave every day.

"I guess I'm the lucky one," he said to Culver. "I flew C-47's for a couple of years. That DC-3 manual looks like duck soup."

"You *are* lucky," Culver replied. "There seem to be considerable differences between a Three and a Catalina."

"They both have two engines," O'Brian said helpfully.

"Drop dead," Culver said rudely. "By the way, I'm Les Culver."

"Bill Mannion," said the crewcut.

"Hi. I'm Paddy O'Brian. This here's Mac McKay. We're rooming together."

"Wish I had met you earlier," Mannion said, looking around before making the remark. "I got an apartment with a real Nervous Nellie. He's told me twenty times he doesn't think he'll ever make it. The damned thing could be catching."

"We're all a little nervous," McKay reminded him. "Where is he?"

"Back in the classroom reading one of the manuals. I'll bet the poor bastard doesn't get any sleep the whole seven weeks. I don't know how he got through the interviews."

They filed back to class, where 201-B watched curiously as Mannion sat down next to a boy who must be the jittery roommate. He acknowledged Mannion's slap on the back with a faint smile and continued to read—McKay imagined it was the company history. Bender already was in front of the class, taking a last sip out of a paper cup, and when he cleared his throat the noise in the room ceased abruptly. Bender, as if pleasantly surprised at the unexpected display of discipline, smiled and then launched into a lecture on the evolution of Midwest's routes which stretched westward to Denver, north to New York, as far south as Atlanta, and to Houston in the southwest.

They finally broke for lunch, Bender guiding the new pilots to a small cafeteria on the lower floor. Apartment 201-B sat down at one table and were joined by Mannion and his roommate, a stocky youngster with unruly black hair.

"Like you fellas to meet Gil Sloan, this is McKay, Mac, that is; Paddy O'Brian and Les Culver."

"Hi," Sloan said.

McKay noticed that all he brought to the table was a glass of milk and a cottage-cheese salad. The kid must have a bowling ball in his guts. He tried to put Sloan at ease. "You an Army pilot?"

"Navigator," Sloan said. "I had a commercial ticket before the war, though. That was enough to get me accepted here. But Christ, that ground school looks tough."

McKay theorized that Sloan, like some navigators and bombardiers, might have flunked pilot training first, but scrapped the theory. Midwest was not likely to take on anyone with that background unless they were desperate for pilots.

"Well, you should have a snap with navigation," he said reassuringly.

"Navigation isn't what's worrying me. It's the rest of the stuff—including flight training."

"Why'd you want to become an airline pilot?" McKay asked, conscious that he was mimicking Shea.

"Because," said Sloan with an intensity that surprised them all, "I didn't want to go back to being a goddamned checker in a supermarket."

"A very good reason," said the practical Culver. They conversed volubly throughout lunch, or at least four of them did. Gil Sloan talked little, although he finally unwound enough to laugh at O'Brian, whose incorrigible cheerfulness worked on gloom like osmosis.

The afternoon consisted of more lecturing by Bender, mostly on Midwest history and policies and a brief discourse on the Federal government's two air agencies, Civil Aeronautics Administration and Civil Aeronautics Board. Intoned the chief instructor:

"The CAA sets the rules for aircraft maintenance. It licenses all pilots including air carrier crews. It lays down the standards under which new transports are designed, built, tested, and certificated. It operates the Air Traffic Control system. It literally is the government agency which deals with the actual operating problems of the airlines.

"The CAB is much smaller but with equal power in different fields. It controls the fares we charge and the routes we fly. If the CAA can be called the operations agency, then the CAB can be called the economic agency. But it also is charged with the responsibility of determining the cause of aircraft accidents—generally speaking, those which involve airlines planes or other large equipment. The Board investigates accidents through its Bureau of Safety. . . ."

Bender droned on through the afternoon, occasionally pausing to answer questions patiently or refer the answers to later in the training. At 5 P.M. he called a halt.

"As I said earlier, we'll have a test on company history tomorrow," he said. "Then we'll head right into navigation on which we'll spend the rest of the week and the first part of next week. Any more questions?"

There may have been, but the class was chaffing at the bit and some men already were getting to their feet.

"That's it for the day."

Mannion suggested they all get together for supper downtown, to which O'Brian was agreeable, but McKay and Culver pointed out that 201-B had been stocked with food the day before and restaurants were a bit of a luxury on $190 a month. They ended up inviting Mannion and Sloan over for dinner, assuring Sloan that all would hit the books right after eating.

Apartment 201-B piled into the Olds. Mannion, who had his own car, followed.

The first day of training was over.

The six weeks of ground school went swiftly and smoothly for McKay. It was more of a refresher course to him, and to Culver and O'Brian as well. For some reason Paddy almost came a cropper on meteorology—an unexpected experience which the Irishman calmly blamed on traumatic experiences with "those weather nuts in England." He claimed all B-24 crews regarded weather forecasting as a vague science remarkably akin to playing the horses.

"It's difficult to pass a subject for which I have so little respect," he explained logically to McKay and Culver following an embarrassing classroom session. An instructor had asked O'Brian to list and describe the various types of cloud formations. O'Brian's list included one legitimate cloud formation and a few others that may have been prevalent either on Mars or in the Hereafter, but definitely were unknown on the planet Earth.

"How the hell can you be so stupid?" Culver asked in frustrated exasperation. "There are only so many formations and all you have to do is memorize them."

"I can't memorize anything I don't understand," Paddy apologized. "Frankly, they all look alike to me. I just can't remember their names."

His roommates tutored him frantically before the final meteorology test. For a while they seriously considered putting crib notes on his shirt cuffs. O'Brian objected on the reasonable grounds that he was low on clean shirts. McKay worried so much over the Irishman's deficiency that his own mind went temporarily blank during the test, but his memory recovered soon enough for a passing grade. Culver passed too, and then both were shocked when O'Brian got his grade. It was higher than theirs.

"Inherent, inbred genius," Paddy said with gracious modesty.

"I'll lay eight to one," Culver growled, "that tomorrow morning you couldn't pass the same test."

"When I am a senior captain and we approach a cloud formation," O'Brian predicted, "I shall ask my copilot to identify same."

"What'll you do if you're flying copilot with a senior captain and he asks you?" McKay laughed.

"By that time my flying skill will have become renowned throughout Midwest and even an incorrect answer will have no effect on my career."

"I may vomit," Culver said. "Let's go out and get a cheeseburger."

Only one man in the class flunked out of ground school, in rather mysterious fashion. It was at the end of the fourth week and nobody seemed to be having any serious difficulty.

Even Sloan, who approached every test with the unbridled optimism of a Kamikaze pilot arranging a postmission social engagement. The flunker simply didn't show up at class one day. Bender announced that he had resigned for personal reasons, but McKay heard by the grapevine that the trainee had been picked up by Alexandria police on a drunk and disorderly charge.

Culver was sympathetic when McKay passed on the gossip.

"Drinking I couldn't tolerate," he said. "But I'm about ready to get picked up on a rape charge. There was a female ship cleaner who passed me yesterday and she looked like Rita Hayworth."

"I saw her," O'Brian commented. "You really must be hard up. She reminded me of a Greyhound bus."

McKay, engrossed in a schematic drawing of the DC-3's hydraulic system, chuckled. His own needs for sex and his approach to sex obviously were less frantic than Culver's. They also, he had gathered, were quite a bit more discriminating. Culver's recounting of numerous past conquests was lurid, explicit, and undoubtedly exaggerated. But O'Brian, like a little boy sitting at the feet of a master storyteller, listened to Culver's bedroom, automobile backseat, and couch exploits with a respect bordering on awe. Paddy, for all of his Irish effervescence and charm, was shy about the opposite sex and admitted it freely. Not that he had to admit it. Culver had asked him bluntly one night if he was a virgin and O'Brian had blushed redder than his hair.

Under the pressure of ground-school completion and the impending flight training, even Culver found it possible to sublimate his natural carnal instincts. Up to a point. One night he asked O'Brian if he could borrow the Olds. McKay figured Culver had latched on to a sure thing, but the innocent Paddy wanted to know if Les was going to a movie. If so, he'd like to come.

"Jesus no, Paddy. I'm gonna get laid if you must know."

"Well," hesitated O'Brian. "It's the only car we've got. . . ."

"I'm not gonna sleep with the car, dammit."

McKay settled the matter. "Let him go, Paddy. He'll be phoning the resident manager if we don't. Lay off the booze, Les."

"Don't worry. I'm gonna ply her with liquor and pour mine into the nearest flowerpot."

He dashed into the bathroom to shave, whistling for the first time in days. He was through in five minutes, put on a clean shirt, and waved merrily good-by to his roommates. They heard the Olds's starter whine protestingly at being awakened, then catch with a roar as Culver headed for his assignation.

"Who's he got a date with?" O'Brian asked.

"I'm not sure, but I think it's some secretary in Flight Planning. He was talking to her at lunch today. It's debatable who was panting the loudest."

"I wish," Paddy said rather wistfully, "I wasn't so damned bashful. You got a girl, Mac?"

"Not now. I dated some in college. The usual stuff. Went steady my senior year but the war came along. She was mostly someone to write to."

"Have you seen her since?"

"Looked her up after I got back from overseas. She met some Navy officer at a dance and they had just gotten engaged."

"That's tough," O'Brian sympathized.

"Not really. She was something to cling to when I was overseas. A picture in my wallet and somebody who made mail call worthwhile. Just as well we didn't get serious. I'd hate to be supporting a wife right now."

"Well, to tell you the truth I kinda envy Les his lechery. I wouldn't know how to seduce a girl. I keep telling myself it's against my religion but that's pure rationalization."

"You probably have the same trouble I do," McKay said. "I believe a girl when she says no. Now Les, he wouldn't take no if she delivered it with a fire extinguisher against his skull."

"But he gets more fun out of life. Doesn't he?"

McKay looked at O'Brian curiously.

"Not necessarily, Paddy. A guy like Les does fine if sex is all you want out of a relationship. It's fine if a guy and gal have the same motive for going to bed—desire or mutual loneliness or affection or love. But when the guy has one motive and the girl another, that's when trouble starts. Call it, well, call it sexual imbalance, Paddy. Like a prop out of sync. It's a warning sign. Anyway, that's been my philosophy —make sure of your motive and her motive and you aren't likely to get hurt or hurt anybody. I don't know if it works for every guy but it has for me—and it may for you. Catholic or not, you'll probably have to get burned a few times before you draw up your personal set of rules."

"Have you slept with many girls?"

"Some. Mostly in England. I lost my virginity my sophomore year in college and I slept with the girl I went steady with. When I was overseas, I suppose I was more like Les. I drank too much and I was scared most of the time. Sex was a barbiturate against fear. You could forget tomorrow's mission with a woman in your arms. You know, Paddy, you can envy Les right now but your chances of winding up happily married are better than his."

"Just the same," O'Brian said sadly, "it's a helluva note to be a twenty-four-year-old virgin."

"Wait till you're flying the line. Some stew'll grab you on a layover and you won't know what hit you."

"What worries me, Mac, is that I'll probably fall in love with the first girl I sleep with. You can get hurt kind of easy that way."

McKay nodded slowly, as if O'Brian had just uttered the wisest of philosophical truisms.

"Yeh. But I've got a hunch, Paddy, that the first girl you sleep with might be in love with you. Don't sell yourself short just because you've never scored. A character like you arouses the maternal instinct."

O'Brian sighed. "I still wonder if I need a nymphomaniac more than a mother," he mused.

"It's possible," McKay assured him, "that you may find both in the same woman. Let's get some studying done."

Two hours later they undressed wordlessly, O'Brian pondering his roommate's observations on Sex and Women. McKay was thinking that despite his rather lofty philosophizing, he secretly envied Culver. Tonight, anyway. Man does not live by bread alone, a man is not made of wood, etc., etc. Well, the hell with it. At least he had made Paddy feel better. He hoped.

They left a light burning in the living room for the Errol Flynn of 201-B. O'Brian knelt for his prayers, crossed himself, and climbed into bed. There was something wonderfully childlike about the way O'Brian approached his religion, completely devoid of affectation. McKay had respect and even envy for a devout Catholic. He wished he had the faith and trust that Catholicism involved, but perhaps without its rigidity.

The two pilots lay silently, each in the citadel of his own private thoughts.

"Good night, Paddy."

"Good night, Mac."

O'Brian lowered the drawbridge of his citadel and let sentiment venture out.

"Mac?"

"Yes?"

"Thanks."

"Okay, Paddy."

O'Brian, who probably would have slept through the San Francisco earthquake, didn't stir when Culver returned, but McKay awoke. He was glad to see that Les seemed perfectly sober, the only residue of his evening being a somewhat smug smirk on his face approximating the saturated satisfaction of a food-gorged lion.

"Feel better?" McKay whispered, half in sarcasm.

"Hell yes," Culver gurgled. "This babe . . ."

"Tell us about it tomorrow. You'll wake Paddy. He's horny enough as it is, and so am I."

"You should have gone with me, Mac. She had a friend, she told me."

"Maybe. But I'd hate to disillusion O'Brian."

"Huh?"

"Skip it. Good night, Les."

Culver gave them a full briefing the next morning, with all the proud air of a group commander disclosing the details of a major and highly successful bombing mission. O'Brian, as usual, was transfixed. McKay was just amused. In the cafeteria after the morning class session, Culver pointed out the girl rather obviously by waving at her, receiving in return a coy smile. Paddy kept staring at her all through lunch as if she was a freak. Or maybe just a Fallen Woman.

"I can fix you up with a friend," Culver told him. O'Brian blushed.

"Well, maybe after we get through ground school," he ventured.

There seemed to be no danger, McKay thought, of Paddy relinquishing his grip on Virtue until some uncertain time considerably after ground school.

That phase of their training ended a week later. By that time the twenty-one survivors knew the guts of a DC-3 as an intern knows the anatomy of the human body. They had memorized the airlines' litany of airport abbreviations—DCA for Washington National, LGA for LaGuardia, LAX for Los Angeles, and a couple of hundred others. They knew how to compute fuel consumption and how to make out a Midwest flight plan and read back an ATC clearance. They could read a Jeppesen approach and airport chart with the ease of a bored housewife digesting a sex novel. They became reasonably familiar—no pilot could recite it from memory—with the Federal airway system. Victor 8 Washington to Pittsburgh. Victor 42 Pittsburgh—Cleveland. Victor 26 Cleveland—Detroit . . .

Some of their training repeated what they had learned in

the military, but it was incredibly more thorough. It had to be. War produced Fords and Chevies and Plymouths, rolling pilots off an assembly line. The airlines had to manufacture Cadillacs and Lincolns and even Rolls-Royces. War made pilots and planes expendable. An airline pilot and plane were no more expendable than the passengers who trustingly paid for their transportation. In a totally unsubtle way, Bender and the other instructors drummed this into their skulls. Safety. You fly by the book. You do this because it's safe and you don't do this because it isn't safe.

At 5 P.M. on a Friday, ending the six-week grind, Bender announced that all had passed and were qualified for flight instruction. This drew cheers and applause, more in relief than self-approval. They had been brainwashed as well as educated, and they were more impressed with air carrier *modus operandi* than with their own accomplishments. A few of them, such as Sloan, resembled condemned men greatly surprised to have won a reprieve.

Bender let the hilarity go on for a few minutes, then banged his ham-sized fist on the desk until he obtained quiet.

"Okay, gentlemen. You've been an attentive class, a good class. But you've just gone through grammar school, so don't get cocky. You're one helluva long way from being airline pilots. Just any one day next week is going to be tougher than all of the last six weeks. You're on your own for the weekend but don't overdo it. And don't get into trouble. There'll be a flight-training schedule posted in Operations at eight o'clock Monday morning. Be there. Any questions? Okay, scatter."

The twenty-one geniuses—at ground school, anyway—emptied the room with the speed of buckshot leaving a muzzle. Culver announced his intention of buying a car, that very evening, by way of celebrating.

"I've got a couple of thousand bucks in war bonds," he said, "and two cars in the family will be a lot more convenient for all of us."

"It'll also help your sex life," McKay theorized with great

accuracy. "But maybe you're right, Les. I oughta go with you and see what I can pick up myself."

"That's silly," O'Brian protested. "We sure don't need three cars."

"We don't," agreed Culver. "You guys come with me and help pick one out."

He talked Paddy into it, but McKay begged off. "You go ahead. I can catch a bus back to the apartment. I'll pick up some steaks and a bottle of good bourbon."

"Get some scotch for me," Culver said. "Pay you when we get back. Come on, Paddy. Maybe you can keep me from getting screwed worse than I was last night."

"Has she really got a friend?" Paddy asked. "Maybe we could ask them over for dinner?"

"Hey, that's a helluva good idea," Culver enthused. "Wadda you say, Mac? I can ask Fay to get two more girls."

McKay had always regarded blind dates as a social version of Russian roulette. But as he hesitated, O'Brian looked at him almost imploringly like a kid who's been told that *maybe* he can go to the movies. McKay drowned his misgivings.

"Go see Fay. I just hope she can produce something other than a couple of dogs. What time will you be back?"

"Not later than eight," Culver said. "Maybe you'd better get some gin and vermouth for martinis."

"I hate martinis," O'Brian advised.

"The martinis are for the girls. A martini is a seduction drink."

"I may drink some myself," McKay said. "Three martinis and Edna May Oliver'd look sexy. And I have a hunch that's what your paramour will come up with—Edna May Oliver or a reasonable facsimile."

"I'll lay the law down," Culver promised. "If her friends aren't passable, no dice."

He and O'Brian marched down the hall toward Flight Planning. McKay, with a couple of hours to kill, decided to have a Coke in the cafeteria. He had just sat down at a table by himself when someone tapped him on the shoulder. It was Shea.

"Hi, Mac. How you doing?"

"Fine, sir." He had seen Shea only once since that first day, when the chief pilot lectured on Communications and ATC. Shea sat down and stirred sugar into his coffee.

"I see where you got through ground school in good shape."

"Yes sir. No particular trouble. Some of it was a little tougher than I expected."

"Worried about flight training?"

"No sir. To tell you the truth, I can't wait for it to start. Neither can Culver and O'Brian."

"That O'Brian seems like quite a character," Shea chuckled.

"He sure is."

"Have you guys thought about where you'd like to be based?"

"Well, some. I like Washington. So does Culver. But I expect Paddy'll want to go somewhere else. He's from Baltimore. I gather he'd like to get as far away as possible."

"You've all gotten pretty close?" It was more of a statement than a question.

"I guess we have."

"Well, I can't promise you anything on a base," Shea said thoughtfully. "But if you three'd like to stick together, we may be able to work out something."

McKay was touched by the offer. He had heard that base assignments at Midwest were arrived at by the scientific method of pulling names out of hats. He already had confessed to himself that he'd really like to stay in DCA—the airline code initials for the capital came naturally, even at this stage of training—and the knowledge that O'Brian probably wouldn't bothered him just a little.

"I suppose we'd better worry about next week before we start worrying about a base," he told Shea.

"I suppose you had, although if any of you flunk out

I'm a lousy judge of potential pilots. I figure there's one weak sister in your class but that's all."

McKay wondered if Gil Sloan was the one Shea had fingered, but he quelled his curiosity and avoided asking the chief pilot. Shea looked almost disappointed that he hadn't asked, gulped down the rest of his coffee, and departed with an admonition to "Come see me if you have any problems."

McKay's most immediate problem was non-aeronautical. He caught a bus back to Alexandria and spent the next hour buying supplies for 201-B's dinner party. When he got back to the apartment, he mixed a batch of martinis—utilizing a vase he carefully washed out—and got the steaks ready for the broiler. He had just enough time for a quick shower and shave when O'Brian and Culver arrived.

"Where are the girls?"

"They're coming over in about an hour," Culver said. "Paddy's date has a car."

"I just hope mine has one head and no hair on her chest. By the way, did you get your car?"

"Didn't have much time to look. But I've got my eye on a '46 Ford with only ten thousand miles on it. We're gonna look at it again tomorrow. Did you get the liquor? Good. I'll go shower."

O'Brian hadn't said a word. He was sitting on the ramshackle couch. At least his body was sitting on the couch. O'Brian himself was apparently at twenty-five thousand feet, a silly grin on his face. McKay thought for a second Paddy had been drinking and sniffed. Not a trace. There was only one other explanation and McKay snorted his disbelief in what he already half believed.

"All right, you adolescent mick. You must have met a girl. I assume from that dying cow look she's a cross between Florence Nightingale and Hedy Lamarr."

Paddy didn't explain. He gushed, like a dynamited dam.

"Mac, you won't believe it. We go down and see this Fay babe and Les says could she find a couple of dates for us. She's a fine kid, by the way, this Fay. After all, her sex life is her own business. Anyway, she says she knows this Midwest stew who's a good friend and has a roommate. Fay calls her but her roommate answers and says she's just about due to come in from a trip. So we shoot down to operations and meet the flight and she gets off the plane and—oh, brother, what a knockout. Where you going?"

"To get a shot of bourbon," McKay said. "I think I'm going to need one. I'm a little mixed up on whose roommate is whose."

"Well, Fay introduces us and she doesn't have a date for tonight. She says she'll call her roommate—the one Fay talked to first—and she doesn't have a date, either. You'll like her roommate. Pat says she's a real nice gal. They're both Midwest stews."

"Pat, I take it, is your target for tonight?" McKay called out from the kitchen.

"Yeh. We hit it off right away. She's . . ."

"Just a minute," McKay interrupted. "How come you latched on to this paragon of pulchritude and I wind up with the roommate?"

He came back to the living room and faced O'Brian with mock anger. Only Paddy took him seriously.

"Honest, Mac, I didn't think you'd go for Pat. Her last name's Donovan."

"So I'm anti-Catholic? What's her roommate's name— Shapiro?"

"Dorothy Martin. No kidding, are you sore?"

Paddy looked so worried that McKay had to laugh.

"Hell no. Just ribbing you. Help me fix up the supper. I've shaved, so you can go in after Les finishes."

"Wait'll you meet her, Mac. She is an absolute living doll. About five-three with a cute pug nose and God, what a smile."

"You want a drink?"

"Bourbon and water. She's been flying for a year. I think I'll ask her to go to Mass with me Sunday."

"While you're there you could save time and get married," McKay suggested as he mixed O'Brian's drink. But when he turned to take it, Paddy was standing there, his lanky frame filling the doorway. And he wasn't grinning.

"Mac, I know I sound like a damned fool. I know I just met her. I know I'm a baby with women. But we—we just hit it off. I could tell it. She even took my arm when we walked her to her car. It was just the way she did it. And the way she looked up at me. I'm not in love, but honest, just wait till you meet her."

McKay gently massaged the Irishman's jaw with his fist.

"Paddy, I just don't want you jumping to conclusions. She sounds like a helluva gal. But don't take anything for granted and play it cool. You'll scare her away. Like wait until you have a few dates before you propose."

"It'll be hard."

"It'll be harder if you don't. You're gonna spin in if you move too fast."

"Even Les liked her," O'Brian said as if Culver's approval was the last obstacle to inevitable matrimony.

"That reminds me," McKay said, "what does mine look like?"

"It's hard to say," explained Paddy. "She had curlers on when we met her."

"I think," McKay said, "it's going to be a long evening."

It was, but not in the way McKay expected. The steaks were succulent, the drinks relaxing, and the girls were good company. Fay Thompson was a buxom, good-natured girl who had no illusions about Culver's having honorable intentions and handled him rather well, McKay thought.

Patricia Donovan turned out to be just as O'Brian had described, but somewhat to McKay's surprise Paddy's optimistic "We just hit if off" came pretty close to the truth. She kept laughing at O'Brian's jokes and after dinner, when they were listening to records on a portable Vic Fay had brought along, McKay was impressed to see Pat's hand slip into O'Brian's as naturally as a glove. Paddy managed to blush and look proud simultaneously.

Dorothy Martin was a tall, not too attractive girl with a rather prominent nose, but a beautiful low voice and a sweet smile. The smile seemed to erase her homeliness and McKay liked her. He got a little high on straight bourbon and made a pass at her in the kitchen, which she avoided neatly and without offense.

"The pass I'll take as a compliment," she said, "but you might as well know I'm engaged."

For some perverse reason, McKay felt relieved. While still in the kitchen, they discussed her fiancé, a boy in her home town of Omaha, and McKay finally got around to her roommate.

"O'Brian's smitten," he told Dorothy. "He's pretty inexperienced and I don't want him to get clobbered. The next few weeks will be tough enough without him beating his head against a female wall. You might tell her, well, Paddy's as fine a kid as I've ever known and it would be a dirty trick to lead him on."

"Pat won't lead him on. She's done nothing but talk about him ever since she met him. She says he arouses the mother in her."

"Mother? Well I'll be damned."

Dorothy raised her eyebrows. "I say something funny?"

"No. Just something I remembered telling Paddy. About not worrying because he doesn't have fangs like Culver. I said he appeals to the maternal instinct in women."

The stewardess put another ice cube in her scotch and nodded. "You know, Mac, until I watched them together I felt like warning Pat not to get serious. Now I gather that Paddy is a bit innocent."

"Very. In a very masculine way, if you get what I mean. He'll be fine with the right girl."

"I think," Dorothy said slowly, "Pat might be the right girl."

The party broke up about 2 A.M. Culver, with rare polite-ness, asked O'Brian if it was okay to borrow the Olds once more. Demonstrating great delicacy, admirable tact, and com-plete bull, he said the only reason he needed the car was because Fay lived a couple of miles beyond the two steward-esses, and naturally it would be inconvenient for them to drive her home. O'Brian threw him the keys with the expansive generosity of a father telling a son he could have his new Cadillac for the rest of the night.

McKay walked Dorothy out to Pat's car and kissed her good night in brotherly fashion. Pat came out a few minutes later, surprised McKay with an impulsive gentle kiss on his cheek, and the two girls drove away. He was almost afraid to go back in and face Paddy, who at this moment must resemble a smitten Andy Hardy. But the O'Brian who was waiting for him, while indeed smitten, had donned a cloak of suddenly acquired maturity.

"Did you like her?" he asked, almost belligerently.

"Very much. And I've got to admit, she seemed to like you."

"We're going to dinner tomorrow night. I thought we could double but Dorothy's gotta fly. How about going with us anyway?"

That was typical of O'Brian, McKay thought. That decent, lovable mick. He wanted McKay along like he'd want a head cold. But he still made the invitation sound sincere.

"No thanks, Paddy. I'll see what Culver's got planned or I'll look up Mannion and Sloan."

While they were getting ready for bed, McKay remembered his conversation with Shea that afternoon. He decided now was as good a time as any to sound O'Brian out on his base plans. "By the way, Paddy, I bumped into Shea today. He didn't promise anything but he said he might be able to keep the three of us together. What'd you have in mind—Chicago?"

"Chicago?" asked O'Brian. "What's wrong with Washing-ton? Hell, Mac, I'd like to see more of Pat. We're going to church this Sunday, incidentally, and then drive over to see her folks."

"Her folks? Where's she from?"

"Baltimore," said Paddy. "Good night, Mac."

Chapter 3

The training schedule McKay and the others found on the Operations bulletin board at 8 A.M. Monday looked foreboding, not for what it said but for what it didn't say. It had two columns, one headed "Link" and the other "DC-3 Time." Every name was on both lists, with different times allotted to each category. The times were Greenwich, and from now on they would live by this twenty-four-hour clock.

McKay found himself listed for the Link at 0900 and did a double take when he saw his name in the other column:

McKAY, McDONALD—2200 (INSTRUCTOR: SHEA)

Culver, much to his delight, was down for one of the first DC-3 flights with Link scheduled for the afternoon. Ditto Mannion. Paddy got the Link at 10 A.M. and a flight at 3 P.M., one hour before Sloan. In fact, McKay was the only one listed for night training.

"Holy cow," McKay said. "They must have something against B-25 pilots. I drew a night test first time out. Well, I'm glad I got Shea."

"It'll probably be smoother," said the ever-optimistic O'Brian.

"It'll probably be tougher," McKay observed.

Regular Midwest crews going in and out of the huge OPS room looked at the trainees crowding around the bulletin board with mixed curiosity and amusement. In came Shea and Bender, totally different and even awesome in their four-striped uniforms. Shea seemed ten pounds lighter and two inches taller with his working clothes on. Most airlines assigned special instructors to flight training, but on Midwest it was still considered one of the chief pilot's duties.

"May I have your attention," Bender called out. "Those men whose names are down for DC-3 time this morning will go with Captain Shea and myself to Hangar 4. All others report back to the classroom for a briefing on the Link."

McKay and O'Brian, accompanied by about two thirds of the class, trudged back to Hangar 6 for the briefing, delivered by an elderly ex-Midwest pilot named Charley Foster who had been beached with a heart condition. He had conducted the course on navigation and was good—informal but thorough and knowledgeable.

"I know you'd rather start right off in the air," Foster acknowledged, "but you'll get your chance. And don't underestimate the importance of Link training. It's primarily to brush up on your instrument flying and you're going to be doing one helluva lot of instrument flying on this airline."

McKay well remembered his Link experiences in the Air Corps. The trainer looked like the tiny imitation plane kids "flew" at amusement parks—which the device was, originally. A young piano manufacturer in Binghamton, New York, named Edwin Link had latched on to the idea that the children's miniature plane, which used organ-style bellows to produce limited motion, could be used for basic flight and instrument training.

The first time he had "flown" one, it was like being locked up in a phone booth with no windows. The motion, simulated as it was, still was real enough to give the illusion of flight. McKay never had any difficulty with instrument flying and the device gave him no trouble. But some pilots actually were scared to death of the dwarf plane which gave them their first inkling of what it was like to fly with no visual reference.

Foster gave one husky trainee a thirty-minute workout in the Link, then put McKay in the trainer for the same period. At first he was a little rusty. He hadn't flown any aircraft for a long time, and while the few instruments were familiar, his coordination was off. By the end of the half hour, however, he was following with smooth efficiency Foster's commands delivered via a mike. The Link nevertheless gave him a twinge of claustrophobia and it was with gratitude that he heard the instructor finally say, "Okay, McKay, nice going. Climb out."

He watched O'Brian climb in later, and unconsciously nodded approval as he saw Paddy manipulate the little monster with effortless ease. The Irishman had a touch that McKay envied. Even Foster was impressed to the point where he decided after only twenty minutes that the Link wasn't even a minor challenge to O'Brian.

"You must have been born in one," he commented when Paddy lifted the black hood and eased his long frame out of the make-believe cockpit.

"Boy," McKay said to his roommate, "they may give you the fourth stripe without even waiting."

"I've got one big advantage," Paddy said soberly and quite seriously. "If you can fly a B-24 you can fly a bloody freight car. That Link is like asking Rubinstein to play 'Chopsticks.'"

It may have been duck soup for O'Brian and McKay, but a few of the trainees were wandering all over the Link's imaginary sky. Sloan was one. Foster was patient for a while, then scolded sharply when Gil couldn't keep its nose up in a simulated turn and fouled up what should have been a routine landing approach. When Sloan got out of the trainer, McKay noticed that his armpits were stained with sweat.

"Jesus!" was Sloan's only comment as he walked over.

"It can be rough," McKay sympathized and felt a throb of hypocrisy as he said it. He recalled Shea's doubts about the one weak sister and sensed that if there were going to be any washouts in this class, poor Gil was a fat possibility if not a pretty solid probability. Yet his trouble seemed more mental than physical, more psychological than aeronautical. Sloan had a commercial ticket and that rating was not easy to come by. McKay had a hunch that being the only nonmilitary pilot in the class had given Gil an inferiority complex. It was an invisible monkey on his back that kept nibbling at his confidence and common sense.

McKay had little time to spend pondering what was wrong with Gil Sloan, however. Before Foster put the next man in the Link, he introduced the trainees to a tiny, wizened man who had just come into the room.

"Gentlemen," said Foster, "this is Ed Weinstock, who's chief of the Washington control tower. He's going to take you men who've been in the Link this morning up to the tower and let you see how the other half lives. Those who still have their Link session coming will get to see Ed's operation later in the week.

"Let me say this before you go. As pilots, you'll curse those guys in ATC. You'll call them a bunch of incompetent slobs. You'll think they're out to foul up your flight deliberately and arbitrarily. There may be a few times when you'll be right." Weinstock grinned good-naturedly at this sally. "But I think when you visit an ATC facility, you'll learn that air traffic controllers have as many problems as you do and probably more. It'll do you a helluva lot of good and it'll make better pilots out of you. Okay, Ed, they're all yours."

It turned out that Foster was very right. The new pilots were taken up to the control tower and got a glimpse of this pressure cooker in a greenhouse. They went down to the basement of a hangar and watched departure and approach control working with the tiny strips of paper on which were marked the flight numbers of the aircraft they were working. They marveled at the unhurried efficiency, the decisions made with so much calmness, yet in an atmosphere of almost electric tension.

Traffic control was something they had taken for granted in the military. Traffic control then was just an unseen, calm voice, usually with a clipped British accent and sometimes a woman's voice, intriguing in its very impersonality.

Weinstock explained that the "shrimp boats"—wooden racks containing the flight strips—dated back to 1936 when the Federal government had taken over control of the airways from the airlines themselves.

"It's still basically the same system we had then," he said. "Now we're getting radar and one of these days—or years— we'll have something to replace these shrimp boats. Maybe some electronic stuff to keep track of flights. But the guys do the best they can. We just want you to realize our own limitations and get across the idea that while your own flight is your whole world, we've got a helluva lot of other pilots and planes to worry about."

McKay had a question, or rather an observation "Mr. Weinstock, it sure as hell impresses me and I guess I'm speaking for all of us. So I don't see why there should be any trouble between pilots and controllers."

Weinstock shook his head almost sadly. "Because," he replied, "this practice of getting new pilots to visit control facilities is something the CAA started only a few years ago on a small scale. The airlines are putting this into their training curricula on more or less of a regular basis, but there are hundreds, maybe thousands of pilots who've never seen controllers on the job. They don't have any idea of why they're asked to do something. They only know that an ATC order can seem arbitrary and unreasonable.

"And it works both ways. We've started what we call a FAM program—FAM for Familiarization flights. We're asking the carriers to let controllers ride jump seats on scheduled flights and get a look at your problems. ALPA is helping with this program and it should do some good on both sides."

The pilots thanked Weinstock for the tour and he escorted them back to the Link, where Foster was finishing up with the final trainee for the morning session. It was lunchtime but McKay and O'Brian were thinking more of Culver than about eating. The lucky bastard must be through with his first flight by now.

They rushed back to Operations but Culver wasn't in sight.

"He must be in the caf," Paddy figured.

He was, sitting with Mannion and another pilot, chomping on a hamburger and looking very pleased with himself.

"How'd it go, Les?" asked McKay.

"No sweat. That sonofabitch Bender is tough, though. He chopped an engine on me and don't let anybody tell you a DC-3 flies by itself. I damned near put my foot through the floor trying to rudder correct."

Mannion said Shea had pulled the same thing on him.

"Hell, Bill took it off and landed," Culver said.

"It figured," Mannion pointed out. "I've got more time on Gooney Birds than anyone else in the class. He just wanted to see how I'd handle it. Guess I did okay. All Shea said was 'See you tomorrow.'"

"All Bender said was something about 'She's different from a Catalina, isn't she?' It sure was. How was the Link?"

"Didn't have much trouble at all," Paddy said.

"He's being modest," McKay added. "The mick looked like he invented Links. Let's get a bite to eat, Paddy."

McKay thought he would just hang around and watch O'Brian's flight that afternoon, but when they returned to Operations at one, Bender had other plans. He sent part of the class to the Link room and had the rest go back to the classroom for an hour's lecture by Midwest's chief dispatcher on the importance of dispatchers. The trainees thought he was a little self-serving. Later they were to find out that a dispatcher could be a pilot's best friend—a sort of built-in conscience composed of experience, common sense, and know-how. They also were to learn that a dispatcher had as much authority as a senior captain when it came to deciding whether a flight should take off.

The chief dispatcher's talk was not nearly as interesting as what followed. The class returned to Operations and observed the dispatching process firsthand. The quiet conferences with captains over flight plans. Fuel load computing. Weather outlook. Alternate airports if the destination was socked in. Up-to-date briefing on NOTAMS (Notice to Airmen). McKay listened to the laconic dialogues and as he had with the controllers, gained everlasting admiration for these apparently minor cogs in an airline's wheels. It was beginning to dawn on him and the other new men that pilots were like actors in a well-made movie. They took the bows and preened their skills and sported the glamorous trappings before the public. But their final performance hinged on a lot of other people. Not even in the Air Force had McKay realized so sharply that a good flight operation involved as much teamwork on the ground as in the air. The seeds of respect had been planted, an inbred safety valve to keep a pilot from getting too impatient with dispatchers and too furious at controllers.

At two forty-five the observation period ended and at two forty-six O'Brian left the ground sans benefit of aircraft. Miss Donovan walked into Operations to report for a flight, demurely sexy in her navy-blue uniform. She grinned at McKay and beamed at Paddy, and the Irishman, as usual, blushed. McKay half wished the encounter hadn't taken place. It probably would take O'Brian's mind off his flying. He should have known better. When Bender called "Let's go, O'Brian," Paddy unconsciously assumed the air of a gladiator entering the arena. A knight preparing to joust for Fair Lady. A halfback charging onto the field with a side glance to make sure the blonde in Row 3, Section A, was watching.

"Lots of luck, honey," Pat whispered.

"Don't worry, I'll knock 'em dead," Paddy assured her.

He did. Bender told Shea after the flight that O'Brian was just a natural flyer, confident without being cocky and with reaction time as lightning-quick as a cobra's strike. McKay himself had time only to witness the takeoff with Pat when he found Shea standing next to him. The chief pilot just nodded and the three of them watched the DC-3 climb smoothly, then turn northwest toward Maryland, and disappear into the overcast.

"Wish we could train down south," Shea said to no one in particular. "Better weather."

McKay didn't answer.

"Good afternoon, Captain Shea," Pat said politely.

"Hi, Pat. Gotta trip?"

"Yes sir. 819 to Cleveland."

"Eight-nineteen? Who's flying it?"

"Captain Billings."

"Oh yeh. Old Wolfman himself. I suppose you can't wait for Mr. O'Brian to get his stripes."

Pat blushed at least twenty shades more crimson than O'Brian ever had. McKay chuckled. Apparently there were no secrets on an airline, even when they involved the new romance of a lowly pilot-trainee. Shea put his arm around Pat and squeezed.

"Tell you what, Pat," he beamed. "The day you get married, I'll fly a DC-4 over the church and drop rose petals outa the landing gear well as you come out."

Pat apparently decided the conversation was getting both too personal and overoptimistic. "Time to board my flight. So long, Mac. Tell Paddy I'll see him tomorrow. Good-by, Captain Shea."

She walked toward a waiting DC-4 two gates down the ramp area. McKay and Shea watched her in silence, Shea paternally and McKay fraternally, and both possibly a little lecherously.

"I see I've got you at ten tonight, Mac."

"Yes sir. Looking forward to it."

"Sorry about the hour."

"No complaints, sir."

Shea started to explain why he had personally scheduled that night reaming job for McKay alone. Then he decided against saying anything. In truth, the chief pilot's conscience was itching just a little bit. There was nothing unique about night training. Most airlines, Midwest included, conducted the majority of training flights after dark and often in the wee hours of the morning because that was the only time planes were available. The only reason for the large number of daylight flights with this class was a current surplus of DC-3 equipment. Midwest was acquiring DC-4's as fast as the Douglas factory could modify them from their wartime cargo configuration. The new pressurized Constellations also were coming off the assembly lines, and Midwest was starting to phase out the old Threes.

Yet with plenty of aircraft available for daytime training, Shea had deliberately thrown McKay a curve. Partly it was to scratch his itching conscience for liking McKay so much on their first meeting. Which, in turn, created a new itch. To quell his natural tendency toward favoritism in McKay's behalf, the chief pilot had figured it was better to err on the side of unfairness and this bothered him as much as the favoritism.

He studied McKay as if he were seeing him for the first time. The new pilot's face was placid, sober, and noncommital.

"See you in OPS at 2145, Mac. Guess I'd better get Sloan ready."

"Yes sir."

Shea headed back toward Operations. He would have felt better if he had known that McKay already had sensed the motive behind the night flight.

The weather had cleared and the stars were bright in their cold blanket when Culver and O'Brian drove him to the airport. They had swapped accounts of their own flights that day, but these gave McKay no real clue to what to expect. Except for Bender's pulling an engine on Les, Culver's flight seemed to be mostly aimed at familiarizing himself with the plane. On the other hand, Bender had tossed at least part of the book at O'Brian—including a couple of stalls, an engine out in a turn, and he had let Paddy make the landing.

McKay had a hunch his own hour's ordeal would be something like O'Brian's, but he kept this misgiving to himself and merely listened to his roommates discuss the idiosyncrasies of the DC-3. When they pulled up in front of the terminal building, he was a little surprised.

"Aren't you guys gonna park and hang around?"

"We thought we'd catch a movie," Culver said.

"Oh. Well, I'll see you back at the apartment."

"Good luck," Culver said.

"Ditto," O'Brian added.

"Yeh. Have fun."

The Olds drove off (Culver never had gotten around to that car purchase) and McKay felt just a mite hurt. It wouldn't have killed them to wait an hour and Culver sure as hell wasn't any moviegoer. Paddy was, but it was totally unlike O'Brian to sentence either of his roommates to a bus or cab ride home. It also was unlike him to display such indifference. But McKay's self-pity evaporated instantly as soon as he met Shea in Operations.

The chief pilot immediately launched into a businesslike briefing on DC-3 handling characteristics and continued the discourse when they were seated in the cockpit. Shea was in the sacred left seat. They went through the pre-takeoff checklist which prodded some B-25 memories in McKay's flight-stale mind. He pulled the yoke back and forth and to either side, testing aileron and elevator response.

The controls felt stiff, but more from the nervousness of the pilot than from any aerodynamic vagaries on the part of the DC-3. McKay heard Shea's voice requesting taxi clearance, granted quickly. They rolled toward the assigned runway and ambled to a halt in the warm-up area where Shea pushed heavily on the brakes and revved the engines until he was satisfied with what the instruments were showing. The tower told them to taxi onto the runway and hold. Shea obliged.

The voice of the controller echoed metallically in McKay's ears.

"Midwest training flight 21, cleared for takeoff. Turn to heading two-zero-oh at fifteen hundred. You are VFR, right?"

"Affirmative VFR. Roger. We're ready to roll. Okay, Mac, you take her off."

McKay hadn't quite expected this jolt but he nodded, took a deep breath without realizing he had taken it, and shoved the throttles forward. The Pratt & Whitneys growled and swelled into a full-throated roar. The DC-3 trembled, then spurted as if a leash tieing it to the ground had been snapped.

At only twelve hundred feet it became readily apparent that it was not to be any familiarization milk run. Shea simply cut the left throttle. McKay felt the torque take hold like a giant vise. He kicked hard right rudder and stepped up the manifold pressure on number two engine to full-rated. The torque pull was stronger than on a B-25, which was something of a minor shock. He figured the DC-3 would be more tractable and docile than the bomber. She wasn't. She was a balky bitch and he was relieved when the power on two surged and the rudder correction responded.

"Good going," Shea said. "Take her up to seven thousand. I'll give you another heading then."

The training ordeal consumed more than an hour and it was a long hour. Mostly, the chief pilot let the rookie absorb the feel of the plane but he never let McKay relax completely. A few miles north of Frederick, while the DC-3 was in a slow, climbing turn, Shea cut an engine again and nodded approvingly as McKay reacted with smooth coordination of throttle and rudder control.

They tried one stall, sufficient to shake the teeth fillings, but the patient DC-3 supplied more advance warning than a B-25 and recovery was easier than McKay expected.

"She's a forgiving airplane," Shea said. "No glamor girl but you'll never fly a sturdier little bird. Just stay away from acrobatics, though. Bender had a student up one day and they were practicing stalls. The kid let it get into a spin and then froze on the yoke. Bender clobbered him with a fire extinguisher but when he pulled out they lost an aileron."

"How'd he land it?"

"Used his throttles—just kept manipulating power to keep the wings level. Helluva job of flying. But it goes to show the punishment a Three'll take. We had one lose three feet off the outer wing panel. Guy brushed a mountain with it. He just turned around and flew back to the airport. Okay, let's see what she feels like with gear and flaps down. We'll simulate an approach."

Back to business again. They finally touched down at eleven fifteen—Shea did the landing, much to McKay's combined disappointment and relief—and taxied directly to a Midwest hangar. They secured the cockpit and climbed out. McKay took a deep breath of fresh, cold air. Every muscle in his body ached. He felt as he had after the first football workout of the fall. But he was rewarded with Shea's warm smile.

"Hope I wasn't too tough."

"No sir. Tough but not too tough. I hope, well, I hope I didn't goof it up."

"You didn't. I've got you down for 1400 tomorrow. Let you try some landings. See you, Mac."

"Good night, sir. And thanks."

Shea waved his farewell. His stubby, solid figure disappeared in the darkness. McKay was about to head for the terminal and a taxi when he noticed the two men standing by the hangar door. Culver and O'Brian, bless their hearts. They were grinning broadly as he approached.

"I see you got it down in one piece," Culver said.

"What's the matter—was the movie lousy?"

"Aw hell, Mac," Paddy said. "We were just ribbing you. We wouldn't let you go up without moral support."

"Moral support my butt," Culver interrupted. "I just wanted to be here if you crashed. You've got two ties I love and that gray suit of yours would just about fit me."

They got in the Olds when McKay had a sudden thought. "Say, does anybody know how Sloan did?"

Culver shook his head but O'Brian gave them a fill-in.

"He flew right after I did. I gather it was pretty bad. He was so damned pale when he got out, I thought he must have been airsick. I tried to talk to him but he wouldn't say a word. Just said he didn't feel like talking. Then I bumped into Bill Mannion later and he said Gil told him he screwed up everything. Said Shea was real patient with him but he still couldn't do anything right."

"Washout," Culver predicted thoughtfully.

"I'm afraid so," McKay agreed.

"He's just scared," O'Brian said. "Maybe if they'd go easy on him and let him work it out. . . ."

"There's no time for him to work anything out," McKay said. "We've all got only one week. Let's face it—if any of us can't cut the mustard, we're gonna find it out in the next four days."

"I feel sorry for him," Culver said. "He wants to make the grade so damned bad."

"Maybe too bad," McKay observed. "That's one of his troubles."

The ax fell on Gil Sloan the next day. Shea had him up for nearly ninety minutes and it was Sloan himself who tossed in the towel. He sat wordlessly as Shea landed. When the chief pilot cut the engines, Gil merely turned to him and wanly smiled a surrender.

"Don't even bother to tell me how lousy I was. I thought I could swing it but I can't and I couldn't if you flew me for another six weeks. Thanks, anyway."

"I'm sorry, Sloan. It's no reflection on you, believe me. A helluva lot of fine men have failed. I'd be willing to let you try it again tomorrow, but . . ."

"It wouldn't do any good. I know it and you know it."

"Look, if you've got an airline bug in your craw, flying isn't the only job around. You didn't do badly in ground school. Dispatch might have something open. Want me to check?"

"Dispatch," Sloan said slowly. "Well, it did seem interesting. I'd appreciate that, Captain. I just . . . I just, well I'd just like to stay with Midwest some way."

"I'll talk to Jamison at Dispatch tonight. Come in and see me tomorrow morning, say about nine."

"Yes sir. And I'm sorry."

"Forget it, Gil. You just had the desire without the knack."

Impulsively Shea put out his hand and after a moment's hesitation, Sloan grasped it. Now that what Gil inwardly had always expected had actually occurred, the dread was gone, replaced by almost a sense of relief. No more Walter Mitty dreams of uniforms and ramp agents saluting and pretty stewardesses respectfully calling him "Captain." But his brief exposure to airline life had sold him on staying in it, somehow and in some way. He wondered how much dispatchers made. And they had authority, too, he rationalized. No uniforms, but they were important, and to every flight that took off.

He followed Shea out of the plane. For the first time in six weeks the constant tightness in his belly was gone. He felt he could almost whistle. And he ruefully confessed to himself he was glad he did not have to think about a flight tomorrow. But because he was only twenty-two and because he was a very normal human being who had been living with an impossible dream, he also decided that tonight he would get very, very drunk.

Apartment 201-B and the rest of the class had little time to mourn Sloan's fate. Each man got fifteen hours of Link time and another fifteen in the DC-3 with about ten of the latter concentrating on emergency procedures. By the end of the week their collective tails were dragging like a tail skid in an over-rotated landing. Late Friday afternoon they got their uniforms—an event which brought decidedly mixed reactions, namely pride followed by panic.

The trainees fingered the three stripes on the jacket sleeves with proud, loving fingers. They caressed the insignia on the hat, gold wings over which were placed in large black letters the words "U.S. Air Mail." Shea had been trying for years to get rid of this anachronism, which he regarded as more or less akin to goggles and a white scarf. But Kane liked the idea of the air mail touch which he insisted had a certain amount of historical dignity. In vain Shea pointed out that only Midwest and Northwest pilot hats proclaimed that their wearers flew the mail. All the other airlines put their own insignia above the visors.

"Goddammit," Shea had argued, "you might as well have us go back to carrying guns so everyone would know we were guarding the mail, not just flying it."

But he lost the argument, and it must be admitted that the class was impressed with the insignia. Also the rest of the uniform. Also, in a negative sense, the price tags. Bender diplomatically waited until they had tried on the uniforms, then broke the news at a final classroom session.

"As we told you at the start of ground school, the cost of the uniforms will be deducted from your pay over a period of one year," he announced.

He paused. As had the last fifteen or twenty classes to whom he had given this grim reminder, these fresh additions to the scheduled air carrier fleet of the United States of America couldn't have cared less.

"The uniform," Bender continued, "is $92.50. Your overcoat is $89. The raincoats you'll get this summer will be $50. The hats are $12.50. Each of the six blue shirts is $5. The two black ties are $5 apiece. And at the little dinner we're giving you tomorrow night, you'll also pick up your brain bags. These are the, well, the briefcases in which you'll carry your operating manuals, airport charts, en-route maps, world aeronautical charts, Part I of the Civil Air Regulations, and—oh yes, a flashlight which Midwest furnishes absolutely free. The brain bag itself is $37.50."

The fresh additions to the scheduled air carrier fleet of the United States of America had started to groan with the first mention of the $92.50. By the time Bender got down to the brain bag, every man was rapidly calculating the total damage and how much of a chunk would be torn cruelly and irrevocably from that $300 a month.

O'Brian's immediate and doleful reaction was a horror-stricken whisper to his roommates, "My God, how can I afford to take Pat out?"

"Go Dutch," Culver advised. "Nobody expects an airline pilot to pick up a stew's check."

Bender charitably waited for the accounting and arithmetic session to finish.

"Okay, let's settle down. I know the bill adds up to more than three hundred bucks—one month's pay while you're on probation. But stretched out over a year, it won't be as bad as you think. And you're going to be too busy to worry about dough for a while. Now, this is our last meeting together. I want to announce first of all the names of those who have succeessfully completed the training."

There was shocked silence at this. Was the roof going to fall on somebody at this late date? And in front of everybody?

Bender milked the moment like a ham actor. He looked sad, then frowned, cleared his throat dramatically, and finally broke into a smile that lit up the room. "You all passed, you lucky bastards!"

Spontaneously the class stood up to give itself a standing ovation. When the applause subsided, Bender continued in a more serious vein.

"You've been a damned fine bunch, from ground school all the way through. There isn't a man in this room I wouldn't want to fly with. I could give you some last words of advice, but Captain Shea will be doing that tomorrow night. Oh yes, the dinner. It's at the Statler Hotel in Washington. Wear your uniforms. It'll be the only time in your whole Midwest career you'll be allowed to take a drink while you're wearing them. Cocktails at 1700. It's stag but if you want to have your dates meet you afterwards, no objections. Or wives—I know a few of you are married. Base assignments will be announced at the dinner. That's it. I'll see you all tomorrow night."

The dinner was a whopping success, although Paddy got bad news before it started. Pat was scheduled to fly that day and said she couldn't get anyone to trade trips. O'Brian sulked all morning, moped all afternoon, and cursed all the way to the hotel. Not even Culver had the heart to either rib him or scold him and McKay felt almost as bad as Paddy. The Irishman had been talking all week about the moment when Pat would pin on his wings.

"She can do it Sunday," McKay tried to comfort him.

"It won't be the same, dammit."

"You're lucky you'll have someone around on Sunday," Culver pointed out. "Mac and me'll pin 'em on each other. So quit acting like a lovesick kid."

"That I am," agreed O'Brian. "That I am."

The big surprise at the dinner was the presence of Midwest President Mencken, who turned out to be a florid-faced giant of a man with a crewcut that made him look ten years younger than his age of sixty-two. He mingled freely with the awed new pilots, downed martinis with absolutely no apparent effect, and stunned O'Brian with the observation that "I hear you're dating Pat Donovan—fine girl."

McKay and Culver suspected that Shea wisely had briefed the president on a few personal items concerning the class, but Paddy assumed the man was obviously and without doubt the Greatest President of Any Airline in the World. Just think, a man with so many responsibilities knowing all about him and Pat. For a sickening second Culver thought the Irishman was going to fall on his knees and genuflect but Shea saved the day by shoving a bourbon and water in O'Brian's fist.

McKay noticed with some amusement that Midwest had no real worries about its new first officers getting loaded while in uniform. The cocktail hour came to a discreetly planned halt in exactly thirty minutes, and if there were any wobbly heads in the room the filet mignons took care of them. When the dessert had been served, Kane gave a blessedly short speech of congratulations, then introduced Mencken, whose speech was also right to the point.

"I've got only one thing to say to you men," the president growled in his rather rasping yet pleasant voice. "I'm damned proud of this airline. So long as you don't do anything to dishonor Midwest, you'll find me on your side. I hope I'll fly with every one of you someday."

Kane rose again but only to introduce "the finest chief pilot of any airline in the world—John Shea!"

"What I have to say tonight is mostly business," Shea began. "I'll get the sentimental crap over with in a hurry. I've never worked with or known a finer training class. If you just keep your damned noses clean, you'll make out fine—professionally and financially.

"Base assignments will be handed you in an envelope when you get your wings. You can quit sweating. I'm happy to say that every man got his choice. That's not because we were kindhearted. It just worked out that way and frankly, you're goddamned lucky. That's the first time it's happened for years.

"You'll all be on reserve status for one month. That means you call Crew Schedule every time you leave your apartment and let them know how long you'll be gone—which had better not be too long. You'll fly with one captain for the first thirty days, unless you hit a reserve trip. And you call captains 'sir' unless otherwise instructed. I suggest you check Crew Schedule first thing tomorrow morning because some of you will be flying by Monday—particularly those based here. Men assigned to Chicago and New York will be going out of here tomorrow. We've got hotel rooms for you and you'll get a chance to find permanent diggings during the week. You'll get your seniority number, by the way, with your first trip.

"It's important for you to check in with Crew Schedule even if you've just come in off a flight. Because when you're not flying a trip, you'll probably be riding a jump seat for observation purposes.

"Now, as I call your name, I'll be proud to give you your wings and your brain bags. Keep the wings shined and the bags full."

McKay was to remember that moment for the rest of his life. Not even the day he got his Air Force wings was more vividly etched in his mind. He knew those would be impermanent and his military flying just a phase in his life. Tonight the wings were a career symbol. A way of living that was to command his allegiance. When Shea called out "McDonald McKay" he had the almost silly feeling that the only ceremony that could have more meaning and involve as much emotion would be his wedding.

When the last pair of wings had been handed out, Shea made a final announcement. "If you're gonna do more drinking in way of celebration, get the hell home first and take off those uniforms. And remember, I'm a sympathetic sonofabitch and I'll try to be fair—but I'll crucify any man caught drinking so much as a beer while he's wearing that uniform. Good luck to you all."

Apartment 201-B shook hands as they did the day they finished ground school. All three of their envelopes contained their names followed by a cryptic "DCA." They had agreed in advance to go back to the apartment and celebrate by themselves, but when they left the dining room all three came to a halt.

Waiting in the corridor, stunning in a dark green cocktail dress, was Pat Donovan. Her eyes were wet, and pride oozed from under every long eyelash.

"Good evening, First Officer McKay. Good evening, First Officer Culver. Good evening, First Officer O'Brian—and may I pin on your wings, darling?"

"Well I'll be damned," Culver marveled. "O'Brian—don't faint!"

O'Brian didn't. He kissed Pat gently on the forehead. "I don't know how you did it," he said softly, "but I'm glad you did. And I think it would be nice if you pinned on all of our wings."

McKay and Culver heard later how she did it. Or rather, how Shea did it. That afternoon he had come across Pat sitting morosely in a corner of Operations; unable to keep the tears from her eyes.

"What's wrong, honey?"

"I wanted to be with Paddy after he graduated or whatever you call it," she sniffed. "Only I've got this trip and I couldn't trade it and—oh—I'm miserable."

"What's your flight?"

"Five-twenty and it's got a Chicago layover."

"Who's your supervisor?"

"Grace Wooley."

"Stay right here," Shea ordered.

She saw him march to a phone and dial a number and she would never forget what he said.

"Grace? John Shea. I'm in OPS and I'm pulling Pat Donovan off 520. The poor little dear is so sick she can hardly move. . . . How the hell do I know if it's her time of the month? She's just sick. You get some girl on reserve down here on the double. That's fine, Gracie. Believe me, Pat couldn't possibly fly today. Thanks, honey."

The chief pilot turned to Pat.

"The dinner's at seven and I suggest you be there no later than eight thirty. Wait for him in the corridor—it's the Empire State Room on the mezzanine."

Pat had burst into tears, as she confided to them later. Paddy almost bawled in mingled sympathy and glee when she told them the story on the way back to the apartment. Culver, he of the "Sentiment is for sissies—I'm all for Les" philosophy, started to make a wisecrack but inexplicably choked up and couldn't get the words out.

"I think," said McDonald McKay, "I'm going to like the airline business."

Chapter 4

Despite what he had mentioned to Shea, Barney Barnwell didn't get McKay for that first month. The lure of higher pay on four-engine equipment was too strong and Barnwell had bid a new DC-4 trip. Crew Schedule called McKay early

Sunday afternoon and told him to report to Operations at 0800 Monday for Flight 221. Hastily McKay checked a schedule, then whistled.

"Boy, what an initiation."

"What's 221?" O'Brian asked.

"Milk run, and I don't mean the milk runs we had in the war. Baltimore, Harrisburg, New York, Hartford, Providence, and Boston. Wonder who the captain is?"

Culver thought he must be pretty junior to bid a Pogostick trip like 221. Les himself had drawn a flight to Richmond, Raleigh, and Atlanta Monday evening. O'Brian was still sweating out word of his first assignment.

"Well, I dunno," reasoned McKay. "He might be junior and maybe he just likes to make a lot of landings. A few trips like that and you're through for the month."

That night they boned up again on the DC-3 manuals, each of them nervous, each unwilling to admit it, and each knowing damned well that all of them were. In training they had heard some weird stories about weird captains who ate new first officers alive. It was a subtle form of hazing, some of it beneficial, some of it cruel. Like the left-seater who deliberately made mistakes just to see if the copilot noticed. If he said anything, the captain would chew him out for correcting him. If he kept his mouth shut, the captain would ream him for not saying anything.

By the time apartment 201-B dropped off to a fitful sleep, the occupants were firmly convinced that their first captains would have the pleasing personality of Edward Hyde and the general appearance of the Frankenstein monster. Paddy was in worse shape than any of them; Crew Schedule hadn't called him at all, which merely gave him more time to worry.

McKay's alarm went off at six the next morning. He shaved carefully and for the first time he put on the gray Midwest uniform for real. Paddy got up to have coffee with him, but Culver stayed in the sack. O'Brian already had promised to drive McKay to the airport. McKay knew he had to do something about a car and soon; O'Brian couldn't keep supplying all the transportation with their schedules varying so much. Culver already had announced his intentions of buying a car that very morning.

They drove to the airport in almost complete silence. McKay lifted his brain bag out of the rear seat, and he wondered how many times in his life would he repeat that move and how many brain bags would he wear out before he quit flying.

"Good trip, Mac."

"Thanks, Paddy. Hope you get one today."

"If I don't, I'll pick you up at ten tonight. That when you get back?"

"Yep, but don't bother. I can get a cab or bus back."

"If I'm not here, you'll know I caught a trip."

"Roger."

They both grinned for no good reason. McKay strode toward Operations. As soon as he entered, he looked at the big blackboard on which were marked the various flights for the morning hours. 221 was toward the top. He read the crew names chalked beside the flight number.

CAPTAIN—H. Snodgrass. FIRST OFFICER—M. McKay. STEWARDESS—Gillum.

Snodgrass. The name sounded familiar, although at this point McKay was jittery enough to have forgotten the name of Orville Wright. He looked around rather forlornly, trying to decide whether he should ask out loud for the whereabouts of Captain Snodgrass or wait until Hyde-Frankenstein paged his new pigeon.

He was about to ask a dispatcher if Captain Snodgrass was in the room when a voice carrying the dulcet tones of an itinerant hog caller boomed through Operations.

"Anybody here named McKay?"

"Here, sir."

McKay turned around to look for the owner of the foghorn voice and saw a slim, rather dour-faced pilot coming toward him.

"McKay?"

"Yes sir." McKay's heart lost altitude. This must be Snodgrass, and he seemed about as cheerful as a dyspeptic under-
taker. His face simply did not go with his voice. But his smile
didn't go with either. When Snodgrass grinned, the dourness
disintegrated so fast that McKay almost expected to hear the
tinkle of breaking glass.

"Hi, I'm Harrison Snodgrass. Otherwise known as Snorkel
Snodgrass. Call me 'sir' until your third trip. After that I'll
castrate you if I hear one more 'sir.'"

McKay's heart regained altitude. This character obviously
was just that—a character. Then it dawned on him that he
had heard the name Snodgrass before. He had been in Shea's
office with Culver filling out an application for probationary
membership with ALPA. Mrs. Gillespie was on the phone,
hung up, and went into Shea's office without closing the door.
McKay and Culver couldn't help hearing her report to the
chief pilot.

"It's Snorkel Snodgrass again, Captain Shea. Passenger Service got a complaint."

"Oh God," moaned Shea. "Now what?"

"He was rolling nuts and bolts down the aisle and one of
the passengers thought the plane was coming apart. Then
when he landed, he asked over the PA if anyone knew . . .
if anyone knew, and I'm quoting Passenger Service, 'Does
anyone know where the hell we are?'"

"That isn't so bad. Last time I called him on the carpet,
it was for boarding a plane with dark glasses, a white cane,
and a book under his arm. The title was *How to Fly* and he
walked up and down the aisle with the damned thing, tapping
that cane ahead of him."

"I suppose you'd like to see him?"

Shea sighed in total resignation.

"Yeh, I guess I'd better. The only trouble is that he gets
six letters of commendation for every complaint. He'll scare
the hell out of one customer and he'll sell twenty others on
air travel. Well, give him a ring and tell him I want to see
him."

Mrs. Gillespie had come out of Shea's office shaking her head and chuckling. McKay and Culver had agreed that Captain Snodgrass must be interesting to fly with. Now he was standing in front of McKay, who was pondering Shea's motives in assigning him to a clown. He had no way of knowing yet that Shea also considered the clown one of the best pilots on the line, one whose incorrigible sense of humor also gave him infinite patience with new copilots. Shea actually had gotten into a mild argument with Bender over the chief pilot's approval of Snodgrass for McKay's first month, when he heard that Barnwell had bid off DC-3's.

"He'll just learn some bad habits," Bender insisted.

"Maybe. And he'll learn some good ones. Snorkel's a nut, but underneath all that horseplay he's a solid pilot. He happens to be a nut about flying by the book. All I know is that every new man who's flown with him picks up *that* habit."

So it was Harrison Snodgrass who was about to introduce McKay to commercial aviation, and the latter wasn't sure whether to rejoice that he hadn't drawn a grouchy martinet, or to wish he could be flying with someone less informal.

"You checked your mailbox yet?" Snodgrass asked.

It hadn't occurred to McKay yet that he even rated one. "No, sir."

"Better. Your seniority number should be in it."

They found the box with a freshly typed "McKay, M" inserted in the slot underneath. There was an envelope inside. McKay opened it and found a mimeographed note from Personnel offering its own congratulations and advising that his seniority number was 1279, which by agreement with the Air Line Pilots Association would be his union seniority as well as his company number. Well, he had only 1278 pilots ahead of him, about half of them copilots who would be entitled to don the fourth stripe ahead of him—no matter how well he did. Seniority, Sex, and Salary—that was the time-honored, half-joking motto of the airline pilot and the priority given the first category was not capricious.

"Ever made out a flight plan?" Snodgrass broke into his thoughts.

"Practice ones, yes sir."

"Well, let's try one. You just watch for the time being."

Snodgrass led him to the dispatch area. He pulled a flight plan form out of a cubbyhole and sat down at a small desk, McKay leaning over his shoulder. He worked rapidly, filling in the airway numbers, planned altitude on each segment, fuel load. . . .

"Hey, Mike, what's my fuel on 221?"

A leathery-faced dispatcher pawed through some papers. "Nine-fifty, Snorkel."

"Okay, thanks. Let's see, wish we could get rid of this Harrisburg dog-leg. Make more sense to stop at Philly."

Snodgrass filled out the rest of the flight plan, and with McKay dutifully by his side went over to check the en-route weather.

"Should be able to make it VFR all the way," he commented after perusing the hieroglyphics that had tumbled off the weather teletype. "Good day for your first trip. Front moving in north of Philly tonight but we'll be practically home by then. Return flight is easy. One stop at LaGuardia then nonstop to Washington. Let's go meet our stew."

They found Jean Gillum chatting with some other stewardesses. She was a pretty, soft-complexioned redhead, but rather plump and it was obvious that she needed the girdle required for even hipless girls.

"Hi, Snorkel."

"Hi, Jeanie. Want you to meet our new copilot, Mac McKay."

McKay thought wryly that even the stewardess got to call a captain by his first name before the copilot earned that honor. He shook hands with her and was mildly disturbed when she gave him a frank going-over.

"Any VIP's aboard, Jeanie? Or company vice presidents?"

"No, Snorkel. Your PA's will be unfettered."

"Next thing you know, we'll have to submit them to Public Relations in advance. Well, Mac, let's climb on our bird. See you on board, Jeanie. I'll take my coffee after we leave Baltimore."

Their DC-3 was parked by Gate 4, a fuel truck alongside finishing up the feeding process. Snodgrass did a walk-around inspection first, pointing out to McKay the items to be checked visually. It impressed McKay that with all his reputation for unconventional clowning, Snodgrass wasn't cutting any corners.

"That walk-around will be your job from now on," the captain said. "And don't ever kiss it off. You never know what you'll catch."

They finally boarded. It was only ten minutes before departure time, and the two pilots began their checklist—McKay reading it and Snodgrass laconically acknowledging each point.

"You'll memorize the damned thing after a while, Mac, but don't rely on memory. We lost one before the war that way. Mechanic forgot to remove the blocks from the elevators and the captain was one of those 'I know the checklist by heart' boys. He started rolling and kept going right into the Potomac."

The passengers were coming through the gate and McKay could hear the departure announcement.

"This is the final call for Midwest Flight 221, DC-3 service to New York and Boston with intermediate stops at Baltimore, Harrisburg, New York, Hartford, and Providence. Final call."

A ramp agent outside signaled an all-clear.

"Okay Mac, start engines. Number one."

It coughed protestingly in the cold, but eventually caught and number two followed suit. McKay contacted the tower and got taxi clearance. He had a minor moment of panic when the tower read their approved flight plan with the pace of a tobacco auctioneer. McKay was supposed to copy it and read it back but he missed whatever airways they were to fly north of New York. Embarrassed beyond words, he looked helplessly at Snodgrass, who just grinned and prompted McKay on the rest of the clearance.

"You'll get used to it," he consoled McKay. "Some of those guys must think we've got photographic minds."

They were airborne a few moments later. Snodgrass leveled off at three thousand and picked up the PA mike. McKay half expected to hear him crack some joke or make a flip comment. He didn't know that Shea had warned Snorkel— it was more of a plea—to "play it straight for the month."

Click.

"Good morning, folks. This is Captain Snodgrass. On behalf of First Officer McKay and myself"—a nice gesture, McKay thought—"welcome aboard Midwest Flight 221. Our en-route weather is good and we should have a smooth trip. I know Miss Gillum will be happy to make your flight as pleasant as possible. Thank you."

Click.

"By the way, Mac, if you have any questions, lemme have them. Don't be bashful. You're supposed to be learning. Even if you think they're stupid, ask."

McKay nodded. He had a couple but they could wait. The old cockpit was too noisy for conversation.

It was routine in and out of Baltimore. But when they left O'Brian's favorite city, Snodgrass endeared himself to the new first officer.

"Wanna take her for a while?"

"Yes sir."

McKay flew the DC-3 with more care than was warranted. Snodgrass leaned back in assumed nonchalance as if he had already accepted the copilot as an accomplished veteran. He buzzed the stewardess who brought him coffee. McKay shook his head when Snodgrass asked if he wanted a cup—he wanted to concentrate on his flying. He appreciated the captain's turning over the controls on the second leg. He knew that a lot of copilots would be lucky to have twenty minutes of flight experience on a first trip.

Five minutes out of Harrisburg, with the snow-covered

hills of Pennsylvania passing under their wings, Snodgrass took over again with a friendly "Good flying but I'd better take it—you're not supposed to make any takeoffs or landings for the first couple of months." He was so businesslike that McKay had trouble associating him with the carefree captain who was something of a Midwest legend. But when they landed in Harrisburg, he learned quickly that Harrison Snodgrass was not likely to let a flight be totally routine.

They were taxiing to the ramp and McKay had finished the after-landing checklist when Snodgrass flicked on the landing lights. McKay hastily consulted the checklist to see if he had missed that item although he couldn't figure out why the lights had to be tested in broad daylight with the sun beaming down. There was no such item. The captain chuckled.

"After we stop," he explained, "look up at the control tower."

McKay did. Through the big windows he could see four or five men looking down on the DC-3. All had field glasses. It still made no sense to the first officer until Snodgrass buzzed the stewardess on the intercom.

"Jeanie? All your passengers off? Okay, the tower's waiting. Mac, sit in my seat and open the window. Look back toward the tail."

He climbed out of his seat and McKay obliged. Stewardess Gillum, standing on the tiny set of DC-3 ramp stairs, lifted her skirt off one shapely leg a good six inches above a dimpled knee. McKay's glance shifted to the tower where the holders of the field glasses were trying to wave and concentrate on Miss Gillum simultaneously. She waved back and re-entered the cabin, laughing. Snodgrass put on the copilot's earphones and spoke into the radio mike, still on the tower frequency. He motioned McKay to put on the captain's earphones.

"Satisfied with that one?" he asked the tower.

"Roger, Snorkel old buddy. She's a honey. Jean Gillum, wasn't it?"

"Yep. I had to make up for the last time. I couldn't have

shown that stew to a CAA inspector. Besides, she had no sense of humor."

"Roger, Snorkel. See you next trip."

Snodgrass rather proudly explained his rapport with the Harrisburg tower.

"Every time I come through Harrisburg I flash the lights on when I've got a reasonably good-looking stew. That's the signal for them to get out the glasses. Hell, I never get stacked up over here. Soon's they hear ole Snorkel's coming in, I get priority. Can't pull it all the time. Depends on the gal. Jean's a good sport, though. Once I turned on the lights and kept blinking them. They figured I had nothing less than a movie queen on board. Then I sent the copilot out. The bastards got even. They made me wait an extra ten minutes before they'd clear me for takeoff. Well, let's get off and check the weather to New York."

That was Snodgrass. A somewhat incongruous mixture of a happy-go-lucky extrovert and a supercautious pilot.

Snodgrass let the copilot fly twenty minutes of the Harrisburg–New York segment and liked his ship-handling when they ran into some mild turbulence. Shea had told him McKay was a mature kid and a good prospect, and Snodgrass had great respect for the chief pilot's judgment. Barnwell had mentioned in OPS one day that McKay had accident investigation experience and might be willing to serve on an ALPA safety committee. Snorkel, for all his propensity for gags, was a hard-working member of the Midwest safety unit—another factor which wrenched from Shea so much patient tolerance toward Snorkel's antics.

For some time Shea's opinion of Snodgrass had not been too high. Sort of an airborne playboy, he figured, with a lot of ability and very little common sense. Then one day he overheard Snodgrass bawling out a copilot for some act of carelessness. The latter had said something like "Why make a Federal case out of a little mistake?"

The Snodgrass who had ripped into the copilot that day was no prank-prone Laughing Boy. Not even Shea had ever dismantled an erring pilot the way Snorkel did on that occasion. Coming from Snorkel Snodgrass, the anger and what might have been charitably called a lecture were even more effective. Snodgrass actually was quivering with rage and the copilot was white with fear.

Yet it was only a week later that a stewardess officially filed a complaint against Snodgrass. Snorkel had been browsing through a novelty store and come across a mask of the Frankenstein monster. Impulsively he bought the gruesome thing and took it on his plane that night. They were cruising peacefully between Washington and Columbus when Snorkel turned the controls over to the first officer and donned the frightful mask. Then he rang for the stewardess, a fresh-faced little thing right out of stew school.

She opened the cockpit door, wondering what her captain might have on his mind.

"Yes, Captain?"

Snorkel turned around slowly. The glow from the red night instruments put spots of blood on the monster's green face.

"Good evening, my dear," Snorkel rumbled in his froggy voice.

The stewardess screamed and jumped back so hard that she bumped her head against a radio rack. This brought tears and the contrite Snodgrass, while he finally stemmed the tears, couldn't placate the angry girl. She refused to speak to him the rest of the trip and reported the incident to her supervisor, who sadly relayed the complaint to Shea.

"I can't figure you out, Snorkel," Shea had said in the subsequent carpet session. "How the hell can a guy who worked seventy-two hours without sleep on our North Carolina crash pull a dumb joke like that on a rookie stew?"

"I dunno, John," Snodgrass had answered. "I didn't think she'd get that scared. Look, I'm truly sorry. But I can't help pulling a gag now and then. I just seem to wanna get some fun out of the job."

Shea's punitive action was an order that Snodgrass write the stewardess a personal letter of apology—and try wearing the damned mask on cargo flights for two weeks. Snodgrass protested the latter punishment as a sentence to an airborne Siberia. He hated a cargo run because there weren't any passengers to talk to. But Shea was firm, and he had hopes that Snorkel might mend his ways at least a little.

He should have known better. On Snorkel's first cargo trip he discovered that one of the items being shipped was a casket bearing the body of a freshly deceased citizen who had died in Washington and was being sent to Atlanta for burial. Snorkel noted that the casket bore the unlucky man's name. He copied it down and when he landed in Atlanta, he obtained one of Midwest's "Write and tell us how you like our service" forms from a seat back in another ship.

He carefully filled out the form, expressing in vitriolic and bitter language a total disgust for every phase of Midwest's service, from food to baggage handling. He signed the name of his expired passenger and mailed the form to Passenger Service.

It took Passenger Service considerable time to locate the passenger who so obviously needed some expert soothing. It took somewhat less time to learn that the passenger who had written "I'll never fly your airline again" quite obviously wouldn't, or any other airline. The circumstances of the incident were such that Passenger Service informed Shea it strongly suspected Captain Snodgrass. Shea confronted Snorkel with Passenger Service's suspicions and he virtuously denied the guilt.

"Off the record, Snorkel?"

"Off the record."

"Was it you?"

"Yep."

"You want off cargo?"

"Hell yes."

"Promise to behave yourself? Like for a couple of months?"

"Promise."

"Okay," Shea said wearily. "I'll put you back on passenger bids."

McKay was not yet aware of all such Snodgrass shenanigans, of course. Right now he was busy wet-nursing the DC-3 through the choppy air and wondering why Captain Snodgrass never offered a word of advice or criticism. He had a hunch he wasn't doing *that* well, but Snodgrass seemed well occupied with ATC communications.

It was when they finally landed in Boston and had a three-hour layover before the return flight that he found out why, along with a new insight into his first captain. Snorkel had suggested the crew have an early dinner together at the airport restaurant.

"Dutch, of course," he added gallantly to Jean Gillum.

"What else?" was Miss Gillum's resigned and naturally cynical reply.

Dinner was like any repast at an airport restaurant, adequate but not exactly inspiring to a gourmet. During coffee Snodgrass lit a cigarette and asked the stewardess, "Mind if we talk shop a little?"

"No, go right ahead and don't mind me."

"We won't," Snodgrass said placidly. "And it's just between the three of us. This here is Mac's first trip and I got a few observations to make."

"Maybe I'd better go for a walk."

"Do that, and I'll pick up your check," the captain offered.

"For such a gesture I'll walk up and down every runway in Boston," beamed Miss Gillum. She snuffed out her own cigarette, patted Snodgrass on his head, and left.

"Well, let me have it with no punches pulled," said McKay. "What did I do wrong?"

"Wrong? You didn't do anything wrong. You handled her fine. Don't get a swelled head—you haven't made any ILS approaches yet. I just wanted to chew the fat with you."

"Look, Captain Snodgrass, I'm no prima donna. I'd really appreciate any tips, criticism, or anything else. I know I've got a lot to learn."

"Sure you do. And you will. Before the month's over, I'll be telling you what I think you should have done, or what

I think you did wrong. And next month you'll fly with someone else and he'll tell you what *he* thinks you should do.
That's just my point."

"I'm not quite sure I follow you."

"Mac, Christ knows how long you'll be flying copilot. If
you're real lucky, you'll get the left seat after five years. It'll
more likely be eight or nine or ten. Until you get that fourth
stripe, you'll fly with God knows how many captains and
every damned one'll have his own ideas how a trip should
be run. How a plane should be flown. One guy'll tell you
your approaches are too long and the next one'll bawl you
out because your approach isn't flat enough. And you'll try
to please every damned one of them. So do you know what
that'll do to your flying?"

Snodgrass didn't wait for McKay to answer.

"I'll tell you what. You'll absorb a helluva lot of knowledge,
a helluva lot of good habits, and a few bad ones because
what's good for one captain isn't necessarily good for another
—or for a copilot, either. On ninety-nine out of a hundred
trips you'll be flying with your hands and the other guy's
brains. You'll be using your eyes and his technique."

"I see what you mean," McKay said slowly, "but there
doesn't seem to be much I can do about it."

"No, there isn't. The big trouble is that a lot of captains
either won't admit this or they aren't even aware of it. And
you can't blame them. Once they get in that left seat, they
acquire more than just a fourth stripe and a few hundred
extra bucks a month. They acquire a very, very large boulder
known as responsibility. Also spelled w-o-r-r-y. So until they're
damned sure of a copilot, they'll take the natural and easy
way out. They'll just try to mold him in their own image
because basically, that's also the safest way most of the time."

"I gather," McKay said, "the best thing to do is ride with
the punches and when I'm a captain I choose my own way
of doing things."

"Right. And when you're a captain, you'll find you're
gonna be a much better pilot than when you were a first

officer. Not because you can fly better, but because you'll be making your own decisions. And that's what airline flying is —decisions. As a matter of fact, I'll tell you something that'll surprise you. Three or four or five years from now you won't be as good a pilot as you are, say, in the next six months. In five years you'll have been overexposed to too many captains."

McKay signaled a waitress to bring two more coffees. He beat a quiet tattoo with a spoon.

"Question," he said.

"Shoot."

"Does this mean I'll fly with you for a month and you won't say anything to me because you figure the next month somebody'll tell me different?"

"Nope. Maybe I overgeneralized. Most of your mistakes will be the kind any captain would correct. It's just when one man tells you something and another tells you just the opposite, you're going to have to make up your own mind which is right. And that'll come with experience. Maybe you'll find out both are right—they just do things differently. I just wanted you to get the general idea. Any more questions?"

"Yeh," McKay grinned. "I'd sure like to know where you got that nickname."

"It's a very interesting story," Snodgrass said, leaning back in his chair and blowing a very expert smoke ring. "I got the name Snorkel because I was the only man in World War II to catch VD on a submarine."

He looked sideways at McKay, who knew Snodgrass must be kidding but wasn't quite sure and hated to admit it. "Is it protocol to ask for the details?" he finally inquired.

"Sure. If you must know, I flew Civil Air Patrol on weekends during the war. One Saturday afternoon I spotted a German sub right outside Chesapeake Bay. I radioed for help and damned if a blimp didn't come out of nowhere and bombed the shit out of it. It was one of their new snorkel types and from that day on, everyone on the line called me Snorkel. Frankly, I like the first version better."

The waitress arrived with the coffee and for the next few minutes both men learned more about each other, swapping accounts of their backgrounds. Snodgrass didn't exactly have one that would have given any inkling he was going to become (1) an airline captain or (2) commercial aviation's Emmett Kelly. He was the son of a high school teacher, raised in a strict Baptist home, and his first exposure to airplanes were the occasional *War Aces*, *Battle Aces*, and *Flying Heroes*—the post-World War I pulps that saturated the newsstands in the twenties and thirties.

"My father was a nut on murder mysteries, of all things," Snodgrass recounted. "He kept insisting that if I wanted some relaxing reading, I should go in for mysteries. One night I brought home a *Spicy Detective* and from then on he let me read the airplane pulps. I worked in a garage and saved up enough dough to take flying lessons and I finally got a job with Midwest as a mechanic. I kept up the lessons and got a crack at pilot training. You know, Johnny Shea was the first captain I ever flew with."

"He's a helluva guy," McKay said.

"He's just that. I remember one day we're taking a flight out and some middle-aged babe walked up to us in the terminal building. She says, 'Are you the captain on flight whatever-it-was to Detroit?' Shea says yes ma'am, and she says, 'you're awfully little to be flying a big airplane.' Johnny just looks at her and says, 'Lady, I'm gonna fly the damned thing, not carry it.'"

The Shea anecdote prompted Snodgrass to reach back in his memory and recall other yarns about the chief pilot— this was when McKay learned Shea was one of the men who had pulled the whiskey bottle stunt at the United ticket counter.

"That wasn't the funniest thing I ever saw happen to Shea," Snorkel continued. "One night during the war we were flying a Three to Raleigh and we had a real old gal on board, must have been around eighty or even ninety. She had never flown before in her life and she was scared to death. I guess we were abeam of Richmond when Shea had to go to the blue room—you know, the can."

McKay nodded. There had been no formal instruction on the traditional terminology assigned to aircraft lavatories, but somewhere through ground school and flight training he had picked up the designation of "blue room."

"Well, it seems the lock on the blue room door was busted and Johnny went in, closed the door, but couldn't lock it. About this time, the old lady asked the stewardess if there was a lavatory on the plane. The stewardess said yes, and she offered to help the old gal to the blue room. She hadn't noticed Shea going back. So she tried the door, it wasn't locked and she pushed it open. There was Shea, sitting on the can.

"There was dead silence. Shea just looked at them and they looked at him. Finally the stewardess blurts out, 'Captain Shea, I'd like you to meet one of our passengers, Mrs. Jones. This is Captain Shea.' Johnny could have killed the stew, but the more he thought about it the funnier it got. When he got back to the cockpit he was laughing so hard he couldn't fly—and that was the time he let me make my first night landing. The only trouble was, I was laughing too and we damned near cracked up. Just as I flared out, I thought about him sitting on that john when the stew opened the door and I nearly caught a wing tip on the runway."

By the time Snorkel had finished a few more airline stories, it was time to return to Operations. Snodgrass let McKay fill out the flight plan, and he also let him fly most of the New York–Washington leg right down to final approach. He made a few suggestions—all of them good, McKay had to admit—and it was with a rather full, happy, and satisfied heart that he bid Snodgrass and Jean Gillum good

night. He felt particularly good when Snorkel had offhand-
edly mentioned, "I'll give you a ring one of these days and
you come over and have dinner with me and the missus—
she's nuttier than I am."

McKay already had learned at their postdinner conversation that Marion Snodgrass was an ex-American stew who
from Snorkel's description was just a female version of himself.

"She trapped me," Snorkel had said. "I told her I wanted
daughters, not sons, and she said every baby born in her
family since 1840 had been a girl. So what have we got?
Three boys!"

Paddy wasn't in Operations and McKay figured he must
have been called for a flight. He took a taxi back to the
apartment and found it empty. He still was on reserve and
he wasn't supposed to drink anything, but he was so keyed
up that he poured himself a stiff shot of bourbon before
he went to bed.

The first month passed quickly. The three roommates flew
observation flights over the system when they didn't fly as
first officers. They studied when they weren't on observation
trips. Les bought a 1941 Chevy convertible and McKay
really splurged—he paid $2095 for a 1946 Ford club coupe
with an alleged 8200 miles on the speedometer and the
salesman assured him he was being generous to an ex-service-
man (the same car brand-new would have cost about $1900
but cars were hard to get). Paddy kept dating Pat Donovan
and confided to McKay that they planned to get married
as soon as he could afford a ring.

They did get engaged after O'Brian disappeared mysteriously on a Friday morning and came back to Apartment
201-B on Saturday with his face looking as if a lawn mower
had run over it. He also had with him a diamond, which he
showed to Culver and McKay with his shy brand of pride.
Both whistled in impressed envy.

"By the way," Culver noted, "where the hell have you been?"

"In Newark."

"On a trip?"

"No."

"You were taking a chance, Paddy, weren't you?" McKay asked. "You're still on reserve."

"I cleared it with Shea. He let me off for the day."

"And what were you doing in Newark?" Culver demanded.

"Getting $300 for the ring."

"What did you do—rent out as a stud?"

"Knock it off, Les," McKay interrupted. "Paddy, where did you get those bruises and cuts on your face?"

"Jumping out of a plane."

His roommates gaped.

"You did what?" said McKay.

"Jumped out of a plane. Some copilot in OPS told me this outfit in Newark was giving three hundred bucks to test a new kind of evacuation seat. He gave me the dope and I deadheaded up to Newark. They took me up to ten thousand in a two-place P-51 and blew the seat out. The wind caught the chute and I landed in a bramble patch and got my face cut up. But they gave me the dough and I went right to a jewelry store and bought the ring."

"Holy Toledo," breathed Culver. "You damned fool."

"Does Shea know why you went to Newark?" McKay queried.

"Nope. I just told him it was important and had to do with Pat and me getting engaged."

"Does Pat know?"

"She saw my face this morning. I told her we went out to a bar the other night and we got innocently mixed up in a fight."

"You'd have done better," Culver advised him, "if you had told her the truth. She knows you wouldn't get involved in a barroom brawl if you heard somebody insult the Pope."

"She believed me," insisted O'Brian. "I think."

Whether she did or not nobody found out for some time. She took the ring the next night. Paddy asked McKay to be his best man and Culver to be chief usher.

"Do they let Protestants be ushers?" Culver asked seriously.

"Sure. And Les, I hope you're not hurt because I asked Mac to be best man. I can only have one."

"Hell no. An old roué like me doesn't deserve to be best man. Besides, it might give me the wrong ideas."

"Have you set a date?" McKay wanted to know.

"Sort of. We figure in about four or five months after I get some more flying in. Maybe six months. Pat wants to start saving up for furniture. I sure won't be saving much outa my three hundred a month."

"I'm real pleased, Paddy," McKay said.

"So am I," Culver added. "Just think, it all started when I got you a blind date."

Despite O'Brian's part-time presence on Cloud Nine, he was too good and too conscientious a pilot to let it interfere with his job. He had drawn a quiet, easygoing, and competent Swede named Tod Thornton for the month and they had hit it off well. Culver had the most trouble of the three, being somewhat more independent and less patient than either of his roommates. In fact, he had real trouble.

His first captain was a fastidious, rather conceited, and ill-tempered perfectionist who, like Culver, was a wolf but not nearly as successful, thus accounting partially for the ill-temper. His name was Fred Laswell and being a perfectionist, he hated to admit the slightest deviation from what he himself considered perfection. He was the type of captain who got along fine with a fawning first officer, which Culver was not.

Their first two flights were uneventful, mainly because Laswell did all the flying. "No rush about it," he told Les patronizingly. "Just want you to relax and get your feet wet slowly."

He kept explaining virtually every move he made, some of it helpful to a new pilot, but much of it so basic or repetitious that Culver got bored. And the lecture was delivered in a tone that indicated Laswell had taught Lindbergh how to fly.

On the third trip he finally let Les take the controls and instantly became hypercritical. Nothing Culver did seemed to please him. "You're not flying a damned fighter plane," he snarled after Culver banked in obedience to an ATC radar identification request.

Two minutes later, when ATC ordered a course change and Les banked again, Laswell snapped: "You're not flying a milk truck, Culver."

Les knew both turns had been identical and competently smooth, but he held his temper. A man who really loved flying, he actually was glad when the captain took over and this bothered him. He said nothing to McKay and O'Brian and even lied when they wanted to know what kind of captain he was flying with.

"Nice enough guy," was his only response. Culver had his faults, such as an overactive libido, but he was a tough, self-reliant youngster with an aversion to whining or the slightest bit of self-pity.

Laswell on one flight surprised him by being cheerful, and even complimented Culver's ship-handling. Les wondered about the sudden change and figured maybe the captain was just moody on occasions. The stewardess brought them a luncheon snack a few minutes later and when she left, Laswell smirked and confided:

"A real swinger. I laid her last night—terrific."

It dawned on Culver that Laswell's moods might be in direct proportion to his bedroom successes—or failures. He quickly learned that his analysis was only too accurate. They had a layover in Buffalo on their next trip and Culver overheard him asking the stewardess to come up to his room for a beer later.

She declined, and rather tartly. The next day Laswell was an absolute bastard. His criticism of Culver's flying dripped with sarcasm and Culver, seething inwardly, took it in silence. It didn't help their relationship when Laswell, coming in too high on a landing at Binghamton, bounced the DC-3 twice before it settled down. Les realized they were too high but he said nothing—and he was rewarded by the captain's turning on him the minute they pulled up to the ramp and chopped the throttles.

"Dammit, Culver, what the hell do you think the copilot's for—sit there like a bloody dummy? You just along for the ride? I made that approach too high on purpose—just to see if you'd catch it. Shape up, boy!"

"Sorry, Captain. It won't happen again."

Something disrespectful in Culver's tone peeked through his mask of deference. He was quite sure Laswell had not deliberately fouled up the landing to test his copilot's alertness.

"And don't get the idea you can sit there and make smart-aleck cracks, either," Laswell barked. "You're no hotshot pilot, buster. I don't give a damn how big a hero you were in the war."

"Yes sir." Culver just managed to get those two words out as a safety valve. It was say something or bust his fist in the captain's face. By the end of the month Culver's ambition to become a captain no longer was confined to such mundane desires as more money. He merely wanted to shove Laswell's brain bag down his throat without getting fired.

Their final flight was the worst, and unfortunately it was Culver who made a mistake. They were coming into National on a snowy night with ceiling and visibility just above minimums. Laswell was doing an ILS approach and Culver was calling out the altitudes. He had just yelled "Seven hundred" when he took his eyes off the altimeter trying to peer through the overcast.

"Five hundred," he called, miserably conscious that he had missed the six-hundred level.

The captain said nothing until they were on the ground. The fact that the ILS approach and subsequent landing were perfect gave his anger even more righteousness.

"And just what happened to six hundred, you dumb bastard?"

"My fault. I looked up trying to catch the runway lights and . . ."

"Try adding 'sir' to that alibi, Culver."

"Yes sir."

They taxied to the ramp and Laswell was about to renew the assault when he looked at Culver's burning eyes and saw the muscles in his prow-shaped jaw tighten and roll. He evidently decided it was unwise to continue the scolding. In fact, Laswell tried to shift gears. "Hate to snap at you, Les, but things are hairy enough as it is on an ILS. I need those altitudes in hundred-foot increments and you just goofed."

Culver relaxed. "I know it, sir. You had every right to jump me."

They seemed to part on friendly terms, but Laswell was to get one last crack at the copilot. At the end of the month all the captains assigned to the new first officers handed Shea what amounted to an airline's version of a Navy fitness report.

Captain Snodgrass said of McKay: "Excellent pilot, excellent attitude. Shows very mature judgment. Can find no criticism whatsoever. He is a very capable addition to our flight crew personnel."

Captain Thornton said of O'Brian: "The best new pilot I've ever flown with. His ship-handling is the equal of many captains, including the undersigned. His only fault is a very infrequent lack of concentration, undoubtedly due to personal reasons. When this was called to his attention, however, he responded with complete cooperation and I am convinced this will not constitute a problem in the future."

Captain Laswell said of Culver: "Had a somewhat disrespectful attitude toward the captain, and seemed to take criticism in a rather sullen manner. Flying ability is reasonably good, but not outstanding. I frankly do not consider him good pilot material for this airline, although his difficulties may have stemmed from more or less of a personality clash with this captain."

When Shea saw Laswell's report, he was not only surprised but shocked. He suspected it was largely unfair, inasmuch as Laswell was not the most popular pilot in Midwest for some well-known reasons—such as his being an unmitigated, pompous ass. But he was a captain, he had never had any trouble on one of his own check rides, and protocol being protocol Shea had no alternative. He had to call in Culver and show him the report.

Les read it, and except for a slight reddening of his face and that tightening of his jaw muscles, he handed it back to the chief pilot with no other show of emotion.

"Do you consider it untrue or unfair, Les?"

"I consider the part about the 'personality clash' a fair statement of the situation, Captain Shea."

"Level with me, Les. What was the trouble? I've fired copilots for less critical reports than this."

"If I tell you what I think of Captain Laswell, I'll sound like a crybaby. He told you his side. As for my side, I've got a small favor to ask."

"Name it."

"Give me a check ride. The worst you can throw at me. That'll be my side of the story."

Shea did, that very afternoon. Culver's performance was not only good but superb. When it was over, Shea said simply: "Thanks for letting me hear your side. I don't want to blow up your ego but you're definitely not fired."

The next day Shea encountered Laswell in Operations.

"Fred," he said softly, "I checked out Culver myself yesterday. You know, in some ways you're a shithead."

Chapter 5

Culver wasn't the only occupant of 201-B who had to fly with a sonofabitch. McKay later hit one grouch on a Washington–Pittsburgh flight. They had just given ATC a position report over Martinsburg and McKay called out the next heading for the airway to Pittsburgh.

"Don't you think I know the goddamned heading?" the captain snarled.

The talk McKay had with Snodgrass was coming home rather forcefully. Snorkel insisted on the first officer giving him heading changes. This captain apparently regarded it as an insult to his ability.

Paddy got into hot water one day with a real boner. He was flying with a rather decent guy named Frank Tennant and they were waiting in a warm-up area for takeoff clearance. O'Brian was having a mildly heated discussion with the tower over Tennant's sudden decision to accept an IFR clearance instead of VFR. The controller, with too many flights requesting IFR, was trying to talk them out of it. Finally Tennant lost his patience and growled, "Cut 'em off!"

He meant the tower. Paddy calmly killed both engines. Tennant nearly had apoplexy and closely approached a fatal stroke when the shattered O'Brian couldn't get number two restarted. The tower picked this opportune time to announce, "You're cleared for takeoff." They wound up watching four more flights taxi around them before the angry captain finally nursed number two to life and took off.

Tennant, however, was not the type to hold a grudge and proved to be a capable and patient teacher. He also told

Shea the story with great glee as the funniest thing to occur in his entire career.

Culver had a story to top this. He came home one night and recounted an incident involving his captain's PA announcement as they flew over Pittsburgh. Whether the captain was hung over or nervous about PA messages or was just having a bad trip, Culver couldn't tell. But the announcement came as a distinct surprise to the passengers.

"Ladies and gentlemen," the captain said pleasantly, "for your information, we're just pissing over Pattsburgh."

Their captains' decidedly varied use of the PA bothered them. Some obviously preferred an engine fire to the mike. Some were hams who did almost as much talking as flying. Some made only a "welcome aboard" announcement with information on route and weather, using the PA from then on only when they figured they had something interesting or essential to report. And then there was the Snorkel type, to whom the PA was a theater stage or a broadcasting studio.

The week before their first month had ended, they had been exposed to the Chinese novel known as the Sequence Bid Sheet. This was a mimeographed sheet of paper listing all the trips out of Washington for the following month. It sounded simple—a pilot merely had to choose a block of flights in accordance with the type of aircraft on which he was qualified. No single block added up to more than eighty-five hours.

The simplicity was purely theoretical. In actual practice, as far as a new first officer was concerned, the Sequence Bid Sheet would have defied a Certified Public Accountant.

Across the sheet at the top were seven horizontal spaces labeled M, T, W, T, F, S, S, for the days of the week. Intersecting these spaces and running vertically to the bottom of the page were the columns containing the flight numbers, with the hours each trip would accumulate. Columns 1 through 5 were DC-3 schedules, 6 through 9 were for DC-4's, and 10 through 12 covered the flights for the new Constellations. A final column was labeled "Reserve" —which nobody bid.

The pilots submitted written bids to Crew Schedule in the last week of each month, choosing a particular sequence with specific days off. The veterans naturally picked the choicest sequences, those with (1) plenty of layover time, (2) the fewest landings possible, (3) weekends off, and (4) four-engine planes, which paid more money. Occasionally a senior captain would bid night trips because of the higher pay. Less senior captains sometimes accepted copilot status on the DC-4's and Connies because the pay was equal to or even more than flying captain on a DC-3 and the trips were better. Seniority ruled the bids, which meant that apartment 201-B was strictly at the bottom of the totem pole.

At this point of their careers they didn't mind, although Paddy had an awful time bidding flights roughly corresponding to Pat Donovan's sequences. She had been flying for two years, which made her relatively senior. But she willingly bid some turkeys just to spend more time with O'Brian.

For the three roommates each flight was a new adventure and a new lesson in airline operations. After their first hundred hours they were allowed to make takeoffs and landings —theoretically and legally every other one, provided the captain didn't object. They discovered anew the individuality of captains. They flew with four-stripers who were generous about giving copilots plenty of experience. They also flew with captains who guarded their takeoff and landing prerogatives with the frigid disdain of a butler looking down on the gardener.

Mannion, who had bid the New York base, told Paddy one day about an incident when they happened to meet in LaGuardia operations. Bill had been copilot on a trip involving quite a few stops. The final landing, with the captain flying, was horrendous—a three-bouncer which left the passengers, let alone Mannion, wondering how the gear stayed on. It was excusable to some extent; it had been a long, tough day and the captain was undoubtedly tired. But he also was embarrassed.

Before they left the cockpit, he asked Mannion to put on the captain's jacket.

"If there are any boos, I'm not gonna be the one to catch 'em," he said to the first officer quite seriously.

Mannion obliged. Sure enough, he related to O'Brian, when he walked through the cabin, four passengers who hadn't deplaned yet stared at him accusingly and one remarked sarcastically: "Have we landed yet?"

McKay, O'Brian, or Culver hadn't encountered a captain with that much foolish pride, but Mannion's experience was an effective reminder of something Bender had stressed during training.

"I've never seen a captain or first officer yet who could make a really good landing every time," he had said. "Nobody expects you to—there are too many variables. But you should at least try, because a passenger ninty-nine times out of a hundred will judge a flight by the landings. That's when he's the most nervous anyway, and if the landing's smooth he thinks he's got Lindbergh flying the ship. I've heard passengers applaud a smooth one, and I've actually heard them boo a rough one."

Culver's natural reaction to that admonition had been "Screw the public—they're lucky they got down in one piece." But he didn't mean it and he wasn't fooling his roommates. All of them quickly learned that every captain—even a happy-go-lucky guy like Snorkel or a somewhat cold professional like Barnwell—liked to be complimented after he painted a ship onto a runway. And all of them, in turn, cherished those words "nice landing" from a captain.

As pilots, they varied little in their skills. O'Brian was the best of the trio, although, as Captain Thornton had noted astutely, his airmanship could get diluted a trifle on occasions. Culver, not very far behind Paddy in sheer natural ability, ranged from brilliance to just plain adequacy depending on how hard he felt like putting out. McKay ranked slightly below them in cockpit proficiency. He could not, for example, land a plane so consistently well as O'Brian. On most of Paddy's landings, a fresh egg tied to the gear wouldn't break.

Yet McKay matched them both in over-all performance. He knew he was more of a manufactured pilot, so he absorbed, digested, and assimilated more from his captains. He mentally catalogued their tricks, their habits, their good points, and their bad points. He discarded what he didn't like and filed away for future use what he figured would make him a better pilot.

His roommates had always loved flying. McKay, as he had told Shea in that first interview, never really had. Yet with Midwest he began to acquire the mysticism of the airman. His military flying had been mostly a game of pure survival. His airline flying sharpened his sense of appreciation of the airman's strange and unique and wonderful world.

He loved a final approach on a clear night, when the city below sparkled and winked back at his plane like diamonds shining on black velvet. He relished, as he never had during the war, the magnificent moment of breakthrough from an overcast or skimming just above the rose-tipped clouds at sunset. He grew to treasure the technical beauty of a well-executed instrument approach, that blending of human skill and electronic miracle with its inevitable build-up of tension before the other pilot calls out—like a trumpeted accolade—"Runway lights in sight!"

This, like a good landing or crisp instrument flying or the technique of maintaining altitude and attitude in the twisting clutches of a thunderstorm—this was achievement. This was professional pride. This was airmanship of a kind that was not a part of him as a B-25 commander. Then it was completing a mission and getting back with as few casualties as possible. The hell with what kind of landing you made so long as you could walk away from it. Never mind about efficient fuel consumption provided you had enough to make it home. Forget about pinpoint navigation unless you were unlucky enough to be the lead plane in a formation.

He never would have admitted to anyone that he enjoyed the respectful gaze of passengers when he strode through a cabin. But he did, because the father image was becoming a part of his physical being and his code of conduct. It still was hazy and embryonic, for he was just a copilot concentrating mainly on trying to please a variety of captains. But it was growing inside him as inexorably as time would add years to his chronological age.

He could get frightened on occasions, as all pilots did. He hated thunderstorms, for example, and he had a special dread of fog. He ruefully learned the truth of the airline captain's axiom: "Flying is hours of boredom punctuated by moments of sheer terror."

He realized that any flying, even in the rigidly controlled airlines, involved a certain amount of calculated risk. The difference between a good captain and one not so good was how much calculating he did in determining a risk. It was hard to spot a borderline pilot because, like a child who behaves beautifully when he knows Authority is watching, a pilot on a check ride generally could shove a wrong attitude under the rug of technical proficiency.

McKay met very few actually careless or indifferent captains, but there were enough of them to jar any feeling of unquestioning hero worship toward the gods who wore the fourth stripe. Most of them could fly as well or even better than their more dutiful brethren, which perhaps was a factor in their straying off the reservation of rules now and then. They bothered McKay, because as he discovered weak or unworthy captains he also discovered that commercial aviation in 1946 was not as safe as airline publicity liked to proclaim so confidently.

He became only too aware of the booby traps planted in the path of too many flights. The badly lit approaches and runways even at some of the biggest airports. The inaccuracies of weather reporting, occasionally so bad it was more of a joke than an admitted menace. The failure of Air Traffic Control to keep pace with the mushrooming postwar traffic, using radar which was fine for tracking twenty-knot warships but dangerously inadequate for guiding and monitoring two-hundred-mile-an-hour airliners. The senseless obstructions erected like deliberate obstacle courses near airports, such as huge radio towers lying evilly at wait on an approach path for an unwary pilot groping toward a runway in choking fog. The incredible lack of modern navigation and landing aids such as ILS, installed at only nine airports in the United States even though electronic guidance was routine during World War II.

Thus, there was born in McDonald McKay disdain, impatience, and even disgust toward the complacent pilot, the careless pilot, the gambling pilot. Thus was born in him, also, a cancer of bitter resentment against those who ignored the pleas of pilots for better tools. Those who made complacency and carelessness and risk far more deadly than they should have been. Those who made a pilot's mistake more likely and even, eventually, inevitable. Those who made an overdue reform a kind of apology to those who got killed. And thus was born in McKay a philosophy toward pilot error that was half sympathetic, half intolerant.

As a pilot, he was most familiar with the razor-thin margin for error when it came time to push the panic button. He recognized that sins of commission in a cockpit might merely be the culmination of sins of omission committed by those outside the cockpit. But he also felt for the passengers, the innocent, the trusting, the totally reliant who had to assume there was perfection and dedication in the cockpit. The father image again. And so McDonald McKay was simultaneously to curse and yet sympathize when the image blurred because a pilot made a mistake.

To a great extent, his code of the cockpit was no different from that of O'Brian or Culver. But the vein ran deeper because he kept questioning what they accepted and even took for granted.

All three joined ALPA and got probationary membership cards for their wallets, which they placed rather proudly next to their CAA pilot's certificate, their CAA medical certificate, and their CAA aircraft radio-telephone operator's authorization. McKay went to union meetings faithfully, unless he had to fly. Paddy would have but Pat was too much of a distraction. Culver expressed sincere interest and noble intentions, but by this time he was busy compiling the phone numbers of stewardesses who Did and stewardesses who Didn't and stewardesses who Might.

At one ALPA meeting McKay renewed his acquaintance with Barnwell, who asked him if he'd serve on the regional safety committee.

"I'd like to. Any time I'm not flying, just yell."

"We won't bother you much for a while," Barnwell assured him. "You've got enough to worry about these first few months. But, God forbid, if we ever drop one I may ask you to work on one of the investigative teams."

"Frankly," McKay said, "at $300 a month I can't afford to take much time off."

"I guess nobody told you. When you work on a crash, ALPA pays your salary."

It was probably just as well that McKay didn't know how many times ALPA was to pay his salary in the years to come. Right now he felt complimented that Barnwell had invited him.

The trio grew to love the DC-3's virtues as they simultaneously bewailed her faults. She was probably the trimmest, most beautiful transport ever built, and on the ground she appeared to blend power and speed with effortless grace. Actually, as every DC-3 pilot quickly learned, she climbed like a runner plodding through ankle-deep mud and her cruising speed left a lot to be desired. Yet she was dependable, rugged, and forgiving of pilot mistakes, and an airman regarded her as he would a faithful wife he couldn't stay mad at.

But Midwest was adding DC-4's and Constellations rapidly and then announced it was ordering the new Convair 240, a pressurized twin-engine job, as the Three's eventual replacement. The old girl was just too small to be profitable. Midwest fitted out a couple with twenty-eight seats instead of the usual twenty-one, but the four-abreast arrangement made the cabin aisle too narrow and the smaller seats drew passenger complaints.

O'Brian was the first to be affected by the new aircraft additions, and only after three months of line flying. Shea called him in, expansively offered him a cigar, and asked how he'd like to transition to DC-4's.

"You've got a helluva lot of four-engine time," he explained, "and we're short of copilots on the Fours."

"Golly," said Paddy. "Sounds fine."

"Means a little more dough, too," Shea added slyly. "Once you qualify."

That clinched it, although O'Brian didn't relish the idea of going back to school for a few more weeks. DC-4 ground school took a full fourteen days and another six hours of flight qualification. But he puffed with unaccustomed luxury on the cigar and nodded assent, sandwiched between two fits of sudden coughing. Nobody had warned him that the chief pilot's cigars were famous, or infamous, for having the delicate, fragrant aroma of burning engine oil. Shea invariably brought them out when he was about to ask a pilot to leave the warm security of familiar equipment for the cold uncertainty of bigger and harder-to-fly aircraft. Most of Midwest's pilots had learned politely to refuse the cigar. O'Brian, who liked cigars but naturally gave them up the minute he found out that Pat detested them, never made the mistake again.

One month later both Culver and McKay also got DC-4 offers, which they accepted with alacrity almost equal in intensity to their rejection of the cigars. Happily, O'Brian had tipped them off.

McKay liked the challenge of the larger plane to his flying skill. Culver liked the fact that DC-4 trips had two stewardesses instead of one, which provided the opportunity of possibly doubling the entries in his address book. None of them was aware of how far they had come or how much they had learned and matured until they saw a new pilot class being shown through Operations. They felt suddenly superior, incredibly experienced, superbly efficient, slightly patronizing, and somewhat older. It also was vastly encouraging to know that a couple of dozen pilots would have lower seniority numbers than theirs. They were a long way from the left seat, but the way Midwest was expanding maybe it wouldn't take the eight years estimated as the industry average.

The DC-4 had much in common with its smaller sister— such as ruggedness and a strange aerodynamic peculiarity. Namely, no two seemed to fly exactly alike. One would be nose-heavy and the next tail-heavy. One would fly with virtually no trim necessary and another would have to be wrestled as much as flown.

By June of 1946 the roommates no longer were worried about drawing reserve trips. Reserve was a strait-jacket status, requiring that they stick around the apartment on constant call, never knowing when Crew Schedule might phone with the message that some pilot was sick or otherwise unable to fly—"So could you get out here fast, please?" Once they were qualified on the DC-4, they could bid longer flights with some fairly decent layovers in cities they had never seen.

They also could fly with one captain for a whole month as they did in their first thirty days. This was a mixed blessing, depending on which captain bid the same sequence as they did. They could get assigned to one who was a good instructor and generous enough to let them do enough takeoffs and landings to keep in practice. Or they might get stuck with an occasional crumb.

McKay was lucky enough to draw Barnwell on his first DC-4 bid and he learned more that month than even Snodgrass had imparted. Barney was one of those rare combinations—deceptively gentle and invariably polite, yet with a no-nonsense air that bred cockpit discipline and respect. If Barnwell raised his voice, a copilot *knew* he was in the wrong and the fact that he raised it so seldom added force to his displeasure.

McKay particularly liked Barnwell's PA announcements. They followed a set pattern—one welcoming the passengers aboard after takeoff, a final one upon landing at destination, and in between an occasional word as to location ("Folks, that's Cleveland off to the right of the airplane") or some historical landmark visible from the air. He was meticulous, too, about using the PA as an anti-fear device. Any rough air would bring Barnwell's calm if high-pitched voice over the cabin speaker: "Folks, it may get a little choppy for the next twenty or thirty minutes because we've going through a front, so why not fasten those seat belts and relax? . . ." Any delay of more than five minutes brought an apologetic explanation from the cockpit—not always truthful, McKay noted, but always diplomatic and logical.

Barney had to feather an engine one day when the oil pressure dropped alarmingly.

"I guess we'd better give the passengers the poop," he said to McKay before he picked up the mike. "Folks, you may have noticed that the propeller on our right outboard engine has stopped. I want to assure you there's no need for any concern. First Officer McKay"—like Snodgrass, Barnwell tactfully included his copilots in many PA announcements because he felt it contributed to their sense of professional pride—"noticed a slight drop in oil pressure which *may* indicate some, ah, potential abnormality in performance. We have shut down the engine and feathered the propeller so it won't windmill and produce a drag. This is purely precautionary, I assure you. We'll fly very easily on three engines and I don't think this'll delay our arrival in Chicago by more than ten minutes at the very most. Thank you."

At dinner on the layover that night, McKay asked Barnwell whether Midwest had any policy about PA announcements. "They seem to differ among captains," he said. "There's nothing in the manual about them."

"Well, I'll tell you something, Mac," Barnwell said

thoughtfully, "personally I think there should be. But I suppose it's not practical. Pilots are personalities, strictly individualists, and a cabin PA reflects a captain's personality. It isn't anything you can force a man to do. I've got my own philosophy about PA's if you're interested."

"I sure am."

"I think an occasional PA is a duty to passengers. The majority of people on any flight are scared to some degree. Or at least a little nervous. I have the notion that if a passenger hears from the captain now and then, he figures things must be going along pretty good or the captain wouldn't have the time to chat.

"If anything happens out of the routine, a captain owes his passengers some explanation—even if it's an outright lie, or a white lie, anyway. Just the fact that he's offering an explanation will allay fear to some extent. Most people who fly are intelligent or they wouldn't be flying. I know that sounds like something Public Relations thought up, but it happens to be the truth. They want to know what's happening and I think they appreciate being treated like adults.

"The 'welcome aboard' and 'thank you for flying Midwest' stuff is just more of the same. Sure, I know the stews make them, too, and maybe I'm gilding the lily if that's the right metaphor or something. But I still have the idea that passengers, well, they feel better if they hear from the cockpit now and then. I don't think an airline captain should be a disembodied ghost. He's not only part of a flight crew but he's part of the airline, too. You know, Mac"—Barnwell chuckled as he said it—"I might let you make a PA on the way back just to guarantee you won't get mike fright first time that you try one as a captain."

"I'd kinda like to, to tell you the truth. Although it may happen—mike fright, I mean."

"It won't be as bad as one of our ticket agents at National. Ever hear the story?"

McKay shook his head.

"Nice kid but he was told to make his first flight departure call and he was scared to death. I was walking through the lobby with two other pilots and they'll swear it really happened. The kid says, 'Ladies and gentlemen, Midwest announces the departure of flight so-and-so. Passengers will please show your tickets to the plane as you board the stewardess.' "

McKay didn't really expect Barnwell to let him try a PA but he did, on the return trip the next day. Barney's usual practice was to wait until they reached cruising altitude for his initial announcement. This time, as the altimeter touched the assigned nine thousand feet, Barnwell grinned at the copilot.

"Okay, chum, tell the customers how lucky they are to be with us."

"You mean it?"

"I mean it. Get those tonsils wet."

McKay was more nervous than he was on his first DC-3 training flight or his first regular trip. He cleared his throat three times before he picked up the mike.

"Ah, good morning, ladies and gentlemen. This is First Officer, ah, McKay. Captain Barnwell and myself would like to welcome you on behalf of the cockpit, ah, flight crew this morning on, ah, Midwest Flight 201. We're at our assigned altitude of, ah, ah, nine thousand feet and our weather ahead should give us a nice, smooth trip. Our estimated flying time is three hours and ten minutes"—he was warming up to the subject now—"and we should arrive in Washington on schedule. Thank you for flying Midwest." *Click.* "How'd I do?"

"Fine. A few too many 'ahs' but that's par for the first time. One suggestion—toss in the temperature at destination if you think of it. People are interested in weather. If the weather's lousy, soften the blow a bit. Don't ever give them the idea that a landing might be hairy. That's when the little white lie helps."

"Roger."

McKay felt almost as proud as if Barnwell had let him

fly the whole trip and make the takeoff and landing. And a little bit of Barnwell had rubbed off, just as a little bit of Snodgrass had rubbed off and a little bit of every captain he flew with. He still was trying to imitate them, as Snorkel had warned he would, but in molding himself in their numerous images, he was unconsciously molding one of his own.

In late September, apartment 201-B came to a partial parting of the ways. Not from a quarrel, but from matrimony. With McKay handing the semipetrified groom a most necessary and extremely stiff slug of bourbon just before the ceremony, thus filling the role of best man admirably if conventionally, and with Culver looking strangely solemn and virtuous in an usher's cutaway, Parnell James O'Brian and Patricia Ruth Donovan were joined in holy wedlock.

The big surprise was Culver, who was even more nervous than Paddy and whose eyes welled up with tears when 201-B's survivors shook hands with their departing roommate. It dawned on McKay that underneath his occasional cynicism Les was something of a sentimental slob himself. He knew Culver was fond of Paddy, but until this day he did not comprehend how deep the vein of friendship ran.

Nor did he guess a secondary reason for Culver's unexpected show of both nerves and emotion. Les would not have admitted it, probably because he wasn't even aware of it except for a vague, uncertain feeling like the spongy, indefinite aches preceding the flu. The truth was, Culver envied Paddy. Like so many men who hide loneliness and insecurity under a flurry of casual conquests, Culver yearned for a deeper and more sensitive relationship with a woman. He had kidded O'Brian about his inexperience, ignorance, and naïveté. But he had sensed, without ever putting it into solid words or even thoughts, that O'Brian in a far more important way had achieved a maturity that he himself lacked.

Paddy invited John Shea to the wedding and was immensely pleased when the chief pilot accepted. Actually, Shea would have been heartbroken if he hadn't been invited. He and his wife loved weddings, especially those which Shea assumed he had had a part in arranging.

His wedding present was an expensive set of cocktail glasses, but an even more welcome gift was a week off for a honeymoon. He never told the newlyweds, but he had gone all the way up to Kane to get Paddy the time off—over the objections of Crew Schedule, which complained bitterly it was too short of pilots and that O'Brian hadn't been with the company long enough to rate a week's vacation.

By coincidence McKay was first officer on Pat's last flight as a Midwest stewardess. They had a layover in Buffalo and the captain had gone all-out with champagne at dinner that night. Knowing that Pat was marrying McKay's roommate, the captain bowed out fairly early. McKay took her to a nearby bar for a nightcap and they talked long and earnestly about O'Brian.

"I loved him the first moment I saw him, Mac. Sounds like a line out of a bad movie, doesn't it? But it's true. He reminds me of the Scarecrow of Oz and he's so damned homely, he's beautiful. One date and I told Dorothy I had found the guy I wanted to have kids by."

"I'm glad, Pat. I've never had a closer friend than Paddy— or anyone I respected more. Les kids a lot but I know he's pleased, too. We didn't want the mick marrying just anybody."

"To use another cliché," Pat said, "when do we find you a wife?"

"I'm in no hurry," laughed McKay, "so don't start matchmaking."

It was only three weeks after the wedding that he met Barbara Deering.

McKay, as he had explained to Paddy the night of their first "dinner party," was no devotee of nonmatrimonial abstinence. Selective, yes. A monk, no. He was healthy, reasonably good-looking, and stewardesses—often in the upper brackets of pulchritude—were available. Some Did—as Culver's notebook phrased it so delicately—and some Didn't. McKay preferred to do his own research rather than rely on Culver's, although he had to admit that Les's recommendations saved a helluva lot of time and money.

He had assumed, from what he had heard about airline people before he became one himself, that pilot-stewardess morals belonged on about the same level as the producer-starlet cliché. He found this assumption to be a gross case of overgeneralization. There were captains who tried to score on every layover and occasionally succeeded. There were captains who treated the girls either with total indifference or like fathers or elder brothers. There were stewardesses who enjoyed frequent sex, those who indulged occasionally, those who had open affairs with married captains, and those who wore figurative chastity belts with locks labeled "marriage only."

He finally deduced that the sex life of flight crews was pretty much like that of any stratum of American society—maybe a little freer because their nomadic existence presented more opportunities. Layovers, McKay learned quickly, can be lonely.

Some captains went about seduction with cold-blooded logistics, as carefully planned as a wartime invasion. Others used bluntness as a weapon. McKay flew with one whose reputation for the frank-and-open approach put Culver's in the amateur class. McKay didn't even believe half of what he heard until a stewardess came up to the cockpit on a summons from this Lothario of the flight deck.

"Have dinner with me after we get in," he said in a tone resembling more an order than a request.

"Oh, come on now, Captain," she said with some trace of sarcasm. "You're old enough to be my father."

The captain turned around to stare at her with a sardonic smile. "Oh really? What was your mother's maiden name?"

McKay expected her to get insulted. She went out to dinner with the captain that night.

Then there was Captain Henry Billings, who wanted desperately to be known as dangerous and actually acquired some undeserved notoriety among a few of the newer stewardesses who didn't know Henry as well as the older ones. He was fifty-two, an age at which a man really worries if he's as good as he used to be and feels compelled to prove it on the right occasion. He fancied himself a smooth customer— a self-delusion which went unchallenged because the right occasion never seemed to happen.

It was Billings' yearning to seduce a stewardess that wound up as a major event in McKay's life. Billings' chief trouble was that he looked like somebody's father, and perhaps to some of the younger girls like their grandfathers. He had more than the suggestion of a paunch, twinkling eyes, and thinning gray hair. Unlike Laswell, he took all rebuffs in good humor, probably because unlike Laswell he never fully realized they were just that—rebuffs. No stewardess had the heart to turn him down too bluntly, and their excuses ranged from having to visit cousins to splitting headaches. His title of "The Wolfman" was strictly honorary.

McKay liked Henry. He was pleased on this warm day in late September when he walked into Operations and found himself posted to Billings' trip—a good DC-4 block involving a flight to Atlanta, back to New York for a fifteen-hour layover, then on to Chicago and return to Washington the following night.

The names of the two stewardesses on the board were strange to McKay: Deering, B. and Salisbury, R.

"New girls?" he asked Billings.

"Nope. They're new to DCA. Transferred from Chicago last week. Good kids. I knew them when I was based there. They've both been flying for two or three years. That Deering's a doll."

She was. A couple of inches shorter than McKay in her heels, a nose not quite thin enough to be called patrician, short-cropped yet soft-looking brown hair just a shade away from being blond, and a slender yet suggestive figure. She was pretty rather than beautiful, intriguing rather than sexy, wholesome without appearing too corn-fed.

All-American girl, McKay thought when Billings introduced them. Her handshake was firm and her smile as spontaneous as a giggle. She was the kind who would look equally good in such assorted apparel as sweaters, tennis shorts, or evening gowns. The kind of girl who would always be type-cast as the third runner-up for homecoming queen, but would never feel the slightest twinge of envy for the two who finished ahead of her.

Barbara Deering's first words to McDonald McKay were not of the deathless prose variety, designed to go down in memory as inexorably hinting of a sudden, overpowering love. "Hi, I'm late. Ruth's already aboard. See you."

For some intangible reason McKay was disappointed. He had yet to meet any Midwest stewardess who piqued anything more than a normal physical attraction. In the few months he had flown he had dated a variety of them—some for mere companionship and a few willing to grant a more intimate relationship. Once he had driven a stewardess named Betsy Bales home from the airport, was invited in to her apartment, and was neatly seduced—complete with the uniform-straight-to-negligee bit, Cole Porter records on her hi-fi, and eventually her hand steering his hand to her uncovered breast while she nearly collapsed McKay's lung with a torrid French kiss.

He had met a Coastal Airways stewardess who was one of those delightful females with armor-plated virtue—until two or three martinis melted the armor like plastic in an oven. She was what Culver always referred to as a "talker"—the greater her passion, the thicker and more frequent her torrent of words until at the moment of climax she screamed her exquisite bliss.

On such delicious occasions McKay was of the opinion that this was really living and maybe Culver had something.

"The best thing about sex," the master told him during one of their infrequent philosophical discussions, "is the first time you unhook her bra and know you're gonna make it."

Thus far, the mysterious chemistry of love, that alchemy composed of half desire, half affection, had escaped him. He found himself willingly settling down in Culver's admittedly pleasant rut until he would go over to Paddy and Pat's for supper, spend three or four hours, and leave feeling restless, empty, and dissatisfied. Happy was the word for the O'Brians' marriage, as inadequate as that adjective may be. With the typical resourcefulness of both a stewardess and a tasteful woman, she had fixed up their tiny apartment in a way that made any visitor feel immediately at home. Their furniture was cheap—Paddy had gone for one of those "your apartment completely furnished for $199.99" advertisements —and it was obvious their marriage was going to last a lot longer than the furniture.

But Pat had added cheerful draperies and Paddy had put up a red, fringed awning over the kitchen cupboard—a touch of dubious interior decorating but one that added blessed individuality to the nondescript room. McKay and Culver went over once a week on an almost regular basis, supplying either steaks or bringing a bottle of good wine.

McKay, in fact, had been there the night before and perhaps he was in a vulnerable state of mind when he discovered that Barbara Deering disturbed him. It was doubly disturbing that he didn't know why. He made out the flight plan, conducted the walk-around inspection, and boarded the plane. The two stewardesses were checking emergency equipment as he walked through the cabin. The second cabin attendant, Ruth Salisbury, grinned at him and said, "Good morning."

McKay stopped and introduced himself, acutely aware of the other girl's presence. He nodded to Barbara and continued his way to the cockpit. Billings came aboard a few minutes later, puffing slightly as he squeezed into the left seat.

"I was right about Deering, wasn't I? Cute gal. That Salisbury's a nice dish, too. I'll ask them to have dinner with us in New York tonight."

The prospect of that invitation already had occurred to Miss Deering and Miss Salisbury. At that very moment Barbara was saying to Ruth: "I expect old Wolfman will ask us out tonight. Wanna go?"

"I don't know anybody in New York," Ruth said. "Might as well. That copilot's kinda cute."

"A little too good-looking," Barbara said. "He's probably a junior version of Billings. He seems like a quiet type, though."

"Dinner with Henry is one thing. When he suggests we have a drink in their room later, I'm going to have lots of letters to write. What'll be your excuse?"

Barbara laughed, a low and mean laugh. "Ruth?"

"What?"

"Let's go to his room."

"Are you out of your mind? The Wolfman will have all fangs bared."

"That's just the point. It's about time somebody called his bluff. And I have a strong suspicion that's just what the lovable old bastard is—pure bluff. I've got an idea. That McKay character worries me—the pilots room together on layovers and he may complicate things. But it's worth trying. Listen . . ."

Fortunately for Captain Billings, he was not aware of the dire plot hatching under Miss Deering's soft brown locks. In Atlanta Operations, he broached the subject of dinner in New York to the stewardesses. McKay was over at Dispatch checking weather.

"I know a wonderful little Italian place," Billings said. "And I'd like you all to be my guests. Sort of a celebration for your Washington transfer, okay? McKay, too. He's a nice, ah, fella." He was going to say "boy" but decided hurriedly this might accentuate the age difference between captain and first officer too sharply.

"We'd love to come," Barbara said, bathing Henry in the warmth of a dazzling smile.

The smile gave Billings just the wrong idea Barbara had intended conveying. He informed McKay that they all were having supper together. He was so pleased that he let McKay make the takeoff and fly the first hour. The first officer, in turn, was conscious of being foolishly proud he was flying the ship when Barbara came up to the flight deck with coffee. *That* feeling was a distinct surprise. A decided, deliberate desire to show off and McKay mentally scolded himself for being so adolescent.

They changed into business suits at the hotel in New York and met the girls in the lobby. Ruth was one of those stewardesses who seemed a little plain and not nearly so attractive as in uniform. It made no difference with Barbara. She wore a beige number with a blaze-orange scarf covering the V-neck. Beige was McKay's favorite color but he resisted the temptation of saying so. He merely confined his greeting to a "You both look lovely" aimed at both girls and Billings didn't have to say anything. He was almost drooling.

He was a wonderful host, though. He kept complimenting McKay on his flying and the girls as exemplary cabin attendants and he really did insist on picking up the check, which, as any stewardess will testify, deserves the same size headline as an outbreak of war. Just before they left, while Barbara and Ruth were in the powder room, Billings decided tonight might be *the* night and what was he going to do with McKay just in case?

"Uh, Mac, I thought I'd ask them up to our room when we get back. Now, uh, I'm a married man and all that, hah, but if something, ah, develops with Barbara, I thought you and Ruth could go back to their room and . . ."

"If something develops," McKay promised (he was secretly nettled), "I'll get out of the way."

He was positive that the captain's development theory was

wishful thinking, but he nodded and muttered something like "I wish you luck." It was an unexpected jolt when once they got back to the hotel, Billings suggested a nightcap in their room and Barbara—impaling Billings on the horns of a suggestive half smile—said to Ruth: "I'd love to, wouldn't you?"

"Sounds wonderful, Henry. Give us a few minutes. What's your room?"

"Uh, 728."

Billings already was congratulating himself for the foresight of packing a bottle of scotch in his suitcase that morning, and he was already calculating what would be a diplomatic and decent interval between the first drink and when he would suggest to McKay that Ruth looked tired.

McKay felt almost sorry for Billings when he saw the captain hurriedly divest himself of his tie, don a plaid smoking jacket, gargle with mouthwash, splash after-shave lotion on his face, and light a virile-looking pipe. The final touch was Billings' request to "Get some soft music on the radio, Mac, while I phone room service for ice."

Shortly after a bellboy brought ice, there was a discreet knock on the door. Billings almost tripped over a suitcase getting over there, but recovered sufficiently to open the door. The girls were standing there in their uniform overcoats.

The captain was puzzled, but this was no time to question their choice of clothes for visiting pilots' rooms.

"Come in, my dears. Let me take your coats."

"Thank you, Henry," said Barbara demurely. She speared him again with that half smile.

They removed their coats.

All they were wearing were shortie pink nightgowns, shockingly transparent.

Billings turned beet-red. He gulped, like a gasping fish trying to breathe. "Uh, maybe you'd better keep, ah, put your coats back on. I, uh, you might get cold . . ."

The stewardesses stayed only for one drink, poured by the ill-at-ease captain who was desperate enough to haul out a picture of his wife and two sons—"One of them's in college," he assured them almost plaintively. McKay was hard put to keep from laughing as the Wolfman ushered the girls out with obvious relief.

"My God," he said to McKay. "I didn't expect them to be so, so frank. It sort of took the, uh, edge off everything."

"You made the right decision," McKay said gravely. "Getting rid of them was the only decent thing to do."

Barbara Deering was eating breakfast by herself the next morning when McKay entered the coffee shop.

"Mind if I join you?"

"Be my guest."

McKay ordered tomato juice, ham and eggs, and coffee. He studied Barbara's face. She still wore a half smile, but it was not suggestive. It was more like a plea for forgiveness.

"That was a dirty trick you pulled on our captain," he finally remarked.

"He's cured for at least six months," she said.

They both started laughing, and then started talking.

"Where's Ruth?"

"Still dressing. She'd rather get an extra fifteen minutes' sleep than eat breakfast."

"Where you living?"

"Potomac Apartments in Arlington. Right near the airport."

McKay took a deep mental breath. "I'd like to see you when we get back. Will you have dinner with me tomorrow night?"

This time she studied *his* face. It seemed guileless, and she liked the masculinity of his good looks. But she was wary. "Let's get something straight, Mac. Just because you saw me in a nightie last night, don't get ideas."

"I'd be abnormal if I didn't get ideas. But that's not the reason I'd like to take you out."

"What's the reason?"

McKay didn't answer right away. He lit a cigarette, stalling for time because he wanted to say the right thing and he wanted her to believe he meant it.

"Okay. I like the way you wear beige. I like your sense of humor. I like the way you look—and not necessarily in a short nightgown. I'd be a hypocrite if I said I didn't like you in that damned thing, but let's *you* get something straight. I'm a red-blooded American male, and I'm also a fairly honorable guy. They are not contradictory."

That apparently was the right tack.

"Got a pen? My phone is Empire 52306. Apartment 721. Pick me up about seven."

"It's a date. By the way, are you engaged or in love or anything like that?"

"Nope. Would it make any difference?"

"Yes, it would."

"Afraid of competition?"

"Not when I'm competing from the same starting line. I just don't like trying to come from too far behind."

"You're starting even-up. How about you?"

"Single and no attachments. Here's Ruth. I'll see you tomorrow night."

Without knowing it, he had crossed another threshold.

Chapter 6

Their courtship and their falling in love were nowhere near as spontaneous and as fast as the affair of Paddy and Pat. They liked each other, but both were suspicious—Barbara of him (and most other men) and McKay of himself. She was afraid that all he wanted was eventually to get her into bed. Which basically was true. He was honest enough to admit it—to himself—and he was decent enough to worry about it.

They double-dated frequently with the O'Brians, also with Culver and whichever stewardess he was trying to seduce. But they also had fun by themselves for two important reasons. They had mutual interests, and they never lagged in conversation. Barbara liked dark cocktail lounges, soft music, frankness, good talk, and sports. So did McKay. More extroverted than Mac, she admired the opposite quality in him.

Their first date was conventional. McKay worried about a choice of tie, realizing as he discarded his first two picks that he usually didn't think of such things. Barbara's indecision revolved around the neckline of her dress. She knew a low-cut number would send any normal, red-blooded American male—as McKay had put it—but in the back of her wily and predatory female mind she also knew that demureness might be better initial strategy. Recalling wryly that McKay already had seen her virtually nude, she finally chose a dress with a high neckline.

He arrived promptly at seven, which pleased her, and she was ready, which pleased him.

He looked over her apartment, simply but tastefully furnished. Some stewardess apartments he had been in were so purely functional that they were devoid of personality and seemed barren even with the usual quota of chairs, couch, and end tables. He noticed Barbara's included some modernistic paintings that picked up the color of draperies and furniture. He himself preferred conventional landscapes, but he admired her selection.

"You pick these out?"

"Some. My roommate bought that flower scene."

"She here? I'd like to meet her."

"On a trip. But you will. Helen Mitchell."

"Midwest?"

"To the core. Where we going, Mac?"

"Olney Inn. Ever been there?"

She had, twice before, but there was something about him that made her realize his choice of restaurant was an unspoken compliment to her.

"Never, but I've always wanted to go there," she said.

"Southern plantation decor," he said. "It's quite a drive but that'll give us a chance to get acquainted."

They got the superficial data out of the way on the ride to Olney, Maryland. Their family backgrounds, education, flying careers, likes and dislikes. Over cocktails at the restaurant, listening to the Inn's Negro pianist, they became more verbally intimate.

"I'd like to pay you a compliment," he said gravely, "but I'm afraid it'll sound like a line."

"I enjoy compliments, so let me be the judge of their sincerity."

He studied the manhattan in his hand, then he studied her, then he lit cigarettes for them both. It seemed to be his habit, she noted, to weigh a remark before delivering it. When he eventually spoke, all the glibness had been strained out.

"Barbara, you're the kind of date who makes a man feel very special."

"That was a very nice compliment, Mac. Now I'll pay you one. I don't think it was a line."

"Unless," he added with that engaging grin, "you figure that trying to impress somebody is a line in itself."

"Depends on why you're trying to impress me."

Again he hesitated, putting his thoughts on a delicate pair of scales before wrapping them up for delivery. "So you'll want to go out with me again. Frequently. Such as next Friday night. I get back from a trip about eight, if you're not flying."

This time it was Barbara who studiously pondered her drink as if it had a message written inside the glass. "You're getting a little ahead of yourself," she remarked. "You don't even know what kind of a date I'll turn out to be tonight."

"If we went home right now," he said in a low voice that bordered on shyness, "it would be a most successful evening. The best I've had in a long, long time."

"Do you eat the cherry in your manhattan?" she asked.

He picked the fruit out of the glass and handed it to her by the stem. "Actually, I love the cherries in manhattans," he informed her, "but I have to prove that chivalry is not entirely dead."

"I hate them," she said and handed it back to him. "But I always give a second date to a man willing to make such a sacrifice. Friday night it is—but I can't stay out too late. I've got a trip Saturday."

"I'll leave a suit in Operations so I can change fast. Barbara, could you meet the flight?"

"Sure. It'll save time."

"I wasn't thinking about time."

"And what were you thinking about?"

His hesitation this time was so long, it came close to being embarrassing. "I've never had anybody meet me since I've been flying. I just wish you would. I guess I'd look forward to it the whole trip. Or am I sounding corny?"

"A little. But it's an attractive brand of corn. I'll be there. Let's order, I'm starved."

When he took her home, she said good night to him at the door and felt like a hypocrite because actually she did not want the evening to end.

"I'm tired or I'd invite you in," she explained. What she was thinking was, I'd love to have you in, but I've got a disturbing idea I could trust you more than I could myself.

He leaned down and kissed her on the cheek. Somehow it flustered her.

"Well," she laughed, "I must be losing my sex appeal."

He took both her shoulders and gripped them firmly. "There's nothing wrong with your sex appeal," he said quietly. "I want to kiss you like I want to keep breathing. I also want to keep seeing you. I guess not kissing you this time is my way of telling you that so you'll believe it. I'll be in Friday on 620. Good night, Barbara."

He strode away quickly, not realizing that he had shaken her badly.

Barbara Deering was twenty-four, the daughter of a Chicago surgeon. She had gone to college for two years, then quit because she felt she was wasting her father's money. Possibly in peacetime she would have stuck it out for his sake but a coeducational campus in wartime was too much of an ivory tower even for a girl. She was about to investigate the WAVES when she bumped into a girl she had known in high school who was now a United stewardess. Until then she had never even considered the airlines but her friend apparently had swallowed a United stewardess brochure whole and regurgitated its persuasive contents so appealingly that Barbara was sold immediately.

Actually, she had intended to apply to United but was detoured by an event that was typical of her. She was heading for an interview with a United Personnel man at Midway Airport when she slipped and sprained her ankle. There were employees of several airlines in the immediate area, but it so happened that the only one who rushed over and offered to help was a Midwest ticket agent.

Once her ankle was bandaged and the pain eased, she calmly limped past the United office and obtained an application form from Midwest. As she explained to the Midwest interviewer two weeks later, "I have to judge an airline on performance."

Up to the last minute she had misgivings. And then there was a final surge of cynicism that maybe she was just going to become an airborne waitress without the incentive of tips. It lasted until she actually reported to the office of the school's chief instructor. The latter was on the phone and Barbara idly read a huge bronze plaque on the wall.

CREED

If you who enter here have come sincerely
And know exactly where your interest lies.
Have tired of office job, or school, or nursing—
Yet thrilled to the flash of silver in the skies;
If you have longed to see our nation's beauty
Not limited to east or western shore,
Can love all people, knowing each can teach you
And make you bigger than you were before;
If you have learned to sympathize with sorrow,
Open your heart to everyone you greet—
And if you honestly respect the culture
Or any creed or color you may meet;
If you have patience born of understanding,
And pride not lessened though the task be small;
If you can gain the joy from helping others,
And have the will to give this job your all;
If you have loyalty unswayed by cynics,
Put kindness far above your own demands,
Can realize all aviation's problems
But aid the vision of its future plans—
Then you will know this miracle of flying,
The comradeship, the progress, and what's more—
You'll feel the very pulse beat of our country.
Welcome to the Stewardess Corps.

Alice Farley 1939

She was reading it over again when the instructor, a handsome, slender woman in her mid-thirties, hung up and rose to greet her.

"I'm Nancy Henderson," she introduced herself.

"I'm Barbara Deering. I was reading the plaque."

"What did you think of it?"

"It gave me goose bumps. I had some last-second doubts about the whole thing, but not now. I suppose Alice Farley was a stewardess?"

"Yes. One of our best."

"Did you know her, Miss Henderson?"

"Very well. I used to room with her."

"Is she still flying or did she get married?"

Nancy Henderson looked at the cold bronze letters as if she were seeing something on the other side of the wall. "Neither," she said. "She was killed in a crash about two weeks after she wrote it. She had sent her father the poem. He had it cast in bronze and gave it to the school. Now then, sit down and tell me all about yourself."

On the day Barbara started Midwest's stewardess school in a ramshackle, ancient Alexandria office building, her knowledge of things aeronautical was confined to the obvious fact that planes fly. She had some vague idea that stewardesses served meals, talked to passengers, ducked the tentacles of octopus-armed pilots, and convinced old ladies it was perfectly safe to travel by air.

At the time Barbara joined Midwest, there were about three thousand girls flying the scheduled airlines in the United States. All carriers cast them in the same mold, and she was no exception. She took courses in simplified aeronautics and company history. She learned how to walk, apply makeup, bid trips, translate the Airline Guide, work galleys, and direct emergency evacuations. She also learned that the good stewardess was the one who knew, either instinctively or by design, how to break the mold.

Her own class was like the few hundred that had preceded it and the many thousands that would follow it. About average in intelligence, above average in looks, and considerably above average in personality.

There were fifteen trainees in Barbara's class and they represented a pretty good cross-section of American backgrounds. Some were from rich families, some from poor, some from middle-class. They came from big cities, small cities, and farm communities. All were eager and petrified simultaneously, with the exception of a trainee named Helen Mitchell.

Barbara became especially friendly with this tall Rosalind

Russell-type from Minneapolis who had been discharged from the WACS for punching, with malice aforethought, a Lesbian sergeant. The discharge was for "not honorable reasons" but she frankly told Midwest the circumstances and her personality was such that she would have been hired if she had slugged George Catlett Marshall.

Only one girl of the fifteen didn't make it. Actually, a second should have flunked but the head of the training school was a superstitious man who refused to send a thirteen-girl class into the world of commercial aviation. The day they received their wings, along with the traditional orchid corsage, Barbara had to admit the three-week ordeal was worth it.

Nobody would have recognized the sharp, poised, smart, and immaculate girls as the same ones who only twenty-one days before had resembled a group of freshly scrubbed college freshwomen. Then Barbara hadn't known an aileron from a girdle. Now she could talk eruditely about piston engines, and explain how planes fly because the prop-wash thins out the air over the curved upper wing while the heavier air under the wing provides the lift. She was more familiar with the map of the United States than a geography teacher. She could make an elderly male passenger feel like Clark Gable, bring a smile to a child's face, and give reassurance to a frightened housewife making her first flight. She learned how to smile when Crew Schedule broke the news that she had to fly on the same day a boy friend invited her to a dance. She became acquainted with that unusual breed of girl-woman known as the stewardess supervisor, a combination of housemother, older sister, top sergeant, and friend.

Although Midwest no longer required that its stewardesses also be registered nurses, she knew the rudiments of delivering a baby if the Lord decided to stage the miracle of birth at seven thousand feet. She also was equipped for that moment when the chips are down—from breathing life into the mouth of a passenger having a heart attack to emptying a burning plane in sixty seconds.

In brief, she was an airline stewardess—with some of the

faults and most of the virtues of Women, and the latter far outweighed the former.

Barbara's father had loudly and angrily opposed this "Damned fool stewardess business." Her mother had cried, in between highly inaccurate statistics concerning the airlines' safety record, but both attended graduation ceremonies and looked as proud as if she were getting a college sheepskin. Mrs. Deering was possibly prejudiced in the unexpected discovery that Barbara really did look sensational in that uniform. Dr. Deering, too, became a sudden but fervent supporter of both air travel and the stewardess profession. His swift conversion, it must be admitted, was not due to any objective analysis of U.S. civil aviation and its impressive accomplishments. It occurred at the precise moment when Miss Henderson asked him to come forward and pin the wings on his daughter. His surgeon's hands, so quick and cool and steady in their profession, trembled as he fumbled with the wings and finally got them pinned—lopsided, much to his embarrassment—on Barbara's jacket. He kissed her on the cheek and strutted back to his chair.

Barbara and Mitch got an apartment together after successfully bidding Chicago for their base. They reported to Chicago Operations for their first flights, an unforgettable occasion stemming from stewardess Mitchell's uninhibited, puppylike approach to life, job, and people. They had just checked in with crew schedule when Mitch overheard some pilots discussing the techniques of jiujitsu. She blithely entered the conversation without invitation.

"I know jiujitsu," she chirped brightly. "It's simple."

The pilots stared at her rudely. Barbara wanted to dig a hole and crawl into it. Miss Mitchell plowed merrily ahead. "I'm Helen Mitchell. I'm a new stewardess and I couldn't help hearing what you said about jiujitsu being hard to learn. It really isn't."

The pilots looked at each other, then back at Mitch.

"You know jiujitsu?" one asked with deceptive politeness.

He was a big two-hundred-pounder built like an inverted mountain peak.

"I'm an expert," Mitch said modestly.

"Okay, throw me."

"Don't be silly. I might hurt you."

"I'll take a chance. Try throwing me."

"Not in here," Mitch protested. "We might break something. We'd better go outside and find a soft spot."

"In here," insisted the pilot.

Mitch shrugged. "Put out your hand," she said. "The rest of you stand back before you get hit by flying objects."

He winked at his colleagues and put out his hand. She smiled sweetly, pumped, jerked, and the pilot was airborne over her shoulder. He landed heavily, but luckily all he hit was the floor. He lay there for a minute, stunned as much by surprise as by impact. Then he climbed groggily to his feet. His uniform was disheveled, but not quite as badly as both his ego and his composure. The room was saturated with silence.

"What did you say your name was?" he almost whispered.

"Helen Mitchell—sir. Are you all right?"

He dusted himself off, felt a few key portions of his anatomy to make sure there had been no structural failure, and shook his head in wonderment. "Miss Mitchell," he said sadly, "you're gonna have one helluva time getting dates on this airline."

She didn't. There was no great social stampede in her direction but pilots asked her for dates out of sheer curiosity. For a while Barbara basked in reflected glory, being known as the roommate of "that nutty stew who nearly killed Bob Strotsky." There was no doubt that Mitch was about as unique a stewardess as ever climbed on an airplane. She had the face of an angel and occasionally the mouth of a garbage pail. The effect was like hearing a nun curse.

Miss Mitchell came close to topping the jiujitsu episode when a conscientious, admirably safety-minded captain decided to quiz her on emergency procedures. She fielded everything in accurate and conventional style until he sternly posed the question: "What would you do if the rear exit door suddenly blew open in flight?"

She paused only momentarily, before giving him an answer that went down in Midwest annals. "I'd shit," she blurted in complete honesty.

It was just as well that Barbara had a personality of her own and did not acquire, chameleonlike, that of her roommate. No airline could have survived two Mitchells. Actually, they both were good stews—Helen because she was unconventional enough to make even the most nervous passenger forget his or her fears; Barbara because she had a natural sense of compassion that led her to do things that were never in a stewardess manual.

Whenever she flew on a holiday, she would get out to the airport an hour earlier than required so she could decorate the cabin in accordance with the occasion. Tiny hearts on Valentine's Day. Bunnies and imitation spring flowers on Easter. Mistletoe, holly, and maybe a tiny tree in the galley around Christmastime. One Christmas Eve she latched on to twenty-one old baggage tags and on the blank side of each one she drew the face of an angelic cherub. Underneath she lettered the words "Merry Xmas from Your Crew" and put the greeting on every dinner tray. Of the twenty-one passengers aboard that Christmas Eve flight, eight wrote letters to Midwest complimenting her on the gesture.

She took in stride the less glamorous aspects of her job, such as supervisors who flicked her fanny to make sure she was wearing a girdle, warned her to get a haircut, or invariably showed up for a check ride on the day she had neglected to remove a spot from her uniform.

She achieved the ultimate in feminine efficiency, namely putting makeup on at 5 A.M. when she was half asleep. Along with this accomplishment, she got used to looking cheerful, friendly, and charming even when she was hung over, suffering from menstrual cramps, or had just received a letter from her supervisor advising her that her stocking seams were crooked on that last check ride.

She stopped speaking in terms of miles between cities—it always was hours, and the hours depended on the type of plane flown between the two cities being measured for distance.

She liked passengers, generally, because she liked people. The exceptions were drunks, overbearing and overdressed women who addressed her as they would an upstairs maid, and men who tried too hard to impress her.

She liked pilots, too. Their cheerfulness, sense of humor, and even their foibles. Just when she decided they all were a bunch of tightfisted, self-centered, selfish finks, a copilot would offer to carry her suitcase or a captain would pick up a dinner check. Most of all, she relished the esprit de corps among flight crews, a kind of under-the-surface sentimentality that always seemed to crop up when it was most needed.

She quickly memorized, although at first she'd write reminders in a little notebook, which captains liked their coffee black or with cream or without sugar or with sugar and no cream. She also learned something she never disclosed to any captain—namely, which ones were the most likely to make sloppy landings, fail to warn the cabin attendants when turbulence was ahead, and take corner-cutting chances. There were a few she dreaded to fly with, and there were some she would have trusted implicitly if both engines were on fire.

If friendly efficiency described stewardess Deering, unpredictable resourcefulness summed up stewardess Mitchell. She won new fame (or notoriety) when an enormously fat woman passenger weighing close to three hundred pounds got stuck in the doorway of a DC-3 as she boarded. Two ramp agents and the copilot tried to budge her without success. They had visions of having to dismantle the plane to get her loose, until Mitch solved the problem. She took a pin out of her cap and jabbed the passenger in the rear. There was an anguished scream of pain, but the woman was propelled inside the plane.

Later, at Mitch's suggestion, she managed to get off successfully by going through the door sideways. Miss Mitchell considered herself a heroine until the woman filed suit for personal damages and public humiliation. The airline took the path of least resistance. It settled out of court.

Inevitably the girls were victims of the practical jokes pilots loved to play on innocent new stewardesses. Barbara was hooked on her second trip. The captain, a grim-faced man, introduced himself and broke the news she had more to worry about than her passengers.

"It's the copilot," he warned. "He's always missing his flights. Be sure he's aboard—I hate to fly these things alone."

She pledged her undying cooperation. But—as the captain knew she would—she forget his admonition. Unknown to her, the copilot had slipped aboard early. Right after takeoff he climbed into a baggage rack just behind the cockpit, pulled the curtain shut, and waited for the captain to ring for the stewardess.

Barbara hastened forward and it took only a glance to realize she had sinned. The copilot's seat was empty.

"I'm sorry, Captain," she stammered. "I was so busy and I . . ."

"Oh, forget it this time," he grumbled. "But don't let it happen again."

Their first stop was 150 miles away. As soon as they pulled up to the ramp the copilot left the DC-3 via the front emergency hatch. The first sight to greet Barbara as the cabin door opened was the first officer, running up with his overnight bag in hand and panting:

"Well, I made it—but God, what a run!"

It was Mitch who reduced the redoubtable Captain Snodgrass to speechlessness. When the weather was good, Snorkel occasionally would let a stewardess sit in the cockpit jump seat during a night landing. It was a typically kind gesture on his part; he knew the girls always got a kick out of the magic moment of flare-out, the runway coming up to meet the wheels, and the first screech of tires on concrete.

He invited Mitch up front one night. She sat enthralled, listening to them go through the approach checklist and watching the bewildering array of fluttering instruments. She was awed when Snorkel saucily asked Approach Control, "Who's handling this flight tonight—Ben Turpin?"

They passed over the final radio checkpoint and the ADF needle—Automatic Direction Finder—spun its accustomed 360 degrees, indicating they were past the beam. Mitch couldn't resist asking a question.

"What's that needle doing?" she demanded.

"That's our virgin indicator," Snorkel explained. "It does that whenever a virgin's in the cockpit."

Mitch shook her head slowly. "Captain," she told him, "if you're using that damned thing for navigation, get it fixed."

When Barbara met McDonald McKay, she had been flying for just over three years, which was a good twelve months beyond the usual stewardess tenure.

After three years some of the challenge and excitement was gone. She enjoyed the freedom of a stew's life, the comparatively easy hours and the relaxed comradeship of the flight crews. But it was getting too routine. Even her attitude toward the passengers was changing. She used to regard them as interesting, unexpected guests. People to pamper and spoil and kid and soothe. Now they were becoming nameless faces, dull nonentities whom she categorized only as potential problems if something went wrong.

Every trip used to be a challenging new experience. Of late, every trip assumed a sameness that was stifling. The introduction of the DC-4 was a welcome change but even her enthusiasm for a new plane palled eventually. She continued to be a good stewardess, but the motivation was superficial—painted on like a chorus girl's smile.

Mitch recognized the symptoms as something peculiar to the stewardess profession, a kind of occupational hazard. They usually afflicted a stew after about three years of flying. Usually a girl quit and got married. Occasionally they would keep flying and get over their restless, vague dissatisfaction to the point where, if they flew for five years, it look dynamite to dislodge them from the job. After five years, overchoosy about men and frozen immobile in an iceberg of independence, they tended to keep flying as long as an airline would let them.

Wisely, Mitch talked Barbara into the Washington transfer mainly as a means of reigniting her sagging interest. It might have worked, too. At a new base and getting acquainted with new friends, Deering seemed happier. Whether the shift of scenery would have had lasting effects, neither was to find out, for McKay changed her from a stewardess into a woman.

She had a sense of humor far more subtle and craftier than Mitch's, and she aimed it directly at McKay's solemnity —which was the smartest strategy she could have employed. It had never occurred to him that a girl could be amusingly and even devilishly clever. It kept him off balance, and a man off balance makes an inept seducer.

Her first stunt was to slip a small rock inside his brain bag. The bag was cavernous and he never looked at the bottom. The next chance she got, she replaced the original rock with a slightly larger one. The process was repeated, each time with a heavier rock.

She was walking out to his flight with him one day and saw him frown.

"Anything wrong, Mac?"

"I must be getting old," he complained. "This damned bag seems harder to carry every time I fly."

Two trips later, she had worked up to two large bricks. This time McKay picked up the bag and put it down immediately. Culver was in Operations and he thought McKay looked pale.

"You feel okay, Mac?"

"I don't know. Am I getting weak or something? I can hardly lift my brain bag."

"Lift it? Are you kidding?"

"No. It feels like it weighs fifty pounds. There must be

something wrong with me. I've been noticing it's been heavier to carry lately."

Culver picked up the bag and grunted. "Jesus, you're not imagining it. It does weigh fifty pounds. What's inside— whiskey?"

"Nothing but my . . . wait a minute."

McKay opened the bag and removed the contents. The last two items he took out were the bricks. His immediate reaction was to accuse Culver but his roommate seemed too sincerely puzzled to be guilty. Paddy? It wasn't his type of joke. It was while he was mentally listing the names of pilots who might have pulled it that the great light dawned.

He had a date with Barbara the next night, after she got off a trip. He met her plane, carrying a magnificently wrapped gift package.

"Little surprise," he said.

"Oh Mac, what is it?"

"Let's go into OPS. You can open it there."

She remarked excitedly on how heavy the gift was. "I'll bet it's something for the kitchen," she guessed. "An appliance?"

"Just open it."

She did. Inside were the two bricks.

One day she found a domino on the floor of the cabin, where a child apparently had dropped it during a flight. Un- doubtedly it was a silly thing to do but she wrapped it in an incongruously huge box and presented it to him.

"Thanks," he said, fingering the little black and white rec- tangle, "but what's it supposed to mean?"

"To ordinary slob people it's a domino. But not many people know that the domino is the Druids' symbol of good luck." This was pure imagination but McKay, whose college courses hadn't included anything relating to prehistoric re- ligion, was impressed enough to show it to Les.

"Did you know a domino was a Druid good-luck symbol?" he inquired.

"She's pulling your leg," Culver informed him out of the vast depths of Druid culture apparently acquired in his one year at Harvard. "I'll admit I don't know much about the Druids except I think they built Stonehenge or something, but the game of dominos was invented in the nineteenth century."

McKay said nothing further to Barbara. Three days later she was opening a half-empty jar of cold cream in her bathroom. She unscrewed the cap and found the domino inside. She reasoned that he must have sneaked it in last night when he and Culver were drinking beer at the apartment. She'd fix him.

McKay was eating breakfast in the airport coffee shop the very next morning. He bit into a blueberry muffin and almost broke a tooth. It was the domino. Barbara somehow had gotten a waitress to let her wedge it into the muffin just before McKay arrived, knowing he invariably ordered blueberry muffins when they were on the menu.

A few days later she was driving her car (a 1939 Plymouth McKay had helped her pick out) to the airport when she felt a spring nudging her buttock most uncomfortably. When she returned from her trip, she took the car to the garage. The mechanic said he'd have to cut into the upholstery to straighten out the spring.

"Go ahead," Barbara ordered. "It's driving me crazy."

It wasn't a spring. McKay, with O'Brian's help, had cut into the seat in a spot where she couldn't have possibly noticed the incision. With much sweating and cursing, they had managed to put the domino in exactly the place where she would have to sit on it.

She kept the domino until just before Christmas when her fertile brain figured out a way to return it with interest. McKay found a letter in his Operations box mailed from Philadelphia and in a totally strange handwriting. Barbara had another stewardess do the mailing and she talked Mitch into writing McKay the crude note.

"Captain Mackay, sir: You dont know me but I know you from a long time ago and I hate your guts. Just open up

lokker 412 in the turmanel bilding and I have a present for
you, you bum. A one time frend."

The locker key was enclosed.

McKay couldn't figure it out. At first he thought it was a
joke but the more he thought about it, the more worried he
got. He finally went to Shea and showed him the apparently
threatening letter. Shea, a man of action, promptly called police who rushed two officers and three bomb experts from the
District of Columbia police department. Airport police
cleared the entire area around the baggage lockers. Gingerly,
the bomb squad opened locker 412.

There was the domino, with a small red ribbon tied
around it.

"What the hell are you trying to pull, McKay?" roared
Shea. "What kind of a gag is this supposed to be?"

McKay, with the eyes of five policemen and his chief pilot
on him in cold accusation, and all of Washington National
Airport holding its collective breath, miserably and feebly
tried to explain.

"Captain Shea, I . . . it's . . . I know what it's about,
and I know who did it . . . it's a joke, I suppose and . . . oh
goddammit, I'm sorry. I've been taken."

"But the domino," Shea demanded. "What does it mean?"

"It's sort of a . . . a code," McKay stammered unhappily.

"I don't suppose you're gonna tell me who did it—wait a
minute, is this one of Snorkel's damned fool stunts?"

"I can assure you, he had nothing to do with it. I—he,
the one I think is responsible, well, I'm sure . . . uh . . .
he didn't realize it would cause all this trouble." (Like
hell she didn't, he thought.)

"It amounts to a false bomb report, fella," one of the bomb
experts said. "You better tell us who it was."

"Now just a second," Shea protested. He was suddenly concerned that a Midwest pilot—he still suspected Snodgrass—
might be getting into hot water. "If you'll read the letter
over, there was nothing said about a bomb."

"You were the one who called us," a second cop reminded him.

"I was trying to play it safe," Shea retorted. "Any prudent man would have done the same."

The police left, possibly wondering if all airline pilots were nuts. Shea handed McKay the innocent-looking domino.

"You won't squeal?"

"No sir."

"I didn't think you would. Wanna tell me what it's all about—just between the two of us?"

McKay hesitated. "No sir. It's . . . it's personal."

"That means a girl. All I gotta do is figure out who the hell you've been dating. . . ." He stopped. The young pilot looked positively sick.

"Well," said Shea, "I hear you're a poor man's Culver these days. No use calling in fifteen stews. So you just tell whoever it was, no more letters."

"Yes sir." It was just as well as he walked away that he couldn't hear Shea mutter out loud: "I'd sure like to know what's with McKay, Deering, and that domino."

The "bomb scare" couldn't be kept a secret, although no one figured out the significance of the domino. Culver remembered the alleged Druid connection and spread the word, slightly garbled, that Deering had given it to McKay because it was an ancient symbol of virility. By the time the story circulated through every Midwest base, the domino had acquired a Sioux Indian background and was known to have had something to do with Custer's defeat. At any rate, McKay had no difficulty in acquiring allies to help him plan its return. Male allies, that is. Mitch flatly refused to collaborate in his first scheme—actually, it was Culver's idea—to sew it into one of Barbara's bras. But Snorkel came through in the clutch.

He was going to Miami for a few days, and knowing that Barbara had a tremendous fondness for fresh orange juice, McKay asked Snodgrass to ship her a crate of the citrus fruit. It arrived at her apartment along with a note from Snorkel that "Mac asked me to send this to you."

"He's probably got the domino at the bottom of the crate," Barbara told Mitch.

She emptied it, but oranges were all that rolled out.

"Maybe it's inside one of the oranges," Mitch said.

"That's it. Let's find one that's been opened and glued back together."

"Just how do you glue an orange?"

"I don't know, but if it's possible Mac would have done it—or gotten Snorkel to do it. Let's look."

They checked every orange and sure enough, they found one with a large patch of peel that obviously had been removed and put back with Scotch tape, carefully painted over in orange to hide the signs of surgery.

"Ah hah!" chortled Barbara. "It's a beautiful job but I knew he'd pull something like this."

She removed the tape and reached inside the fruit. No domino. But her exploring fingers touched a folded piece of paper. She opened it. In Mac's handwriting was this message: "Curious little wench, aren't you? Love. MM."

She was positive he would give her the domino back in some way for Christmas. They seldom flew together but Mac drew a Christmas Eve flight with a Chicago layover and Barbara traded trips to be with him.

Snorkel was the captain—he, too, had graduated to fairly regular DC-4 schedules by now—and naturally Captain Snodgrass could not let a Christmas Eve trip go back without some special commemoration. They left Washington National at 6 P.M., nonstop to Chicago. Only thirty-one of the fifty seats were occupied but the lack of a capacity audience didn't deter Snorkel.

He gave the takeoff to McKay, having already informed the first officer that "You're gonna do all the flying on account of I have plans to further this airline's public relations."

He furthered them farther than Public Relations would have desired. They leveled out at eight thousand and the captain, winking at McKay, clicked on the PA.

"Good evening, ladies and gentlemen. This is Captain

Harrison Snodgrass. First Officer McKay and I would like to wish all of you a Merry Christmas. Now, once a year Midwest has what we call a mystery flight. You folks just *think* you're going to Chicago. You will, but after we treat you to another trip all at Midwest's expense. Some of you may still want to go to Chicago, but not when you hear our real destination.

"I won't keep you in suspense any more. This aircraft is heading for Los Angeles, where we will be guests of movie star Jimmy Stewart. I flew with good ole Jimmy during the war and if he told me once, he told me a thousand times, 'Harrison, someday you bring a planeful of passengers out to Hollywood and I'll really show them the town.'"

Some of the passengers were stirring uneasily, a few were grinning, and all of them were anxiously awaiting additional news from the cockpit.

"Is he serious?" a middle-aged woman asked Barbara.

"I don't think so," Barbara said dubiously, unwilling to tell a customer that with Captain Snodgrass *anything* was possible. Snorkel, satisfied that he had shaken up the entire passenger list, not to mention his crew, continued.

"We know you want to get back to Chicago, so we won't spend too much time in Hollywood. Jimmy's taking us to dinner at Chasen's and then out to his estate for a swimming party. Let's see, I know he's invited Claudette Colbert, Clark Gable will be there, and Rita Hayworth, of course."

Three bachelors in the cabin instantly decided they hoped the captain wasn't kidding.

"Let's see, who else did Jimmy invite? Well, Spence Tracy, naturally. Greer Garson . . ."

He rolled out a list representing half of M-G-M's stable with a few from Paramount and Warners thrown in. By this time he had even the stewardesses concerned—or perhaps intrigued was a better word. The second stew, a tiny blonde who was on only her fourth trip, already was mentally composing what she'd say to Gable and why didn't Captain Snodgrass give them some advance warning so she could have packed her bathing suit?

McKay was the only one who knew that Snorkel was having a ball. He had the advantage of knowing that Snorkel's wartime experiences hadn't included a bosom friendship with Colonel James Stewart. Mostly he was curious to know how Snodgrass was going to get out of this. He was unprepared for what followed.

"Now folks," Snorkel continued, "maybe some of you think I'm kidding. I'm going to radio ahead and get Jimmy on the horn . . . he's at the Los Angeles airport waiting to hear our plans. And I'll hook this mike up so you can hear the conversation."

He paused to take a deep breath. Then he said into the PA mike: "Hello, Los Angeles. This is Midwest 314, Captain Snodgrass here. Is Jimmy Stewart there in the tower? Good. Put him on."

Back in the cabin, there wasn't a sound. Both stewardesses were wide-eyed. Barbara still had doubts, having been exposed to Snorkel before, but this time—who knew?

Snorkel looked over at the flabbergasted McKay and winked again. He put a handkerchief over the mike, keeping his mouth a few inches farther away than usual. What came from his lips was a perfect imitation of James Stewart's nasal drawl.

"Hullo, Harrison old buddy. Uh, this is Jimmy. Where are you?"

"Eight thousand, about ninety miles east of Pittsburgh, Jimmy." This in Snodgrass' normal voice, with the handkerchief removed. "Uh, we should be in LA in about ten hours."

Back went the handkerchief. Stewart's voice again. "Uh, Harrison. I've got some bad news for you. M-G-M wants me to start a new picture first thing tomorrow morning. Uh, we're leaving for location in the next half hour."

Snorkel again. "That's too bad, Jimmy. Golly, I'd already told all these passengers about the mystery flight and the party. They'll be disappointed but I know they'll understand. The movie must have come up real sudden, like."

Stewart: "Very sudden, Harrison. They, uh, didn't give me

even ten minutes' notice. Will you apologize to everyone for me?"

Snorkel: "You can do it yourself, Jimmy. I've hooked you on to the cabin PA. Go ahead, Jimmy. This is Jimmy Stewart, folks."

Stewart: "Wal, now, folks, I'm just as sorry as all get out. Uh, about all I can say, folks, is that I wish you a very Merry Christmas from Hollywood. You, too, Harrison. He's really a wonderful pilot, folks. He taught me everything I know about flying. Uh, he's a real modest guy but he saved my life four different times, didn't you Harrison? Uh, you should wear all those medals on your airline uniform. Well, Merry Christmas, uh, Harrison."

McKay was doubled up over the yoke, with tears streaming from his eyes and his face scarlet from trying to hold back the laughter so he wouldn't give Snodgrass away.

Snorkel: "Merry Christmas to you, Jimmy. Midwest 314 out."

Click.

The passengers sat back, sighing half in relief and half in disappointment. The junior stewardess was almost crying. Bathing suit or no bathing suit, she was positive that Gable would have flipped.

The stewardesses served dinner and had the trays stowed when Snorkel flicked on the PA again.

"This is Captain Snodgrass again, ladies and gentlemen. I want to add my own apologies to those of Jimmy. We're heading for our original destination, Chicago, of course. I suppose a lot of you are kinda glad we can't go through with our mystery flight. After all, it's best to spend Christmas at home. And to keep all of us in the Yuletide spirit, I'm going to ask the stewardesses to lead us in a few Christmas carols. First Officer McKay and I will join you, although you may not be able to hear us too well. Miss Deering?"

Barbara was caught by surprise but the passengers were smiling in anticipation. She nodded to the other stew and in her untrained but clear and sweet voice she began.

"'Silent night . . . holy night . . .'"

Hesitantly at first, then with growing volume the passengers joined in, their voices drowning the sound of the engines. Snorkel's own singing was interrupted by ATC asking for a position report. He provided it, but before ATC could sign off he held them on for a minute.

"Chicago, I'm gonna open the cockpit door. Listen."

The voices, young and old, were booming forth in that most magnificently sad and sentimental carol. The captain held the mike as close to the cabin as he could.

"ATC—did you hear it?"

"Roger, Midwest 314. Sounds real fine. Merry Christmas."

"Merry Christmas, you guys, Over."

Snorkel, without telling his crew, had arranged for a small Christmas tree in his room and invited McKay and the two stewardesses up for some after-dinner eggnog. He even had presents for them. Sterling-silver cuff links for his copilot and perfume for the girls. He also confessed to the latter that mimicry was one of his lesser-known talents, which made the younger stewardess feel much better. She was still brooding over her failure to meet Gable.

They sang some carols, softly so the desk wouldn't relay any complaints from other guests. Snorkel phoned his wife to make sure she could set up the new electric train for their middle son without his aid.

"It's up already? Fine, honey. We'll be in about noon. If the kids can't wait to open the presents, it's okay. Maybe they could open half of them and wait till I get there for the rest. And don't open yours. See you tomorrow. I love you too, honey."

McKay had always hated Christmas from his boyhood. Maybe not hated it, but it always had been more of a sad than happy occasion after his parents died. He never had felt happier than he did right now. He and Barbara held hands as they sang "Silent Night" again—"A good way to end the evening," Snorkel said.

McKay walked the two girls back to their room. He said good night to the junior stew but was reluctant to let Barbara go.

"You sleepy?"

"No, Mac."

"Let's go down to the coffee shop. Would you mind if I gave you your present tonight?"

"Is it the domino?" she asked, her eyes twinkling.

"No," he smiled.

"Meet you downstairs in ten minutes. I happen to have *your* present in my suitcase."

Over hot, steaming coffee, they laughed anew at Snorkel's Jimmy Stewart imitation. McKay finally pulled a package out of his pocket and watched Barbara's face as she opened it.

It was a seventeen-jewel traveling clock. On the alligator-skin case McKay had had the jeweler glue a pair of Midwest stewardess wings—with the pin cut off and the back of the wings smoothed so they would fit on the case.

"Mac, it's . . . it's beautiful."

"I wanted to get you something you could use, but something special. Grace Wooley gave me the wings."

Barbara leaned over the table and kissed him. Then she handed him his package. "After this, I wish I had thought of something better," she said.

He always felt embarrassed about opening a present in front of the giver. He was so essentially honest that never in his life had he been able to hide disappointment or disapproval if he didn't like the gift. And he was afraid he might offend Barbara. But he removed the Christmas wrapping and his fears were gone. Hers was a leather traveler's kit, with sterling-silver receptacles for shaving cream, toothbrush, toothpaste, and razor. But she had added a final touch—a small desk portfolio with a picture of her in uniform that he had asked her for.

"That's so you'll remember me on layovers," she said.

He, too, leaned over and kissed her with a gentleness that

spoke his gratitude and more than gratitude. Her eyes were glistening and their greenness was like the reflection of a fire in the eyes of a cat.

He gulped. He took her hand. "Merry Christmas, Barbara Deering."

"Merry Christmas, Mister McKay."

"I never want to take things for granted, so I'll ask you now. I'd like a date with you New Year's Eve."

"Accepted. Provided I'm not flying or you're not flying or both of us aren't flying."

"If you are, or I am, or both of us are, then we'll have our own New Year's Eve later."

"I hope you like your kit half as well as I like my clock."

"Twice as much. We'd better get some sleep."

"Yep, I guess we'd better." She paused.

"Mac?"

"Yes?"

"I wish I could go to bed with you tonight."

Her directness upset him. "I'm afraid we might disturb our captain." He was trying to joke his way out of an almost frightening emotion. His heart was pounding and he could feel the tightness rising in his loins.

"Are you shocked?"

He pondered her question gravely, because he sensed his answer was all-important—to himself as well as to Barbara. "Shocked isn't the word. It's what I've wanted for a long time. But now that you said what you said, I feel more protective than . . . than lecherous."

"Protective?"

"Yes. Protective. Tender. I'm not much with words, Barbara, but I just want you to know you wouldn't be just a casual . . . affair."

"I hope not. I'm no slut, Mac. I don't sleep around. I'm not a virgin, either. I enjoy sex with the right person. I think you're a right person. What happens next, I don't know. I guess I should have been coy and played hard to get. It's

just hard to be coy with a guy like you. I'm probably cutting
my throat, but I decided you'd appreciate honesty more than
some phony 'I'm not that kind of girl.'"

He was still holding her hand. Now he squeezed it. They
got up and walked wordlessly to the elevator. When they
kissed good night at the door of the room she shared with
the other girl, it still was tender but with a tenderness that
was electric and promising and as intimate as sex itself.

They went over to the O'Brians' on New Year's Eve with
Culver and Jean Gillum. It was their first date since the
Chicago layover. He had wanted badly to ask Les if he were
going to stay out all night but knew he couldn't ask. It was
Barbara who settled the matter. When he picked her up, she
mentioned almost casually that Mitch had four days off and
had gone to Minneapolis to see her family. She stared at him
almost defiantly as she said it.

It was a fine though relatively quiet party. They drove back
to Barbara's apartment with only a few inconsequential remarks breaking the silence. She gave him the key as if the
gesture was a symbol of surrender and his hands shook as he
opened the door. He helped her out of her coat.

"I'll be right out, Mac." She said it in a whisper.

He poured himself a straight shot of bourbon and then
another. He sensed rather than heard her coming back into
the living room. He turned around. She wore a white negligee
and her firm young breasts were only too visible through the
silk veil. Yet she looked strangely virginal rather than seduc-
tive.

"Hello." Her voice was soft and scared.

He moved to her and started to kiss her when he felt wet
tears against his taut face. He cupped her face in one hand
and looked at her long and hard.

"Barbara?"

"Yes?" Again, she was whispering as if she were having
trouble with her voice.

"I have a feeling I should go home."

"Because I'm crying?"

"Because you're crying. And because . . . because there comes a time in a man's life when he has to decide whether walking away is going to hurt a girl more than not walking away."

She lowered her eyes but there was not a trace of coyness in the gesture. "That's quite a decision. What have you decided?"

"I haven't yet. Come sit down on the couch."

She put her head on his shoulder. Neither spoke for a while, but McKay knew he had to take the initiative.

"Barbara, God knows I'm no angel. I want to stay. I was ready to stay. Those tears scared me. Maybe it'll help if you tell me why."

"Why am I crying or why do I want to sleep with you?"

"Try answering the first one. Maybe that'll answer the second."

"I already asked myself the second question. I wanted you to make love to me. I wanted you inside of me. And that's when I asked myself the first question. The answer I got—it isn't what you should hear."

"I think I'd better."

"Okay, Mac. I'm in love with you."

His arm involuntarily tightened around her. "Is that a reason to cry?"

"It is when I'm not sure about how you feel. A girl takes a chance going to bed with a guy she loves. I don't know what your reaction will be. It could mean everything to you or it could spoil the whole thing. That's why I was crying. I want you and I'm scared. Not of sex but of what happens after sex."

"So you'd like to know how I feel."

"I'm not worried about how you feel now. You could probably say 'I love you' and mean every word of it. But tomorrow morning you might regret it. I wouldn't blame you for it."

McKay took his arm away, rose, and went over to the

chair where he had flung his overcoat. His back was to her and she couldn't see what he was doing. He returned to the couch, sat down, and handed her a small box. Her immediate thought was that it couldn't be what she wished it was; the box was too oblong. She opened it.

Inside was the domino. Attached to its top by a small, almost invisible string was a diamond ring.

"That," said McKay firmly although his voice cracked just a shade, "that should answer all your questions. And now, Miss Deering, I believe I will go home. A newly engaged pilot needs his sleep."

Being feminine, Barbara cried. Being feminine, she also was curious.

"Suppose," she asked many minutes later, "we had gone to bed without my knowing you had a ring. Just when were you planning to propose?"

"Tomorrow morning. I figured it was the surest way of convincing you my intentions were honorable."

"You're cute. You're also wonderful. And I'm happy."

"I'm glad. So I am. Your negligee, by the way, is driving me nuts so good night, Mrs. McKay-to-be."

They walked to the door and embraced before and after they kissed.

He felt her breasts against him and she felt his arousal. She knew the decision was now hers. She made it with no equivocation or hesitation. She broke away from him and looked at him as if she were seeing him for the first time. Then she spoke, and it was no longer a whisper.

"Don't go, sweetheart. I'm not afraid any more."

He stayed and confirmed what up to now had been a hopeful theory—that sex was far better with someone you loved, because there was a residue of affection left over in the wake of satisfied desire.

They were blissfully and busily planning their wedding when McKay was plunged into his first airline accident investigation.

Chapter 7

It happened only a week after Shea had called him in on the occasion of his first anniversary with Midwest. The probationary period was over and the chief pilot had gone over with him all the required reports filed on McKay's performance by each captain after every trip.

"I'm very, very pleased, Mac," Shea had said. "There are a couple of minor negative comments—both involve landings —but on the whole these reports are excellent. You're off probation. Welcome to the fraternity."

They discussed the reports (McKay was rather pleased that Barnwell's had been the most laudatory) and the copilot got around to telling Shea that he and Barbara Deering were going to get married in June, an event of which the chief pilot had been informed via the company gossip circuit three days earlier. The next day McKay passed his six-month CAA physical with no sweat and life had never seemed brighter. He and Les still shared the apartment on Bennett Street and decided to stay there until McKay's wedding, when Les planned to get a place by himself.

His pay went up from the $300 a month during probation to 56 per cent of a captain's basic salary, and by holding DC-4 bids he now was earning a neat $6800 a year. He was almost as happy as O'Brian at this overnight affluence—almost, because Pat picked the day Paddy got off probation to announce that she was pregnant. They celebrated with dinner at the Statler's Embassy Room—McKay and Barbara, the O'Brians, and Culver. Les brought a United stew who irked the hell out of both Culver and Barbara by paying slightly too much attention to McKay. It was McKay's first exposure to the frightening phenomenon known as the Jealous Woman, but the occasion was too special for anyone to stay mad very long. Not with the O'Brians' forthcoming parenthood.

Paddy, who forgivably got a wee bit high, decided at 1:30 A.M. that their son would be christened McDonald Lester O'Brian, which collided somewhat with Patricia's equally firm decision that McDonald Lester O'Brian was a lousy name for a daughter.

"Come to think of it," Culver said, "it's a lousy name for a boy. Negative on that middle handle. I'll bet if Hitler had a kid, he'd have named him Lester."

"Lester Hitler," Paddy burped. "Sounds very euphonious."

"Leslie O'Brian wouldn't be bad," Pat said. "But that leaves Mac out of it. Anyway, I've always promised my family I'd name my daughter after my grandmother."

"What was her name?" Barbara asked.

"Teresa. We could call the baby Terry for a nickname."

"Terry's short for Terence," Paddy said. "Terence O'Brian, now. I like it."

The christening debate broke up at two, when the Embassy Room closed. Driving Barbara back to her apartment, McKay broached a subject they had only casually discussed in the first flush of their courtship and engagement. She was snuggled up to him, warm and content like a sleepy kitten.

"Barbara, you have any solidified prejudices about kids? Boy versus girl, I mean?"

"Nope, I just want babies. Two definitely, maybe three. I suppose you'll demand a son, like Paddy?"

"You may think I'm nuts, but I'd rather have a girl."

"I don't think you're nuts, but I'm surprised. I thought all men wanted sons more than daughters. Paddy may move out if Pat gives him a daughter."

"I doubt it. Anyway, I've got a logical explanation for my preference. Mostly, it's the job. I'll be away too much. That'll be a little rougher on a boy than a girl. A daughter'll be easier for you to raise."

"Not necessarily. But continue."

McKay hesitated. As usual he was molding his thoughts before putting them into words.

"I'm not trying to be dramatic," he said. "But you're a stewardess. You know the birds go down occasionally. If anything happened to me, you'd be better off with a little girl. I've always heard it was harder for a, ah, widow to bring up a son."

He was surprised when Barbara noticeably shivered, then snuggled even closer. She said nothing, and McKay was worried.

"Honey, did I upset you?"

"Yes."

"I didn't mean to. But hell, darling, it's just something I thought about ever since I fell in love with you. Kids and how to raise them and . . . well, planning ahead."

"It's something I've thought about ever since I fell in love with you."

"Kids?"

"Yes. And what I'd do if you didn't come back from a flight."

"The safety statistics," McKay said soothingly, "are very much in my favor. And they'll get better. There's a helluva lot we can do to make flying safer."

Barbara pulled away from his arm and looked at him. "Give me a cigarette, darling."

McKay obliged. He started to get out a match but she shook her head and used the dashboard lighter. She returned to his encircling arm and suddenly began to cry. McKay was shaken, but he let her continue to cry until the tears had flushed away the debris of whatever had been dammed up.

"I have a feeling," he said gently, "the possibility of my crashing someday is not all that's involved."

"Mac, would you mind if I quit flying?"

"Not if you wanted to. But I thought you loved it. And we're not planning to get married until June. I take it something's wrong."

She sat up again and looked straight ahead. She puffed nervously on the cigarette.

"I don't really know what's wrong. No, that's not true. I do know what's wrong. I'm ashamed to admit it. I'm just scared. I'm frightened to death every time I take a trip. I shudder at takeoff. I want to hide in the blue room when we land. I hear sounds from the engines I never heard before. When you change pitch on a prop, I think we're in trouble. And I can't explain it. A stewardess for three years and all of a sudden I'm petrified of flying. Isn't that the stupidest thing you ever heard of?"

"Nope. The stewardess menopause."

"The what?"

"Stewardess menopause. That's what Snorkel called it. He and Shea talked about it one night. We were having a beer at the Marina with Grace Wooley and Shea brought it up. Only he was talking about pilots getting afraid. Said every pilot reached a point in his life when all of a sudden he was afraid to fly. Then he gets over it. He can't explain either why he got scared or why he snapped out of it. Then Grace said it's true of stewardesses, too. Only it happens to them a lot earlier—usually after three or four years. It might not hit a pilot for ten or twenty. But it happens to damned near every crew member, male or female. And from what Grace said, I gather you're at the point where it's hit you."

"Did Grace say stewardesses get over it?"

"They either get over it or they quit, according to Grace. She said she carried it around in her gut for about a month, and just like that—it went away. She's never had the feeling again. So it's nothing to be ashamed of, honey. Shea said it happened to him the year before he became chief pilot. It was so bad he couldn't sleep the night before a trip. Then he snapped out of it. Snorkel, too. Can you imagine that nut being afraid of anything? He told us that for two weeks, he didn't even feel like making a PA."

"Well, how about that?" said Barbara. "I thought I was having an exclusive phobia."

"Nothing very exclusive about it. Feel better?"

"I guess so. I'll know more next time I fly. I'm glad I said something to you."

"So am I. It helps just to talk about it. Actually, you should have talked it over with Grace."

"I wanted to but I was afraid. Afraid of being afraid. Catch?"

"Affirmative. When are you flying again?"

"Day after tomorrow. Same as you, oh future husband. Mac, if I find out I still want to run away from an airplane, would you mind? Get me a job in reservations, maybe, until June?"

"That's up to you, sweetie. To be honest, I'd like to see you try and lick it."

"So would I," she murmured.

It turned out McKay was the one who asked her to call it quits. Two days later he had come in from his trip and was checking out of Operations. Barbara was in Atlanta on a layover, so he planned to spend a quiet night reading. He had put his brain bag in its assigned rack and was examining the pilots' bulletin board, noting with amusement the latest entry:

ALL PILOTS: THERE HAVE BEEN COMPLAINTS THAT FLIGHT PERSONNEL HAVE BEEN WEARING THEIR COATS UNBUTTONED AND/OR TIES ASKEW WHILE WALKING THROUGH CABIN AREAS AND IN AIRPORT LOBBIES. PRIDE IN PERSONAL APPEARANCE IS THE HALLMARK OF A CONSCIENTIOUS AIRLINE PILOT. FURTHER VIOLATIONS WILL RESULT IN DISCIPLINARY ACTION.

BENNETT KANE, VP
FLIGHT OPERATIONS

Underneath, Shea had endorsed the warning with a handwritten scrawl: "Shape up, slobs, or else. J. S."

McKay glanced over the rest of the bulletin board, as usual crowded with such vital aeronautical items as automobiles for sale, a captain imploringly inquiring if any crew members had teen-agers willing to baby-sit, and a hopeful announcement from a first officer that he was willing to part with an outboard motorboat for the ridiculously low price of $250 "or best offer," which meant he knew $250 was too high for a boat with approximately the same seaworthiness characteristics of the sunken *Titanic*.

McKay stopped by the dispatch desk to say good night to the dispatcher on duty, a quiet, middle-aged man named Ken Hemmingway, who naturally was called Ernie.

"Hear you're getting married. Congratulations, Mac. That little Deering gal's a honey."

"Thanks. I agree—she's quite a girl. Everything quiet?"

"So far. We've been lucky with weather this winter. I remember one January when . . . wait'll I answer this phone. Midwest Dispatch, Hemmingway."

McKay could hear a voice on the phone without distinguishing any words. He had a sudden chill when he noticed the dispatcher frown.

"Keep me posted," Hemmingway said and hung up. "Mac, you busy?"

"I was just going home. Anything wrong?"

"We may have trouble. ATC says they can't raise 312. Last they heard he was leaving Martinsburg. He should have been in range by now."

There were five other pilots in Operations besides McKay, plus two stewardesses. The dispatcher must have spoken louder than he intended, because all seven gravitated toward Hemmingway's desk—and all eyes automatically sought the big crew schedule board to see who was flying 312.

The names stood out like Braille. CAPTAIN—J. Steele. FIRST OFFICER—G. Minotti. STEWARDESS—D. Martin.

"Jim Steele," said a captain. "Maybe his radio's out."

"Maybe," the dispatcher said dourly. "My ulcer's telling me different. Mac, this phone's a direct line to ARTC. Stay by it in case they call. I gotta get hold of Shea."

"How long since they've heard?" McKay asked as he moved behind the Dispatch counter.

"About thirty minutes. Hell, he should be pulling up to the ramp right now."

McKay watched the ATC phone as if a fixed stare would make it ring. Its very silence was evil, diabolical, menacing. A pilot switched on an intercom and tuned it to the Approach Control frequency. The metallic voice filled the room.

"Midwest 312. Midwest 312. Do you read us? Over."

There was no answer, except crackling static.

"Midwest 312. This is Washington Approach Control. If you are unable to read us, you are cleared for final approach via the Springfield fan marker. All traffic below you has been vectored away. Repeating, Midwest 312 this is Washington Approach Control. If you are unable to read us . . ."

Hemmingway, who was dialing Shea, called out to keep the volume down.

"Captain Shea? Hemmingway in Dispatch. 312's overdue. No sir. He checked in over Martinsburg. That's the last we heard. Just a minute." He glanced up at the crew schedule board. "Captain's Jim Steele. First Officer, let's see—Minotti. That's George Minotti. Want the stewardess? Martin. Dorothy Martin, I guess. No meal service flight. Just one stew."

McKay felt ice on his spine. The "D. Martin" on the board hadn't rung any bell until now. Dorothy Martin. The girl who had been his blind date the night they finished ground school. She was supposed to be quitting next month to go back to Omaha for her long-delayed marriage. The dispatcher was still talking to Shea.

"Yes sir. I'd appreciate your notifying Mr. Kane. Right. See you later."

He pulled up a drawer and took out a mimeographed sheet of paper. McKay peeked over his shoulder and saw the heading at the top. EMERGENCIES MANUAL. Underneath was a list of names and numbers to call, and instructions on procedures. Hemmingway dialed a number, but his finger slipped. He swore and dialed again.

"Mr. Barker there? Yes ma'am, it's Dispatch. Very important."

Russ Barker was Midwest's Public Relations director. An ex-Marine combat correspondent and a nice guy. McKay had met him when he asked Barbara to pose for some publicity shots.

"Mr. Barker? This is Hemmingway in Dispatch. Afraid we may have one down. You're on the list to call. Dunno. It's 312 from Cleveland and Pittsburgh. Just a second."

He fumbled nervously at some papers, and finally produced a teletyped message from Pittsburgh Dispatch.

"Jesus, it ain't good. Forty passengers, three crew. They haven't been heard from since they checked in at Martinsburg. Yes sir, I'll try to call you back when we hear something but I'll be pretty busy. Be better if you came in. Thanks. Good night."

"How about a search plane?" McKay asked.

"Hell," said a burly captain. "Take a look outside. What's that last weather—six hundred feet and a mile and a half. We'd have a helluva time spotting anything."

"We could if they were burning," said another pilot quietly.

"Well, I'm game to go up if a ship's available," McKay offered.

"Better wait till Shea gets here."

They began pacing, occasionally walking outside to peer at the silent sky as if looking could produce the sound of 312's engines. Shea showed up twenty minutes later, his face grim.

"Kane's on his way. Anybody phone our PR?"

Hemmingway said Barker had been advised, and the CAA already had notified the CAB's Bureau of Safety.

"Good. We'll have newspapermen up to our butts soon's this gets out. Well, anybody wanna go looking?"

They all volunteered. Shea picked two senior captains. "Mac, phone Hangar 5. I'm pretty sure we've got a spare DC-3 in there. Tell 'em to fuel full up and taxi her over here in a hurry. Let's see. Gate 1's available."

McKay found the interoffice number for Hangar 5. He

relayed Shea's instructions. Shea turned to the two search pilots.

"Wait'll we find out how he was coming. Then take the same airways to Martinsburg and double back. And for Christ's sake, watch yourselves. Don't start playing hide and seek with those Blue Ridge tits. About all you can do is watch for fire. Ernie?"

"Yes sir."

"What clearance did they get from ATC? Airway 20?"

"No sir. Sixty-one. Over the Arcola range."

"Sixty-one? What the hell are they doing on that? That's the new route. We haven't even published minimum altitudes on it yet. Did Steele ask for it?"

The dispatcher's face was pale. He swallowed hard.

"Yes sir. I relayed his request to ATC. I didn't know it was illegal. I just assumed . . ."

"Goddammit," Shea said in an almost matter-of-fact voice. "Why would Jim . . . that reminds me, he's married. If we don't hear anything pretty soon, we'd better call his wife. How about Minotti?"

"Single," a pilot said. "Lives alone."

"How about the stew? Somebody call Grace Wooley. Tell her to get her ass down to her office. I got an awful feeling we'll be notifying next of kin. Christ, I hate those words."

The ATC phone rang. Before Hemmingway could pick it up, Shea intercepted it.

"Yeh. Nothing? We've got a DC-3 going up in about . . . make it twenty minutes. Give 'em an emergency clearance over 61 to Martinsburg. That reminds me—did you clear 312 on that airway? You did? Never mind, friend. I think we've all got troubles. Keep us posted. Yeh, we'll try to raise 'em on company radio. I dunno. Ernie, what's fuel exhaustion time?"

The dispatcher hurriedly did some calculating. His still-pale face looked up. "Forty more minutes."

A phone rang. One of the pilots answered, listened a few seconds, and turned to Shea with his hand over the mouthpiece. "It's Mrs. Steele, John. She wants to know if Jim's in yet."

Shea shook his head helplessly. "Tell her, tell . . . oh hell, I'll talk to her. What's her name—I can't think . . . Betty? That's it. Betty. Hello, Betty? John Shea. Look, honey, we may have some trouble. Jim's a little overdue. We don't know a thing yet. His radio may be out."

He listened to her say something.

"Well, it wouldn't hurt. Be a lot easier waiting here than at home. Got someone to stay with the kids? Fine, Betty. Come right over to Operations. And don't get upset. Nothing's definite yet."

He hung up.

"How'd she take it?" a gray-haired captain asked.

"Calm as hell. Just said she figured she'd better come down."

Barker, the PR, walked in. Shea drew him to one side and filled him in.

"Okay to call the wire services and papers?"

"Might as well," the chief pilot said. "I'm pretty sure it's down. Tell 'em to go to my office. I don't want 'em cluttering up this place. You can park there and I'll have someone phone you soon's we get anything."

"We'll need a passenger list. And crew."

"Copy the crew off that board. You'd better phone Pittsburgh for the manifest. Where'd they originate—Cleveland? Phone them, too. And whatever you do, keep those goddamned reporters out of here. We've got enough troubles. CAB guys should be here before long, too."

"Okay," said Barker placidly.

Shea called McKay over.

"Mac, phone Barney Barnwell. Snorkel, too. Where's crew sked?"

"Here," said the crew scheduler.

"Billy, check Barney's and Snorkel's skeds. If they're flying tomorrow, pull 'em off and make it indefinite. They'll have to be in on this. Get some guys from reserve to fly their trips. Let's see—who else we gotta notify?"

The chastened Hemmingway said he'd finish the emergency list. McKay felt sorry for him, although he wasn't sure what was involved in the exchange over Airway 61. All he knew was that it apparently was shaping up as one large goof by somebody—and that suddenly he didn't want to be around when Betty Steele came in. That thought reminded him of Dorothy Martin, and that in turn made him think of Barbara.

Maintenance phoned to advise that the DC-3 was on its way from the hangar. Shea rebriefed the crew and sent the two pilots on their way. There was nothing to do now but wait. Kane arrived, followed a few minutes later by Mrs. Steele. Her eyes were bloodshot, but she had herself under control and greeted the pilots she knew with a faint smile. Shea led her into the pilots' lounge—mainly so she couldn't see the crew schedule arrival board with the line reading: "312. CAPTAIN—J. Steele . . ." He assigned two pilots to stay with her, conversed with Kane, and began pacing around the room.

Someone turned up the intercom volume again. The set still was on Approach Control frequency. The strangely patient, calm, and impersonal voice echoed through the room.

"Midwest 312, this is Washington Approach Control. If you are unable to read us, you are cleared for final approach. . . ."

"Turn the damned thing off," Shea growled. "How about the ticket counter? There'll be people waiting for that flight."

Hemmingway said counter personnel had been notified. In accordance with instructions, the agents were to post next to the flight arrival time the words: DELAYED. SEE AGENT.

"I called Frank Reed," Kane said to Shea. "He should be up there now."

Reed was a senior vice president. On his shoulders would fall the task of telling the relatives and friends awaiting 312's arrival that it would never arrive.

The big clock on the wall of Operations ticked loudly, like the beating of a huge heart. McKay felt as if his own heart

was keeping time. Hemmingway's voice shattered the silence.
"Captain Shea," he said. "Fuel exhaustion time."

The chief pilot made the sign of the Cross. He slumped
into the nearest chair, his face gray. Kane moved swiftly to a
phone and dialed.

Upstairs, in the lobby, an agent took down the words:
DELAYED. SEE AGENT.

In their place, he hung just one word next to the flight
number. CANCELED.

A search plane found 312 the following day, a DC-4 with
its carcass splattered obscenely against the side of a Blue
Ridge peak known aptly as Devil's Peak. A search plane
radioed "no survivors."

Mac had slept little that long night. He kept thinking of
Dorothy Martin, remembering the pass he had made at her
in the kitchen . . . the way she had talked about the boy she
was going to marry when they both had saved up enough
money . . . their discussion of Pat and Paddy. He had seen
her a couple of weeks ago at the airport and she had gleefully
told him, "Just one more month and I'll be a housewife,
Mac."

At 7 A.M. he couldn't stand it any more. He called Barnwell.

"Mac, Barney. Sorry if I woke you. Look, I'd like to help
any way I can. Search team or anything. I'm off today."

"Meet you at Operations in—say an hour. Okay?"

"Okay."

Barnwell was waiting for him when he arrived.

"Anything yet?"

"Nope. Too dark. There'll be four or five planes up soon
as dawn breaks. Thank God the weather's clearing."

McKay went up to the restaurant to get them some coffee.
When he returned, Shea was there, his eyes heavy with fatigue. He hadn't been to bed at all. He nodded brusquely at
the pair.

"Snorkel coming?"

"I never got around to telling you last night," McKay said. "He had an Atlanta layover."

"I called him after Mac called me," Barnwell said. "He'll be in on 516 this afternoon."

The wreckage was spotted about 9:30 A.M. Devil's Peak was an angry-looking ridge just above the town of Leesburg, Virginia. At 9:40 Barnwell and McKay were in the latter's Ford, heading for Leesburg at illegal speeds. Shea said he'd wait and go out with the CAB investigator-in-charge.

They had some trouble getting by a state police roadblock just outside the village, but while they were arguing with the cop, a CAB car pulled up alongside and the driver recognized Barnwell.

"Let him through, Officer. He's okay."

"And who the hell are you?"

"Bengsten, Civil Aeronautics Board. Here's my credentials. Captain Barnwell's with the Air Line Pilots Association."

The policeman waved them through.

"Thanks, Al."

"Don't mention it. Looks like we've got a bitch. Who's that with you?"

"McKay. He's a copilot. On our safety committee. Mac, this is Al Bengsten of CAB. We might as well get going."

They had to leave the cars at the foot of the mountain. Trudging their way up, McKay found himself next to Bengsten, a burly man with iron-gray hair.

"This your first one?"

"First one since I've been with an airline. I saw a few overseas."

"I'm afraid you'll find these a little different."

McKay did. Not only different, but far worse. Death in the war was something you expected. So was the sight of a mangled B-25. You even took it for granted. And there was nothing mysterious about it. His first glimpse of 312's twisted, burned, and battered corpse made him catch his breath. He almost gasped aloud. It was strewn about in a few thousand pieces, and all he could think of was that it resembled the half-devoured remains of a prehistoric beast. It was unbelievable, incomprehensible, that the symmetrical beauty of a mighty transport plane could be so totally destroyed. Only the DC-4's tail was intact, towering against the sky like an impromptu monument to disaster. The blue letters MIDWEST were incongruously clean and unmarked.

"Jesus," he said to Barnwell.

"Take it easy. They usually look this bad. Let's see if we can find the crew. Al—okay if we look for the cockpit?"

"Sure. Tell your boy not to touch any wreckage. What team do you wanna work on?"

"Operations, probably. Whatever you guys say. McKay here was an aeronautical engineer. Good bet for Structures."

"Fine."

Bengsten had been referring to the CAB's method of assigning teams to work on various phases of a crash investigation. The so-called "interested parties"—Midwest, ALPA, the aircraft manufacturer, CAA—their representatives would serve on groups, each group headed by a CAB Bureau of Safety investigator. A sort of probe-by-committee arrangement. There would be a team to interrogate eyewitnesses, if any. Structures would go into the possibility of any structural failure or malfunction. Power Plants would be responsible for the engines. Operations would check 312's last flight—its handling by ATC, its communications, etc. Another team would review the plane's entire maintenance record. Still another would go into the backgrounds of the crew.

This was the "team concept" of the CAB's accident investigation process. In the early stages of a crash probe the CAB would draw on the skills of the interested parties up to the point where their objective technical knowledge might be affected by their subjective motives. Namely, in the writing of the final verdict.

McKay and Barnwell found the cockpit, or rather what had been the cockpit. There was nothing left of the basic structure. The DC-4 had rammed the mountain almost head-on. McKay almost tripped over a section of instrument panel, the glass in the dials pulverized. He bent to examine them and his eyes caught the charred remnants of a brain bag off to one side. Just beyond it was a mud-stained first officer's hat. McKay shivered.

"Wonder where the cockpit seats are?" Barnwell muttered. "They could have been thrown a hundred yards ahead, on the other side of this damned ridge."

"Want me to look?"

"No. We'd better wait. We'll be marking and charting every piece of this wreckage when they get the teams organized. My God, she really splashed. They never knew what hit 'em."

"I guess I'll just wander around," McKay gulped.

"Okay. You all right?"

"I may get sick."

"Go ahead. I did first time I saw one of these messes. You'll never really get used to it. Just immune."

McKay stumbled away, too ashamed to throw up in front of the captain. He tried to keep his eyes off the blackened stumps that were the bodies. He wondered which ones might be the crew. The odor of burned flesh was in his nostrils and it would stay there—and in his mind—for many more days. For the first time in his life he saw the pitiful and poignant residue of an airliner crash. The luggage with seams ripped open and leather hides slashed as if by a wanton knife. A gaily colored scarf. The charred pieces of mail, already being guarded by a postal inspector. A grimy, dirt-spattered girdle. A baby's rattle. A woman's dress shoe and a man's loafer. A bottle of aspirin, the pills mysteriously ground into white powder. A shredded, partially burned copy of *Time* flipped open to the Foreign News page. A toy airplane someone had picked up at an airport for his son. A coffee cup with the grounds still at the bottom. Inanimate objects that in a mute way spoke of sudden death.

He was wandering around when he spotted something that was only too familiar—a stewardess' handbag. He knelt and opened it.

Inside was a wallet. Inside the wallet was Dorothy Martin's Midwest identification card. Her half-smiling picture on the card was like seeing a ghost. As he put the wallet back his hand touched a piece of paper. He took this out, for no reason except blatant curiosity. It was a copy of a charge slip from Garfinckel's department store. There was only one entry.

"WEDDING GOWN . . . . $75.89"

McDonald McKay vomited.

Fortunately, he was kept busy for the rest of the day. He was part of a group that mapped the wreckage distribution and tagged various pieces of structures with tentative identification. Rescue workers arrived with big rubber blankets into which they unceremoniously dumped the remains. They carried their burdens down the mountainside into Leesburg where a chapel had been set up as a temporary morgue. An FBI disaster team, which already had pulled the available fingerprint files of those aboard, went to work trying to make positive identification. The air reeked with the sweet, sickish odor of formaldehyde.

Late that afternoon McKay and Barnwell returned to the car and drove to the chapel. Relatives of the victims had begun to arrive. The FBI would occasionally admit one inside the chapel. One, a youth in his twenties, emerged tight-lipped and walked over to an older man.

"She wasn't so bad, Father," he said. "She . . . she lost some teeth."

McKay felt pity. But he also mused, with perhaps subjective and intolerant bitterness, there was no one there to mourn the crew. This was unfair, he conceded. Why should Betty Steele be there? Dorothy's family or fiancé couldn't have arrived from Omaha this soon. First Officer Minotti was a bachelor—McKay didn't even know where he was from. So how come the feeling of what was almost resentment? The nagging, persistent belief that the crew was the forgotten factor in tragedy—until it came time to point the finger of blame.

"Want some coffee?" Barnwell's voice interrupted his thoughts.

"Sure could use some. Where?"

"There's a Red Cross mobile canteen over there."

They were walking to the canteen when Barnwell stopped.

"Mac, that guy by the truck. What's he carrying?"

McKay looked where Barney was pointing. A man in overalls was putting what seemed to be a piece of metal into the back of a pickup. A shaft of sunlight suddenly reflected off the metal.

"Aluminum," Barnwell said. "I'll bet the bastard's got a piece of wreckage."

He ran toward the truck, McKay sprinting behind him. The man had just closed the rear panel and was climbing into the cab when Barnwell grabbed his arm.

"Just a minute, buster. What did you put back there?"

The man was evidently a farmer, with an unshaven, weather-beaten face and filthy coveralls that stank of manure.

"Jist a hunk offa that airyplane," he drawled. "Found it up on the hill. Takin' it home for a souvenir."

There was the rank, stale odor of whiskey on his breath.

"Get it off." Barnwell's voice trembled with suppressed anger.

The farmer looked at him rudely. "Screw you," he said. "I got as much right to a souvenir as anybody else."

"You got no rights, you scavenging sonofabitch. Mac, get it off the truck."

McKay hesitated. The farmer outweighed Barnwell by forty pounds. McKay sensed a fight brewing and he didn't want to leave Barney's side.

"Take it off," Barnwell repeated.

"You touch my souvenir and I'll kick the hell outa you," the farmer warned.

"Get it out, Mac," Barnwell ordered.

McKay complied. As he opened the back panel he heard the sound of a scuffle. Alarmed, he ran back to the cab but it was immediately obvious that Barnwell needed no help.

The tall captain had slammed the farmer against the side of the truck and was shaking him as a dog shakes a stick. McKay went back and removed the piece of aluminum, cutting his finger on a sharp edge in the process.

"You got no right to take that," the farmer protested. "It ain't gonna hurt nobody. Who's gonna miss a little piece?"

"Get the hell out of here before I break your goddamned neck," Barnwell growled.

The farmer got into his truck. McKay and Barnwell had started to walk away, McKay carrying the hunk of wreckage.

"Jist a minute, friends."

They looked around. The farmer was out of the truck. In his hand was a pistol.

"Gimme back my souvenir."

The two pilots stopped, anger wrestling with discretion.

"Give it back," the farmer said in an ugly voice.

McKay mentally calculated if he could throw the piece hard enough and far enough into the farmer's leering face, and gave up the idea as quickly as it occurred. Instead, he dropped it on the ground.

"Come and get it," he said quietly.

"Oh no you don't. Pick it up and put it in my truck."

McKay saw red. He started toward the farmer when Barnwell put a restraining hand on his elbow.

"No need, Mac. The Marines have arrived."

Behind the unsuspecting farmer loomed the towering figure of a Virginia state trooper. He didn't know that was going on, but the gun in the farmer's hand was all he needed to know at this point. In one swift move he encircled the man's neck with one huge arm and grabbed the wrist of the gun-holding hand. A sharp twist. The farmer yelped with pain and dropped the gun.

"What's going on here?" the trooper inquired in a matter-of-fact voice.

"I'm Captain Barnwell of Midwest," Barney said. "We caught this scummy bastard trying to haul away a piece of wreckage."

"That true, Mister?"

The farmer was holding his aching wrist. "I don't mean no harm. All I took was that little piece, there. For a sourvenir. Ain't nothin' illegal about that. Who'd miss it?"

"It's about as legal as your carrying that gun. Got a permit?"

The farmer muttered something under his breath, which the pilots couldn't hear but which the trooper did.

"I thought not. You wait here until I can get a deputy sheriff to handle you. Get in your truck and give me the keys."

The farmer obeyed, still grumbling, "I didn't mean nobody any harm. . . ."

"Thanks, Officer," Barnwell said.

"Don't mention it. The old goat's all boozed up. Say, your friend's hand is bleeding." McKay had forgotten about the cut, but now it began to hurt.

"Jesus, Mac, let's get a bandage on it. Red Cross should have some first aid. Thanks again, Officer."

There was a first-aid kit at the canteen. A Red Cross worker cleansed the cut and bandaged it. The two pilots gratefully accepted hot coffee, both more shaken over the incident than they wanted to admit.

"Scavengers," Barnwell said. "They're part of every crash. They're like jackals. So help me, when I see people like that I wonder about the human race."

McKay, his anger diminished, said they probably didn't realize they were doing anything wrong. "I don't suppose somebody like that farmer knows a single piece of wreckage might be the key to the accident," he added.

"It's more than lack of knowledge. It's lack of common decency. I remember reading about the *Shenandoah*—the Navy dirigible. They were late getting a security guard around her after she crashed. People stripped damned near all the wreckage clean and they even took the Annapolis class ring off the commander's finger. What the hell was his name? . . ."

"Landsdowne, I think. Zachary Landsdowne. Funny I should remember his name. I guess I must have read about every word about the *Shenandoah*."

Barnwell gave his cup to the Red Cross girl for a rare refill.

"That was one they didn't blame on pilot error," he said dryly.

"Nope. I guess they will this one."

"Probably. You see anything remotely resembling structural failure?"

"No, but don't overestimate my aeronautical engineering background. I don't think I could recognize metal fatigue now if it walked up and bit me. Anyway, I don't think anything came off the airplane before she hit. Elevators, ailerons, horizontal stabilizers—they're all located. Ditto the wings. I'm afraid she was all in one piece when it happened."

Barnwell nodded unhappily.

"Well, I guess—hey, there's Snorkel driving up."

They ran down to the road where Snodgrass was parking his car. Snorkel, who hated cold weather, had dressed warmly enough to embarrass an Eskimo. He had on a parka, huge storm boots, and thick mittens.

"Where did you think the crash was—the South Pole?" Barney asked.

"I didn't want to take any chances," Snorkel said. "Find out anything?"

Barnwell shook his head. "Nope. Nobody walked away."

"Last night," McKay put in, "Shea seemed pretty upset over the clearance. They were 61 via Arcola."

Snorkel whistled. "That ain't good," he said ungrammatically but earnestly. "Wonder why Dispatch let him use an unauthorized route."

"Or why," Barnwell speculated, "ATC cleared him."

Or why, McKay thought, a veteran like Steele asked for an illegal clearance in the first place. Airway 20 would have been the usual approach. Sixty-one had all its navigation aids operating, but its minimum-altitude rules had yet to be published in the *Airman's Guide*. Until they were published, 61 was off-limits to Midwest pilots—even though they knew the new airway was in operation technically.

"That reminds me, Mac," Snodgrass said. "Were you planning to work on this?"

"I was if it's okay with everybody. I've got a trip tomorrow."

"Crew sked asked me before I left for here," Snorkel informed him. "They're short as hell, as usual. Said if Shea tells you to stay, okay, but they'd rather have you fly your trip."

"Hell, I figured this would be a good one to break him in on," Barnwell said. "Mac, I guess you'd better go back tonight. Unless you wanna ask Shea."

McKay was torn and indecisive. "I'd like to stay," he said finally. "Guess I'll let Shea settle it."

They started back up the mountain and met the chief pilot coming down, accompanied by Al Bengsten. McKay remembered how young Shea had looked the first time the young pilot had seen him in uniform. Right now Shea seemed ten years older. The chief pilot merely grunted a hello and Bengsten nodded.

"We'll be organizing the teams in about an hour," the CAB man said to Barnwell. "No use going back up—everything's about cleaned up and it's getting too dark."

"They get all the bodies?" Barnwell asked.

"Yes. What was left of 'em. Hello, Snorkel. McKay. You wanna stay on Structures?"

"I'm supposed to have a trip tomorrow. Captain Shea, I'll leave it up to you. Crew sked says they're short but to check with you."

Shea sighed, with all the sorrow and weariness of the last few hours underlined by that one exhaling of breath. "You need him?" he asked Barnwell.

"We could use him. But it's not vital."

"Guess you'd better fly your trip, Mac."

On impulse, the chief pilot turned to look at the mountain ridge above them. "Yeh," he said to no one in particular. "We're short of pilots. I know we're short two."

McKay was disappointed but in one way, he was glad. As soon as he drove back to town, he rushed over to Barbara's apartment and announced his firm, unequivocal decision that she should quit flying. This time, it was Barbara who was coolly logical.

"I know you're upset about Dorothy Martin," she said, "but you just got through saying the other night you wanted me to work out my problem. I think I have. I had a touch of the jitters this last trip, but nowhere near as bad as they've been. Come on, Mac—it makes about as much sense for me to quit now as for you to quit. Because of one accident?"

"It's different," McKay argued. "Flying's my profession. It isn't for you."

"Honey, you're being ridiculous and too emotional."

"I know it," he admitted. "That damned crash—and Dorothy—it shook me up."

"Let's talk about it later. Right now I'd like to neck up a storm with you and we'd better get started because Mitch'll be home in about thirty minutes."

They did talk about it later, namely over the next three weeks, during which time some of McKay's more vivid and painful memories of Devil's Peak and Flight 312 diminished to a dull ache. His protests against Barbara's continuing to fly also diminished in direct proportion to those memories. As she knew they would.

Although he never got back into the investigation, he was off the day after the CAB's public hearings opened in one of the eyesore temporary buildings that botched up the landscape between the Lincoln Memorial and the Washington Monument. It was a structure, built during World War I, that reminded McKay of a military barracks—a squat, two-story affair as ugly and Spartan inside as outside.

He went to the session with Snorkel. The hearing was in an almost airless, overheated room whose only touch of color was the American flag draped listlessly on a standard in back of the long table where the CAB investigative panel was parked at one end of the room. Presiding was Vice Chairman Warner Hampton of the CAB, a man eminently qualified to head a fatal accident investigation by reason of his eighteen years in Congress, his eventual appointment to the Board as a lame-duck lawmaker who needed a job— furnished promptly by a grateful President from his own party—and his vast experience in aeronautics which consisted of taking at least seven airline flights annually.

Fortunately for the integrity and efficiency of the accident investigation process, as McKay was to learn, CAB members usually were mere figureheads at a crash hearing. The questioning was performed mostly by Bureau of Safety personnel who knew what they were doing. Presiding officer Hampton actually was not as bad as one of his predecessors who thought that the "DC" in DC-3 stood for some kind of District of Columbia airplane license—and embarrassed the Bureau immensely when he asked about the letters at a hearing. Hampton, a pink-cheeked little man with sad spaniel eyes and a melodious voice, privately conceded his non-aeronautical background and publicly let the Bureau run with the ball.

The Bureau was running wild with it on the day McKay sat in on the Flight 312 hearing. The opening session the day before had disposed of such possibilities as structural failure, sabotage, in-flight fire, and weather. Today's session began with the testimony of a scientist from the National Bureau of Standards who had been assigned the task of determining whether there could have been any chance of altimeter malfunction. The Bureau, with virtually no technical facilities of its own, farmed out to other agencies any laboratory work involved in an accident investigation.

McKay and Snodgrass sat down at a table on which was a little sign reading ALPA. Barnwell already was there, along with a stocky, pixie-faced man whom Barnwell introduced as Tom Dayton, safety representative for the pilots' union in Washington. McKay glanced curiously at the other small tables facing the panel. They, too, bore identifying cards. Douglas. Pratt & Whitney. CAA. Midwest. Weather Bureau. The "interested parties" present to aid the CAB in arriving at the truth.

There also was a press table, occupied largely by men unfamiliar with air safety problems but enormously skillful at draining from a mass of technical testimony—which they seldom understood—an indicting headline or snappy lead. And in the back of the room, feverishly taking notes, were lawyers representing relatives of the crash victims—all waiting to pounce on the slimmest inkling of negligence on somebody's part, especially Midwest, that would lead to an easy lawsuit or a fat out-of-court settlement. Naturally, many of them already had filed damage claims charging criminal, inexcusable negligence. The fact that the probable cause of crash hadn't been determined yet made no difference. When their 30 to 50 per cent share of the damages collected was involved, there was no point in waiting for the solution of the accident. As Al Bengsten had once bitterly remarked to Barnwell, "If those legal vultures were told a crash was an act of God, they'd find some way to sue Jesus."

The Bureau of Standards expert was sworn in and sat nervously in the witness chair directly in front of the panel's table. The interrogator was the Bureau's investigator-in-charge, Robert Pool, an ex-air-mail pilot himself who, except for a mane of graying, almost white hair, startlingly resembled John Shea.

Pool, doing his questioning from the panel table, where he sat at Hampton's right, quickly established the witness' technical qualifications. Mr. Frederick Snow, it appeared without doubt, was an expert on the workings of the aneroid altimeter—which is a version of the aneroid barometer used in homes. It does not really measure height. It merely measures the weight of the air, and translates that weight into terms of feet instead of pounds per square foot.

"You bench-tested the altimeters from N-7402, Mr. Snow?" Pool asked, referring to 312's aircraft serial number.

"Yes sir."

"Did you find any evidence of malfunctioning?"

"No sir. The tests showed the altimeters were within proper tolerances,"

"By proper tolerances, how much of an error would have been permissible?"

"About twenty-five feet at the most."

"Are these the altimeters subjected to the bench tests?" Pool picked up two black cylindrical objects from a table behind him. He handed them to Snow. Everyone in the room craned forward to look at them. McKay had the weird feeling it was like seeing a ghost from the crash site.

"Yes sir, they're from the plane." Snow handed them back.

Pool fondled one altimeter as if he expected it to speak in its own defense. "No further questions, Mr. Chairman," he said to Hampton.

The CAB member whispered something to Pool who whispered back. Hampton lubricated his tonsils with a "ah, hmmmmm" and officiously peered around the room. "Any questions from Douglas?" he demanded.

"No sir," boomed the factory representative.

Hampton also drew negative responses from the CAA, the engine firm of Pratt & Whitney and the Weather Bureau.

"Midwest?"

Bennett Kane was conferring with a company lawyer and Shea. He finally emerged from their huddle and said, "No questions."

"ALPA?"

Barnwell had been scribbling notes furiously on a sheet of foolscap and talking to Dayton. He looked up from the pad and announced, "I have a few questions."

Witness Snow, who figured he was through with the ordeal, stirred uneasily. But Barnwell disarmed him with a pleasant smile.

"Mr. Snow, as an expert on altimeters, do you regard a bench test as infallible?"

Snow stared at him.

"Are bench tests infallible?" Barnwell repeated. "Or perhaps I should put it differently. Would the tests you conduct in a laboratory always reflect the behavior of the same instrument if it were on an aircraft, in actual flight?"

"I would say so," Snow said in a rather nettled voice.

"I'm not challenging the, uh, integrity of your very fine technical facilities, Mr. Snow," Barnwell went on diplomatically. "I'm merely wondering if a laboratory or so-called bench test, under what must be carefully controlled conditions, would show an altimeter the way it may have operated, say, the night of this accident."

"I see no reason to question the test results," Snow replied firmly.

"I would like the Board to turn to page 3 of the communications transcript, marked 'Prehearing Exhibit 5-C,'" Barnwell said.

There was a rustle of papers throughout the room.

"You'll note," the pilot continued, "that when Flight 312 was cleared to begin his descent from Martinsburg, he was told to report each time he left another one thousand feet of altitude. From this transcript of communications between the flight and Approach Control, I'd like to call your attention to what may be significant. As you can see, he reported leaving six thousand, five thousand, four thousand, three thousand. That three thousand was his last reported altitude."

"And what exactly is the significance, Captain Barnwell?" Hampton asked.

"In testimony yesterday, Mr. Chairman, it was established that the aircraft impacted Devil's Peak at exactly 1425 feet. I'm just wondering, in view of Mr. Snow's insistence that Captain Steele's altimeter was functioning properly, why there was no report of his leaving two thousand. It seems obvious that the crew believed they were higher than two thousand feet or they would have reported leaving two thousand."

Neat point, McKay thought. Except it might have more holes than a fishing net. He was well aware that altitude reports were not always made at the exact second a plane passed through an altitude level.

The Chairman whispered again to Pool, who nodded. Hampton peered over his old-fashioned square glasses at the ALPA table.

"Thank you, Captain Barnwell, the Board will take this, uh, apparent discrepancy under due consideration."

Another conference at the panel table, and Hampton summoned dispatcher Hemmingway to the stand. Obviously unhappy and frightened, he took the oath and eased himself gingerly into the witness chair. Pool drew from him his full name, dispatching experience and the admission he had relayed Flight 312's request for an illegal clearance.

"Specifically, what did Captain Steele ask for?" said Pool.

"Well, actually I was talking to the copilot, Mr. Minotti, who . . ."

"I understand that, Mr. Hemmingway. But I'm assuming that the request came from the captain, even though the first officer was handling communications. Is that assumption correct?"

"Well, most of the guys . . . most of the captains let the copilot handle the radio. Yes, I guess Captain Steele wanted . . . what he asked for."

The dispatcher was putting off the admission as long as possible, but Pool pressed on.

"And what exactly did he want?"

"He asked for a visual clearance down . . ."

"Just a minute, Mr. Hemmingway," Pool interrupted. "I think the Board would appreciate knowing what constitutes a visual clearance."

"Well, it means he'd follow the route only as long as he could see the ground."

"Thank you. Continue."

"He asked for a visual clearance down the west course of the Arcola range on Airway 61, on into Washington."

"And had your company authorized the use of this route?"

"Well, all the pilots knew it was operating with nav aids and everything. It was only a question of time . . ."

"That's not what I asked you. Had Midwest authorized the use of Airway 61? Had the minimum altitudes been published in the *Airman's Guide?*"

"No sir."

"Your answer is negative to both questions?"

The dispatcher rubbed the back of his hand across his mouth. "The clearance request was illegal," he answered.

"Did you know, or realize it was illegal?"

For the first time Hemmingway bristled a little. "If I had realized it that night, I wouldn't have relayed it," he said bitterly. "I just wasn't thinking. I was busy and . . ."

"Thank you, Mr. Hemmingway. Mr. Chairman?"

Hampton called the roll. There were no further questions. Pool summoned en-route controller Joseph Sandusky to testify. Sandusky was a youthful, sandy-haired individual with thin lips and what would have been an ingratiating smile except that he was as scared as Hemmingway and hadn't smiled since the night of the accident. There were dark circles under his eyes and his hands trembled.

Pool was rather gentle with him, but it was a deceptive gentleness that was merely an anesthesia for the hide-tearing that was to come.

"Mr. Sandusky, you've read the transcript of communications between en-route control and Flight 312?"

"Yes sir."

"Do you consider it an accurate record of those transmissions?"

"Yes sir."

"You were en-route controller working Flight 312 on the night of the accident?"

"Yes sir."

"At what stage, Mr. Sandusky, would the flight have passed from your jurisdiction to Approach Control?"

"When he checked in over the Arcola range, Approach would have taken over."

"Then the clearance the flight received occurred when you were handling it?"

"That wasn't the clearance I gave him originally," Sandusky said hastily.

Pool nodded patiently. "Yes, according to the transcript you originally cleared him to Washington National via Airway 20 to the Herndon fan marker. Let's see, at seven thousand feet."

"Yes sir. Then I advised him that at Herndon he could expect a delay of about an hour and twenty minutes before getting final approach clearance."

"And the flight subsequently requested Airway 61 via Arcola?"

"Yes sir."

"Let me read from the transcript. 'ATC clears Midwest 312 Airway six-one via Arcola. Cross the Arcola range at or below two-five-hundred in accordance with visual flight rules. If unable maintain visual contact, hold at Arcola at two-five-hundred and advise.' Is that correct?"

"Yes sir."

"In other words, you told him he could descend from seven thousand to twenty-five hundred *or lower*—I repeat, *or lower*—in attempting to maintain visual contact with the ground?"

"Or lower?" asked the controller.

"Yes. Your clearance—I'll read it again—your clearance specified that he cross the Arcola range *at or below* two-five-hundred. Is this correct?"

"Yes sir, that's what I told him."

"You cleared this flight to descend below twenty-five hundred feet over mountainous terrain on an airway for which no minimum altitudes had been published?"

Sandusky, as had Hemmingway, tried to fight back if only in a futile flurry. He came close to glaring at Pool before answering. "The airway might have been illegal for Midwest, but it wasn't for us. It was in operation. The nav aids were all in."

"With no published minimum altitudes," Pool reminded him.

"No sir. But that's not my job. As far as ATC was concerned, it was a legal clearance."

Pool's gentle voice hid the next question like flowers draped around a lead pipe. "Mr. Sandusky, were you aware that no minimum altitudes had been published for Airway 61?"

The controller did not answer for a full five seconds. His face was pale and his thin lips colorless. "Yes sir, I knew it."

"I'm informed, Mr. Sandusky, that in such cases controllers must consult an aeronautical map before granting a clearance on an unpublished airway. Did you follow this required procedure?"

Sandusky bit his lips. "Yes sir," he said finally.

"You actually looked at a map before you told the flight to descend below two-five-hundred and maintain visual contact?"

"Yes sir."

"Mr. Sandusky, we're not trying to hang anybody here. We're simply trying to determine the truth. The cause of this terrible tragedy. So I must ask you, sir, could you explain why you allowed this aircraft to descend, at night and in an overcast, into a mountainous area where the terrain in question was as high as two thousand feet?"

The controller bowed his head and suddenly began sobbing. The room was deathly still. A raucous horn from a passing truck outside sounded so loud that a few spectators started in surprise.

"Would you like a brief recess to compose yourself?" Pool asked.

Sandusky took out a handkerchief and wiped his eyes. "No sir. I'd rather get it over with."

Pool looked at him sympathetically. "As I said before, Mr. Sandusky. We're here to determine the truth. I know you feel as badly as anyone over what happened. We appreciate your honesty. Now, if you feel you can give us your explanation . . ."

"I looked at a map," the controller said in a low voice. "I just misread it. I looked at it . . . I thought there wasn't any terrain over one thousand feet. That's when I told him to descend below twenty-five hundred. I figured he'd see the ground long before he reached one thousand."

Pool leaned back in his chair. Hampton asked for questions. When he came to Barnwell, the pilot started to speak, looked at Sandusky's expression of total misery, and said quietly, "No questions."

The next and final witness was Shea, who testified briefly on Midwest's rules regarding acceptance of clearances on unpublished airways. He also read into the record, with belligerent emphasis, the excellent results of Captain Steele's last check ride and his over-all, spotless record with Midwest.

"I should like to point out to the Board, if I may, that Captain Steele had more than eighteen thousand hours in the air," Shea said. "As his immediate superior and supervisor, it is incomprehensible to me that a pilot with such experience would descend blindly into known mountainous terrain."

"Previous testimony has brought out that the flight was nearly an hour late," Pool suggested. "Don't you think there might have been an element of impatience involved? After all, it was obvious that when he was told there would have been a further delay on Airway 20, and that he would have to hold for more than an hour at Herndon, he requested what amounted to a shortcut."

"I can't read the mind of a dead pilot," Shea said testily. "All I know is that a guy with eighteen thousand hours doesn't go around playing Russian roulette with a DC-4 and forty passengers."

"Captain Shea, as chief pilot can you tell us if Midwest has an official, or perhaps unofficial, uh, policy regarding the making up of lost time on a late flight?"

"If you mean do we pressure pilots to take shortcuts if they're late, the answer is hell no!"

A spectator laughed nervously.

"I wasn't suggesting that was the case, Captain," Pool apologized. "I was just asking the question. I was trying to establish the reason for Captain Steele's decision to take a shortcut."

"Let me put it this way," Shea said firmly. "He was not operating under any implied or subtle pressure from management regarding the maintaining of schedule. Nor was there anything in his record to even remotely suggest he would take a deliberate chance just because he was so damned late."

Shea was excused with no other questions. At noon Hampton declared the public hearing was concluded.

Dayton returned to his office, but McKay, Barnwell, and Snorkel went to lunch at the Occidental. The younger pilot was noticeably quiet and Barnwell was curious.

"What did you think of it?" he asked.

"Well, interesting. Seemed pretty thorough and objective. Is Pool a good guy?"

"Competent enough. He loves that prosecutor role a little too much. His mother must have been frightened by a lawyer. Tell me, Mac, if you had to write the verdict yourself, what would you say?"

"I didn't hear the first day's testimony," McKay said cautiously.

"No matter. You heard enough and you know all the facts."

"Dammit, Barney, I don't know what I'd decide. ATC really goofed. So did our Dispatch, to a lesser degree. Pilot error? I'd have to buy it on the basis of circumstantial evidence. Yet it's like Shea said—why would a pilot take an unnecessary calculated risk with eighteen thousand hours in back of him?"

"I still think he had a bum altimeter," Snodgrass said. "Nobody can tell me a bench test is worth a damn."

"I doubt it," Barnwell said.

"Then why did you raise the issue?" McKay asked.

"Smokescreen, mostly. The whole hearing was pointing straight toward the cockpit. Sure, ATC pulled a rock and Dispatch shouldn't have passed on the clearance. But you gotta come back to why he was flying that airway and what the hell he was doing at around fifteen hundred over mountains and in clouds. And for that matter, why he still was descending. He hit in a slightly nose-down attitude."

"Do you think it was pilot error?" McKay asked. "Would you put that down as *your* verdict?"

"No."

"But you just said . . ."

"I said I'd like to know why he was on that airway and why he was trying to establish visual contact in the middle of some goddamned mountains. I'm looking for a logical explanation to an illogical crash. I don't think pilot error is a logical explanation . . . not for a guy like Jim Steele. You take all the evidence that says the captain made a boo-boo, and the CAB will stop right there. I say you go farther—you ask how the hell could a good captain pull such a bonehead and maybe you'll find a logical explanation. Some reason nobody ever suspected. Like a lagging altimeter. Sure it was a shot in the dark, but it's more logical than Jim Steele being so impatient he started playing footsies with the Blue Ridge."

"And yet," McKay observed, "you've admitted you don't think the altimeter had anything to do with it."

"Correct. I don't know what happened. A nav aid could have been off. They were tested the next day, but there could have been some unusual, intermittent interference at just the wrong time. My point, Mac, is that while I'm representing ALPA at a hearing, I'm really representing the guys who can't defend themselves. Steele's the only man in the world who'd be able to tell us what happened that night —and he's dead. So it's our job to raise possibilities other than pilot error. And I'll raise them every chance I get. And someday, my young friend, so will you."

"Even," McKay said, "when I know pilot error was responsible?"

"Yes, because that's your job as a pilot. Or don't you agree?"

"I think," McKay said slowly, "if I was sure a pilot made a mistake, I'd try to find an explanation for the mistake but I wouldn't defend him for making it. That's the whole trouble with your . . . well, your philosophy."

"Continue," Barnwell said good-naturedly.

"You seem to assume that pilot error itself is illogical. Maybe it was with Steele, but even in one year I've seen some stupid things. Not by you guys, but as green as I am, I haven't gained any impression that a pilot is infallible."

"I never said he was," Barnwell protested mildly.

"Then let me ask you this. Suppose you were investigating an accident in which a pilot just out and out messed things up. There weren't any extenuating circumstances. Only plain and simple pilot error. Bad judgment or bad flying or both. Would you defend him? Would you still try to raise other issues?"

"Good question, Barney," Snorkel said.

Barnwell toyed with the remnants of the veal cutlet on his plate. "I guess I would," he replied.

"But why, Barney?"

"Because he can't defend himself, that's why. Because he's the only one who could tell what really happened. Because somehow, somewhere, there must be a reason for the mistake. You've got to raise doubts about pilot error because once that verdict is reached, nobody gives a damn about finding out the why—and that's how you keep some other joker from pulling the same mistake."

"Okay, suppose the pilot survives. I'll buy your argument in a fatal accident, but would you feel the same way if he lived?"

"If there were cockpit survivors," Barnwell said, "it would be fairly easy to determine the reason for the mistake. And I'd concentrate on the reason, rather than the mistake itself."

"That's one trouble," Snorkel objected. "Now you're assuming a pilot would admit the mistake. I never knew one who did. Hell, I don't think I would."

"I wonder," said McKay, "what Steele would have said if he'd been able to walk away."

His question produced silence at the table.

"He was the kind of guy who would have told the truth," Snodgrass said eventually.

Barnwell shook his head. "No, I don't think so, Snorkel. A pilot's natural reaction would be to rationalize—particularly if people got killed. He'd have his whole career on the line. He'd have a helluva tug of war—between honesty and self-interest. I think self-interest would win out. A pilot's only human. He's try to find an excuse, a good out. It would be a rare bird who admitted everything. Maybe one like Mac, here."

"I hope," said McKay, "that I never find myself in that situation. But I don't think I could live with myself if I lied."

"You think that now," Barnwell said. "I've heard pilots say the same thing you just did—but when it came time to throw themselves to the wolves, they denied they goofed. They didn't really lie, they just convinced themselves they had a good alibi. Rationalization is the best word I have for it. And I suspect I'd rationalize."

"For a new copilot, I'm probably off base," McKay said. "But I still have the idea that blind defense of a pilot can, well, interfere with getting at the truth. Isn't that the most important thing?"

"Sure," agreed Barnwell. "But the whole truth—and pilot error isn't always the whole truth."

"Then, one more observation and I'll shut up," McKay said. "It seems to me that if you defend any pilot, regardless of the circumstances, you weaken your case when you protect one who really deserves defending. You're just creating the impression that ALPA will fight a pilot-error verdict, no matter what the evidence. You're literally crying wolf too often."

"Good point," said Snorkel.

"Whose side are you on?" Barnwell laughed. "Yeh, you do have a point, Mac. But I find myself constitutionally unequipped to go along with you. I suppose I keep thinking I'd want someone to defend me if I clobbered one, for any reason. So we come back to my first question, Mac. How would you pass judgment on Steele?"

McKay didn't hesitate. "Pilot error," he said quietly. "With contributing factors."

"I like your frankness," Barnwell said. "As a matter of fact, that's exactly what the CAB will decide."

As a matter of fact, that was exactly what the CAB did decide. Six months later McKay got a copy of the accident report and read the verdict.

"The Board determines that the probable cause of this accident was poor judgment by the captain in descending through clouds at night over known hazardous terrain, resulting in impact with obstructing terrain. Contributing factors were the relaying of an illegal clearance by the carrier's dispatcher and the failure of the Civil Aeronautics Administration's Air Traffic Control system to advise the pilot of minimum-altitude restrictions."

Or, as Snorkel phrased it, "They ran out of altitude and information simultaneously."

One man who didn't read the report was controller Joseph Sandusky. The week after the public hearing, he put a gun to his right temple and pulled the trigger.

Chapter 8

Eventually McKay had to face the prematrimonial obstacle course known as Meeting Her Parents.

They flew to Milwaukee on one of his rare weekends off, McKay being just a little bit apprehensive about the ordeal. Barbara was more fortunate. She enjoyed that delicious privilege understood and appreciated only by stewardesses— namely, watching other stewardesses work a trip.

"I think Culver dated that blonde once," McKay said.

"Is there anybody he hasn't dated?"

"You," grinned McKay. "And Mitch."

"Mitch would be good for him. She'd scare him to death."

"It would be interesting," McKay agreed. "Sort of the irresistible force meeting the immovable object. Wonder what would happen if she pulled jiujitsu in the middle of one of his passes."

"He'd probably seduce her as he went over her shoulder," Barbara conceded. "Anyway, I hope Mitch meets the right guy someday. Like I did."

McKay took her hand and was about to lean over and kiss her when he thought he heard an engine miss a beat.

"Number four sounds a little rough," he worried.

"Sounds all right to me," Barbara said. "Say, are you nervous?"

It hadn't really occurred to McKay until she said it, but he actually was. This was the first time he had sat in a cabin since winning his airline wings. Barbara's reaction to off-duty flying was to be critical. His was a feeling of helplessness that by the end of the trip threatened to turn into abject misery. He kept wanting to rush up to the cockpit to reassure himself that everything was under control.

Barbara was delighted in a perverse way.

"I've heard you pilots were babies when you rode back here," she told him. "Now I believe it. Honey, you act like you've never flown before."

"Doctors make bum patients, too," he said defensively. "It's just . . . just different when you're not up front. Anyway, I'll bet that copilot's pretty green. I hope the captain makes the landing."

He squirmed, frowned, fussed, and complained for a half hour. He was positive at least two and possibly three props were out of synchronization and he practically put his head through the window when number-two engine threw a little oil.

"Do you think I should go up and tell 'em about it?" he asked.

"No, I don't," she said. "But if it'll make you feel any better, go ahead."

"I'll just go up and say hello," McKay promised. "I'll be right back."

"Good-by, my brave pilot," she chided. "And hurry back —chicken."

McKay spared himself the luxury of a dirty look. He was too anxious to make sure the cockpit was in the hands of two breathing, physically fit airmen who were not suffering from (1) food poisoning, (2) heart attacks, or (3) sudden onslaughts of insanity. He strolled nonchalantly up the aisle and opened the door to his world.

He was no sooner inside than he realized how foolishly he was acting. The "green" copilot (who had exactly two months' less seniority than McKay) was flying the ship and the captain was Tod Thornton. The very sight of them in the familiar cockpit calmed him.

"Hi, Mac," Thornton said cheerfully. "Couldn't you stay away?"

"Guess not," McKay said.

"You know Ozzie Eskin?"

McKay shook hands with the first officer and while doing

so, sneaked a look at the oil pressure on number two. Thornton's sharp eyes didn't miss it, however.

"What's the matter?" he laughed. "Think you saw an oil leak?"

McKay was embarrassed but nodded. "It's sure different back there," he admitted. "I'm discovering I'm a backseat driver at heart."

"Join the club," the captain said. "There isn't an airline pilot in the United States who likes to fly as a passenger."

He examined the oil pressure gauge briefly. "Everything normal," he announced.

Reassured temporarily, McKay stayed on the flight deck for a few minutes, then returned to his seat, where he relaxed for the unusually lengthy period of a full ten minutes before starting to listen to the engines again and feeling the motion of the plane through the seat of his pants. In a way, it was just as well he was experiencing the tremors of a pilot unhappy in the role of a passenger. It kept his mind off what awaited him in Milwaukee.

His concern over his introduction to his future in-laws was unnecessary. Dr. and Mrs. Deering met the flight, and the doctor put McKay at ease immediately by referring to him as "Mac" instead of "son." Barbara's father was a handsome man, about a half inch shorter than McKay and without even the suggestion of a middle-age paunch. His handshake was firm, his smile warm and his manner friendly.

Mrs. Deering kissed McKay—and like every male who examines a prospective mother-in-law in terms of wondering what her daughter will look like twenty years hence—he saw with satisfaction that she was still beautiful. Except for her graying hair, she was more of a slightly blurred carbon copy of Barbara than a woman precisely twenty-six years older.

McKay, who hadn't the vaguest notion that Barbara's father was wealthy, was a bit jolted by his car—a shining new Cadillac. He was further shaken when they arrived at the Deering home. The uncle who raised him had lived in an ordinary wood frame house in Columbus, which McKay had always regarded as large. The Deerings lived in an English Tudor dwelling which to McKay's awed eyes seemed a few cubic feet smaller than Yankee Stadium. The tree-lined grounds were enormous and McKay had a sudden sinking spell when he realized that their wedding reception—it would be held here, Barbara already had informed him—probably would involve a crowd approximating Midwest's weekly passenger traffic.

He worried briefly over the expectation that there would be a butler or two. There wasn't—merely the family maid who gushed over Barbara and giggled over McKay and was more flustered than anyone else.

He was shown to the guest room, which was larger than his entire apartment, taken on a tour of the house—during which time he was pleased to see several pictures of Barbara on various tables and mantelpieces—and finally, much to his relief, offered a drink which he accepted without giving a damn whether the doctor was opposed to drinking. The doctor wasn't, if his liquor supply was any indication, and he mixed himself a highball twice as strong as McKay's.

They went out to dinner that night and McKay was even more impressed with the parents than on their initial meeting at the airport. They had the knack of being rich without being self-conscious or patronizing about it. They obviously worshiped Barbara, yet despite her being an only child raised amid wealth, McKay knew she was completely unspoiled. Through the evening he discovered that this admirable achievement was the product of two intelligent people with a high sense of values and the knowledge of where doting should end and discipline begin.

He remembered that when Barbara first suggested the weekend, he had seriously considered wearing his uniform— for the same security-grasping motive that afflicted him the day he reported to Midwest for his first interview with Shea. He wanted desperately to impress her parents, yet the fact that they openly liked him was almost forgotten in his discovery that he also liked them.

Dr. Deering asked him some intelligent questions about flying, and they got into an interesting discussion on fatigue and how it affected proficiency. They had an even more interesting and vital discussion later on, after Barbara and her mother went to bed and the doctor took McKay into his den for a nightcap.

"I hate to sound like the conventional father-in-law-to-be asking for the proverbial man-to-man chat, Mac," he said, "but I think you know Barbara's our whole world. She's told us all about you. Your family background, your military experience, and while she's possibly prejudiced, she insists everyone is convinced you've got a great future with the airlines."

"I think the airlines have a great future," McKay said. "I enjoy my work, I'm proud of my job, and I figure it's just as important to work at a marriage as to work at your profession. If that helps answer your questions."

The doctor tapped tobacco into a beautifully grained pipe, lit it, and sipped his drink, studying McKay closely. "What I have in mind," he said, "is not so much a question but an impression. Perhaps a prejudice. Let me put it this way. I have a great deal of respect for what you do. At the same time, I have some qualms about it."

"If you're worried about how safe . . ." McKay started to say.

"No, not safety. We've been concerned about Barbara's flying. But it's what she wanted and I'll have to confess we've been proud of her choice. And we wouldn't worry about you. I'm very much aware that you don't pay any higher premiums for life insurance than, well, say a stockbroker."

"Or a doctor," McKay said with a slight smile.

"Touché. Matter of fact, I'd have to admit a doctor's life expectancy is less than an airline pilot's. No, Mac, it's not the safety aspects of your job. It's the life you lead. You're away from home a lot—no, let me finish—you're exposed to many attractive girls, and to be completely candid, I don't want Barbara hurt. I'm being honest with you, Mac. This is our main concern about a marriage which in every other respect seems ideal. I know Barbara loves you, so I wouldn't even raise the issue with her. Hell, my boy, she wouldn't listen to me."

"Doctor, let me be candid, too. I don't think you're being fair to pilots. I don't say they're all angels. I know some of them cheat. I also know many who would just as soon fly a ship into a mountain. My point is that if you're worried about Barbara getting hurt, infidelity could be a problem no matter what her husband's profession. Sure some pilots are unfaithful. So are some lawyers, or bankers—or even doctors."

"Touché again," chuckled the doctor. "But my point is that a pilot is exposed to more frequent temptation. Isn't he?"

McKay thought that one over a minute. "True," he said. "But exposure doesn't necessarily mean infidelity actually takes place. And are you judging it by its existence or by the number of times it occurs?"

"I would suggest," Dr. Deering replied, "that infidelity could become a habit with an airline pilot, whereas another man might stray infrequently or perhaps once or twice. I could excuse the latter, depending on the circumstances. I could not condone the former."

"Infidelity must depend on the individual, Doctor. All I can say—assuming I'd agree with your generalization—is that there are exceptions, many exceptions. All I can promise you, Dr. Deering, is that I have the utmost respect for the marriage vows."

Barbara's father started to say something, but McKay interrupted.

"I'd like to add one more thing, sir. It took me a long time to fall in love. It took me a long time to decide to get married. One of the reasons was my belief in the sanctity of marriage. I fell in love with your daughter because she has every quality I think a man would want in a woman. I'm human. I have human weaknesses. Barbara is the kind of girl who's the best guarantee against those weaknesses. And the best guarantee you could have, too—against your worrying about them. I hope I'm not sounding too Pollyanna-ish."

"No, Mac, you're not. You've made me feel much better. Want another drink?"

"Very light, sir."

The doctor mixed it, handed the glass to the pilot, and sat down again. "What's your goal in life, Mac? Getting to be a captain?"

"Immediate goal, yes. Long-range—I haven't thought about it in specifics. I'd like to be a chief pilot, I suppose. I'd like to do more work in safety. I've already told Barbara I'm going to work on ALPA—that's the Air Line Pilots Association —on ALPA safety committees. I have a theory about my job, Doctor, if you'd like to hear it . . ."

"I certainly would."

"Well, it's something the chief pilot told me the first day I went with Midwest. That too many airline pilots like to think of their job as a profession, exactly as you think of medicine as a profession, but they don't do anything about making it a profession. They just fly their trips. There's an awful lot to be done in aviation outside of getting a plane from Point A to Point B. Pilots bitch . . . complain . . ."

"'Bitch' sounds fine."

"Pilots bitch about what's wrong with commercial aviation. They know what's wrong, too—better than anyone else. But try getting them to serve on some committee or commission or attend conferences or meetings. I don't say all pilots should be running around crusading. I don't blame any man for trying to forget an airplane when he gets off a trip. For leading a normal life away from an airport. But a few of us have to take the lead. Maybe if just 10 per cent of us, or even 5 per cent fought for what we believe in, we'd get the reforms we keep crying for. Or some of them, anyway. I may —and I hope this doesn't worry you even more—I may be away more than the average pilot. I don't want to be one of the guys who talk but don't act. Barbara understands how I feel. You asked about the long-range future. It's a long way off . . . I've got a lot to learn just about getting from Point A to Point B, so to speak, but I also want to do something about getting from Point A to Point B more safely. I'm afraid I'm being too vague. What do you think?"

"I think," said Dr. Deering, "you're going to make us one helluva son-in-law."

They were married in a Presbyterian church on June 15, 1947, with Paddy O'Brian best man, Pat O'Brian matron of honor, Mitch maid of honor, and always-an-usher-and-never-a-bridegroom Les Culver performing what was threatening to become an avocation.

"I'm glad I've finally run out of roommates," he told Shea during the reception.

"You should settle down, Les," the chief pilot advised, knowing full well that this might take an act of Congress in Culver's case. "This is quite a layout, isn't it? I didn't know Deering came from a background like this."

"Neither did I," Culver said. "If I had known it, I'd have chased her myself."

Snorkel and his wife were there and so were the Barnwells —the only other pilots McKay and Barbara had invited. Even this took some doing, with crew schedule insisting that marriage or no marriage, trips had to be flown. McKay had suggested asking Henry Billings and his wife, but Barbara turned thumbs down.

"That's how we met," McKay reminded her. "If it wasn't for Henry . . ."

"I know," said Barbara. "I couldn't look his wife in the face."

She had flown her last trip with none other than Snorkel. She was feeling properly sentimental about her final trip in a Midwest uniform and even a little blue, but it was a full ship and she was too busy to think about it except in nostalgic spurts.

They were on final approach to Washington National when Snorkel came on the PA.

"Ladies and gentlemen, this is Captain Snodgrass. Before we land in Washington—on time, which is not unusual for your highly skilled captain—I'd like to let you in on a little secret. That pretty ash-blonde who's been serving you is going to be walking up another aisle in just three weeks. Miss Deering is going to marry one of our pilots—a fine young man who learned everything from me. I think it would be nice if we gave her a round of applause when we touch down."

The passengers didn't wait for the landing to applaud. Barbara blushed, Snorkel rolled the DC-4 up to the ramp, and the cabin door was opened.

Virtually every off-duty pilot and stewardess from the Washington base was lined up outside—led by Captain Shea, who was carrying a huge bouquet of red roses. Three weeks later, as she stood before a holy altar, she thought about that last flight and was grateful for having been a part of aviation with its sentiment and friendships and laughs and even its occasional tears. She even had a moment of regret until she looked at the face of the man standing beside her and knew that through him she would always be a part of it.

They spent their honeymoon in San Francisco, which neither had ever seen. They held hands at the Top of the Mark and took a side trip to the Grand Tetons in a rented car and trailer. They made love with the uninhibited desire of two people discovering that marriage, rather than shackling them, offered a new kind of freedom unmarred by feelings of guilt or fear.

They returned to Washington July 1 and settled in a brand-new apartment building near the airport. Barbara's parents had given them a $3000 check as a wedding gift to be used for furniture. Barbara spent only $1500 of it and put the rest in a savings account to which McKay systematically added. This was their "house fund" for both agreed that they would buy a home as soon as they could. Over McKay's mild objections, she went to work a month later as a Midwest reservations clerk and banked her entire salary in the house fund.

"It'll build up faster that way," she argued. "And I'll get bored just sitting around."

"No night shifts," he warned.

"No night shifts," she promised.

They had agreed not to have a baby for at least the first year, which wasn't easy inasmuch as Barbara's passion surprised her husband and his virility surprised her. In pure sexual satisfaction their few premarital experiences had fallen far short of their matrimonial ones. Barbara found out quickly what aroused him and deliberately seduced him on sufficiently frequent occasions to keep him not only happy but worn out.

For his part, McKay was determined not to let their marriage settle in any kind of a rut where they took each other for granted. He was by nature sentimental and affectionate, although until he had met Barbara he had tended to keep it bottled up like a vintage champagne to be opened on a special occasion. He got into the habit of bringing her little gifts after every trip involving a layover. Usually they were inexpensive and of the "gag" variety. Sometimes they were expensive, bought on impulse when he would go window-shopping in a layover city. He particularly liked to buy her clothes and he had excellent taste for a man—or perhaps the instinct of a husband who knew what his wife would look good in.

When Barbara protested once, although not very hard, that he was spending too much money, he very honestly gave her an explanation that made her glad she had picked this first officer for a husband.

"Yeh, I know I went overboard on that damned blouse," he said. "Like I did on that cocktail dress I picked up in Atlanta. But, honey, did it ever occur to you it's the only way a guy like me can say 'Barbara, I love you and I miss you' without sounding sappy?"

Her only complaint was that McKay invariably picked out apparel in beige.

"You'd buy beige underwear if you found it," she laughed

after he had brought home a beige negligee, which closely followed a beige dress.

"Do they make it?" he asked innocently.

"I suppose so. But let's be practical. I've got enough beige in my wardrobe. Anyway, I found out why you go ape for it. Did you know that Jack the Ripper's mother always wore beige?"

"That bit of historical data," said McKay, "is probably as accurate as the domino being a Druid symbol. By the way, where is our domino?"

"I've got it hidden away for when we buy a house."

"When we buy a house? You gonna nail it to the front door?"

"I'm going to put it on our fireplace mantel. Then people will always ask what it means. And I'll tell them it's a symbol of how I got you to marry me."

"It's a symbol of how you almost talked me out of marrying you. I'll never forget that day you put it into the locker. Shea was ready to kill me. And I felt somewhat the same toward you."

"Love and hate are virtually indistinguishable, I've read someplace," Barbara said. "Let's go to bed and you can hate me."

They saw a lot of the O'Brians, which was something of a will-power test for Barbara because as she witnessed Pat swelling with pregnancy, her own "no kids for at least a year" resolve wavered. They also became friendly with Snorkel and Marion Snodgrass and with Barney and Donna Barnwell. As McKay acquired more experience in the right seat, both the professional and social gap perceptibly lessened between him and his captains.

His relationship with Shea changed, too. The chief pilot invited them over for dinner and McKay took Shea and his wife to a Washington Redskins' game for which he had acquired some last-minute tickets. He even broke down and started calling Shea "Johnny" although the first time he used his superior's first name he felt like apologizing. He was rather surprised to sense that the Sheas were frankly grateful for an occasional social contact. Then it dawned on him that many of the younger pilots avoided those contacts deliberately for fear they would be regarded in an apple-for-the-teacher category.

This, of course, was unfair to a man like John Shea. He was scrupulously fair, rigidly objective, and ruthlessly impartial on a check ride. Yet he was the kind of chief pilot who could wear the stern peaked hat of discipline and the soft felt hat of friendship with equal ease. With McKay, as he had with other pilots for whom he had ungrudging respect, Shea achieved a curious blending of comradeship and command.

Culver was a minor problem. McKay was enough of a recent bachelor to know that the prospect of "Come over and have a home-cooked meal" really had an insipid appeal. He did not want to lose touch with Les, yet he realized that with his own marriage their friendship had to go through something of a metamorphosis. Not in deepness nor strength, but in emphasis—a kind of shift to an awareness that both would be ready in any test of loyalty, even as personal contact lessened somewhat. McKay never forced the issue. He merely made it clear to Culver that he always was welcome, invited him over on anything resembling a special occasion, and—at Barbara's urging—even attempted to get Les and Helen Mitchell together.

This was strictly a matchmaking effort on Barbara's part that dropped its hopeful seeds on barren ground. Culver's chief fears in life were thunderstorms, shotgun weddings, in-flight fires, unexpected impotency, and women who were smarter than he was. Mitch's sharp tongue would have sent Casanova to a monastery, quivering in humiliated frustration. Actually, Les liked her cheerful, bombastic personality and he even thought she was good-looking. But he also was a little afraid of her, never grasping that she also was a little afraid of him.

Culver told McKay, "She's a swell gal, but clever women aren't my type."

Mitch told Barbara, "He's a swell guy, but wolves aren't my type."

Which freely translated meant that if the McKays had left well enough alone, the Clever Woman and the Wolf might have gotten together on their own.

The three ex-roommates checked out as first officers on the Constellation and came to appreciate the luxury of a pressurized aircraft that was not shackled to lower altitudes. Their only complaint was the Connie's cockpit visibility. The DC-4 was no flying greenhouse, but compared to the peepholed Connie it was like flying in the open. Not that they flew the triple-tailed, sharklike beauties very often. They still were too junior, so they continued to plod along with the older Fours and watch the maddening slow changes in the seniority list.

Of all the captains McKay flew with, Snodgrass was his favorite. He respected Barnwell and learned much from him, but a trip with Snorkel usually was just pure fun. Snodgrass had a pentagon-sided personality unlike anything McKay ever had encountered.

He could use the cabin PA as a pilot's propaganda weapon, skillfully mixing sarcasm and humor in a way that got his point across without getting anyone mad. One night he was coming into an airport that had just dedicated a new eighteen-million-dollar terminal building, but hadn't gotten around to putting ILS on its undersized runways. The weather was miserable and they were about number nine in the holding stacks with at least an hour's delay before landing clearance.

They had finally worked down to number three when the tower informed him the field was now below minimums and to proceed to an alternate airport. Snorkel acknowledged this welcome bit of news and advised the passengers. Then he added: "I wanna compliment all you folks from this city on your new eighteen-million-dollar terminal building. It's the most beautiful terminal building I've seen in all the years I've been flying. I just wish I could put this bird down in the damned lobby."

As did so many pilots, he regarded the miracle of flight almost as a religion, touching even the agnostic with its awesome dignity; its cool, clean, so totally detached splendor. The great silver creatures he flew were altars on which an airman worshiped the unsullied sky and whatever or whoever created this world of beauty and man-dwarfing enormity.

He gave McKay a glimpse of his feelings one day. They had a solid bank of thunderheads in their path, and Snorkel was climbing above the boiling, darkening cauldron, evil yet magnificent. The storm was being spawned by a cold front colliding with the heat of a mid-September afternoon. The two pilots watched the hatching process.

"Boy, that'll drop the temperature down about twenty degrees by the time we land," McKay commented.

"God's air-conditioning," murmured Snorkel.

Like so many men who get a kick out of life, he was unafraid of death. Or perhaps he merely was afraid to show fear. McKay had the privilege of seeing him perform in an emergency—on a trip when they couldn't lower the wing flaps and finally had to come in over the runway boundary at 140 knots. It was like trying to dock the *Ile de France* in a trout stream. Before they made their flapless landing, Snorkel joked with the passengers even as he told them frankly what was wrong. He also called the stewardesses up to the cockpit and made sure they knew their emergency procedures. When he saw one of them wavering on the precipice of tearful panic, he got out of his seat and grabbed her roughly by the shoulders until she cringed from both the pain and his anger.

"I'm getting paid to land this bucket in one piece, flaps or no flaps," he said in a low voice. "You're getting paid to keep your goddamned head. If something goes wrong, every blessed man and woman in that cabin will have their lives in your hands—not mine, but yours. So you march right back there with your head up and you put a smile on your face—

and if we come out of it okay, I'll buy you the driest martini and the fattest steak this side of the Mississippi. Do you read me?"

"Loud and clear, Captain Snodgrass," she said huskily. "And thanks."

She walked back to the cabin with her head up and the smile on her face, as ordered. They blew out every tire on the main gear and Snorkel had to ground-loop the DC-4 to keep from going off the edge of the runway. When they finally came to a stop, with fire engines clustered around them in a worried convoy, Snorkel merely grinned at McKay and announced: "Naturally, they may make heroes out of us. It's the least they can do."

It was while McKay was congratulating him that the first officer noticed the captain's hands were trembling. At that precise moment McKay understood, as he never had before, the loneliness of the left seat and the symbolism of the fourth stripe.

That was Snorkel Snodgrass, airline captain.

On their next flight together Snorkel became intensely interested in the activities of a brand-new ramp agent he had never seen before. The youngster was bustling around with the unvarnished dedication of a man to whom the fate of Midwest Airlines had been personally entrusted by President Karl J. Mencken and the entire Board of Directors.

When Snorkel asked him if the caterer had loaded the food yet, he replied:

"Yes *sir*, Captain Snodgrass. I saw to that myself, sir. Everything's in order for a fine flight. Is there anything else I can do for you, sir?"

"No," grunted Snorkel.

He hung back before boarding and watched the agent examine the passenger manifest as if it listed the Presidential Cabinet, J. Edgar Hoover, the head of the Civil Aeronautics Administration, and his own mother. Snorkel finally got on the plane after witnessing the new man greet every boarding passenger with a dazzling smile and sugary farewell. The captain shook his head.

"Troubles?" McKay asked as Snodgrass slumped sighing into his seat.

"Naw, it's just that new ramp agent. I never saw such a gung-ho kid."

Outside, the agent closed and locked the cabin door, rolled away the stairs, and marched in stern military fashion to the nose of the plane. The engines coughed and growled. The agent stiffened. Chest out. Belly in. Shoulders back. He saluted Captain Snodgrass with a disciplinary fervor that would have embarrassed a four-star general. Snorkel rolled back his window and crooked his forefinger several times.

The agent blanched. He must have forgotten something important—and on the first departing flight he had ever worked. He hastily pushed the boarding ramp back to the plane, ran up the stairs, opened the door, and ran down the aisle with the stewardesses staring after him.

"Is there anything wrong, sir?" he panted.

Snorkel turned around and smiled sweetly, benevolently.

"You forgot to kiss me good-by," he said.

And that also was Snorkel Snodgrass, airline captain.

Early in October, the McKays' telephone rang at 2:48 A.M. McKay sleepily answered, then sat upright. It was Paddy.

"Mac, Pat's having labor pains. Can you come over and drive us to the hospital?"

"Sure, but what's wrong with your car?"

"The damned thing won't start," O'Brian said. "I've been trying for fifteen minutes. It just won't turn over."

"Who is it?" asked Barbara.

"It's Paddy. The baby's coming and he can't get his car started. Paddy, I'll be over as soon as I can. Do you think you oughta call an ambulance?"

"I wanted to, but Pat says the pains aren't too bad yet. I hate to bother you, Mac, but . . ."

"Forget it. I'll be right over."

He hung up and jumped out of bed.

"I want to go, too," Barbara said.

"You've got to be at work by seven," he reminded her. "You won't get much sleep."

"I'll be all right. Is Pat okay?"

"I guess so. But Paddy sounded like he was losing three engines on final. Where the hell are my shoes? . . ."

Four hours later Pat gave birth to a daughter. Twenty minutes later she achieved what her doctor had predicted but which she hadn't told Paddy. She also presented him with a son.

O'Brian reacted with the same calm, unruffled equanimity that had marked his leaving the apartment without his shoes—an oversight which McKay had to force him to correct. When the obstetrician broke the news, Paddy kissed him and shook hands with a passing nurse.

"I thought new fathers acted this way only in the movies," McKay told him. "Relax, mick. Pat did all the work."

"Yeh," said O'Brian. "But I did all the worrying."

Later, when Paddy had been reassured that Pat was fine and after McKay drove Barbara to work, they returned to the O'Brian apartment.

"Lemme take a look at the Olds," McKay offered. "You can't be without a car. It's probably the battery or the starter brushes."

O'Brian, who at that point couldn't have sharpened a pencil, readily accepted. McKay got into the Olds.

"It's an accelerator starter, Mac. Remember? Just put your foot down on the gas pedal."

"Yeh, I know. Gimme the key."

"The key?"

"The ignition key. Come on. What's the matter?"

O'Brian's face was sunset-red. Wordlessly he took the ignition key out of his pocket and handed it over. McKay inserted it, turned it, pumped the gas pedal, and the old engine coughed into life instantly.

"I forgot to use the key," O'Brian explained unnecessarily.

McKay just looked at him.

"I'm sorry as hell, Mac. Getting you outa bed and all that."

McKay grinned. "You can pay me back if and when ours arrives," he promised. "I just hope to hell Barbara has a baby after midnight so I can get even. You flying today?"

"Yep—430. Cleveland turnaround."

"You're in no shape. We'll call crew sked and swap trips. I've got 430 day after tomorrow. I'll take yours today and you fly for me Friday. Give you a chance to spend the rest of the day with Pat."

"I'd sure appreciate it, Mac. Guess I wouldn't be much use to anyone. Hey, how about that? Twins!"

The O'Brians named their daughter Teresa Leslie and their son Mark McDonald. The girl had Pat's features but Paddy's red hair. The boy was dark like Pat, but the first time McKay and Culver saw him, they burst out laughing. Even at the tender age of two days, the baby's ears already had assumed the jug-handle proportions of his father's.

When they were baptized, the O'Brians asked Culver to be Teresa's godfather and the McKays to be Mark's godparents. Culver regarded his newly acquired godfather status in the same spirit as an ensign promoted overnight to rear admiral. He even volunteered for baby-sitting.

McKay was amused. "For a confirmed bachelor, you're displaying an unusual love of children," he remarked.

"It's easier to like kids when you're a bachelor," Culver said. "A bachelor doesn't have to put up with all the headaches. Besides, I don't necessarily like all kids. I just happen to be nuts about these. Being a godfather is probably the closest I'll get to parenthood."

"Wanna bet?" said O'Brian.

"Tell you what," Culver offered. "The day I get engaged I'll buy Terry the biggest doll on the eastern seaboard and I'll get Mark an electric train."

"There should be a time limit," Barbara said. "Like if you're not engaged in five years, we'll all chip in and buy you a new suit or something. Personally, I can just see Mark playing with his new electric train."

"Five years," McKay repeated thoughtfully. "Wonder how close we'll be to captains by then. It's hard to imagine sitting in that right seat for five years."

"You'll get the fourth stripe ahead of Les and me," Paddy said. "You're just above us in seniority."

"My God," Culver suddenly realized, "by the time we're captains these kids will be walking. Hell, they'll be in school."

"Some of the older copilots are bidding the smaller bases," McKay said. "They'll move up faster that way. Barbara, maybe . . ."

"Maybe," she replied. "Right now I'd rather stay here."

She was probably right, McKay admitted to himself. True, the bigger the base, the longer the seniority list. But for someone like himself, the airline's headquarters city had its advantages. McKay already had begun a kind of self-education process in accident investigation. He dropped in to see Bengsten at the CAB one day and asked if he could read over some past accident reports.

"Figured I might get a better feel of what you guys are doing," he said.

Bengsten was pleased. "I've got some spare copies you can have," he said. "There's that 1942 TWA crash in New Mexico —the one that killed Carole Lombard. Helluva interesting case. If you can wait about ten minutes, I'll have a girl get a bunch together for you."

"Got all morning," McKay said. "What are you working on now?"

"Coastal DC-4 near Baltimore," Bengsten said. "Last July fourth. Familiar with it?"

"Read all the details in the papers. Went into the first half of an outside loop, didn't it?"

"Yeh. Funny thing, but we had two of our own guys in a Beech just behind them. They saw the whole mess. She went into a dive from four thousand and just kept going. Just before they hit, they were almost on their back. Like you said, looked like an outside loop."

"Sounds like elevators."

"That's what I thought. But it was one of the first things we checked out. No sign of elevator trouble. Hinges were in good shape. Matter of fact, the horizontal stabilizers were hardly dented. Damndest case I ever saw."

"Well, I wish you luck," McKay said.

"We'll need it on this one. First time we ever had two Bureau of Safety guys actually witness a crash and they couldn't even give us a clue. Lemme go and tell my secretary to dig some stuff out of files."

While Bengsten was out of the room, McKay glanced curiously around his office. Spartan was the word for it, except Spartan was too plush a description. The furniture apparently was a hand-me-down from possibly as recent an administration as Lincoln's. One item of interest was an ashtray on Bengsten's desk. It was metal and looked like half of an engine piston. He was still examining it when the CAB investigator returned carrying a stack of crash reports.

"Recognize it?" he asked.

"Looks like part of a piston."

"That's what it is. Salvaged it from an accident I worked on back in '40. See the fatigue crack? That little bastard started an engine fire and killed fourteen persons. We learned a helluva lot from that one. They redesigned the whole firewall and the carrier shook up its maintenance system."

"I guess you learn something from every accident," McKay said.

"Just about. Accidents are the mistakes of aviation. There are damned few we can blame on the Almighty."

Bengsten handed McKay the reports. "That oughta keep you busy a few evenings, Mac. I'd like to know what you think of them."

"I'll give you a critique when I bring them back," McKay said.

"No need. They're extra copies. If you're interested, I'll

put you on the mailing list. We send a batch to ALPA and the airlines, but we never know how much distribution they get."

"I'm interested," McKay said.

He wrote out his home address, shook hands with Bengsten, and departed just as another CAB investigator walked in.

"Who was that?" the second Bureau of Safety man asked.

"Kid named McKay. Copilot with Midwest. Wanted some back accident reports. I gotta hunch we'll be seeing more of that boy."

His hunch was correct, and sooner than either McKay or Bengsten expected. Exactly four weeks later to the day, a Midwest DC-4 flying at eight thousand feet from Cleveland to Washington went into a half-outside loop in a maneuver identical to Coastal's. Paddy O'Brian was the copilot.

McKay was at home reading the Washington *Post* when the call came. It was Shea, who wasted no time on formalities.

"Mac, Johnny. We damned near lost a DC-4. Barney's on a trip and I can't reach Snorkel. Get the hell over to my office on the double."

"Right away," McKay said. "What happened?"

"Tell you when you get here. Paddy was the first officer."

McKay's heart skipped two beats. "Is he okay?"

"Yeh, he's fine. Little shook up but matter of fact, he's a hero. You're listed as third man on ALPA's safety committee, so move!"

Barbara was at work. McKay scrawled a hasty note in case he wouldn't be back when she returned. Then it occurred to him that she had the car. He had to call a taxi and by the time he got to Shea's office, it was filled with pilots, CAA men, and Al Bengsten.

McKay spotted O'Brian, who was sipping coffee and talking to Bengsten and Shea. Paddy looked up as McKay walked over.

"Hi, Mac," he said cheerfully. "Heard the news?"

"The hell with the news," McKay answered. "Are you all right?"

"I'm fine."

Shea gave McKay a hasty briefing. The DC-4 had been cruising normally. George Shub, a fairly junior captain, was in the left seat. Occupying the jump seat was a check pilot named Ed Allen, giving Shub a final route qualification ride. The nose of the DC-4 had started to climb for no apparent reason and Shub was trimming it forward when the bottom dropped out. The plane plunged into an almost vertical dive and was going over on its back when Paddy got it under control.

"He was the only one whose seat belt was fastened," Shea recounted. "Shub and Allen were thrown out of their seats and that's what saved the plane. Their heads hit the feathering buttons. It cut the power on three engines and O'Brian pulled it out. If he had had full power, they'd have kept on going down."

Both Shub and Allen had bandages on their foreheads. They were telling Bengsten the autopilot inadvertently must have kicked in and caused the unwanted climb.

"I applied full down trim," Shub said. "The autopilot must have disengaged right at that minute. I can't figure out why the nose kept climbing unless the autopilot somehow engaged."

"You weren't using the autopilot?" Bengsten asked.

"No. I was flying her manually."

"Sounds like the autopilot malfunctioned," the CAB man conceded. "You guys were plain lucky. Jesus, that outside loop —just like Coastal. I wonder . . ."

Allen said nothing. He was a recent transfer to DCA and few pilots knew him very well. He was pale and subdued, which was natural under the circumstances. Twelve passengers had been hurt, the DC-4 cabin was a shambles, and Paddy—with the other two pilots groggy and helpless—had landed the ship with one aileron torn. But McKay, who seldom missed anything, noticed Bengsten glancing at the check pilot with what amounted to a querulous look bordering on suspicion.

"Well," Bengsten said, "we'd better go down and have a gander at that autopilot. O'Brian—you go along with this autopilot business?"

"I don't know what else it could have been," O'Brian replied. "It sure felt like the autopilot just took over—kicked in and then out."

Bengsten took the CAA inspectors out with him to yank the autopilot. Shea, O'Brian, and Shub followed, leaving McKay alone with the check pilot. Allen, waiting until the room had cleared, rose and walked over to McKay.

"McKay, I understand you're sorta representing ALPA."

"I'm on the safety committee, yes," the young copilot said.

"Well, I think it would be a good idea if we closed ranks on this autopilot malfunction."

McKay was puzzled and there was something he didn't like about Allen's remark. He wished Barnwell or Snorkel were there, but some vestige of his B-25 command days suddenly took over. "We'll close ranks if that's what happened," he said curtly.

Allen looked at him, then lowered his eyes. "I guess I'd better tell you what happened," he said. "It wasn't the autopilot. It was the gust lock."

"The gust lock?" asked McKay. He was referring to a DC-4 cockpit lever that automatically locked the rudder and elevators while the plane was on the ground, to protect against winds.

"Yeh, the gust lock. Remember that crash at LaGuardia a few months ago? They tried to take off with the gust lock engaged and never got off the ground."

"I remember."

"I got to wondering what a DC-4 would do if you engaged the gust lock in flight. I moved the lever without Shub seeing me. The nose started to climb. When I saw George applying trim, I disconnected it. So help me, I never dreamed she'd dive like that."

"But why? Why did you try it in the first place?"

"Curiosity, mostly. And I wanted to see how Shub would handle it. If he'd recognize the symptoms."

"Symptoms my ass," McKay snapped. "You didn't know the symptoms yourself."

"Now I do. I know I goofed. Look, McKay, I'm a check captain but I'm still an ALPA member. If they find out what I did, they'll cut me up in little pieces and feed me to the CAA. I won't be able to fly a Piper Cub, let alone a DC-4."

"There's one thing wrong with your reasoning," McKay said, completely forgetting their difference in rank. "They're gonna find out in one helluva hurry there wasn't anything wrong with that autopilot."

"I know. But they won't suspect that gust lock, either. Unless"—he looked at the younger pilot squarely—"unless you tell them."

"It isn't my business to tell 'em. It's yours."

Allen walked over to Shea's desk and idly fingered a paperweight. "I can't," he muttered. "It would mean curtains. The first mistake I've made in sixteen years of flying and if I admit it, there goes the whole damned sixteen years. You think one lousy mistake is worth it? You think I'd ever pull anything so stupid again? Don't you think I've learned my lesson?"

"Yes," McKay said. "But how about the guys who haven't?"

"What other guys?"

"The ones who might get curious about engaging a gust lock in flight someday."

Allen was silent for a long while. "You have me where the hair is short," he said. "But put yourself in my place. I just can't do it."

McKay shook his head, half in sympathy and half in anger. "Captain Allen," he said quietly, "if you don't, I will."

Allen said not another word. He sat down heavily in a chair. After a while Bengsten and the others returned.

"CAA's checking that autopilot," the CAB investigator announced. "Didn't seem to be anything wrong with it but we'll give it a good going-over. I still keep thinking about Coastal. If you didn't have the extra four thousand feet, you'd have bought it. Even with the power cut, nobody could have pulled it out from four thousand. Well, anybody got anything else to say?"

"I guess I'd better call my wife," O'Brian said wearily.

"Nice job, Paddy," Shea complimented him. "Take a few days off. I'll tell crew sked."

"Thanks, Johnny. Mac—coming?"

"Just a minute." McKay was staring at Allen.

The check pilot rose to his feet. A beam of sunlight coming through Shea's window illuminated the burnished gold stripes on his uniform coat like a spotlight. He stood straight and tall and his shoulders were back.

"Mr. Bengsten," he said, "I think we'd all better sit down."

When the confession was over and the room was emptying, Bengsten motioned McKay to stay behind.

"I've got a strong feeling you wormed that out of him," he said. "Thanks."

"Don't thank me," McKay said bitterly. "I've got a strong feeling, too. Like I stabbed him right in the back. And while I'm at it, I suppose you figure this solves Coastal."

"No."

"No? The maneuvers were identical. Only the altitudes were different. Paddy wouldn't be alive if the dive had started at four thousand."

"There's one additional difference. That Coastal captain was a former test pilot. I doubt very much if anyone with a test pilot background would go screwing around with a gust lock at four thousand feet. So if you think you've just stabbed two pilots in the back instead of one, forget it."

McKay was only partially convinced. "I'll wait till your report comes out," he said. "It won't surprise me if you call Coastal pilot error."

Bengsten wasn't offended at McKay's tone. "If you got just a minute, sit down," he said. "I know you wanna go home with O'Brian—damned fine pilot, by the way—but I'd like to get something straight in your mind. Okay?"

McKay sat down. "Shoot."

"Mac, I've been investigating carrier accidents for years. I know pilots think we try to hang everything on them. I guess a few of us do. That guy in the cockpit is the most natural target in the world. And pilot error is the easiest answer in the world. There are men in my own bureau who automatically assume pilot error—guilty until proven innocent. I dunno, maybe they resent a captain's earning fifteen thousand bucks a year while they're pulling down seven or eight or even less. My friend, they're just as wrong as you'd be if you tried to cover up for a pilot who goofed. We've got to work together."

"I read over those reports you gave me," McKay said. "There's quite a flock of pilot-error findings—and some of them look pretty damned circumstantial. They sounded like you couldn't figure out what really happened, so you blamed the crew."

"Granted. Circumstantial evidence is all we've got to go on, too many times. That's why we always wind up with that phrase—'the probable cause.' If anyone can come up with new evidence, we'll reopen an investigation. We never close a file."

"Mr. Bengsten . . ."

"I think you can start calling me 'Al.'"

"Al, I did what I thought best in this case. But I give you my word, I'll fight you any time I think there's even the slightest doubt about the guys up front."

"Fair enough. We'll get along fine. Now go meet O'Brian—and tell him thanks from the Civil Aeronautics Board. I hate fatality statistics."

McKay had one more question as they walked down the

hall. "What do you think will happen to Allen?" he asked.
"They'll throw the book at the poor bastard. Bound with
iron spikes. He'll never fly for an airline again."
"That," said McKay, "is what I was afraid of."

He carried the Allen incident around in his conscience and
craw for weeks, until the more prosaic problems of "flying
from A to B" eventually diluted the pain. And those problems were not exactly minor. The business of being an airline pilot was one long, continued process of learning, testing,
and requalifying.

"It seems to me," Culver observed one day, "that I fly
trips in between times I'm being checked to see if I can
continue to fly trips."

It wasn't that bad, but Culver had a point. The CAA
gave a check ride every six months and so did Midwest. There
was the medical examination twice a year. There were daily
NOTAMS—Notice to Airmen—to be digested, absorbed and
duly recorded. "NOTAM: Runway 22 LaGuardia last 200
feet unusable account construction . . . NOTAM: Deer may
be encountered on north-south runway Syracuse . . ." There
were Manual Revisions to be studied, memorized, and duly
entered into bulging brain bags. There were the Jeppesen
charts always being brought up to date as new navigation aids,
runway lighting, and airport construction made changes necessary.

It was a standard joke that no pilot could take off until the
weight of his paperwork equaled the weight of the aircraft.
McKay came to understand why so many pilots resisted such
extracurricular activities as attending ALPA meetings. It
simply was a lot easier to go home to one's family and forget
airplanes until the next trip. Even McKay felt like weakening
at times.

Barbara never complained. She did remind him that he was
not getting enough exercise and talked him into taking up
golf, a game she had loved since high school and played fairly

well. For a while her husband suffered the ego-shattering tortures of being bested by a woman in an athletic contest. But he took a few lessons and before long was playing acceptably—which means that a few well-kissed drives, towering iron shots, and long putts compensated for the remaining eighty shots which weren't so good. Later he remembered only the better shots and conveniently forgot the bad ones. He finally could beat Barbara consistently—but not Culver, who started playing about the same time and often made it a threesome. Culver had more natural skill, his chief trouble being that he took the game too seriously.

"You're the only man who throws a club farther than he hits the ball," McKay remonstrated one day when Les had topped a nine iron and angrily fired the offending club twenty yards away.

"You look like you didn't get much sleep last night," Barbara said. "Are those circles under your eyes?"

"Probably," Culver said. "I was studying until about 2 A.M."

"Studying?" McKay asked. "Sex manuals?"

"Nope. Been fooling around with lawbooks. At one time I thought I wanted to be a lawyer. I can't fly forever, so I figured it wouldn't hurt to get some background in something else."

He marched off to retrieve his iron.

"Well, that surprises me," McKay said. "I didn't think he had it in him."

"Maybe he's getting serious with somebody and doesn't want to admit it," Barbara wondered.

"Maybe, but I doubt it. I'm not complaining, though. I'm glad he's got more on his mind than bedrooms."

By mid-June of 1948 there wasn't time to devote too much attention to golf, bedrooms, lawbooks, or accident reports. The new Convair 240's were put into service. Midwest acquired twenty of the snub-nosed planes, sold all but two DC-3's which were kept for occasional charter purposes, and converted a pair of Fours into freighters.

McKay and Culver couldn't wait to get assigned to Convair school. Some of the older pilots, still faithful to the DC-3, expressed large doubts and loud criticism in the 240's direction. It was too fast, the wing was too stiff, and the controls were too light.

"I feel like I'm skidding, not flying," one veteran complained—not remembering that fifteen years before, he had firmly denounced the DC-3 as being too fast and too light on the controls.

But most of the crews liked the Convair and a few—as pilots will—fell in love with it. Barnwell, senior enough to bid Constellations, took a check ride in a 240 and swore he'd be happy if he never flew anything else.

"It doesn't have one bad habit," he enthused to McKay. "The aileron control is beautiful, even when you're near stall speed. Wait till you handle her in a crosswind—she flies like she's glued to a railroad track. She tells you what she's gonna do ahead of time and she always does it."

For a while McKay had to be satisfied with just looking at the 240. He invariably stopped to watch every time one pulled up to a ramp or finished loading. The Convair was the first airliner equipped with integral loading stairs which eliminated the necessity for an outside boarding ramp. It took a long time for McKay to get used to the sight of the cabin door opening or closing by itself, mysteriously folding and unfolding in a way that made the aeronautical engineer in McKay pay silent tribute to the genius who designed the contraption.

It was late in 1948 when he and Culver finally were ordered to report to Convair ground school. One day Bender was lecturing on the plane's navigation system.

"This next chart," Bender said, "is a diagram of the new fluxgate compass installation. As you know, the fluxgate is designed to provide you with headings that are not affected by changes in attitude. An ordinary magnetic compass would read incorrectly in any kind of bank, climb, or dive. The two fluxgates on the 240 are located in the wing tips. Like the installations on our other aircraft, they're perpetually stabilized by a spinning gyroscope. The gyro on the Convair is a new type, but basically the whole system works the same. Your compass indications are fed to the cockpit and appear on the Radio Magnetic Indicator, or RMI. Question, Mac?"

"I notice," McKay said, "that on the diagram it shows both the captain's and copilot's RMI's are hooked to the same circuit. If your gyro tilts for some reason, wouldn't you get an erroneous reading on both instruments?"

"They are," Bender agreed. "But there's not much chance of a fluxgate malfunction. Dirt in the gyro bearing might give you a phony heading. Or a short circuit. But it's not likely. And if you get a bad heading, you just cage the gyro to bring it back to level."

"You might not know you've got a bum heading until it's too late," McKay said. "Why not do it like we do on the Fours—hook the captain's RMI to one compass and the first officer's to the other? Then if you had one gyro tilt, you wouldn't get the same error on both RMI's."

Bender scratched his head at this logic. "It would be a pretty damned expensive modification," he pointed out, "and these Convairs cost $235,000 apiece to begin with. But I don't think this wiring is any reason for concern. Look at this next chart, Mac. This is the Convair's new course deviation indicator. If you had a gyro give you an erroneous compass reading, the discrepancy would show up immediately on the deviation indicator. There also is an automatic erection mechanism that pushes the gyro back to level even if it does become tilted."

McKay abandoned the argument. After class, however, Culver commented that "You sure had a hair up your butt on the fluxgate."

"It still bothers me," McKay said thoughtfully. "It could lead somebody right into a mountain."

It took quite a while for his prediction to come true.

Chapter 9

Time moves in differently paced dimensions for a man living in two worlds.

It moved too quickly in McKay's personal world, his life with Barbara. It moved too slowly in his professional world, his life with an airline. The latter became a blurred kaleidoscope of flights and paychecks and sequence bids and friendships and laughs and proficiency checks and medicals and faceless passengers and the beauty of flying.

The only trouble with this kaleidoscope was that the view was always from the right seat. His impatience with first-officer status was no exclusive emotion. All copilots shared it. But for McKay, it had an added frustration—it affected his air safety work.

He found it difficult to stand up in ALPA meetings and expound on safety issues and problems. He was too conscious of his being a first officer to inject himself wholeheartedly into a controversy. The absence of the fourth stripe was an uncrossable void separating strong beliefs from strong expressions of those beliefs. He tried it once and was slapped down.

On this occasion, he raised an issue stemming from the death of a sixty-one-year-old Midwest captain who suffered a heart attack during an ILS approach. The copilot had landed the plane. McKay got up to propose that the union consider making retirement mandatory at age sixty, with a strong pension plan part of every future contract package.

"It seems obvious that the chances for an incapacitating heart attack increase after sixty," he argued. "Our aircraft are getting bigger and more complicated. In a few years it may be extremely difficult for one man to land a plane, particularly in bad weather. I think we're underestimating this hazard and I also think some day the government will get around to a maximum age limit for airline pilots. If we take the initiative ourselves, along with some financial protection for the pilots affected, we'll soften the blow."

A grizzled captain, two months beyond his sixtieth birthday, arose and transfixed McKay with a baleful glare. "No snot-nosed, wet-eared copilot is gonna tell me when I should quit flying," he roared. "I'll quit when the medics and chief pilot tell me I'm not safe to handle a ship any more. And as for you, McKay, don't give me any of that 'this is for safety' crap. You first officers would just like a way to compress that seniority list."

He sat down,. amid a ripple of applause from every captain in the room within ten years of that magic number of sixty. The younger pilots sat on their hands and also their convictions. Barnwell decided that McKay, whose face was flushed, needed some help short of outright support. He got the floor.

"I think it's unfair to assign any selfish motive to Mac's suggestion," he began. "His deep interest in the safety committee's work is sufficient evidence to warrant my resenting any impugning of his integrity. But I'd also like to point out to him that he has made this proposal without any medical data to support his contention of heart attack probability after sixty. Mac, just the other day I read about a copilot having a fatal attack at age thirty-eight. I think it's best to let the physicals—and as Captain Waterman just said—let the chief pilot decide when a man should retire. There's no way to predict a heart attack, whether a pilot is thirty or seventy."

McKay knew he was licked, and he wished he had not spoken at all, but he did not want to surrender abjectly. "I want to assure Captain Waterman I was not thinking of the seniority list—at least, not this time. I think of it all the time when I'm in the right seat."

Even Waterman managed a chuckle. McKay continued: "I agree with Barney that there's no way to predict a heart attack, and that I could have one just as easily, and without warning, as the oldest man in this room. I merely want to emphasize that in the absence of any means of predicting incapacitation, chronological age is the only standard of measuring probability. This was the basis of my proposal. I sense a fair-sized lack of agreement so I'll withdraw it. But with one last word—I repeat, it's going to be a government order some day. And I still think a mandatory retirement rule would be easier to swallow if we put it into effect ourselves. Captain Waterman, I apologize for giving you any idea that my motive was ulterior."

This time the pilots applauded McKay.

"The apology should come from me, McKay," Waterman said graciously. "You just hit an old man's sensitive spot."

It pleased McKay considerably when Waterman accosted him after the meeting and dropped the "McKay."

"Mac, I've never flown with you but I've heard a lot about you. I wish you'd bid my sequence some month. I'd like to get to know you better."

McKay had heard a lot about Waterman, too, namely that he ran a cockpit like a Marine drill instructor. Culver had drawn him once and reported, "He was tough enough to make me stop thinking about sex," which coming from Les was more than adequate motivation to keep McKay and O'Brian from ever bidding a Waterman trip.

The veteran captain, McKay thought, didn't seem like the flight-deck ogre of such frightening repute.

"I'd like very much to fly with you, sir," he said. "If it's okay with you, I'll try to get your sequence next month. Guess Barney and Snorkel have had enough of me for a while, anyway."

He did fly with Waterman and learned anew the fallacy of judging anyone either by reputation or first impressions. Waterman *was* tough. He also was fair, a fine pilot, and— McKay found out on their second trip—a lonely old man. McKay asked him about his family.

"Boy and a girl, both grown and married. My wife died six years ago. Cancer. I still have our house but it's an empty

place. Been thinking of moving into an apartment. Just can't
sell myself on it. It'd be like transitioning from a Connie to a
Cessna. Watch your goddamned heading, Mac."

McKay, with some misgivings, invited him to supper.
Waterman accepted and the evening was a huge success.
Barbara could cook spaghetti and meatballs the way Paddy
could land an airplane (it was illogical, but she also could
mangle a simple meat roast beyond all culinary recognition,
and never could explain it).

Culver picked that night to drop in for a late drink and
almost did a 180 at the sight of the stern captain, whose
opening greeting was a growled "Have you learned how to
handle your rudder in a crosswind yet, Culver?"

"Want some spaghetti, Les?" Barbara asked.

"No thanks, I've had supper. Just stopped in to chew the
fat. But you've got company . . ."

"Oh hell, don't mind me," Waterman said. "Gives me a
chance to know you younger pilots better. After all, if McKay
had his way, I'd be out to pasture before I had a chance."

His eyes actually twinkled as he said it, and McKay grinned
at him. They all sat around sipping brandy, and Waterman
inevitably began recalling the old days.

"You think Snorkel Snodgrass is a character? You should
have known Bill Chambers. He was flying a DC-2 trip once
and he had a cocky copilot on board. The kid didn't know it,
but Bill had met some Army pilots the night before and told
them where he'd be flying the next day. He turns the ship over
to the copilot just about the time he catches an Army pursuit
job coming up in his starboard wing. The Army guy, exactly
as Bill had planned it, rolled just before he came alongside.
So when he pulled up even, he was on his back. Bill tapped
the copilot on the shoulder and pointed to the other plane.
'Don't look now,' he says, 'but I think we're flying upside
down.' The copilot fainted."

"Is he still with Midwest?" McKay asked.

"No. He went over with a B-17 squadron during the war.
Bought it on a Berlin raid. I think we lost about ten Midwest

pilots before it ended. Either in combat or with the Ferry Command. The best man at my wedding disappeared flying the Hump. They never found his plane. I always wanted to ask you young squirts, isn't airline flying pretty tame after what you went through?"

"Not tamer," McKay said. "Different, certainly."

"The flying is tamer," Culver said with a mischievous grin. "The captains are more dangerous."

Waterman laughed. "You've got to be tolerant of us old guys, Les."

Culver warmed to the use of his first name.

"I hate to sound nostalgic, but I envy you. Chances are the Connie, or maybe the DC-7's coming up pretty soon, they'll be the biggest and fastest planes I'll ever fly. You kids can look forward to stuff that isn't even on the drawing boards yet."

"Like jets," McKay ventured. "Turbines are the coming thing."

"I'll probably still be a copilot," Culver predicted sourly, "in the year 1970."

"Well, I know it's a long haul," Waterman sympathized. "I chopped Mac's head off the other day for suggesting retirement at sixty, but seniority does keep some guys out of the left seat longer than they deserve."

"Has there ever been a case where a copilot never made captain?" Culver wanted to know.

"Not that I know of, but I suppose it could happen if the seniority list got too long. Those on the bottom might grow beards before their names came up. That reminds me, ever hear the story about me and the copilot who couldn't fly?"

"If they have, I haven't," said Barbara.

McKay and Culver shook their heads.

"It happened before the war. I went into OPS and knew I was supposed to have a kid fresh out of pilot school named Harris. I didn't know him from Wilbur Wright so I just called out 'Where's Harris?' This kid walks up to me and says 'I'm Harris, sir.' I told him to get his butt on the airplane. He had on a blue uniform shirt and no coat, but I figured he already had hung it up in the plane. I tell him to read the checklist and he wants to know what's the checklist. I thought he was kidding. He looked absolutely petrified. We finally take off and I tell him to fly her for a while. He wanders all over the sky, can't maintain altitude, and when I yelled at him to follow the heading, he doesn't know what a heading is. When we finally landed, I told him to go the hell back to school because he's the worst copilot I ever saw. He just looks at me and tells me he isn't a copilot. He's a ramp agent named Harris. I asked why the hell he got aboard and he says because everyone said to obey captains no matter what they ordered. Two weeks later I met the real Harris and he asks me how come I went off and left him."

Waterman indulged in more reminiscences. Most of the evening was shoptalk, and McKay wondered if Barbara was bored. She wasn't. She had the admirable knack of never staying out of a conversation completely, yet never injecting herself at the wrong moment. McKay, as he had been on more than one previous occasion, was enormously proud of her. She had enslaved the captain, treating him with a deft mixture of deference and teasing.

It was after one when Waterman left, after extracting from them a promise to be his dinner guests the following Saturday. "You, too, Les," he added. "I can afford it on my captain's pay. Bring along a date."

"Matter of fact," Culver said, "I do have a date for Saturday. That's what I came over to tell you. I wondered if you'd like to double."

"Sure," McKay agreed. "Anyone we know?"

"Yeh," Les said—and Barbara could have sworn he was very close to blushing. "Helen Mitchell."

What with Mac's busy schedule, neither he nor Barbara was aware that Culver had been seeing Mitch. Their earlier attempt to get them together had been an abject failure, and they had abandoned any further matchmaking efforts.

It actually started when Les and Mitch drew a Chicago trip together and for the want of nothing better to do—compounded by the fact that the other stewardess was engaged and therefore off limits—Culver asked Helen to have supper after they got in. They were drinking coffee when Mitch pulled a newspaper clipping out of her purse.

"Look at this," she said.

Culver read the story. It was a little item announcing that a Midwest Personnel man would interview stewardess applicants the following morning at the Hotel Illinois, room 704.

"So what?" Les asked. "That goes on all the time."

"So I did some phoning while I was in my room. This Personnel man is from New York and he's fairly new. I'm gonna go over and apply."

"Apply? What for, Mitch? You're already a stewardess. I don't get it."

"Frankly, I'm not sure I get it either. But I've been a stew for about six years and I just want to see if I could get the job if I applied all over again. Under an assumed name."

"Lots of luck," Culver said. "I'll bet you a dollar against a kiss you're turned down."

"Not necessarily. Because I'll bet they take me. What was that wager—a dollar against a kiss? Which way?"

"If you're accepted, I'll pay you a dollar. If not, you owe me a kiss."

"You're on."

She had the interview the next morning. She said she was from Washington and was in Chicago on a vacation when she happened to see the newspaper story. She gave the Personnel man her Alexandria, Virginia, address with the right apartment number but under the name Hedy Mitchell. She tried hard to simulate a legitimate applicant, yearning for the life of a stewardess, and gave the same answers she had given six years before when she actually was hired. It was not easy to keep a straight face, because the interviewer kept making remarks like "You understand, Miss Mitchell, this life is not all glamor."

Only three days later a letter addressed to Miss Hedy Mitchell was delivered bearing a Chicago postmark. Apparently the interviewer had not even bothered to check references or her background—she had told him she worked for the Agriculture Department in the livestock division. She tore open the envelope and read the contents, which were brief and to the point.

Dear Miss Mitchell:

I regret to inform you that your application to become a Midwest Airlines stewardess has been rejected.

This should not be regarded as a reflection on your personality, appearance, or other qualifications. It is merely my studied judgment, without going into details, that you would not be happy in this type of career.

I wish you luck in your job with the livestock division of the Agriculture Department.

Sincerely,

Bailey Buchanan
Personnel Department

Mitch showed the letter to Grace Wooley who laughed and passed both the story and letter on to Midwest's Director of Passenger Services who laughed and passed them on to the vice president of Personnel who laughed and passed them on to President Karl Mencken who didn't laugh and fired Mr. Bailey Buchanan.

Mitch called Culver a few days later. "I owe you a kiss," she said. "When would you like to collect?"

"Tonight. I'll be over at eight."

They dated steadily for seven weeks, during which time they got over being afraid of each other. One night they asked the McKays to meet them at the O'Brians'. They arrived with Mitch carrying one large box and Les an even larger package, both gift-wrapped.

"Are the twins in bed yet?" Culver asked.

"They're sound asleep by now," Pat said. "What's in the boxes?"

"The biggest damned doll east of the Mississippi and an electric train," Culver said. "Mitch and I are getting married. And I hope you four lovebirds are bloody well satisfied."

As McKay's seniority improved along with his proficiency, his relationship with the captains gradually changed. He became more of a flying partner than a junior member of the flight-deck firm. Discipline and command still ruled him, but they were sugar-coated by growing friendships. Barnwell and Snodgrass were the first to start treating him as an equal in the cockpit as well as on the ground. Snorkel's acceptance was the most informal. McKay was making out their flight plan, and Snodgrass was telling a joke to a dispatcher.

"What altitude do you want, Snorkel?"

"How the hell should I know?" Snorkel called back. "You're flying most of the trip. Pick your own."

Even Captain Waterman softened as he came to accept McKay's professional skill as something to be taken for granted instead of a trial performance to be monitored constantly. Waterman was the last captain McKay called "sir," and this symbol of pilot protocol went out the cockpit window one stormy night when McKay made a particularly well-executed landing in a stiff crosswind.

"Nice job, Mac," Waterman said gruffly. "Take her to gate three."

"Yes sir."

Waterman put a hand on the younger man's shoulder as McKay spun the nose wheel control.

"I think, in fact I'd rather, you started calling me Bill," the captain told him.

Bill Waterman became one of his closest friends. From the older man's vast reservoir of flying experience McKay drew countless lessons of technique and judgment. Nor was it a one-way street. The captain saw in Mac and Barbara the same mature love he had enjoyed with his own wife. Being with them occasionally was almost like going back in time. He had never wanted to live in the past, yet they stirred in him memories that were pleasantly and warmly nostalgic, rather than sad.

On Christmas Eve of 1951 they were heading home from Columbus and McKay asked Waterman to come over for eggnog after they landed.

"Thanks, Mac, but I'm getting right on another flight soon as we get in. Gonna spend the holiday with my daughter and two of my grandchildren. That reminds me, give this to Barbara tonight, will you?"

He took out of his brain bag a small package, Christmas-wrapped.

"Dammit, Bill, you didn't have to do that. Barbara'll be pleased but she'll raise hell, too."

"She won't. Not when she sees it. Just something I thought she'd like to have."

Barbara opened the package that night. Inside was an old but beautiful pendant, exquisitely delicate. McKay read the enclosed note over Barbara's shoulder.

Dear Barbara:
This belonged to Mary, my wife. It's been gathering dust in a drawer for years. I know she would want you to have it and so do I. Forgive an old man's sentiment, but you are so very much like her. A Merry Christmas to both of you.
Bill Waterman

"It's the sweetest thing that's ever happened," Barbara gulped. "I could cry. Isn't he a dear?"

"That he is, honey," McKay said.

Later, when Barbara had gone to bed, McKay decided to have a last eggnog. He was disturbed and worried, and he knew why without wanting to admit it. Waterman's landing tonight had been incredibly sloppy. Too high an approach and a premature flare-out that came close to a stall when they still were fifty feet over the runway. Touchdown had been a gear-jolting jar. Bill had muttered something like "Needed more manifold" but McKay knew the power settings were adequate.

All pilots made bad landings occasionally, but this was the fourth consecutive one for Waterman, and each had been at night.

"Mac, aren't you coming to bed?"

"In a minute, honey."

The pendant that had been Mary Waterman's was on the coffee table in front of him. He picked it up and looked at it for a long time before he put it down and went to bed.

He continued to fly with Waterman for another month and noticed that Bill began letting him make all the night landings. He said nothing. Toward the end of the month they were coming into LaGuardia and Waterman was flying. He started the letdown and said, "You take her, Mac."

"No," McKay replied.

The captain bristled with a show of his old authority. "I said take her, Mac."

"You land her, Bill," McKay said firmly. "And you know why."

Nothing more was said. The approach again was too high and the landing rough. Waterman taxied to the gate, leaned back in the seat, and rubbed the back of his gnarled hand against his eyes.

"So now you know," he said softly.

"I'm sorry, Bill."

"Loss of depth perception at night, I believe it's called. Sign of old age."

"Maybe not. How about seeing an eye doctor? It might be something temporary."

"Guess I will." Waterman hesitated. "Mac, I'd appreciate your not saying anything to Johnny Shea about this."

"I won't, but promise me you'll see a doc."

"I will."

He didn't, because he knew what the doctor would tell him. He also should have known that Shea would have found out eventually. It was partially by accident, although Shea was already suspicious. He could smell a pilot who was beginning to falter. The chief pilot was in Operations when Waterman checked in for a flight. He didn't notice Shea in the room and sat down to make out a flight plan. He had to squint to see what he was writing, and he finally rubbed his eyes in weariness.

When Waterman left, Shea walked over to the crew scheduler. "Mike, who's been flying with Bill Waterman lately?"

"McKay, mostly. Six trips the last month."

McKay found a note in his box the next morning asking him to see the chief pilot. As soon as he entered Shea's office, he sensed something was wrong. Johnny was frowning.

"Mac, has Bill Waterman been having any trouble that you've noticed?"

"Trouble? You mean personal trouble?"

"I mean flying trouble. Like his eyes. What kind of landings has he been making?"

McKay decided to sidestep rather than lie. "Well, he usually lets me make the landings. So I wouldn't have noticed anything wrong."

"Landings like at night?"

McKay still didn't want to lower the boom. "Sure, but in the daytime, too. Bill's always been swell about giving me experience."

Shea looked right through the pilot. "Suppose you quit protecting him, Mac. I couldn't get an old geezer like him to admit a damned thing. I'd have to carry him to an eye specialist."

"I'm not protecting him, Johnny."

"Mac, I'm gonna tell you a little story. Once upon a time there was a Midwest captain who was the best-liked guy in the company. He'd been flying since the days of Orville Wright. He was a father to every copilot who joined the line. The word beloved is not too strong. When his eyes started going bad on him, they kept protecting him. He never had to make a landing, the first officer would do it for him. Then one night he drew a brand-new copilot who didn't know him. It was lousy weather and the captain trusted a greenhorn less than he did his own eyes. He overshot, went into a ditch, and caught fire. Sixteen people didn't get out—including our captain who was too proud to quit flying. What's wrong with Bill?"

McKay, sick at heart, didn't answer right away. Shea let him wrestle with his conscience and knew who would win. When McKay finally spoke, his voice was shaky. "His depth perception seems gone. I asked him to see a doctor. I thought he had by now."

"That's what I figured. I watched him in OPS the other night. He could hardly see the flight plan in front of him. I might have bought just eyestrain and told him to get glasses for reading. But his landings were lousy on his last check ride."

"Why didn't you ground him then?" McKay asked with some bitterness. "Why make me the stoolie who turns him in? He's been wonderful to Barbara and me. And he's still one helluva pilot—landings or no landings."

"Don't be foolish, Mac," Shea said. "What goes up must come down. I said his check ride landings were bad, but they could have been called borderline. I stretched a point for him and thought maybe he just had an off day. You don't ground a guy like Bill Waterman without being sure he's had it."

"Now you're sure?"

"I'll send him to an eye doctor for a complete examination, including a depth-perception test. Meanwhile he's grounded."

"Fine. I won't be able to look him in the face."

"You couldn't have looked yourself in the face if you hadn't told me—and if Bill had cracked up a plane full of people some night. He's been getting by because senior copilots were bidding his trips. Sooner or later he would have hit a junior he couldn't have let make a tough landing."

"I still feel lousy," McKay muttered.

"A long time ago, Mac, you sat in this very office and talked to me about feeling a sense of responsibility being a part of an airline pilot. Who deserves that more—Bill or the passengers? What comes first—blind loyalty to a fellow pilot or loyalty to your profession?"

"You know the answer," McKay said. "But it wasn't too long ago that I threatened to turn in a pilot if he didn't come clean on his own. I'm beginning to wonder if I'm fated to be a stool pigeon."

"You're not a stool pigeon. And I'll tell you something else. If I told Bill Waterman you reported he couldn't land a plane at night—which I won't, by the way—he wouldn't hold it against you."

"I wish I could believe that."

"You can. Because he's the same kind of person you are. The only difference between you and Bill Waterman is about thirty years and twenty thousand hours."

Shea was right. The doorbell of the McKays' apartment rang two weeks later. Waterman stood there with a broad grin on his face.

"Come on in," McKay said. "Barbara, Bill's here."

"Can't stay. I'm packing."

"Packing? For where?"

"Denver. Shea just told me. I'm taking over as chief pilot there. Guess you heard I was grounded."

"I heard. Bill, I've got to tell you something that's been eating at my craw."

"You don't have to, Mac. I know you turned me in. You should have. You did me a favor."

"That sonofabitch Shea. I asked him . . ."

"Shea didn't tell me. You did."

"I did? I haven't seen you for two weeks."

"Yeh, I know. When you didn't call me, I figured you were feeling guilty about something. Hi, Barbara—come kiss the old man good-by."

The move from the right seat to the left seat was a matter of inches measured in terms of hundreds of flights and thousands of hours.

Every time a pilot moved to another base, quit, or was retired, the first officers at DCA would scan the revised base seniority list to see how far up the ladder their names had progressed. Forward progress was the equivalent of a sick snail moving through molasses.

By his sixth anniversary with Midwest, McKay had logged just under forty-five hundred hours as copilot. He mentioned it to Barbara with some pride. "It'll be five thousand by June. How about that, sweetie?"

"Very impressive, lover. How many hours are there in about seven and a half months?"

It went right over his head. "You mean flight hours? Well, let's see, eighty-five a month. Say about five hundred in round figures."

"Good. In somewhat more than five hundred hours I'm gonna have the roundest figure you ever saw."

What had gone over his head turned around and landed hard. He rose out of his chair and stood over her. He took both her hands in his and kissed her so gently she hardly felt the touch of his lips.

"We're gonna have a baby?"

"Roger and affirmative, my beloved airman. I've been thinking all day how to break the news dramatically. You gave me a beautiful opening. Happy, honey?" She asked the question as a few billion women had asked it before her. Expectantly, proudly, and a little bit uncertainly.

"Totally and with no reservations. I suppose I'd better get conventional—like have you seen a doctor and hadn't you better stop work? And if you think you can get me to do the dishes tonight, you're right."

"Yes to all inquiries. Want a boy or a girl?"

"Triplets. I've gotta go that bastard O'Brian one better."

"I'm serious, Mac. We talked it over a long time ago and you said a girl. Still feel the same way?"

"Sort of. But I won't send you back for refresher training if you hand me a son."

McKay's Midwest logbook read five thousand, two hundred, and three hours and Barbara's logbook read nine months and two days when she handed him a child. Unfortunately he wasn't around for the event. The night it occurred, he and Snorkel were battling an early September thunderstorm 120 miles out of Washington. Knowing the baby was due, he had tried to trade trips, but the usually compassionate Shea turned him down.

"Too shorthanded, Mac. But she'll be okay. First babies always come late anyway."

McKay had a premonition that the chief pilot was no authority on gynecology. Now, at twelve thousand feet in a Convair which he wished was a faster Constellation, he would have gladly accepted a ten-year sentence as first officer to be with Barbara.

Snorkel insisted on McKay flying the ship on the theory that it would keep his mind occupied. So it was the captain, handling the radio, who got the news first.

"Midwest two-oh-two, this is Washington Center. You got a first officer named McKay on your flight?"

"Affirmative, Washington Center."

McKay thought he heard his heart pounding through the headset.

"Midwest two-oh-two, your Dispatch has been trying to raise you on company frequency. They asked us to relay a message."

"Go ahead, Center."

"Here it is, two-oh-two. Tell McKay Barbara had baby girl. Six pounds, eight ounces. Both doing fine."

"Roger, Washington Center. And thank you, sir."

"Just a minute, two-oh-two, there's more to the message. Advise McKay Barbara says the baby's name is Nancy Helen and if he doesn't like it, not to bother landing."

"I'll pass the word along," Snorkel assured the Center. "Midwest two-oh-two, out."

"Hey, two-oh-two. Tell him congratulations from Air Traffic Control. We're glad it's a girl."

"Okay, Washington Center. By the way, how come you're glad it's a girl?"

"Because," said the unknown voice, with as much feeling as could be transmitted through an impersonal mike, "a boy might grow up to be a controller. Over and out, Midwest two-oh-two."

"Well, well, congratulations, Papa Mac. I . . ."

Snorkel took over the yoke without finishing the sentence. McKay had a silly grin on his face and might as well have been sitting in the cabin with the passengers.

Their daughter, a tiny edition of her mother, was ten months old when the Great Event occurred. It was June of 1953 and McKay found an envelope in his company box. He had been carefully watching the seniority list and it was not a complete surprise, but he still was excited when he read the notice from Flight Operations:

> McKay, McDonald:
> You are hereby advised that you are eligible for upgrading to captain pending completion of qualification training. Please contact the chief pilot to arrange the necessary scheduling for the aforementioned training. Until further notice you are relieved of regular line flying duties.

It took him less than three minutes to race to Shea's office. The chief pilot was amused. "I just got through telling Mrs. Gillespie you oughta be coming through the wall any second. I'm a little disappointed. You came through the door. And what took you so long? That note went into your box two hours ago."

McKay was panting. "I just saw it, Johnny. When do I start?"

"Whoa, boy. Not too fast. Number one, trot down to Doc Hall's office and take a first-class physical, or make an appointment for one."

"First-class physical? I took the CAA's six-month physical only last week."

"Makes no difference. Take it again. Company rule. On second thought, sit down and have some coffee. If you went down now, your blood pressure would ground you for a month."

McKay sat down. Shea sent his secretary down the hall for coffee and phoned the company medical director. He arranged an appointment for McKay at two that afternoon. Then he discussed the forthcoming training curriculum.

"You'll fly captain on the smallest equipment, Mac. That's the Convair. Which means five days of ground school on the 240 to start with. Add another thirty hours for route examinations. Twenty-five hours jump-seat observation time on every segment the 240 serves. Two proficiency check rides of ninety minutes each, mostly emergency procedures stuff, plus a two-hour oral quiz on emergencies. And you'll be taking a quiz on each of these subjects."

He handed McKay a mimeographed sheet which listed such items as Captain's Duties and Responsibilities, Civil Air Regulations, Navigation, Meteorology, Communications, Air Traffic Control, Company Rules, Equipment Review including all systems, operation, and performance, and Emergency Equipment.

"My God, Johnny, am I gonna be flying President Eisenhower around? I've done all this before."

"I know. But you'll do it again. And just to qualify for a Convair's left seat. You'll repeat it every time you upgrade equipment. Oh yeh, toss in four hours of Link time, too. Still wanna be a captain?"

"When do I start?" McKay repeated.

He started that afternoon with the first-class physical. He finished some three months later. The ground school and written examinations came easy. Most of it was refresher training. The toughest part of qualification were the two proficiency flights, one with Shea and the other with Bender. They threw everything at him but an actual crash.

He sweated through simulated hydraulic failures, engine fires, wheel-well fires, cargo-compartment fires, total electrical-system failure, smoke evacuation drill, explosive decompression, inadvertent prop reversal, and propeller feathering malfunctions.

He went through for-real emergency landing-gear extensions, emergency flap operation, emergency descents, emergency fuel dumping, and emergency control failures. He was exposed to so many engine-out landings and takeoffs that it seemed a luxury to have both engines running simultaneously. First-officer training was grammar school, almost kindergarten, compared to the captaincy qualification ordeal.

At the end of three months he felt as if he could land a 240 if both wings had fallen off. And even then Midwest insisted on voicing the suspicious belief that new captains had to be watched and their passengers protected. For the first hundred hours he was to fly as captain, the minimum ceiling for all landings would be one hundred feet higher than normal and visibility would be a half mile longer.

He took his final route qualification ride with Shea, sitting for the first time in the left seat on a regularly scheduled flight. But he still wore his three stripes and he knew he was not really a captain yet. Shea acted as copilot, let McKay make all landings and takeoffs, handle the PA's and fly every leg of the multistop trip. They left Washington National at 8 A.M., returned at 7 P.M., and went into Operations to check out. McKay was tired and worried.

Shea hadn't said a word of praise, criticism, suggestion, or advice all day. McKay signed his flight pay sheet, entered the elapsed flying time in his logbook, and turned to the chief pilot.

"Okay, Johnny. I couldn't have been that good—or that bad. For Christ's sake, say something."

Shea's craggy Irish face wore a frown that blended disappointment with disgust. McKay almost wanted to cry. Then Shea grinned and stuck out his hand.

"Sure. Congratulations—Captain McKay."

As soon as the new captain had left to go home to wife and daughter, Shea dialed McKay's home phone.

"Barbara? Johnny. You can keep the decorations hanging —he came through fine. He's on his way now. Have a fine party. What? Hell, I'd better not, honey. Leave management out of this shindig. Just tell O'Brian and Culver to stay sober. They're right in the middle of what your boy just finished. Good night."

He hung up. For no reason in particular, he felt wonderful. On second thought, he knew why he felt wonderful.

McKay drove home at slightly above legal speeds. He was bloated with plans. Tonight he would tell Barbara they could buy a second car, start looking for a house, or maybe even build one from scratch, and the first thing tomorrow morning he would call a Midwest captain selling life insurance on the side and take out an education policy for Nancy. The route qualification trip he had just finished automatically added $300 a month to his income. Cautiously, in the past, he had ended all discussions on such things as cars and homes with "Let's wait till the fourth stripe." The waiting was over.

He didn't even get mad when he couldn't find a parking spot near their apartment—a too-frequent occurrence which usually exasperated him. He ran up the stairs to the second floor, fumbled for his key, and finally got the door open.

Culver, Mitch, and the O'Brians were there, Paddy and Les on their knees bowing with hands outstretched in humble supplication. Mitch and Pat curtsied. And Barbara stood there, her eyes glistening as they had on that Christmas Eve so long ago when he had first sensed her love. Now it was love and pride, mingled in overwhelming proportions.

"Welcome home, Captain," she said.

It was a magnificent party. O'Brian had brought champagne. Culver handed him a package which turned out to be a pair of pajamas with four stripes sewed onto each sleeve.

The laughter woke up Nancy and Mac carried her into the living room to be fussed over before he put her uncomplainingly back to bed. At ten, a Western Union boy rang the doorbell to deliver a telegram. McKay read it aloud amid more laughs.

WE HAVE JUST PURCHASED STOCK IN THE PENNSYLVANIA RAIL-
ROAD. LOVE AND CONGRATULATIONS. MARION AND SNORKEL

When the Culvers and O'Brians had left, they peeked in on Nancy and poured themselves a final glass of champagne, sitting on the couch holding hands.

"Sunday," McKay said, "we'll go house-hunting and it's time we got a new car. I can use the old one just to run back and forth from the airport."

"Let's get a station wagon, honey. If we're gonna go suburbia, we might as well go whole hog."

"Know something, Barbara? I've never been happier."

"Just because of the fourth stripe?"

"The fourth stripe and you and Nancy."

"Incidentally, Captain McKay, when do you officially get the stripe?"

"I forgot to ask Johnny. There's usually a little ceremony in Kane's office, or maybe even Mencken's. You get your captain's wings and some kind of certificate."

"You also should get yourself a new uniform, honey. The pants on your old one are so shiny, it reflects."

"Guess I will. Costs like hell but I sure need one."

Two days later he was summoned to Mencken's office with two other new captains and presented his gold captain's wings and a certificate.

THIS CERTIFICATE IS AWARDED BY

MIDWEST AIRLINES, INC.

TO

MCDONALD MCKAY

WHO ON OCTOBER 3RD, 1953, WAS DETERMINED TO BE FULLY
QUALIFIED TO SERVE AS AIRLINE CAPTAIN, HAVING COMPLETED
THE REQUIRED QUALIFICATIONS FOR THE HIGH RESPONSIBILITIES
AND PUBLIC TRUST OF THE POSITION.

Karl Mencken
President

Into McKay's wallet went the little slip of paper that was
his precious ATR—Air Transport Rating—which proclaimed
the United States government's finding him "properly qualified to exercise the privilege of airline transport pilot." This
was his license to command. This was his passport across the
cockpit border to the left seat.

The next day he flew his first trip as captain.

Flight 263 was not exactly one of Midwest's glamor flights.
It was Washington to Chicago via Charleston, Cincinnati,
and Indianapolis—a prosaic puddle-jumper. For McKay, he
might as well have been Lindbergh crossing the Atlantic,
and the Convair was the Sacred Cow carrying Roosevelt to
Casablanca.

Mike Shelley, a bright youngster not too junior to McKay,
was his copilot. It was Midwest's policy to assign new captains relatively experienced first officers.

"Do me a large favor, Mike, and don't call me 'sir'," Mc-
Kay told him. "Flight plan ready?"

Shelley handed him the form. McKay studied it and signed
"McDonald McKay" with a self-conscious flourish in the
space marked CLEARANCE ACCEPTED.

"Hi, Captain McKay, sir, you hero of the airways."

McKay turned around. It was Helen Mitchell, in uniform,
bright and chipper as usual.

"Morning, Mitch. What trip you working?"

"263, what else?"

McKay took another look at the flight plan. Sure enough, "H. Mitchell" was the cabin attendant. He hadn't even noticed her name.

"You're a bit senior to be working Convairs," he remarked.

"I traded—just to be with you on your first flight as captain. Besides, Barbara thought it would be a good idea."

"I'll beat her when I get home. Knowing you, you'll probably ask every passenger if he took out insurance."

"Naturally. I just took out some myself. What's our load?"

"Forty—full ship."

"Thanks a heap, Mac. That means forty breakfasts between here and Charleston. See you on board."

She grinned at him, saluted in a mock gesture resembling a child trying to imitate a soldier, and left.

McKay and Shelley walked out to the plane fifteen minutes before boarding time. He actually would have preferred to go out sooner but didn't want to appear too eager. Or nervous.

And he was nervous, in a totally new and strange way. Now, as never before, he grasped the meaning of the fourth stripe, with its awesome responsibility. He performed the walk-around himself, remembering that was how Snorkel had done it on their first trip. He came close to mentioning the importance of the preflight inspection to Shelley, as Snodgrass had, then decided against it. He already had been unfair to the copilot, who was perfectly capable of the walk-around—and who knew why McKay was doing it himself.

They walked down the aisle and went into the cockpit, McKay smiling at the song Mitch was humming behind them. "Nearer My God to Thee," no less.

"A character," Shelley said.

"Sure is." McKay lowered himself into the left seat. The nervousness suddenly left him, replaced by a tangible sense of excitement and an intangible sense of authority. The years of training, the accumulated knowledge of the scores of captains with whom he had flown, the doctrines of discipline

and safety drummed into him by Shea and Bender and Snodgrass and Barnwell, all took over in one magic moment.

"Checklist, Mike." He had given his first command. He
heard the PA announcing the flight.

"Midwest Airlines Flight 263, to Chicago with intermediate stops at Charleston, Cincinnati, and Indianapolis, is
now ready for boarding. Midwest Flight 263."

He could not resist peeking out the cockpit and watching
the passengers filing toward the plane. Finally the ramp
agent signaled "all on," and the engines whined and snorted
grumpily into their impatient idling. McKay closed his window. The ramp agent waved all clear and with a broad grin,
saluted.

They had reached cruise altitude when McKay figured it
was time for his first PA.

"Ladies and gentlemen, welcome aboard. Our en-route
weather is good and we anticipate landing at Charleston, our
first stop, on schedule. Miss Mitchell will be serving a hot
breakfast shortly so settle back, relax, and enjoy your flight.
Thank you."

Mike Shelley looked at him with amusement. "Why didn't
you tell 'em your name? 'This is Captain McKay.' "

"Because," McKay said seriously, "after all these years I
can't believe it."

He got back to the apartment about nine that night, still
too excited and happy to be hungry.

"How'd it go, honey?" Barbara greeted him.

"Fine. No sweat. Nancy okay?"

"Small case of sniffles. Peek in on her while I fix you something to eat. Hungry?"

"Not very. Sandwich'll do. You can pour me a stiff shot of
bourbon, though."

He looked in on his sleeping daughter, took off his uniform
coat, and went into the kitchen where Barbara was slicing
some cold ham.

"Your drink's over there, darling. Double shot. Tired?"

"Yeh, a little. But everything went okay. I guess you know

Mitch flew the trip. She kept saluting me every time I reboarded at a stop. By the end of the day I was ready to break her arm."

Barbara hugged him. "Honey, how did it feel? Being a captain for the first time."

"Like I was ten feet tall," he said.

Chapter 10

They bought a home in a new Virginia subdivision, a three-bedroom rambler about a half-hour drive from the airport. It was of the architectural design builders liked to call contemporary on the theory that some buyers were scared by the word modern. The lot was wooded, there was a pine-paneled den and a finished basement including a built-in bar. They especially loved the living room, with a huge fireplace and a cathedral ceiling. One of Barbara's first tasks was to place their domino on the fireplace mantel.

McKay teased her about it, pointing out that it would require an explanation from every non-Midwest friend who visited.

"I don't care," she insisted. "I'll just look mysterious. Maybe I'll hint I won you in a domino game."

Thus, they settled down to the existence of an airline captain and his family, a mixture of glamor and inconvenience that brought from their neighbors an equivalent mixture of envy and sympathy. The wives who told Barbara how lucky she was being married to a handsome pilot also clucked with dismay when she had to turn down invitations because "Mac's flying this weekend."

He flew a good many weekends, being merely a junior captain. O'Brian and Culver joined that status in short order. The O'Brians also followed them into suburbia, buying a home not too far away, but Culver and Mitch preferred apartment living for a while.

Les and Helen were married a month after he got his fourth stripe. She had to quit flying, of course, but Midwest offered her a job as stewardess supervisor under Grace Wooley, which she filled with admirable efficiency. Being a nonconformist stewardess, she had wormed through enough regulatory loopholes to know exactly how they should be plugged. No girl pulled anything on Mitch, who at one time or another had violated every rule in the Midwest manual.

She could be funny and firm simultaneously. She joked, teased, and listened to their most intimate confidences with the detached wisdom of a priest. Up to a point she let some of them get away with murder. But she knew where to draw the line between intelligent leniency and impractical softheartedness. She could be ruthless, for example, about weight checks—scales being a worse menace to stewardesses than flying through thunderstorms. Yet she protected her girls with the fierce zeal of a mother lioness when she thought the circumstances warranted protection.

A Midwest vice president once sent her a curt note ordering her to fire a stewardess for rudeness and insubordination. She called the girl in first and got her side of the story. She had been upset by news that her father had cancer, and when the VP on her flight had remarked that food service was a little slow, she had snapped, "Keep your shirt on till I feed the paying passengers."

"I shouldn't have said anything to him, Mitch," she sobbed. "But the pompous bastard was making sure everyone around him knew he was a vice president. I was already coming apart at the seams because of that call from home and when he made that crack about service, I lost my temper."

"Go home and mix yourself a stiff drink," Mitch said. "I'll call you later."

"Am I fired?"

"Not as of now. Let's not worry. I'll have a little talk with our boy."

She marched into the VP's office. With rare humility she explained the circumstances and asked him to give the stewardess another chance.

"No," he ruled. "If she can lose her temper with me she could lose it with a passenger. I'm sorry about her father but Midwest stewardesses aren't supposed to take their troubles into aircraft cabins."

"Crap," said Mitch. "Those kids are human, which is more than I can say for you. You still want her fired?"

"Yes—and if I hear any more insubordination out of you, young lady, you'll be joining her in unemployment."

"Fire her yourself," Mitch said. "And I suggest you do it by letter. That's so Mr. Mencken can study both reports—yours and the one I'll be sending him. About a stewardess who's had a perfect record for three years and seven commendations from passengers. Plus a gold watch from Mr. Mencken for giving first aid to a passenger with a heart attack. Plus a little item I've been waiting to unload on you—complaints from five of my girls who say if you pinch their fannies once more when they're working behind a galley curtain, they'll crown you with a fire extinguisher. I'm going back to my office. If I don't hear from you in thirty minutes, I'll assume you had a change of heart. And a very pleasant good afternoon."

No call came in the next thirty minutes. Mitch tore up his original note and phoned the stewardess.

"I talked to him and he agreed that he was being hasty," she said. "You be a good girl and write him a little note of apology. Don't spread it on too thick—the sonofabitch doesn't deserve it."

McKay attended one of her stewardess emergency procedures recurrent training classes. She had posted a notice on the pilots' bulletin board inviting all who were interested but McKay and Shea were the only ones who showed. They sat in the rear of the room and admired Mitch's technique of teaching—bawdy, blunt, and tremendously effective.

"Miss Mitchell," asked one fresh-faced stewardess, "why

can't we use the pilot's cockpit escape hatch for another emergency exit?"

"Because if things go wrong, the hatch'll be full of pilots' asses," Mitch explained.

Her marriage, unfortunately, was a disaster. She had married Les with misgivings, knowing his reputation for being promiscuous, and she had bluntly warned him she would not tolerate infidelity.

"My playing days are over," he assured her. "You're all the woman I want."

He believed it, too, but he began straying from the matrimonial reservation only three months after their marriage. He loved Mitch, but he discovered he could no more stay away from other women than an alcoholic can stop drinking. Sex to Culver was the thrill of the chase and the excitement of a new conquest. For a while he kept his sinning from Mitch but eventually she caught him and under circumstances that hurt her deeply.

She had retained her maiden name on her job, and some of the new stewardesses reporting to her did not know she was married. It was one of these girls who lowered the boom on Culver. Mitch was going over a check ride report with her and mentioned that she didn't seem to have had much sleep the night before.

"I guess I didn't," the stewardess confessed with a giggle. "To tell you the truth, I had a layover in New York last night and wound up in bed with the captain."

Culver had been in New York the night before, Mitch thought. But she was jumping at conclusions. There must have been a half-dozen other Midwest pilots on a layover, too.

"Well, I won't ask you his name," she said dryly. "It's none of my business who you shack up with unless it shows up in your work."

"I shouldn't tell you this," the girl confided with what amounted to pride, "but he was an absolute living doll. Les Culver. Do you know him?"

"Quite well," Mitch said icily. "He's my husband. Now get the hell out of here before I either slug you or start crying."

After the stewardess left, shaken into tearful apologies, Mitch had her own cry. Then she went home, slapped the surprised Culver in the face, packed her suitcase, and moved into a hotel. Culver begged her to return, pledging undying faithfulness, and even the McKays asked her to give Les another chance.

"No," she told Barbara. "I don't really blame the bastard. I'm to blame for marrying him. Some wives can forgive infidelity. They accept it like they accept the inevitability of menopause. But I'm not one of those gals. Les is congenitally incapable of sleeping with only one woman and I'm not going to get hurt the rest of my life. Besides, I've lost respect for him—I didn't think he was stupid enough to crawl into the sack with one of my own girls."

She filed for divorce. Culver, feeling like an AA who had fallen off the wagon, found himself suffering from a double burden. Not only had he been a damn fool, but Mitch's own popularity placed everyone's sympathy with her. Some stewardesses would speak to him only in the line of duty. He finally asked Shea for a transfer to Chicago. He told McKay and O'Brian it was "just to get a change of scenery" but he told himself the truth—he could not stay at the same base as Mitch. McKay got a letter from him after Les settled in Chicago.

Dear Mac and Barbara:

Just a brief note to advise I found a reasonably pleasant apartment and am flying Convairs out of here to Denver.

I'm honestly sorry for what happened. It may seem hard for you to believe but I love Mitch and always will. I even miss her terribly and I only wish I was the kind of man who could accept the responsibilities of marriage. I'm a good-for-nothing heel and I'll probably go through life hurting people who don't deserve to get hurt.

I suppose the basic trouble is that unlike Mac and Paddy, I was never able to distinguish love from sex. I thought I could with Mitch but I was so very, very wrong. Maybe someday I'll grow up.

Love,
Les

Les Culver never got his chance to grow up. Two months after he wrote that letter, he was dead.

On the last morning of his life he and a copilot named Ben Pellington were sipping coffee at the Denver airport. They were heading east to Chicago via Platte, Colorado, Topeka, and Kansas City.

The leg from Denver to Platte was routine. After landing, the two pilots got out to stretch their legs and Pellington commented on the clear, crisp weather.

"That visibility must be about forty miles," he said.

Culver nodded but pointed to the mountains to the east. They were almost obscured by the gathering snow clouds. Only the foothills were visible.

"I'll be glad to get out of here," Les said. "That storm's coming in fast. Let's get back on board."

They rolled away from the ramp a few minutes later and began the checklist litany.

The voice of the Platte tower sounded through their earphones. "Midwest three-six-three, you are cleared to Topeka at nine repeat nine thousand Airway one-seven. Climb northbound on the back course of the Platte ILS localizer."

Pellington read back the clearance. It meant that they would take off toward the southeast and make a right turn —away from the gathering clouds—and continue the turn to a northerly heading. They would follow this heading on a radio course line until they intersected Airway 17.

"Okay, Midwest three-six-three," the tower said, acknowledging the readback. "Report passing the Comstock intersection to Approach Control, please."

"Comstock intersection?" Culver muttered. He picked up his own mike.

"Midwest three-six-three," he said. "Our departure procedure chart doesn't show any Comstock checkpoint."

"Comstock is correct," advised the tower. "It's the old Weller intersection. It's been renamed."

"Okay, Platte. But I wanna make sure. Comstock is where the localizer crosses your zero-two-six radial off the omni station—is that right?"

"Roger, zero-two-six radial from the Platte omni. Got it?"

"Affirmative. Midwest three-six-three rolling."

The Convair thundered down the runway and broke ground, swimming gracefully upward.

"Gear up," Culver called out.

The wheels tucked themselves into the landing gear well. Les reduced power. Pellington asked the tower for permission to make the required right turn. Flight 363 continued to climb. The Convair was just out of the turn when it entered the overcast and Culver went on instruments, watching his RMI until it showed the desired heading. They leveled off, still climbing, and entered the takeoff time in the navigational logbook. They leveled at nine thousand but still were in the overcast. An alarm bell rang in Culver's mind.

"Where the hell did this stuff come from?" he grumbled. "That storm was to the east—we shouldn't be getting this much of it."

The words were hardly out of his mouth when Pellington almost rose out of his seat.

"Ground at three o'clock!" he shouted.

Off the right wing barely visible through a weak spot in the overcast was a sheer cliffside which should have been ten miles away. Les rolled hard to the left and pulled the nose up. His hands shoved the throttles forward and the engines howled with the power surge. The RMI in front of the captain spun crazily. Culver's eyes were on the instrument panel but he still couldn't have seen what lay ahead even if he had been looking out the cockpit window. Lurking malevolently in the gray clouds was another cliff. Pellington must have caught a split-second glimpse of it just before they hit. His scream was the last sound Les Culver heard.

Nobody saw them crunch into Bald Eagle Mountain and explode. The tower controller first realized something was wrong when a Pioneer DC-3 requested takeoff clearance and he decided to make sure of Midwest's position.

"Midwest three-six-three, are you northbound on the back course yet?"

There was no answer. The tower repeated its query several times, gave Pioneer permission to take off, then paged 363 again and again. He phoned Midwest Dispatch in Denver. Dispatch notified the nearest Civil Aeronautics Board regional office in Los Angeles. Over Midwest's teletype system, the impersonal keys clucked out 363's epitaph.

ALL STATIONS . . . INFORMATIVELY FLIGHT 363 UNREPORTED
AND OVERDUE AFTER TAKEOFF FROM PLATTE EASTBOUND FOR
TOPEKA. THREE CREW FIFTEEN PASSENGERS. CAPTAIN L.
CULVER . . .

Reporters rushed to the scene and phoned in fresh bulletins when the wreckage was sighted on the edge of a precipice, 9250 feet above sea level and 1879 feet from the top of Bald Eagle Mountain. The newsmen then clustered around the CAB investigator from Los Angeles. Phil Baldwin was a good-natured, rather stout man in his late thirties who never wore anything but bow ties. Despite his bulk, he moved with the peculiar grace common to some fat persons.

"Do you have any theories about the crash?" AP asked.

Baldwin glared at him before he replied.

"We haven't even reached the wreckage yet. No comment and it'll be no comment for a helluva long while."

The UP staffer, out of the Denver bureau, found a CAA official bustling around trying to look simultaneously concerned and important.

"Any idea what caused the crash?" said UP.

"Well," said the CAA man, "he was supposed to be at nine thousand heading north and he hit Bald Eagle which is at least eleven thousand and to the northeast. I guess it's fair to say the pilot must have had a hair up his ass."

And that was Les Culver's epitaph.

McKay wasn't in on the investigation from the start. Barnwell flew to Platte along with Midwest's chief pilot in Chicago and the union's safety chairman for the western region. Barney returned a week later and gave Snodgrass and McKay a fill-in.

"They'll never get the wreckage off the mountain," he related. "About the biggest piece left was the tail. We couldn't find anything that would give us the slightest clue. Les just flew right into that damned peak."

"How about the nav aids?" Snorkel asked.

"CAA checked them the next day. Everything was working fine."

"How about his instruments?" said McKay.

"Didn't show a thing that wasn't normal, far as we could tell. They'll be running bench tests but I doubt if they'll come up with anything. I'm going back to the hearing in Denver in about a month. Maybe we'll have more to go on by then."

McKay said nothing. That night he came home with several sheets of paper stuffed in a manila envelope. Right after supper he began studying them.

"What are you reading, honey?" Barbara asked.

"The wiring of the fluxgate compass system."

She wasn't sure what a fluxgate compass was, but she changed her mind about asking him to go to the movies. "Is it something to do with Culver's crash?"

"Could be."

He was still reading the diagrams and technical data when she went to bed. She awoke when he finally crawled in beside her. He tossed uneasily all night, which was unusual for him, and she had trouble sleeping soundly herself. She found herself thinking of Mitch and what made a woman fall out of love with a man. Was Mitch grieving inwardly now? Did she have any feeling of guilt, let alone sorrow? Then Barbara caught herself wondering why there should be any sense of guilt. Except she could not brush an ugly word out of her own mind. Suicide.

As a matter of fact, the CAB a month later obviously was entertaining similar thoughts. Barnwell attended the public hearing on Flight 363 and was disturbed about one aspect. Testimony had been introduced concerning the breakup of Culver's marriage. Several Chicago-based pilots were called as witnesses and asked about the captain's apparent mental state in the weeks preceding the accident.

"Everyone insisted Les was perfectly normal and seemed happy," Barney reported to McKay on his return. "They dropped the subject but it still bothers me. It sounded like they were reaching for a motive instead of an explanation."

"Did they concentrate on anything in particular? Instruments, for example?"

"That worries me, too," Barnwell frowned. "Most of the testimony was on weather. The gist of it was that he had plenty of visibility up to a couple of minutes before he hit the mountain. There was one guy—an Army captain who was leaving on a hunting trip right around the area. He said only the top of Bald Eagle Mountain was obscured by clouds. And he claimed he saw the plane just before it went into the overcast."

"How long before the crash?"

"He wasn't sure, but he thought it was only a couple of minutes—after they told him the impact time. But he said something that seemed to impress the Board. He said the plane passed right over him and he remembered thinking that if it was eastbound, it was too low and if it was northbound, it must have been off course."

Up to that point McKay had never mentioned his old fluxgate compass concern to anyone, including Barnwell. But he did now, repeating mostly what he had discussed with Bender in Convair ground school. Barney was interested but not convinced.

"It's a good theory, Mac. But there's a hole in it. Even if his RMI had been off, his course deviation indicator would have shown them they were on the wrong heading."

"If Les had seen it, or Pellington."

"There's no reason why they wouldn't have. Or is there?"

"I don't know," McKay admitted. "But I'd sure like to find out. Maybe there'll be something in the CAB report when it comes out."

There wasn't. The verdict on the Platte accident was issued six months later. The pilots were stunned. It implied suicide.

The Board determines that the probable cause of this accident was a lack of conformity with prescribed enroute procedures and the intentional deviation from airways at an altitude too low to clear obstructions ahead . . .

There was no evidence of any malfunction or failure of any component including basic flight and navigation instruments. Even assuming this unlikely factor, all the captain had to do was look outside to determine that he was not following the airway. There was no understandable reason why the pilots would not know, by reference to the conspicuous terrain features, that they were not on the planned course. In brief, he should have seen the mountain ahead of him in sufficient time to avoid it. Therefore, from all available evidence and the lack of evidence to the contrary, the Board can only conclude that the course taken by the flight was intentional.

Intentional. Les Culver had deliberately left an assigned course, and flown at an altitude of only nine thousand feet directly toward an eleven-thousand-foot mountain clearly visible for most of the elapsed time from takeoff. Or so decreed the CAB. McKay couldn't believe it. Not Les. Especially not Les. Not with his curiosity, his enjoyment of his senses, certainly of the sensual aspect of life. It just didn't ring true.

A few weeks after the CAB report was made public, Barnwell was flying a Convair into Dayton one night and had just been given final approach clearance with the necessary heading toward the assigned runway. They were in an overcast. Barnwell banked the 240 until his RMI swung to the heading, then nosed down through the clouds. When they broke out, he was bewildered. There were no approach lights ahead. For that matter, there was no airport. And the city of Dayton was off the right wing. It should have been to the left.

Barnwell caged the fluxgate gyro to bring it back to level. The RMI spun to a different heading—the correct one. They had been flying southeast instead of south. And his copilot's RMI also had shown the erroneous southerly heading.

When Barney returned to Washington, he marched right into Shea's office and talked to the chief pilot for more than an hour. Then he phoned McKay and told him what had happened on the Dayton approach.

"If the terrain wasn't flat, we could have flown smack into a hill," he said. "I've talked to Shea. Told him you've been studying fluxgate malfunctions. He says to spend as much time as you have to—even if you have to miss a trip occasionally. And incidentally, Johnny's already called Ben Kane. They're modifying that fluxgate wiring the way you suggested a long time ago."

McKay went to work the next day. He first called on Al Bengsten and related the details of Barnwell's Dayton experience.

"Interesting," the CAB man agreed, "but hardly conclusive. All you've got is one example of fluxgate error. We don't reopen a case unless there's new evidence, Mac. This isn't new evidence. It's just a theory."

"All you've got is circumstantial evidence," McKay retorted. "What we've got is a damned strong conviction that no pilot in his right mind would fly northeast from Platte for five minutes at nine thousand feet."

Bengsten looked at him sharply.

"Maybe he wasn't in his right mind. You know . . ."

"Bull. That suicide implication was a phony, dammit. I've read your own report. He was at nine thousand. He hit the mountain at ninety-two-fifty. So he climbed two-fifty feet in the last split second. Would a guy trying to commit suicide do that?"

"No," sighed Bengsten. "I hate to admit it, Mac, but that word 'intentional' was hitting below the belt. I tried like hell to get it cut out but I don't run the Bureau. Tell you what, you keep me advised of any more fluxgate malfunctions. Or better yet, I'll have CAA ask all the carriers to watch for 'em and feed 'em in here. If it looks like there's a pattern, we'll take another look at Platte."

In the next three months Bengsten received five reports of erroneous fluxgate headings. He figuratively beat his chief over the head with them and got the case reopened. But when the CAB issued an amended report, the only change was the elimination of the word "intentional." It dismissed the possibility of fluxgate error in these words:

The possibility of navigational instruments having contributed to or having caused this accident was considered at great length. In judging this possibility, however, it is necessary to keep in mind a number of important factors.

One is the relatively good visibility prevailing from the takeoff to the point where a competent witness, an Army officer, saw the aircraft enter an overcast near the area of the crash. The Civil Air Regulations require crews to be visually alert. If these pilots were, there is no reason why they should not have known, by reference to the terrain below them, that they were not on the planned course.

If we are to believe that undetermined and highly unlikely malfunctioning of the aircraft's navigation equipment actually occurred and led the flight into the crash area, we almost must presume a number of instrument failures—failures which would be more or less simultaneous, of similar magnitude and in the same direction.

Furthermore, it should be pointed out that this extreme unlikelihood would have to be accompanied by the crew not looking beyond the cockpit. An additional rebuttal of the instrument malfunction possibility is that these theoretical malfunctions would have had to prevail from the very start of the flight up until it entered the overcast within two or three miles of the impact site. These malfunctions thus are based on unbelievable possibilities, compounded to such an extent that the Board must reject them as being too tenuous to warrant their serious consideration as a possible contributing factor to this accident.

McKay was on a trip the day the amended report came out. Shea got a copy and left word in Operations for McKay to see him as soon as he landed. When McKay walked in, Shea merely tossed the report at him and waited wordlessly for him to finish reading it. When McKay finally looked up, Shea grunted, "You licked?"

"Wounded but not dead. I still think it was fluxgate."

"That's not the point, Mac. Even if you could prove fluxgate, you'd still be left with pilot error. They've hung their goddamned hats on that visibility business. They're saying if Les had been looking out of the window, it wouldn't have happened. How the hell do you refute that argument?"

McKay shook his head in frustration. "I don't know, John. That Army captain's testimony did more to convict Les than anything else. Yet it still doesn't make sense. If he could see the mountain, why did he keep flying toward it? And don't *you* give me that suicide business."

"I don't buy it, either, Mac. But let's face facts, my friend. The CAB won't reconsider an accident unless it has fresh evidence. You don't. So where do you go from here?"

"Well," said McKay, "for one thing I'd like to look at their whole file. All I've read are the two final reports. Maybe there's something in the transcript that'll give me an idea. I'll let you know."

He phoned Bengsten and asked if he could borrow the entire file on the Platte crash.

"You can come over here and read it, but you can't take it out. CAB rule."

"Do you know anybody else who might have the whole business?"

"Tom Dayton at ALPA would have the public hearing transcript, but that's only part of it. You'd better resign yourself to a few hours in our docket section. Or days. That file is the size of two New York telephone directories."

It was. McKay took one look at it and phoned Barnwell.

"I'll need two or three days to comb through it," he explained. "Could you ask Shea to authorize some time off for ALPA business?"

"Consider it done. And good luck, chum."

He examined the file for two full days. At first it was discouraging. Particularly the testimony from the Army captain who was being questioned at the public hearing on the weather the day of the crash.

"Only the upper portion of Bald Eagle was obscured by clouds," the captain had testified.

Well, that was definite. And damning. Curiously, McKay turned to a section containing the depositions taken from the various witnesses before the public hearing. He found one from Captain Harvey Lindell, U. S. Army, and was rather idly perusing it when he came across a sentence that glared up at him.

"I would say that the altitude of the cloud base adjacent to Bald Eagle was lower than seventy-five hundred feet mean sea level. Offhand, I would estimate that the upper third of the mountain was obscured by clouds."

Upper third. McKay reread both CAB reports on the accident. Each one quoted the captain as saying "only the upper portion of Bald Eagle was obscured by clouds." There was a helluva lot of difference between "upper portion" and "upper third," McKay thought. Then he found these quotes from four ground witnesses interrogated after the accident.

"The clouds were right down to where the terrain starts leveling off."

"All you could see were just little parts of the foothills."

"I could see the base of Bald Eagle, but the rest of it was completely covered."

"The height of the cloud layer over the mountain I'd say was around eight thousand feet and it lowered as you went south along Bald Eagle."

These estimates showed an irregular cloud base, McKay conceded. But that was to be expected, and it occurred to him quickly that the degree of mountain obscurement would be far greater from Culver's cockpit than what ground witnesses observed.

He continued the search for any further evidence that would shoot down the excellent visibility claim. In the two CAB reports indicting Les, he had underlined a sentence reading, "The flight had visual reference to the ground during the turn around the airport and for approximately five minutes thereafter before entering the overcast."

Now he inspected a deposition from the crew of the Pioneer flight that had left Platte eleven minutes after Midwest 363. The pilot had written that approximately three or four minutes north of the field he had been skimming through the tops of a fairly solid overcast at ten thousand feet. A thousand feet above Flight 363 and yet the CAB had insisted Culver had visual contact with the ground for fully five minutes flying in a northeast heading.

Carefully, McKay copied from the bulging file and the mass of exhibits all the data that would reconstruct Culver's collision course. Wind velocity. Temperature. Reported flight path. Gross weight. Climb capabilities of the Convair 240. Elevation of the Platte airport, one mile above sea level. All the testimony concerning the cloud cover. He got out the little pocket computer that is as much a part of a pilot's uniform as his pants. For fully thirty minutes he scrawled figures in a notebook. He computed that Les had entered the overcast immediately after rolling out of his initial right turn, and disappeared into the clouds within two minutes after the turn.

That night he gulped down supper—with Barbara frowning at his obvious impatience with anything as prosaic as eating.

"You're gonna get indigestion," she remonstrated.

"I know, honey. But right now I've got indigestion of the mind."

He went into the bedroom, picked up the phone on the night table, and dialed long distance. "I'd like to place a person-to-person call to Captain Harvey Lindell in Platte, Colorado," he said. "No, I don't know his address."

The next day he notified Barnwell to put him on temporary ALPA payroll and caught the first Midwest flight to Chicago and Platte.

He took a taxi to the address Lindell had provided over the phone. It was a small but attractive ranch-style house with that easy yet gracious informality of Western architecture. Lindell met him at the door and proved to be hospitable as well as likable. He insisted on pouring McKay a drink and also that he stay for dinner.

"Wife loves company," he said. "She'll be fixing dinner while we talk. Come on into the den."

The Army man was a lean, leathery-faced career officer assigned to the Platte Ordnance District. He told McKay he was renting the house but hoped to move to Platte permanently someday.

"I love the West," he said. "I'm from Lansing, Michigan, originally, but these mountains get me. Now, what's on your mind?"

"Mountains," said McKay. "Bald Eagle, specifically. I told you on the phone I was working on a theory about that crash. Like I said, your testimony is somewhat in conflict with the theory. So I had to see you personally."

"Shoot."

McKay briefly told him about the fluxgate compass and the

part he believed the instrument played in the accident. Then he went over Lindell's testimony.

"The discrepancy about the degree of obscurement doesn't concern me," McKay said. "What hurt Culver the most was your statement that you saw the plane just before it entered the overcast."

"Culver? Oh yeh, the pilot. Well, I don't know what to tell you. I did see the plane. I know you wished I'd say I was mistaken, but I did see it."

"Just before he entered the overcast near Bald Eagle?"

"Not more than a minute or two at the most."

McKay took a mental deep breath and asked the next question. "How clearly did you see him?"

Lindell was puzzled. "I'm not sure what you mean. I saw the plane clearly enough. Intermittently through the clouds. Then he . . ."

"Through the clouds?" McKay pounced like a hungry panther.

"Sure, through the clouds. It was cloudy as hell and I saw him going in and out of them. I never said I had him in sight all the time."

"For God's sake, why not? From your testimony, it looked like you saw him flying VFR."

"VFR?"

"Visual flight rules. It means he had contact with the ground, visual contact. But you said you spotted him intermittently. I wish you had told the CAB that."

"They didn't ask me," the Army man said. "They wanted to know if I had seen the flight and exactly when. I guess I should have been more explicit."

"The CAB should have been more explicit," McKay said angrily. "You couldn't have known the significance, but they should have. Anyway, you've been a big help."

Lindell shook his head. "It's still a little beyond me," he said, "but I'm glad if I helped straighten something out."

"You did. I won't bother you with the details, but what you told me refutes the crew's being VFR for all but the last two minutes. They must have gone on instruments right after they broke ground. And that means the fluxgate error must have occurred when they rolled out of their turn. It led them right into the mountain."

They discussed the crash and then had dinner. The Lindells wanted him to stay overnight but there was an eastbound Midwest flight coming through around midnight and McKay was anxious to get back. He couldn't wait to confront Al Bengsten with the Army captain's newer account. He didn't know that fate had decreed a turn of events almost as important as what Lindell had told him. While he had been en route to Platte, the director of the CAB's Bureau of Safety had resigned and Bengsten was appointed his successor.

McKay got the word as soon as he returned. Barbara had gone shopping but left a note.

"Honey. If you get back before I do, Barney wants you to call him. I love you. P.S. I missed you last night."

McKay phoned Barnwell who told him about Bengsten.

"Maybe we'll get somewhere on Culver's crash," Barney said. "Did you come up with anything?"

"Plenty. I'm going over to the CAB now. I'm gonna ask Al to sit down and go over the whole thing again."

He stopped in Bengsten's office long enough to congratulate him. Then he disappeared into the dockets room and resumed his study of the file. He took copious notes and became so engrossed that he forgot to eat lunch. His hunger pangs were massive, but he still did not want to take the time to eat. By 5 P.M. he had completed his task and caught Bengsten just before the CAB investigator left his office.

"Al, is it okay if Barnwell and I come over to see you tomorrow afternoon?"

"Sure. Got something hot on the Platte business?"

"I think so. How about two o'clock?"

"Let me check my schedule. Two's fine."

He conferred with Barnwell and Shea most of the next morning. At two sharp he and Barney sat down with Bengsten. First, McKay told him what Lindell really had seen the morning of the crash. Then he began reading from his notes.

Lucidly and dispassionately he dissected and demolished the "excellent visibility" finding. He read the quotes from the ground witnesses. He emphasized again that the CAB had pinned almost its entire case on Lindell's testimony which now admittedly had been incomplete.

"Okay," he continued, "now we come to the reason he flew northeast instead of north for five minutes. First, we have to establish that he actually intended to fly north. Why you didn't establish that yourselves I'll never know. The transcript's loaded with evidence.

"First, there was a record of the radio conversation Les had with the tower. Culver specifically questioned the reference to the Comstock intersection. He asked the tower to define its exact location. Question: would any pilot have gone to that much trouble if he didn't plan to comply with the clearance?

"Second, I found in the file a report by the systems team that checked the radio control panel. It says the radio navigational equipment had been set up to follow the prescribed route and to check the required Comstock intersection.

"So, we have two definite indications Les did not mean to fly northeast. He did—for nearly five minutes—and this can be explained by one thing. Fluxgate malfunction. Al, you guys just didn't do your homework."

Bengsten looked at him and a wry smile flicked the corners of his lips. "Neither did you, Mac," he said.

He rang for his secretary, who poked her head into his office.

"Go down to dockets and bring back the file on the Platte accident," he ordered. "You won't need the docket number —McKay's had it out enough the last few days so they won't have any trouble finding it."

The three men sat silently until the secretary returned with the file. Bengsten opened one of the two huge volumes and thumbed through it until he discovered what he was looking for. He sighed almost as if he were sorry he had found it.

"All right, Mac—you too, Barney—come around to my side of the desk so you can see this. It's a report on the only RMI dial we recovered. We never did find the other one. But we don't need the other, do we—because McKay's been arguing that both RMI's would have the same reading in a fluxgate malfunction. Correct?"

The pilots nodded.

"Okay, let's read from this report. Quote. 'Impact had caused the dial to seize. Upon disassembly of the dial, there were no marks found to show that the indicated RMI heading at the moment of the crash was changed by impact forces.' End quote. Follow me so far? You agree that the RMI heading shown on this dial reflects the course Culver took?"

"Yes," muttered McKay. "Dammit, how could I have missed that report?"

"Now," continued Bengsten, still almost sorrowfully, "Phil Baldwin established the actual heading at time of impact with a sun compass. You can't question its accuracy. I won't bother to show you all the data on that finding. It's in both the accident reports. The exact impact heading was 260 degrees. So let's go back to the RMI analysis."

He ruffled through the pages quickly. Then he pointed his finger at a single sentence. The very gesture was a knife stuck into McKay's heart.

"The RMI heading on the seized dial was 273 degrees," read the sentence.

"Jesus," murmured Barnwell. "Only thirteen degrees off the actual heading at impact. That wouldn't be a fluxgate malfunction."

"No, it wouldn't," Bengsten agreed. "In fact, the thirteen-degree difference easily could stem from the evasive move Culver took in the last second. There isn't the slightest doubt in the world his RMI showed a northeast heading right up to the time he hit. And there goes your fluxgate theory, Mac.

We said we found no evidence of instrument failure and you just didn't bother to learn why we said it."

McKay said nothing. He was thinking. Bengsten misinterpreted the silence for surrender and decided it would be decent to ease the pain a little.

"Don't feel badly, Mac," he said. "You raised some good points. Provocative ones. But they don't refute the evidence. The flight wasn't on a north heading, it was flying northeast. Off an assigned course. On a heading selected by the captain. At nine thousand feet toward a mountain eleven thousand feet high. And assuming we were wrong about the so-called excellent visibility, even assuming he couldn't have seen Bald Eagle, he still shouldn't have been where he was. Why, only the good Lord knows."

McKay smacked a fist into an open palm. "The 'why' is still the hole in your whole damned case," he said.

"You're grasping," Bengsten said patiently. "He probably was taking a little short cut. To intersect Airway 17 involved a dogleg. He could have decided at the last minute to knock off the dogleg and pick up 17 on a direct course. And that fits what you've developed yourself—that he never saw the mountain until it was too late. I'll admit our analysis of the weather stank. So that's it—and I'm sorry, Mac. I don't like to hang pilot error on you guys. But Culver pulled a rock. Agree?"

"No," said McDonald McKay politely but firmly.

It was Barbara who gave him the clue that cracked the case of Flight 363 wide open.

He went home that night feeling far less confident than his final remark to Bengsten would indicate. After supper, a disconsolate affair during which he told Barbara about the defeat in Bengsten's office, he got out the well-thumbed manual on fluxgates. He was rereading it when Barbara came over and perched on the arm of his chair.

"What's the gizmo on the diagram?" she asked.

"That? Let's see. That's the automatic erection mechanism."

"Sounds pornographic," she said. "And just what, lover, is an automatic erection mechanism?"

McKay didn't really feel like explaining, but one of the things he loved about his wife was her interest in his work. He didn't always welcome discussing it with her, particularly technical matters, but he never brushed her off impatiently. Nor did he now. He tried to give her a simple idea of how the device worked.

"When your gyro is tilted for some reason," he finally concluded, "this pornographic gizmo, as you so delicately phrased it, automatically cages and brings it back to level. Understand?"

"Affirmative. Can I ask a stupid question?"

"The only stupid question you could ask me is whether I still loved you. So ask."

"I've gotten it through my female skull what you think happened to Les. So why didn't this erection thing work in his case?"

"Probably because it took too long to cage automatically. By the time it caged and corrected the bum heading, he already was at Bald Eagle."

"How long does this . . . this caging take?"

"Oh, I suppose maybe about five minutes. Depends on the degree of tilt. It would . . ."

Something flashed in his mind, like a fire warning light suddenly glowing blood-red on an instrument panel and the angry alert bell going off simultaneously. He jumped out of the chair, dumping the manual unceremoniously on the floor, and grabbed Barbara.

"Holy Orville Wright!" he shouted. "That's it. The erection mechanism. That's why the RMI reading they found and the impact heading were almost the same."

Barbara was pleased but puzzled. "Did I say something clever?"

"Clever, my wing flaps. Honey, you said something bordering on pure genius. You beautiful, brilliant wife. You just dropped an A-bomb."

The next morning he asked Shea who in Midwest was considered an expert on fluxgates.

"Herb Dillman, head of Engineering," Shea told him. "Hey, are you still on Culver's accident? I thought Bengsten clobbered you."

"He didn't exactly pat me on the head. But I've got a notion we can reopen the case, depending on what I can get from this guy—Dillman?"

"Yeh. Wanna unload on me?"

"No, not yet Johnny. This time I'm gonna make damned sure."

"You'd better be damned sure," the chief pilot said bluntly. "They've already reconsidered it once. If they reopen it again, it'll be like the second coming. I'll give Herb a ring and tell him you're on the way down."

McKay found Dillman in his office. The Engineering chief was surprisingly youthful in appearance, a slim, bespectacled, rather scholarly type who greeted McKay in friendly fashion.

"Shea told me you wanted to know something about flux-gates," he said. "From what I've heard, I'm not sure I can teach you anything. That was a damned fine idea you had for hooking the Convair RMI's to different compasses."

"Thanks, Mr. Dillman, but I'm still in grammar school on that instrument. What I need from you is some dope on the automatic erection mechanism."

Dillman raised his eyebrows to half-staff. "Like what?"

"I guess you know the details of our Platte crash?"

"Only too well."

"What I'm after is a way to prove that a tilted gyro fluxgate could create a serious compass error, bad enough to steer a pilot into a mountain, and yet correct itself by the time he actually impacted."

Dillman looked at the young pilot with fresh respect. "I see what you're driving at. You figure Culver's fluxgate went haywire, then the erection mechanism corrected the error."

"Right. But the correction wasn't soon enough. We lost our case because his RMI at time of impact showed a northeast heading. That hung him. I've been studying that automatic gyro-erection setup all night. I'm positive Les had a compass error that gradually disappeared over a period of five minutes, but I gotta have a way to demonstrate it to the CAB."

Herb Dillman whistled. "It won't be easy," he warned. "We'd need the maximum and minimum rates a tilted gyro will erect. Of course, we could get those from the manufacturer's maintenance manual. Then we'll have to study every compass error that's possible from different degrees and direction of tilt. It's tough, but not impossible."

"Could you show all this data on some kind of a chart?" McKay asked.

"Sure. I have a guy in this department who's a crackerjack at that kind of thing. If you'd supply him with Culver's ground speed at various stages of the flight, he could plot you a series of curves representing different flight paths."

"I only need one flight path," McKay said. "The one Les took."

"Oh no," cautioned the Engineering chief. "You need a whole series of flight paths. Each one will have to represent what would happen from your various combinations of gyro tilt, the gyro erection rate, and the effects on the indicated heading. You're trying to prove something to the CAB, not just yourself. Follow me?"

"Not quite."

"Well, it's impossible to determine exactly the degree of tilt Culver had. So what you have to show is a whole flock of different tilts, with different erection rates, each capable of steering that plane into a mountain at just about the moment the tilt was corrected. If your theory on the erection mechanism checks out with these flight path curves, you'll be showing the Board not just one possibility but several."

"That," said McKay, "is exactly what we need. How long will it take?"

"Oh, I dunno. Give us about a week. Better plan on spending a few hours with Joe Burnett. He's the one who'll be making up that chart. How about tomorrow night? That'll give me a chance to brief him on the project."

"Tomorrow's fine. And I'm sure grateful."

"Forget it," Dillman said with a slight smile. "You know, some of you pilots think Engineering sits around figuring ways to keep from spending money on whatever flight crews suggest. I just want you to realize that every man in this department would like to help get Culver off a hook."

Twelve days later Dillman called McKay, who had been getting impatient.

"Come see your display," Dillman said. "Took a little longer than I figured but Burnett did a helluva job."

It was just that. He had taken the crude plotted curves worked out with McKay and redrawn the graphs in color. Dillman had gone a step further, mainly with McKay's hoped-for session before the CAB in mind. He took the graphs to the airline's photographer and had them reproduced as slides.

McKay was not only delighted but vastly encouraged. Dillman ran off the slides through a projector. Each had red lines representing the gyro tilts, green lines portraying various flight paths, and blue lines showing different erection rates. On each slide the red, green, and blue lines all converged on a tiny X. The X marked the location of Bald Eagle Mountain.

"Satisfied?" Burnett asked.

"They're beautiful. Can I take them with me?"

"Sure," Dillman said. "Keep me posted. I'd like to sit in on your presentation if the CAB gives you another shot."

"I will," McKay promised. "It won't be for a while. I've got a few more shells I wanna load."

He showed the slides to Barnwell, Snorkel, and Shea, all of whom sat fascinated as the neatly drawn graphs told the story of Les Culver's last five minutes of life. For every set of colored, curving tracks ended at the tiny X.

"Boy, you've got something," Shea said. "Wonder why none of us thought of that erection business."

"I should have," McKay conceded. "I was just too cocksure about his having fluxgate trouble to begin with. When Bengsten lowered the boom, I had to backtrack. Barbara opened the door that night when she asked me about the erection mechanism."

"What'll you do now, Mac?" asked Snorkel. "Ask the CAB to reopen it?"

"Not till I line up a few more ducks. Johnny, you think we could borrow a Convair for a couple of hours?"

Shea hesitated, thinking how he could justify this to Kane. Then he thought the hell with it, Kane was a pilot once himself and he was just as anxious to clear Les Culver as anyone else.

"Got a good reason?"

"Yep. I'd like to simulate a flock of fluxgate malfunctions. Take a movie camera along and photograph the instrument panel. Matter of fact, I'd like to do it at Platte. It would be damned effective."

"Well," Shea said, "I'll ask Kane and keep your fingers crossed."

He did and Kane asked a blunt question: "Will it help Les?"

"I think so," the chief pilot replied. "McKay is really on to something. The better his presentation, the better our chances."

Kane thoughtfully tapped a pencil on his walnut desk. "You know, John, if McKay clears Culver with this fluxgate theory, he could wind up shifting the blame from the cockpit to the front office."

"Probably. But what's the difference? The legal eagles'll be getting fat no matter what the verdict."

"Sure. But the Board of Directors—and Mencken—would rather have pilot error than a management mistake. Dammit, John, McKay's already cost us a bundle with that fluxgate wiring setup."

"Agreed," Shea said sympathetically. "But you gotta admit it was a good idea to modify the wiring. Remember, I told you what happened to Barney coming into Dayton. We could have dropped two, not just one."

Kane swiveled his chair around and stared out the window overlooking the Midwest ramp area. *Tap, tap, tap* went the pencil on the arm of his luxurious, leather-upholstered chair. Shea didn't say a word. The vice president swiveled back and faced his chief pilot. "Tell McKay he can have the Convair. Even if we have to cancel a flight to give him the ship."

"Thanks, Ben. I sorta figured the pilot in you would see the light."

Kane laughed. "Get the hell out of here, Shea, before I change my mind."

Four days later a Midwest Convair—with McKay riding the jump seat and acting as "director"—took off from the same runway as Flight 363 and on a clear day for nearly three hours went through the various malfunctions, induced by tripping the fluxgate to an uncaged position, that were depicted on Burnett's slides. A Midwest captain with a flair for photography shot both the instrument panel and the chilling view of Bald Eagle looming up fast through the cockpit window.

Two weeks later McKay called Al Bengsten and requested another meeting on the Platte accident.

"You must be kidding, Mac," the CAB man said. "I thought I got you off that fluxgate crap."

"Look," McKay said quietly. "The Board will reopen a case provided there's new evidence. Right?"

"Yeh, but . . ."

"We've got new evidence. Yes or no?"

"Yes, you persistent sonofabitch. But you'd better have something really new."

McKay was tempted strongly to ask if Bengsten was aware of the automatic erection mechanism and resisted the impulse. He set a date for the following week. It arrived alarmingly soon, but McKay was ready.

Armed with both a slide and movie projector which Dillman volunteered to run, he faced not only Bengsten and four Bureau of Safety associates, but the chairman of the Civil

Aeronautics Board and the investigator-in-charge of the Platte accident, Phil Baldwin. Bengsten had said nothing to McKay, but the instinct nurtured by years in the crash investigative field—and the subconscious feeling that not all was kosher about Les Culver's accident—had prompted him to summon Baldwin from Los Angeles.

McKay plunged into a review of the refuting facts concerning the supposed "excellent visibility" the crew of 363 had enjoyed. He emphasized the precautions Culver had taken to make sure he understood the clearance via the Comstock intersection. He cited the finding that the radio navigational equipment had been set to follow the assigned route. He admitted the apparent connection between the heading on the impact-seized RMI dial and the final impact heading determined by an unimpeachable sun compass. Then he went into the workings of the automatic erection safeguard and showed the slides and movies.

When Bengsten turned on the lights in the darkened room, nobody spoke for a full two minutes. Then Baldwin posed a question.

"Okay," he said, "you've raised a good possibility. But you still haven't explained why the malfunction wouldn't have shown up instantly on their course deviation indicators."

"Because," McKay said quickly, "to comply with the Comstock clearance, one of the two indicators had to be set to that intersection. Only the other one would have been available for checking their position. And there were a lot of reasons why it wouldn't have shown a wrong course."

"Like what?" asked Baldwin with a trace of sarcasm.

"Like a malfunction in the indicator itself. They depend on some pretty complicated electronic circuits. Or the radio transmitter at Platte might have transmitted a temporarily false signal. I have here depositions on two separate reports from a Continental flight just five weeks ago and a TWA pilot the following day that the Platte localizer seemed to be giving false signals."

"The Platte localizer," Bengsten reminded him sharply,

"was checked the day after the Midwest crash. It worked perfectly."

"I asked the CAA about the Continental and TWA reports," McKay said. "Checks were run right after they filed their false signal reports and everything was normal. The false signal apparently was intermittent. I'd like to point out there are a number of highly secret military installations in the Platte area. The localizer transmitter could have been distorted by interference from an unknown radio transmission."

Baldwin still wasn't buying it. "Wait a minute," he interrupted. "There's a localizer monitoring system at Platte. If that signal had been phony, the control tower would have gotten an alarm."

McKay mentally thanked himself for the advance planning he had performed before the meeting. He pulled out of a briefcase a piece of paper. "There should have been an alarm in the tower," he replied. "But this is a communication from the CAA in connection with the two Continental and TWA false signal reports. In both cases there was no alarm recorded. We've been advised by the CAA they're overhauling the entire Platte localizer antenna system."

The CAB chairman stirred restlessly in his chair. "Mr. McKay," he said, "it seems to me all this would involve quite a few coincidences. Your automatic correction of a compass error at just the right time. One of your course deviation instruments going bad. Your false localizer signals. All would have to occur just about simultaneously. As I said, this would add up to a mighty unusual series of coincidences."

"It was a mighty unusual accident," McKay answered soberly. "May I point out, sir, that all the evidence points to Captain Culver's *intending* to take the assigned course? This leaves us with the necessity of determining why he did not. I submit there is only one possible explanation—unless you fall back on deliberate suicide. A faulty fluxgate compass must have decoyed the flight to destruction. I'd also like to remind you that Midwest has considered this possibility sufficiently serious to modify the RMI installation on all our

Convairs. Speaking for ALPA, if not for Midwest, we respectfully urge the Board to evaluate the evidence presented today and consider the issuance of a new probable cause."

McKay put all his papers and notes back in the briefcase and sat down. He was physically and emotionally exhausted. He looked at his watch and discovered the entire presentation had taken a little over two hours. It felt like twenty.

"Speaking for the Board," the chairman said, "I'd like to compliment you. I want to assure you the Bureau of Safety and the full CAB will consider this evidence on its merits."

"I'll second that," Bengsten commented. But what was more satisfactory to McKay was Bengsten's whispered remark as they left the room. "Nice going, Mac."

McKay went back to flying the line on a regular basis. Twice he called Bengsten to ask when an amended report might be issued. Both times the CAB man chided him for impatience. Approximately two months later Bengsten asked him to come to his office. As soon as McKay walked in he handed him the draft of the third report on the Platte crash. The pilot's eyes focused immediately on the key paragraph.

> The Board determines that the probable cause of this accident is unknown. But the possibility of fluxgate compass error, while unproven, is a strong likelihood according to all available evidence.

Chapter 11

The Culver case brought McKay a minor measure of fame and a major measure of respect from his flying brethren. The CAB report, of course, had made no mention of his role. But the airman's grapevine, as mysteriously effective as that of a prison, quickly spread the word that a young Midwest captain named McKay had almost singlehandedly cleared a fellow pilot and forced the CAB into one of its rare reversals.

McKay thought the story would remain pretty well confined within Midwest's own borders. But sometimes he met pilots from other carriers who would say, "McKay . . . McKay . . . aren't you the guy who cracked that Platte accident?" He even got several pilot letters commending him, and at the first ALPA meeting he attended after the revised CAB report came out, the members gave him a standing ovation as he walked into the room.

He was human enough to be touched and proud. He also was smart enough to know he had been lucky as well as persevering. His failure to grasp the significance of the impact-seized RMI dial had nearly been his downfall, just as over-reliance on that one facet of the case had been the Board's downfall. It had almost beaten him, and he was well aware that only Barbara's chance remark had given him the opening through which he finally glimpsed the truth.

It was typical of him that he spent considerably more time worrying about the mistakes he had made than patting himself on the back for the successful outcome. He had learned a great deal, such as the folly of pinning everything on a theory without going the vital step farther and buttressing theory with some facts. He also recognized that in a reverse fashion, this had been the CAB's weakness—they had pinned almost everything on a single fact, which ran contrary to a logical theory, and then had largely failed to follow up the theory.

Al Bengsten told him as much one day when the CAB man invited him to lunch. They got into a discussion of the philosophy of accident investigation and McKay, perhaps a bit too flushed with victory, remarked that the Bureau hadn't exactly been objective or even thorough in the Platte inquiry.

"You weren't too thorough yourself, Mac," Bengsten said. "You could have beat us over the head a lot earlier if you had read that complete file. You skipped over the RMI report like it was an ink blot—and yet our whole indictment of Culver revolved around that one item. Frankly, my eager young friend, you damned near blew it. Although I might add, we *did* blow it. But good."

"You're right," McKay admitted. "I think I learned a few lessons. Maybe some you'll wish I hadn't learned."

"You're wrong there," Bengsten said earnestly. "I've said it before and I'll say it again, get rid of the idea that we're always ready to lower the boom on the crew."

"From the events of the last few months," McKay couldn't resist saying, "I kinda got that impression."

"I can't say that I blame you. It was about the sloppiest handling of an investigation I can remember. We screwed up with that half-ass suicide assumption, we mishandled the weather factor, we let that RMI impact heading override all the evidence that Culver wanted to head north, and to cap our fine performance we never even thought of the erection mechanism. Which reminds me, you happy with Midwest?"

McKay was startled at the question.

"Sure. Very happy. Why?"

"I wish you'd come with the Bureau."

McKay felt as if Bengsten had just pinned a medal on him. He was touched, pleased, and a little embarrassed. "You mean it?"

"I wouldn't have said it if I hadn't meant it. Don't get a swelled head, but you'd make one hell of an investigator. You've got brains, guts, curiosity, and you don't mind digging. And you're a pilot."

"The latter qualification escapes me," McKay said with a half smile.

"It shouldn't. We need pilots in our business. Men who know how airline crews think and work. Who know their own weaknesses—and their own strengths. That's one reason we invite ALPA to be on our teams. We always can use a pilot's viewpoint as well as his professional skill. Maybe we do make too many assumptions about pilot error—and maybe it's because we don't understand pilots as well as they understand themselves. Let me put it this way, Mac. If Phil Baldwin had been an ex-airline pilot, you wouldn't have even gotten into the act. And we wouldn't have written three different reports. Culver's accident was a perfect example of how a pilot mentality would have kept us out of the wrong detours we took."

"Believe me, Al, I'm flattered. But I'd hate to leave the line right now."

"Too much of a salary drop?"

"Partially. But I like my job, too. And I'm going to be learning a helluva lot more about flying and aviation as a captain. I don't think I could get the same education just figuring out why somebody or something went wrong."

"Well," Bengsten said grudgingly, "I guess you'd make a better investigator if you were a more experienced pilot. But the offer still stands. You've got a job with me any time you want it."

"I appreciate that. More than you'll ever know."

McKay started to get up but Bengsten motioned him to sit down again. "Mac, I've been kicking around an idea. Like to sound you out on it."

"Shoot."

"These teams we have—Structures, Power Plants, Witnesses—you know the setup. Well, what I was thinking about was adding another team. Call it the human factor, or human factors. Delve more into crew personalities. Their home life. What kind of people they were. See if we can find out anything about a pilot to explain why he pulls a rock, not just that he pulled one. Was he taking pills or seeing a psychiatrist or sleeping with too many women or worrying about a mortgage? What do you think?"

"It sounds," McKay said cautiously, "like you're going to solve crashes with some retroactive head-shrinking."

"No. That's not what I mean. Barney Barnwell's been telling me for years that we shouldn't stop at a pilot-error verdict. I agree. If we had a pattern of engine malfunctions or structural failures that caused crashes, we'd examine the pattern to find out why it developed. Yet even though human error is the leading cause of accidents, we've ignored investigating the facts that might have led up to the error."

"Now you're making sense," McKay said.

"I think so. It's my theory that with pilot training what it is today—and it's going to get better—with good airplanes and competent crews, normally there shouldn't be any reason for a really serious bonehead. It's also my hunch that the seeds for a lot of cockpit mistakes are planted long before the actual accident. It might be something that happened during training. Maybe some subconscious, inbred fear about a certain phase of flying—a fear a pilot doesn't even know exists. It lies dormant inside him until one night he runs into a runway that's too short and too slippery and the approach lighting is lousy and all of a sudden this fear, or lack of self-confidence in just this one set of circumstances, takes over and bang! Six months later we say pilot error."

"Are you saying that most crashes have a psychological base?"

"No. I'm saying that some crashes *might* have such a base. And it's the one area where we're doing absolutely nothing. I don't mean to imply that we have to psychoanalyze in every case. The possibility of some subconscious fear or weakness was just one example. It's more likely that a pilot's mistake could be traced to something as simple as an apparently minor deficiency in a training curriculum."

McKay was getting thoroughly interested. The discourse reminded him of his debate with Barnwell after the Leesburg hearing, when Barney had defended the belligerence of airmen toward a pilot-error verdict. Now he could not help challenging Bengsten in a different way.

"The main trouble with this human factors gimmick—good name, by the way—is the unavoidable fact that the front end of the plane hits the ground first. You don't get much chance to interview pilots who don't walk away."

"Granted. I admit there are a lot of problems. A human factors team would be strictly experimental to start with.

Most pilots who do survive a crash are in a state of shock. I've seen them so affected by the traumatic experience of an accident, they can't even recall driving to the airport that morning—let alone what happened in the air. That reminds me. Remember that Dixie Airlines' DC-3 that hit the mountain down in southern Virginia a few months ago?"

McKay nodded.

"The report isn't out yet, but it'll be pilot error. The poor bastard was letting down ten miles to the left of his course. We're calling it a navigation mistake. There were some survivors but unfortunately not from the flight deck. You heard any scuttlebutt about the captain?"

"No," McKay said. "We don't see many Dixie crews."

"Well, I heard some. That captain was a damned fine pilot. Perfect safety record. Excellent reputation. He had about as much chance of committing an inexcusable navigation error as I have of becoming president. Yet he did. So I went around and did some informal human-factors checking, so to speak. I found out his wife was shacking up with anyone wearing pants. It was common gossip around the airline, but I couldn't latch on to any indication that the pilot knew about it. I'm out of cigarettes, Mac—got one?"

McKay handed him one. Bengsten went on.

"I had to take it easy—that kind of prying isn't exactly welcome. But luckily Dixie's chief pilot is an old friend of mine. He introduced me to some of the other pilots and they finally talked freely. They didn't think the captain was aware of his wife's being a nympho. They figured she kept him so damned busy in bed he never dreamed she was playing around. But I'm not so sure. So I got to thinking. Suppose he had survived the crash. We might have found out if he had real personal problems, serious enough to detract from his flying proficiency."

McKay nodded. "I see what you mean. Mental distraction could have caused the navigation mistake."

"You're on the beam, friend. His was a case where if he had survived, a human factors team might have added an extenuating circumstance to pilot error. In other words, we would have determined not only what happened but why. Don't quote me, Mac, but that Dixie crash is what helped get me off course on Culver. I never bought the suicide bit, yet I kept thinking there was a parallel in the two accidents. Culver was known to have domestic troubles. I figured mental distraction might have been involved at Platte, too."

"You still think so?"

"No, guess I don't. You've proved your point very well. Jesus—it's almost two. I gotta get back to work."

McKay insisted in picking up the check, over Bengsten's protest. "I consider talking to you part of my aviation education," he laughed. "You said only one thing that bothers me."

"What's that?"

"I wonder if I'm walking around with the seeds of an accident inside me, waiting for a set of circumstances to make 'em sprout."

"I doubt it. Shea runs as good a training lash-up as there is. You're happily married and you're well adjusted, far as I know. Remember, this seed theory—if you wanna call it that —applies probably to about one out of five thousand pilots. Let's hit the road."

They went their separate ways outside the restaurant. Bengsten, standing by the curb waiting for a taxi, watched the tall figure of the pilot moving away down the street. McKay was one fine person, he thought. Then he had an uncomfortable notion. He wondered how objective he could be if he ever had to investigate an accident involving McDonald McKay.

By early 1957, Midwest had acquired twenty-five new DC-7's, the O'Brians had acquired three more children, and McDonald McKay had established a real reputation as an authority on air safety.

The airline itself was maturing from its hectic, sometimes makeshift days of the immediate postwar years into a sprawling, slickly run giant. It won from the CAB an extension of its

Chicago–Denver route to Seattle, giving it transcontinental status. It built a new eighteen-million-dollar headquarters building two miles south of National Airport, on the banks of the Potomac. The structure included magnificent crew training facilities, complete with flight simulators for pilots and elaborate cabin mock-ups for the stewardess school which had been moved from Chicago.

The simulators were reproductions of Midwest's Convair and new DC-7 cockpits. The controls were hooked to electronic tubes and wiring in big metal cabinets outside the marvelously realistic flight deck. An instructor pushing a button on a panel could send to the controls and instruments a signal re-creating every known flight situation, normal and abnormal, from engine fires to a seventy-mile-an-hour crosswind on landing. Hydraulic jacks supplied motion and there were even engine sound effects.

The pilots greeted the simulator with suspicion at first, then admitted it was the best training device they had ever seen. They gave it such affectionate names as "The Monster" and "Captain Humbilizer." For the airline, it meant a flight training cost of $125 an hour compared to $1200 an hour for using an actual airplane—not to mention the fact that the company wasn't risking one of its new $2.5 million DC-7's on risky maneuvers. For the pilots it meant better training, not only during initial qualifications but for recurrent emergency checks and upgrading.

O'Brian invested some money with another captain in a filling station near his home. Not that he needed an avocation. Raising five children was avocation enough, and the twins— growing up fast—could be double-barreled trouble. They actually got him into hot water by nearly causing him to miss a trip—a cardinal sin with Midwest or any airline.

He had asked crew schedule to phone him at five for a six-thirty flight because their clock radio-alarm was on the blink. The twins hid the phone in the closet and Paddy never heard it ring. Pat woke up at five forty-five, fortunately, and O'Brian just made it to the airport in time. He spent at least part of the day thinking up punishment to fit the crime, finally settled on a one-week television moratorium, and arrived home to be informed that the twins both had chicken pox.

"Well, they've still got to be punished," he decreed to Pat.

"Sure, honey, but while you're thinking up their sentences, move the TV set into their bedroom."

McKay's nonflying, nonfamily world was wrapped up in various ALPA safety projects and assignments. He succeeded Barnwell as chairman of the Midwest council's safety committee and six months later was named safety chairman for ALPA's eastern region.

He hesitated before taking the latter job because he feared it would take too much time away from line flying. But Barnwell begged him, Shea encouraged him, and Tom Dayton—ALPA's safety and engineering representative whom he had met at the CAB hearing on Jim Steele's accident—settled the issue.

"I won't give you any soft soap, Mac," Dayton said. "It's a crummy, thankless job. It sure as hell won't help your own flying. But somebody's got to do it. And in the long run you'll be helping ALPA and pilots and even every airline in the country more than you would be flying all your trips."

McKay liked Dayton. He was a rather short, slightly potbellied Georgian who had been an air traffic controller and a damned good one. He was blunt, scrupulously honest, and not a little cynical—a quality which, when he had too much to drink, he extended to pilots. "The troops," he called them, half affectionately and half sarcastically.

It was Dayton who introduced McKay to what might be termed the Public Eye. On June 30, 1956, a TWA Constellation and a United DC-7 collided over the Grand Canyon. It was out of McKay's technical jurisdiction as eastern region safety chairman, but he got involved in the case when a Senate subcommittee decided to investigate the tragedy—somehow ignoring the fact that the CAB already was investigating the same accident.

ALPA was invited to appear at the Senate hearings. Dayton asked McKay to represent the pilots' union, because ALPA's president was out of the country.

"But why, Tom? Let some pilot from TWA or United do it. Their airlines were the ones involved."

"That's exactly why a pilot from a third carrier would be more effective. No ax to grind. Besides, you have a more impressive title—regional safety chairman. I'll help you with your testimony. And you'll look good on the witness stand. You're even getting a little gray around the temples."

Barbara could not have been any prouder if he had told her he was going to the White House to advise Eisenhower. McKay was not so sanguine. He still had a high school civics class notion that United States Senators were very sharp, learned persons a lot more intelligent than a mere airline captain.

"I'll probably make an ass out of myself," he warned her. "I hope you're not planning to be there."

"I wouldn't miss it. My husband—before a Senate committee!"

Dayton, as an ex-controller, was particularly good on Air Traffic Control problems and wrote most of McKay's testimony. He sat down in the walnut-paneled hearing room on the first day of the hearing, expecting to listen to numerous other witnesses before he was called. The committee chairman delivered a flowery oration on the purposes of the hearing—none of which included his strong conviction that with an election coming up in the fall he could use some publicity. The chairman then announced:

"Our first witness will be Captain McKay of the Air Line Pilots Association. Is Captain McKay present?"

The startled McKay rose, walked to the witness chair conscious of Barbara's eyes on him, and was sworn in.

"My name is McDonald McKay," he began reading. "I am a captain with Midwest Airlines and I am regional safety chairman for ALPA. We appreciate the opportunity to present ALPA's views on what we believe is a growing collision menace. . . ."

The statement Dayton had prepared was largely a recitation of the Grand Canyon circumstances and why the same circumstances could occur again unless corrective action was taken. Both TWA and United had left Los Angeles heading east and flying "off-airways"—in airspace uncontrolled by ATC centers. The controlled airways were not as direct or had too much traffic, McKay explained, so in choosing to fly in uncontrolled airspace, the pilots assumed sole responsibility for avoiding other planes.

TWA, originally assigned to a lower altitude, had been given permission to climb a thousand feet above the clouds. In doing so, he had to reach twenty-one thousand feet—the same altitude as United. TWA was told United was at twenty-one thousand, but the undermanned ATC centers along the route were too busy to warn United of TWA's presence. They had their hands full with traffic on controlled airways and could not accept responsibility for off-airways traffic.

"Thus," McKay continued to read, "the pattern was set. Insufficient Federal airways, inadequate ATC facilities, and obsolete regulations that completely ignored the visual handicaps of pilots.

"Let me give you a few facts about those handicaps, and the fallacy of expecting flight crews to follow this rule of 'see and be seen.' The cockpit has about the same proportion of visibility in all directions as the human eyeball. In other words, from the cockpit you cannot see directly below or directly behind your aircraft, any more than you can see the top, base, or back of your head.

"Now, you combine these limitations of visibility with the speed factor. A .45-caliber bullet travels at 522 miles per hour. The closure speed of two modern transports is more than six hundred miles an hour. Tests have shown that when a pilot approaches at three hundred miles an hour an object that is standing still, he has only twelve seconds from the moment he spots it to complete an evasive maneuver. If the object is approaching him at the same speed, he has only one tenth of a second to make up his mind what to do. That one tenth of a second means he must start his evasive action from a distance of at least two miles. At one mile, he could not avoid collision.

"Complicating both the vision and speed factors is another problem associated with high-altitude flight. At such altitudes and in clear skies, a pilot can be affected by an optical phenomenon known as empty field myopia. Literally, he suffers temporary nearsightedness and tends to focus his eyes on a location less than six feet in front of his cockpit windshield.

"Grand Canyon was an impossible accident. It occurred in clear weather, at a high altitude, and in virtually empty airspace. ALPA believes if such a tragedy could happen over the Grand Canyon, it is far more likely to happen in congested areas—unless the Air Traffic Control system is modernized, given such tools as en-route radar separation, strengthened with more personnel and supplied with a network of aerial superhighways instead of obsolete two-lane roads. And this must be done in the next few years because things are going to get worse before they can get better. By 1960 the airways will be filled with turbo-props and pure jets, with closure speeds of up to twelve hundred miles per hour. The reforms must be started now or the forthcoming jet age will be blackened by more Grand Canyons. Thank you."

There was a hum of reaction throughout the room as McKay put the prepared statement back in a briefcase.

"Thank you, Captain, uh, McKay," said the chairman. "Are there any questions from members of the committee? I see my distinguished colleague, Senator Brunswick, has one."

Brunswick was a large, florid-faced man with snow-white hair and a syrupy voice.

"A very interesting statement, Captain," he said in a tone of voice indicating that he felt the statement was full of prune juice. "However, the points you raised and your suggestions for correcting the situation seem to ignore the facts. What you'd like to do is have the Federal government spend millions on the airways to keep airline planes from running into each other. I fail to see the necessity for undertaking huge expenditures for the sole purpose of protecting a couple of thousand civil transports. If the airlines need such protection, they should be paying for such protection themselves. Now, it also is . . ."

"Just a minute, Senator," McKay interrupted. "Modernized Air Traffic Control is needed for more than just our two thousand commercial transports. We also have approximately twenty thousand military aircraft and about sixty thousand general aviation planes sharing this limited airspace. It's not a question of keeping just the airliners from colliding. They also could collide with military planes or private planes. The 128 deaths at Grand Canyon could be multiplied a few dozen times."

"Young man," Brunswick boomed oratorically, "I share with the American people a tremendous sense of sorrow over the tragedy of last June thirtieth. But my deep, personal, and most sincere grief and concern does not blind me to the facts. As a member of this committee, I was one of the first on the scene of that accident. I investigated it firsthand. I remind you, Captain McKay, that there has been considerable speculation that both pilots were sightseeing. Sightseeing, I repeat. Your remarks about limited cockpit visibility were most provocative, but perhaps we should not be pointing a finger of blame at the alleged inadequacies of Air Traffic Control. Perhaps we should be asking why those two pilots were indulging in sightseeing activities."

"Are you quite sure, Senator, that they were sightseeing?"

"As I said, there was considerable speculation, based on very logical evidence. Airlines crews have been known to maneuver their planes in the Grand Canyon area to give passengers a better view and to allow picture-taking."

"There was a cloud cover over the Grand Canyon that day, Senator, at approximately twenty thousand feet and the cover extended downward to about twelve thousand feet. Both aircraft were at twenty-one thousand. The possibility of sight-seeing has been thoroughly discarded."

"It hasn't been discarded in my mind, Captain," Bruns-wick remarked with an air of rock-ribbed certainty. "Perhaps we should wait for the Civil Aeronautics Board verdict on this unfortunate accident before drawing any conclusions."

"Perhaps you should have waited for the CAB verdict before you held these hearings," the pilot snapped.

Dayton thought, Now he's done it—he's insulted Congress. Barbara thought, Oh brave husband, I hope you know what you're doing. The press table thought, The guy has guts but heaven help him.

The chairman started to say something but Senator Bruns-wick held up his hand.

"One moment, Mr. Chairman. Let me ask the witness if he is challenging the right of this committee to investigate what amounts to a crime against the American people."

Pencils at the press table were scribbling furiously. McKay knew he was in hot water up to the top of his rudder, but he also was mad.

"Senator, I do not challenge the right of the Congress to investigate anything it pleases. But it was you who pointed the finger of blame at the cockpit. I'd like to point my own finger of blame for 128 deaths. At Congress. At every man in Congress who ever voted against appropriations that would have meant greater air safety."

Brunswick's florid face turned scarlet.

"You owe every member of this committee an explanation for that libelous, totally unjustified remark, Captain. Along with an apology, I might add."

"I'll be happy to explain, but I won't apologize," McKay said with almost deadly quietness. "Grand Canyon happened because Congress has failed to give the CAA adequate funds to modernize the Air Traffic Control system. The ATC appropriation for this fiscal year was sixteen million dollars. Every study done on the problem has pinpointed the need for spending at least four times that much just to start with. Sixteen million merely keeps the system going as it is—there are no funds for improvement or modernization or even research."

"I am well acquainted with the spending program for the CAA," Brunswick said. "You say four times the current appropriation is needed. The CAA itself never asked for that amount."

McKay was glad he had done some legislative research. Actually, he had wanted to incorporate the money angle into the prepared statement but Dayton said it might raise some hackles unnecessarily. McKay had the facts at his fingertips and Brunswick had just handed him a fat target to fire at.

"No," the pilot agreed. "The CAA did not ask for what it needed. But it also failed to get even what it did ask for. And never has—not in the last decade. Senator, believe me, I'm not trying to make wild accusations against you or any other Congressman. But I'd like to remind this committee that ALPA and the airlines themselves have been warning Congress for at least the past five years that a Grand Canyon was going to occur. It did. We don't ask that you do any breast-beating over the past. We merely plead that you do some soul-searching for the future."

Brunswick started to launch into a rebuttal but another Senator broke in. This was Maloney, a Westerner with a suntanned, leathery face and piercing eyes.

"Let's not turn this into a personal debate," he remarked. "There are a good many other witnesses to be heard from. Captain McKay, as far as I'm concerned, has given this committee some very frank views and I don't think they call for any apology. If we're here to prevent future Grand Canyons from happening, and Congress is in the least way responsible for the events of June thirtieth, we'd better accept that responsibility like men. Captain, I'd like to ask one more question, or perhaps make one observation, if I may."

McKay nodded gratefully.

"Captain, I agree with you that funding for the Air Traffic

Control system has been, to put it charitably, inadequate. But Senator Brunswick has raised a very good point. The CAA has never come to Congress and requested the money you say all the experts agree is necessary."

"I know that, sir. I'm no expert on this subject, but it's my impression that the trouble lies in the CAA's being part of the Commerce Department. Its own budget requests are watered down even before they get to Congress."

"I take it, then, that pilots believe the CAA should be independent of the Commerce Department?"

"In this area," McKay answered, "I can't speak for all pilots. I do know that some of us would rather see an independent air agency, just as the CAB is independent. It seems obvious that the CAA's efforts are diluted because it is part of a larger government department that has no overriding interest in aviation."

"Very interesting," Maloney commented. "Mr. Chairman, I suggest we call the next witness."

"Any more questions of Captain McKay?" the chairman queried.

There were none. A couple of Senators stared at him rather reproachfully, Brunswick, unmollified, glared at him. Maloney had a tiny smile on his lips and began writing in a notebook. McKay sat down next to Dayton, looked around for Barbara, and was rewarded by her smile and wink.

"Nice going," Tom whispered. "I thought for a minute you were in the soup but you climbed out—and thank God for Maloney."

The next witness was the president of the Air Transportation Association, trade organization for the U.S. scheduled airlines. In somewhat politer, more diplomatic language, he said the same things McKay had. When the hearing recessed for lunch, McKay found Barbara in the crowd.

"You were great, honey. I wanted to spit in that Senator's eye. Brunswick, I mean. The tall man with the tanned face, he was nice."

"Thank you, ma'am," said a voice in back of them.

The McKays turned around to find Senator Maloney smiling at them.

"I agree with you, Captain McKay did an exemplary job. This, I take it, is Mrs. McKay?"

"My wife Barbara, Senator. Darling, this is Senator Maloney."

"My pleasure, ma'am. I wonder if you both would do me the honor of lunching with me. Perhaps you haven't had the opportunity to sample the Senate restaurant's famous bean soup."

Dayton already had gone off to another luncheon appointment. McKay accepted, feeling flattered and also knowing that Barbara would have shot him if he had declined. Maloney took them to the restaurant and was kept busy pointing out to Barbara various Senators, whose names were household words but most of whom she never could have recognized in person.

While she was thrilled at the experience (although she privately considered the Senate's vaunted bean soup overrated), she was even more pleased at the way Maloney and McKay got along. The Senator was surprisingly knowledgeable about some aviation technical matters but was not hesitant to admit when one came up he didn't understand. He had heard, for example, that the DC-7 was having a higher-than-normal rate of engine failures and he questioned McKay closely on the design of the Seven's power plants.

They had finished dessert and had ordered second cups of coffee when Maloney broached the problem uppermost in his mind.

"I'm glad you slapped down Brunswick," he said. "He had it coming. For one thing, he never should have gone trotting off to that Grand Canyon crash. That's a habit of ours I wish we'd eliminate. We just get in the way of legitimate investigators and we have no business making public statements in the course of an investigation. But aside from that, Captain, he was right about the CAA. They've shown no aggressiveness in pushing for Air Traffic Control reforms. And please don't take offense, but I've heard they also show no aggressiveness in their regulatory duties. Particularly with pilots."

"Don't quote me, sir," McKay confessed, "but I agree with you. There are times when I think CAA inspectors should be a lot tougher. Pilots can get complacent."

"Do you think that the trouble lies largely in its satellite status?"

"Satellite? You mean because it's part of Commerce? I think that's the heart of the problem. Frankly, Senator, when that was brought up this morning, I felt somewhat inadequate to discuss it intelligently. It's not a subject I've thought through. More of an impression than a flat opinion."

Maloney nodded. "I haven't thought it through, either," he said. "But I think I'd better start thinking about it. I have a rather vague idea in the back of my mind. A bill I'd like to propose one of these days, and perhaps I should devote more time to it. Briefly, I'd like to have Congress create a new independent agency to regulate civil aviation. As I say, I haven't crystallized my views, but I have gone so far as to think up a name for it."

"Okay," smiled McKay. "I'm curious. What would you call it?"

"The Federal Aviation Agency," said the Senator.

It was two years later that Congress passed and President Eisenhower signed into law a bill establishing the Federal Aviation Agency. For McKay and fourteen thousand other airline pilots, the FAA meant a new way of life—more regulated, more harassed, and, when they finally got around to admitting it, somewhat safer.

Eisenhower named as the first Administrator former Air Force General Elwood R. "Pete" Quesada, who rocked ALPA back on its collective heels with such unpopular edicts as—slightly paraphrased—stay the hell in the cockpit unless you have to go to the blue room, and retire when you're sixty before you have a heart attack in the middle of an ILS approach.

McKay publicly supported ALPA's battle against such new FAA regulations. As a regional safety chairman he dutifully wrote letters and made speeches denouncing them. Privately, he had a strong suspicion that both he and ALPA were wasting their time. The union couldn't sell the traveling public on any notion, for example, that with the skies becoming more crowded with faster planes, pilots still had time to go back and chat with passengers. The sixty-year-old mandatory retirement rule he knew was unfair to a lot of older captains, but until science came up with a means of measuring physiological age as contrasted with chronological age, the regulation made sense.

McKay thought ALPA would be better off expending energy on more pertinent and less personal issues. As a pilot, he sympathized with fellow airmen who resented the tougher, stronger, and too frequently autocratic new agency with the natural enmity a motorist displays toward a traffic cop. But he realized that the greater authority and stricter regulation had to come. He felt pilots could live with it, if only because along with the newborn bureaucratic power came spending for safety.

Spending on new navigation aids. Radar for Air Traffic Control. Blueprints for an ATC system of the future. Approach and runway lighting. New airports. A trickle of water in a desert at first, then gradually a flood. Inevitably some of the money was poured down drains of undirected research, inefficiency, and wrong decisions. But for every step backward, the FAA was taking two steps forward and McKay settled for that progress even while he stirred restlessly against its slowness.

That there were abuses he could not deny. Too often FAA would order some air safety reform already informally adopted by pilots and airlines alike—then take public credit for merely legalizing it. Too often there were FAA actions aimed at relatively minor problems, attacking them with the ponderous weight of government *noblesse oblige* like an elephant declaring war on a mouse—while major problems went ignored and unsolved. Too often pilots were harassed, persecuted, and hamstrung by FAA inspectors who substituted Authority for their own inexperience and even incompetence. Too often FAA regulations issued in the name of safety could not be fought on any reasonable basis because to fight them was to denounce Virtue. And the FAA supplied the only definition of Virtue, permitting little argument, virtually no compromise, and seldom any rewrite.

The new agency reflected the personality of Quesada, who ran civil aviation like the ex-general he was. Autocratic, arbitrary, occasionally unreasonable. But also courageous, devoted to the job and its goals, and with an unyielding sense of integrity and public service. McKay attended one ALPA safety forum where Quesada was invited to speak. The atmosphere was not only chilly but icy with unspoken animosity. Quesada spoke for thirty minutes and left with a standing ovation.

"I admire his guts," Snorkel said to McKay after the speech. "He walked into a den of wolves, patted us on our heads, and told us to be good or else."

Snorkel's statement of grudging admiration was a fair summary. What the general had said was that the dawn of the jet age had brought new responsibility to the cockpit—and pilots had to assume it or have it forced on them like medicine. With which McDonald McKay agreed.

He himself was literally a stepchild of the jet age. While the senior captains bid the new Electras and 707's, the juniors continued to fly the Convairs and Constellations and DC-7's. Midwest had put the DC-7 into service in 1955 as the queen of its fleet—and in four years it was relegated to the status of a dowdy lady-in-waiting.

Midwest had been flying its jets for a year when McKay finally checked out on the DC-7. It brought him his first real exposure to a three-man cockpit crew. He had worked with flight engineers briefly on a few Connie trips, but it was entirely different issuing them orders instead of secretly sympathizing with them, as he had when he was a lowly first officer, for the overbearing attitude of a few captains toward the two-stripers.

They were a strange breed—independent, proud, and stubborn. Many were ex-mechanics with encyclopedic minds and an incredible knack of improvising. The knack was somewhat wasted in these days of more efficient maintenance and even stricter "do it by the book" rules than McKay had been taught in his early training days. He kept urging the flight engineers who flew with him to take pilot training.

"You're like cavalrymen in an army starting to re-equip with tanks," he told one FE. "You're a throwback to the days when you had to be able to fix a DC-3 starter with a piece of chicken wire. But in less than ten years we won't be flying anything except jets. We'll need three-man crews but the third man will have to be a pilot, not an FE sitting around poking an occasional button."

Sometimes the younger flight engineers agreed with him. The older ones, even if they agreed, pointed out they were too old to expose themselves to the ruthless rigors of pilot school. Whatever their views, McKay made a special effort to treat all FE's with courteous discipline, accepting them as crew members who had their own dignity and place in aviation. He even climbed down the throat of one arrogant first officer who snapped at a flight engineer with unjustified sarcasm. The FE barked back.

"Knock it off," was all McKay said when the tiff broke out in the cockpit. But later he got the copilot alone and let him have it.

"There aren't going to be arguments on any flight deck I'm running," he said quietly but with open anger. "If we ever get into a real nut-twister, I want teamwork and complete cooperation from every guy in that cockpit—or we'll all buy it."

"I'm sorry, skipper," the copilot apologized. "Those guys just rub me the wrong way. They're too damned clannish. They've even got their own union."

"They've got their own union," McKay reminded him, "because we wouldn't take them in ours. Which for my dough was the stupidest decision we ever made. Now we're talking about absorbing them and they want no part of ALPA, for which I don't blame them. So let's make sure you understand me—when those wheels break ground, all feuding and fighting and friction get left behind or the man causing the trouble gets off my airplane. Whether he's a first officer or a flight engineer makes no difference. Read me?"

His crews did read him. As he grew in experience he came to resemble Barnwell in the way he ran a flight deck. He asked—but it still was a command. He gently chided—but it still was a reaming. He suggested—but it still was an order. They knew it, appreciated it, and gave him their loyalty and affection as he had bestowed on his own favorite captains when he sat in the right seat.

He saw too little of Barney, who had gone on to the jets. Snorkel was flying Electras, a plane he declared to be the greatest piece of flying equipment ever designed. McKay was dead-heading once to an ALPA safety conference and Snorkel let him fly the ship. McKay, used to the comparatively stodgy and sluggish DC-7, nearly snap-rolled the big prop-jet the first time he banked.

"My God," he marveled. "She's like a fighter."

"A pilot's airplane," Snorkel agreed. "If we chopped three engines, she wouldn't lose a foot of altitude. If we had to abort a landing, you wouldn't believe what this baby'll do. Just touch the throttles and she'll climb like a goosed eagle."

Snorkel's love of the Electra was a large help in easing the pain of a traumatic experience on the ground. Captain Snodgrass was what the marketing experts would call an "impulse buyer"—meaning he was a sucker for anything that happened to catch his eye or fancy, particularly if there was a sale price on it. He was lackadaisically glancing through the classified section of the Washington *Star* one night when he came across an item advertising a 1949 Rolls-Royce for $4995. He ran into the kitchen to advise Marion they were about to become the proud owners of a Rolls for "only four thousand bucks."

Marion had lived with him too long to do anything but offer a few logical though futile arguments against it. Snorkel went over the next morning to the dealer who had advertised the car, and bought it in five minutes. He had been driving it for exactly two weeks when he happened to pull into a filling station for gas. Marion was with him, suffering in unspoken misery at the naked conspicuousness of the whole thing.

He got out of the Rolls and felt a fresh surge of unmitigated pride as the attendant walked around the car in obvious admiration.

"Like it?" Snorkel smirked, almost bursting with the sheer joy of possession.

"Sure do," said the attendant. "You really keep this old Packard in good shape."

Snorkel climbed back in. "Marion, if you say one goddamned thing I'll wrap this steering wheel around your neck."

He drove home in crushed, dejected silence. He sold the Rolls a week later, took a $500 loss, and threatened to leave his wife if she uttered one word about the episode to any Midwest pilot. Naturally, she told the story to everyone possible.

McKay missed flying with Snodgrass, but it was the kind of nostalgia one bestows on something like college days. It was fun and even wistful to recall them, but not with any great desire actually to relive them. He was too happy with Barbara and Nancy, with his flying and his safety work.

He sometimes worried about the latter being fair to Barbara, not only because of the too frequent times it took him away from home but in the knowledge that he could not fly forever. He envied Paddy's gas station as a solid symbol of future security and wondered if he, too, shouldn't be thinking of preparing himself for some kind of other business.

He took out loss of license insurance, a policy that would pay $25,000 if he was grounded through no fault of his own. But this was an inadequate sop to conscience, and one night he decided to resign as safety chairman—the night Barbara told him they were going to have another baby.

"This time," she announced, "it'd better be a boy."

"Boy or girl," McKay said, "it's about time I started being a real father. I'm gonna tell Snorkel they can start looking around for another pigeon. I might as well be married to ALPA and I've had it."

"If that's what you really want, honey," Barbara said gently.

"It's what I want. Isn't it what you want?"

She came over and perched on his lap. "Captain McKay, you are a very sweet and wonderful person and I love you very much. I also miss you very much when you're away. But I don't think you should quit the safety job."

"But I thought . . ."

"You think too much. Mac, I'd be proud of you if you were just a captain flying his trips. I've never told you this, but I'm even prouder of you because you're so much more than that. The day you testified before that Senate committee, I fell in love with you all over again. A wife's pride in her husband can be a very important part of a marriage."

"I'm grateful for your saying that, Barbara. But it's still not fair to you or Nancy or our next baby."

"Mac darling, if you're giving up safety work because of me, forget it. The first time, God forbid, there'd be a crash, you'd want to go running off and you'd feel guilty about not going. I'd rather be a little lonesome than know I was keeping you from something you felt you should be doing."

"Is this an order, Mrs. McKay?"

"No, it's not an order. It's still your decision. But I don't want you making a decision without knowing how I feel about it."

"It isn't just being away from home. I should be doing some planning for the future. Like Paddy and his gas station. Barney's selling real estate on the side. Snorkel's bought himself some property down on Chesapeake Bay—four cottages just to start with. The point is, I can't moonlight like that and keep up this safety business. I love you for saying it's important, for being proud of me, but you're important, too."

Barbara climbed off his lap and went into the kitchen for

a Coke. She brought him a beer. "How'd you know I wanted a beer?"

"Female intuition. Just like the female intuition that's telling me we shouldn't be worrying about your selling real estate or pumping gas. You're no dope, husband. If you had to quit flying tomorrow morning, you'd get a good job. Besides . . ." She paused.

"Besides what?"

"Well, I kinda have an idea that without your realizing it, maybe safety is your future when you have to leave the line. I don't know in what capacity or what kind of job, but I don't think you'll ever leave aviation."

"That's funny," McKay said. "I remember telling your father something like that the night I met him. Well, I'll think about it. Promise me one thing. If you ever get too lonesome, tell me."

"Promise. What'll we name our baby? McDonald junior?"

They named her Deborah and there were times when the McKays wondered if the genes of Captain Harrison Snodgrass had somehow wandered into their second daughter. Nancy was a quiet, solemn child with much of her father's personality. Debbie was 50 per cent imp and 50 per cent clown. Barbara worried that McKay might have preferred a son, but one look at his face when he came home from a flight and greeted his daughters was enough to convince her he worshiped them.

"You may never get to raise a pilot," she reminded him.

"So we'll raise stewardesses. Can you imagine me pinning wings on these two?"

"Nancy, no. Debbie, yes. She'll probably grow up to be another Mitch. Honey, will you answer the phone?"

It was Snorkel. Barbara heard McKay say, "You're kidding. That's wonderful, Snork. Hell, we'll have to throw him a party. When's he take over? Thanks for telling us, boy."

He hung up and blurted out the news to Barbara.

"Mencken's resigned. Kane's the new president and guess who's the new vice president for operations—Johnny Shea!"

"Oh, Mac, that's great. But we'll miss old K. J."

"He'll still be around. Chairman of the Board. But Ben Kane's a good man. And he's always worked well with Johnny. Now I wonder who'll be chief pilot? Barney, I hope."

It was Barnwell, a popular choice among all pilots. They threw Shea and Barney a stag party, at which they presented Shea with a gold-plated altimeter off a DC-3, mounted on a mahogany plaque. An engraved inscription underneath read:

TO JOHN SHEA—AIRMAN, BOSS AND
FRIEND, WHO TAUGHT US TO FLY AND LIVE STRAIGHT
May 5, 1962

Perhaps the emotional backwash of that evening still was in McKay two weeks later when he was called to the airport. A Midwest Convair landing at night had clipped a nav aids shack with its wheels, the gear collapsing as the pilot touched down. Nobody was hurt, fortunately, but the captain understandably was shaken when McKay talked to him in Operations about an hour later. Tom Dayton was there, too, listening laconically as the pilot explained what happened.

"Well, it's like I told that CAB guy, we must have had a crosswind nobody told us about and then the ship seemed to sink faster as if we weren't getting rated power."

"We've been trying to tell FAA that localizer shack is too close to the runway," Dayton commented.

"Maybe," McKay said, "but it's been there for God knows how long and nobody ever hit it before."

Dayton looked at him somewhat in surprise. McKay's voice had seemed unnecessarily sharp. McKay said to the copilot: "The approach seem normal to you? Good rate of descent, glide path okay?"

"Yes," the first officer said, glancing sideways at the captain rather ruefully.

"Were you satisfied with it?" McKay asked the captain.

"What the hell, how can you be satisfied with a landing that washes out a ship?"

"That's not what I asked you, Norm. Could that approach have passed a check ride?"

"Well, I was too low," the captain admitted. "I was trying to keep my airspeed up so we wouldn't undershoot, but then she seemed to start drifting to one side. I started to correct to keep the runway lined up and next thing I knew, I felt the gear brush that damned shack."

"How about the crosswind you said you had?"

"There must have been one. I can't explain the drift. Wadda you want me to do—tell the FAA I screwed up?"

"Norm, I'm afraid that's exactly what you did, so why not tell FAA the truth? Nobody got hurt so they aren't gonna lift your ticket. A fine, probably. Maybe thirty days in the right seat and a stiff check ride. I think they'll go easier on you if you just admit you goofed. Tom, you agree?"

"I hate to admit anything to those bastards."

"Maybe we ought to try it sometime," McKay said. "I'm sorry, Norm, but that's my advice. If nobody has anything else on their minds, I'm going home. Good night, all."

After McKay left, Dayton bit off the end of a fresh cigar, lit it, and puffed away meditatively. "Mac's getting a little tough these days," he said finally.

"Yeh," the captain sighed. "Should I do what he said? Hell, it *was* a lousy approach."

"He may be right. You'd probably shock 'em into being lenient."

Dayton's observation about McKay was most accurate. He would fight for a pilot he considered wronged, he would fight for a pilot whose mistake involved extenuating circumstances, but he was getting impatient with brethren who were just careless. He could condone an error in judgment forged under the white heat of an emergency, but he could not excuse one that flaunted training, specific rules and common sense.

In his mail one day there arrived a copy of a press release put out by ALPA headquarters in Chicago shortly after the

CAB had issued a pilot-error verdict against the captain of another airline. McKay had gone to the crash scene and attended the hearings. Ten passengers and both pilots had died. The captain had elected to take off in the teeth of a thunderstorm. The plane went out of control in turbulence at an altitude too low to permit recovery. When investigators pried the wreckage apart, they found the captain sitting illegally in the right seat and he apparently was letting the copilot make the takeoff.

The CAB's criticism of the captain's judgment was sharp. But the ALPA statement denounced the Board's findings and claimed the crew hadn't been given adequate weather information. McKay read the ALPA release, sat down, and wrote the union president a letter.

Dear Clayton:

I cannot understand why Headquarters saw fit to issue a release attacking the CAB's report on the Indianapolis accident. The ALPA statement attributing the crash to inadequate weather information is patently ridiculous. The storm already was hitting the airport area when the captain chose to take off. It obviously was vicious and dangerous—and only too visible to the naked eye. His decision to take off virtually in the middle of it was, to put it charitably, questionable.

Furthermore, the statement totally ignores the CAB's justified criticism of a captain who in an admittedly marginal weather situation, moved over to the right seat for no apparent reason.

I always regret any pilot-error finding. In this case, it appears to have been warranted. We do the cause of objective accident investigation no service if we try to protect crew members who do not deserve protection. The ALPA statement cannot help but foster the impression that we will defend any pilot, and attack the CAB, no matter what the circumstances and no matter how fair a verdict the Board renders, when that verdict involves pilot error.

We literally are placing ourselves in the position of crying wolf when there is no wolf in sight. And this tendency certainly will weaken our efforts to obtain reconsideration or reversals of unfair or inaccurate accident reports. We have enough troubles with Bureau of Safety personnel without handing them ammunition fortifying their belief that ALPA is not impartial in its own investigative work.

Sincerely,
McDonald McKay

He sent copies of the letter to every safety chairman of every airline in the country. A few wrote back notes complimenting him. Several questioned his sanity. The safety chairman from the airline involved in the Indianapolis accident mailed him a fourteen-page tirade defending the dead captain and calling McKay "a traitor to the memory of every pilot who has gone to his grave carrying the stigma of a false CAB accusation."

That one hurt. McKay showed the letter to Snorkel. "Think I should answer it?"

"Wouldn't do any good, Mac. You'll just get into a long-range debate that'll go on and on. He won't change his mind and I doubt if you'll change yours."

He answered it anyway—a carefully composed, friendly yet firm exposition of his views on the investigative process and ALPA's role. He must have hit exactly the right combination of forceful argument and gracious apology, because the reply was equally cordial. The captain said he agreed thoroughly with McKay's stand, except that it did not apply to this particular accident. McKay decided not to continue the correspondence, satisfied he had won a partial victory.

His line flying was becoming generally routine. He was not overly fond of the DC-7, particularly after tasting—if only briefly—the intoxicating power of the Electra. The DC-7 was a dependable, somewhat dull and aging spouse taking on weight in the wrong places as she grew older. The Electra was an exciting young mistress, an almost sensuous airplane that flew with effortless ease and nimble response.

It occurred to him there always seemed to be a greener patch on the other side. He had grown impatient with the

DC-3 and yearned for the faster, bigger Fours. He outgrew the DC-4 in his desire to fly in pressurized equipment. The Convair's virtues dimmed as he waited impatiently for a chance to qualify as captain on Constellations and DC-7's. And he knew that when he finally got to fly the Electra, he eventually would be unhappy until he went on to the mighty jets.

He never stopped marveling at the progress in commercial aviation achieved since he had joined Midwest, even while he criticized some of the slowness of that progress. Nav aids were incredibly improved and ILS no longer a rare luxury. ATC facilities had mushroomed to the point where controllers were handling more than twenty thousand IFR movements every twenty-four hours. Now they were at least talking about all-weather landings and automated Air Traffic Control. Weather-warning radar was on every Midwest plane, sending its invisible signal as far as 150 miles ahead of the plane, piercing the black clouds in its path, and measuring the amount of turbulence that lay lurking in wait.

McKay felt better when threading his way through a storm because he could peer into the hooded radar scope and swiftly analyze the pattern of the return signal that told him the smoothest course. He would call out the heading changes to the copilot as he picked his way through the clouds and took tremendous pride in a flight that reduced bouncing to a minimum. He got a laugh out of one flight when he inadvertently left the cockpit door open and an elderly woman passenger sitting in the most forward row of seats stared curiously into the cockpit, where she could see McKay hunched over the radar set.

After they had left the storm area, McKay came back to the cabin and was about to enter the blue room when the woman tapped his arm.

"Young man," she said sternly and with more than a touch of indignation, "haven't you pilots anything better to do than watch television in the middle of a storm?"

He became an author of sorts, thanks to Tom Dayton. Tom had received a request from a Sunday supplement magazine for an article titled "What Pilots Don't Like About Flying."

"How about batting me out a few hundred words, Mac? They want a pilot's byline on it. I'll touch it up a bit when you finish, but you can write whatever you like. Strike some blows for liberty."

McKay would have turned him down but thought that Barbara would be excited to see his name in a national publication and, he added to himself, for that matter so would he. For four nights he sat in front of his old typewriter suffering the pangs of composition. He started the article six different times, rewrote it completely twice, and finally felt pride of authorship sufficiently to show it to his wife.

"I think it's great. Your spelling stinks but I'll correct it. Mail it just as it is."

After he got Dayton's okay, he sent it to the magazine and spent the next four weeks asking Barbara daily in what he thought was a nonchalant tone, "Uh, any mail today?"

Finally, a letter arrived thanking him for the manuscript along with a check for $200—a modest sum that somehow looked larger than his monthly paycheck from Midwest. The article was published two months later, carrying an editor's note identifying him as "a veteran airline captain who is regarded as one of the nation's leading experts on air safety."

He hated to think of his colleagues' comments on that line. Maybe he could be considered a veteran—it was customary for all reporters to refer to *any* airline captain as a veteran—but he winced at the "expert on air safety" bit. Nevertheless, it wasn't a bad piece and Barbara quietly bought ten extra copies, putting one of them carefully away in her scrapbook.

It was to be expected that Snorkel addressed him for the next month as "Oh veteran Captain McKay." Shea sent him a complimentary note, characteristically neglecting to mention that he himself had received a not-so-complimentary note from President Kane suggesting "you might tell our pilots writing articles that might frighten the public to clear them first with Public Relations."

Shea crumpled the advice into an angry wad, tossed it in a

wastebasket, murmured "Bullshit," and looked sadly around his new plush office wondering if he really was making a good vice president. The VP in him tended to sympathize somewhat with Kane's sensitivity, but the pilot in him agreed with most of McKay's points. He figured he might tell McKay one of these days that the president wasn't exactly happy about the article, but the next time he saw Mac was at a conference with Barnwell. And the occasion was a near-accident.

A Midwest DC-7 landing at LaGuardia had encountered unexpected and thick fog just before touching down. The captain decided on a go-around but as he tried to climb out, numbers one and two propellers touched the ground. Number one separated completely and number two was damaged. The captain flew the staggering plane to Newark, which had no fog, and landed safely. He was in Shea's office the next day with his first officer and flight engineer when McKay and Barnwell arrived.

"Barney, Mac," Shea greeted them. "You know Captain Runnion? This is his first officer, Phil Gates, and flight engineer, Marty Lynton."

Sam Runnion was a tall, graying pilot whom McKay had seen in DCA operations a few times. He was Chicago-based, but Barnwell had known him for years. They exchanged greetings with a marked absence of levity.

"Okay, Sam, give us the poop right from the start," Shea said. "I already know they screwed you on the weather. Your last advisory was three quarters of a mile visibility with some ground fog and smoke. Right?"

Runnion clasped and unclasped his hands nervously before replying. "That's right, Johnny. Everything was normal. We were making an ILS approach. I saw eight to ten runway lights just before we touched down—must have been about a thousand feet from threshold. Then all of a sudden we hit that damned fog. Christ, it was like moving through oatmeal. I hit full throttle, yelled 'Gear up' and then 'Flaps 20.' We . . ."

"What speed were you at when you applied full power?" Barnwell asked.

"Approximately V₂—one hundred knots. We were a little beyond V₂ when I rotated. I thought we were out of it and I told Phil to raise the gear the minute I knew we were airborne. Then we heard this noise and felt a kind of impact. That's when the props hit. We finally got up to five hundred. We feathered number two and I decided to head for Newark. I wouldn't have tackled that fog again if Kim Novak was waiting for me at the end of the runway."

"Sounds like you followed the manual right to the letter," McKay said.

"Yeh," Shea acknowledged, "but maybe there's something wrong with the manual. No reason for those props to hit. Did you have a positive rate of climb?"

"Johnny, I think so. But I couldn't swear to it. I had my hands full trying to maintain airspeed and attitude. All I know is that I followed the book, so help me."

"He sure did," Gates broke in. "Gear up and flaps at 20—I can't see why we didn't make it."

"Gear up," Barnwell said thoughtfully. "John, I wonder if that's where the manual might be wrong."

"You gotta trim for takeoff in a go-around," Shea pointed out. "Power, gear and flaps—that's S.O.P. You got something better?"

"A gear wouldn't give you much drag at V₂. The point is, maybe we ought to leave that gear down until we establish a positive rate of climb."

"Why?"

"To give you a cushion if the ship settles on you. Look at what Sam ran into. He had a helluva time maintaining one hundred knots. In the fog he didn't have any visual reference. His gyro horizon was all he had to give him attitude and that damned thing'll stick if you have sudden acceleration. The Seven climbs like mush anyway. Why don't we change the manual?"

Shea looked interested. "Leave the gear down until you have

a positive rate of climb," he repeated. "You know, you might have something. If Sam had done that, the props never would have touched. And you're right about the drag. I don't think the gear would give you more than 1 or 2 per cent drag."

Barnwell warmed to his theory. "With a DC-7 and no visual reference, it's gonna be hairy starting a go-around no matter what you do. I'll bet fifty times out of a hundred you'll tend to settle at least a little before you get your speed up. And once you settle, that gear is all that's between you and impact."

"Okay," Shea said. "You've sold me. I'll give FAA a ring and tell 'em about the manual change. They'll wanna pass it on to the other carriers. Everyone satisfied?"

"Fine with me," said Runnion.

"Mac?"

"Sounds logical."

"Consider it done. I wanna talk to Sam and his crew a little longer. I'll see you guys later."

It was only a week later, toward the end of February, that McKay found the revision in his operations mailbox. Section 1, page 50, emergency procedures of the DC-7 Operating Manual, labeled "4-engine go-around," had read:

> Execute pull-up in the following manner: Captain should advance throttles to takeoff power and simultaneously order "Props full forward." Obtain and maintain at least V_2 speed. Order "Gear up" and give palm-up hand signal. Order "Flaps 20."

McKay took out this part of the sixty-two-page section on emergency procedures from the two-inch-thick manual. Into the loose-leaf black book he placed a new page 50. The item on 4-engine go-around technique now read:

> Captain should advance throttles to takeoff power and simultaneously order "Props full forward" followed by the order "Flaps 20." Obtain and maintain at least V_2 speed. When positive rate of climb has been established, call "Positive rate of climb, gear up," and give palm-up hand signal.

Chapter 12

On the morning of March 28, 1963, the alarm clock by McKay's bed went off with that rude, persistent, impatient clamor known only to alarm clocks. It was five-thirty.

He groped for it in the darkness, finally made connections with the off button, and climbed out of bed reasonably awake. He was conscientious about getting at least eight hours' sleep the night before a trip, but he had never gotten Barbara to observe the same rule. She had stayed up to watch a late movie on TV, and now she groaned in protest.

"I'll fix your coffee in a minute," she mumbled.

"Stay in the sack, honey, I'll get it myself."

He went into the bathroom, shaved, and showered. Barbara still was in bed but watched him sleepily as he dressed.

"I think I'll take you up on your offer," she said. "I haven't the energy to lift that damned coffeepot."

"Sure. What turkey were you watching?"

"It wasn't a turkey. It was *The High and the Mighty*."

"I think we've seen it five times."

"I know, but it's all about how brave airline captains are."

"It's all about how brave copilots are," McKay reminded her. "John Wayne was a first officer."

He carefully knotted his tie, slipped into his uniform coat, and sat down on the edge of their bed.

"You're better-looking than John Wayne," Barbara informed him.

"Thank you. You're better-looking than the stewardess in the movie. Even with two kids."

"Doe Avedon," Barbara said.

"Doe Avedon? Who's Doe Avedon?"

"She played the part of the stewardess. Imagine, one girl working a Honolulu–San Francisco trip."

"That wasn't the only technical error," McKay said.

"I know. The first time we saw it, you were so busy looking for mistakes that you forgot the plot."

"Well, it kinda got me when Wayne slapped the captain's face. I kept thinking how many times I've wanted to, but didn't. Barbara, that's where we oughta go on our next vacation."

"Around slapping faces?"

"No, my sarcastic little former flygirl. Hawaii."

She sat up. "Mac, I'd love it. Do you think we could?"

"Don't see why not. Wouldn't cost much. Use a Midwest pass to Seattle, hop down to LA, and take United over to Honolulu. The kids would love it. We could see Disneyland while we're in LA."

"Disneyland would never be the same after Debbie got through with it."

McKay grinned. "She's a character. Like her mother. I'd better get going. I'll fix a cup of instant. No, honey, stay in bed."

"I'm wide awake now. I'll have one with you."

They drank coffee together in the bright little breakfast nook, chatting excitedly about the Hawaii trip. In all their married life they had never found the swamp of silence that traps so many couples who run out of mutual interests, or who never had any to begin with. They were happy because they never stopped communicating with each other, whether it was about sex, budgets, children, or airplanes.

McKay gulped down the last few drops of coffee and put on his overcoat. "Go back to bed, sweetie. Kids won't be up for another hour. I'll call you when we get to New York. Be around ten-thirty."

"Is this the Atlanta trip?"

"Yep. Down there this morning, back to New York tonight, Atlanta, and home again tomorrow. Say good-by to Nancy and Debbie."

"Will do. Have a good trip, honey."

She heard him start the engine of their 1951 Ford, which he used purely for driving to and from the airport. She put their coffee cups and saucers in the sink and went back to the bedroom. She paused to glance surreptitiously at a framed picture of McKay, in uniform, which had been on her dressing table since the first year of their marriage. She had done this so often, every time he left for a flight, that she was not even aware of the habit, or that it was a habit.

The last conscious thought of Barbara Deering McKay, before she dropped off to sleep again, was that her husband was quite a guy. Hawaii, with Mac and the kids . . .

His copilot and flight engineer were waiting for him when he arrived in Operations. The first officer was a slightly built, eager kid named Jerry Kohlmeir, one of the few Jewish pilots Midwest had on the roster. He had been flying with McKay all month and McKay liked his alertness and willingness to learn. The captain had not a semblance of anti-Semitism in him and had even asked Kohlmeir curiously why the airline profession didn't attract more Jews.

"You don't see many Jewish stewardesses, either," McKay had mentioned.

"Search me," Jerry had said. "Outside of the pilot level, the salary scale's probably too low. Me, I've wanted to be an airline pilot ever since I was a kid."

Flight Engineer Wesley Scott also was a comparative youngster, a crewcut graduate of Georgia Tech whose only fault was his persistence in calling McKay "skipper." Like most captains, McKay hated it but he didn't have the heart to discourage the FE. Scotty was one of the best engineers McKay had ever flown with. He worked the engineer's panel as a master pianist manipulates a keyboard. McKay actually had found himself watching in admiration as Scotty's long fingers moved expertly and lovingly over the myriad switches and buttons. His power settings were instant and smooth and sometimes he seemed to anticipate McKay's commands, so fast were his responses.

A good crew, McKay thought. Young, ambitious, light-hearted, and cooperative. No captain could ask for anything more.

"Flight plan's all made out, Mac," Kohlmeir announced.

"You guys get here at four?" McKay grumbled in jest. "Let's take a look. They gave us sixteen thousand. What's our weather?"

Jerry handed him the forecast.

"Looks good. I wish I could say the same for the way back."

"Yeah," Kohlmeir said. "Idlewild's flirting with minimums right now."

"We'll recheck in Atlanta. Who'd we draw for stews?"

"Fletcher and Drum. Must be fairly new. Their names don't ring any bells."

"Are they around yet?"

"Haven't seen them."

"If you spot 'em, tell 'em I'd like to see them before they board."

"Right. Flight plan okay?"

McKay studied the flight plan again, checked the allotted fuel, signed the clearance, and nodded. "It's fine, Jerry. By the way, it's almost the end of the month. Better give you some takeoff and landing time. You fly her down and I'll take her back tonight."

Kohlmeir was delighted. "Thanks, Mac. Hey—these might be our girls. They both look bewildered."

McKay went over to the two stewardesses, who were staring around Operations much as he had that day he was looking for Captain Snodgrass. "Good morning. You girls on 517?"

"Yes sir," said one stewardess. She was a honey-haired blonde.

"I'm Captain McKay. You'll be flying with me today. Thought I'd just introduce myself."

"I'm Norma Drum," said the blonde. "This is Mickey Fletcher."

Miss Fletcher was a tiny brunette with a baby face. Both the girls looked young, or maybe all of a sudden McKay felt old.

"How long have you been with Midwest?" he inquired politely.

"We just graduated from stewardess school," said Norma. "This is our first trip."

That was not in accordance with Midwest policy, but on rare occasions Crew Schedule was desperate enough to assign two brand-new girls to a DC-7 flight.

"Oh? Well, we'll try to make your inaugural flight a good one. Any questions on emergency procedures? Anything not clear?"

"I don't think so," said Miss Drum doubtfully.

The captain was tempted to quiz them briefly, such as asking them where the portable oxygen bottle was stored on the DC-7. But he relented, figuring it wasn't fair to make like a martinet when they probably had a case of the jitters on their first trip. McKay had a disconcerting habit of tossing an occasional emergency procedures question at stewardesses before a flight, just to keep them on their toes. It had given him a kind of "watch-out-for-Captain-McKay-he's-a-nice-guy-but" reputation.

This time, he confined himself to a friendly "Glad to have you with us—if you have any problems or anything you don't understand, don't be afraid to ask."

"Yes sir," said Norma Drum. "He's nice," she whispered to Mickey after McKay walked away.

"Thank God," said Miss Fletcher. "I was afraid we might hit Captain Bligh the first time out."

The trip to Atlanta that morning was routine. The crew had a late lunch in the airport coffee shop, although the two new stewardesses were too excited to eat.

"Dammit," McKay said when they both ordered a fruit salad and nothing else, "I'm gonna pick up your check. This'll probably be the only time in your flying career it'll happen. The least you can do is order a hamburger or something."

"I'll probably regret it," admitted Miss Drum, "but a salad's all I want."

"Me too," chimed in Miss Fletcher.

"Are you picking up our checks, too, skipper?" Scotty asked.

"Hell no. You and Jerry have flown with me before. I was trying to be nice to the girls on their first trip."

"I seem to remember my first trip with you," Kohlmeir said. "You didn't offer to pay for my lunch on that occasion."

"You weren't built like a stewardess, Jerry. And I also remember that occasion—you didn't wanna eat any lunch, either."

"I was scared to death, Mac," the first officer admitted. "When I heard you were ALPA regional safety chairman, I took it for granted you were going to chew me out if my tie wasn't straight."

"It's your ILS approaches I worry about, not your tie."

The stewardesses listened in what amounted to awe at the banter.

"Are you married, Captain McKay?" Norma couldn't resist asking.

"Very much so. Two daughters and my wife was a Midwest stewardess. Like to see their pictures?"

"Yes," lied Miss Drum, thinking that it figured—a captain this charming, handsome, and decent must have been hooked long ago.

She and Miss Fletcher dutifully looked at the snapshots in McKay's wallet. They were prepared to issue a conventional "She's very attractive" but one look at Barbara's picture and they didn't have to be conventional.

"She's beautiful," Norma said, mentally consigning Captain McKay to the Don't Waste Your Time category.

The girls still were nibbling at their salads when McKay called for their checks and excused himself.

"Wanna take a look at that New York weather," he apologized.

"Thanks for lunch," Miss Drum said.

"Don't mention it. See you in OPS."

He left and the stewardesses looked with open admiration at his tall, straight figure standing by the cashier's counter.

"Gee, he's real nice," Mickey said.

"The best," the flight engineer agreed. "There isn't a more thoughtful guy on the line."

"He's more than thoughtful," Kohlmeir said. "He's a damned fine captain. I hope I learn to run a flight deck like he does. He makes a crew feel like they're . . . well, like they're part of a team instead of just nonentities taking orders. Right, Scotty?"

"Right. And don't you kids ever think you can take advantage of him because he's a nice guy. If he ever asks you something about emergency procedures and you don't know the answer, watch out. He'll stand over you while you look up the answer in your manual. And if you keep giving him wrong answers, he'll turn you in to your supervisor like a rabbit makes love. Wham, bam!"

Miss Drum looked dubious. "What is he—a nut on safety?"

"Yes," answered Kohlmeir. "Which is why I like to fly with him."

"I think," said Miss Drum to Miss Fletcher, "we might glance through our manual before we leave tonight."

In Operations the "nut on safety" was examining the weather outlook for New York with a bit more optimism than he had indicated at the luncheon table. The mumbo jumbo on the weather teletype he translated quickly into a fairly favorable outlook.

From 1800 Greenwich time (6 P.M.) March 28 to 0600 March 29, Idlewild would have partial obscuration, three miles visibility in haze and smoke with occasional two-mile visibility. He took the airman's cynical view of the "HK" that signified haze and smoke. The Weather Bureau invariably assigned "H" (haze) to atmospheric conditions which should have been more accurately labeled "K" (for smoke). To pilots, there was a significant difference. Haze normally was a temporary visibility obstruction, whose evaporation could be predicted with some degree of certainty. Smoke was the product of air pollution. It might be local or it might be the waste material spewed from factory smokestacks a thousand miles away, carried in the arms of a weather front, and left to squat in stagnant ugliness over some metropolitan area. Mixed with fog, it could be deadly, for it tended to transfuse the fog with continued life.

McKay therefore was suspicious of the HK on the Idlewild forecast, yet over all the outlook was not too bad. He compared it to the supplemental forecast issued by Midwest's own meteorology department. It was about the same and the captain relaxed.

His crew arrived a few minutes later and they settled down to killing the three hours they had before departing Atlanta. This was the most boring segment of their flying lives—the waiting period on a turnaround. Too much time to waste and not enough time to really do anything. Kohlmeir announced he was going to take a nap in the pilots' lounge. The stewardesses, who had never seen Atlanta, asked McKay if they could go downtown. The captain admonished them to keep track of the time, then decided to go with them.

"Come on along, Scotty," he urged the flight engineer.

"Well, I dunno, I thought I might browse through the bookstore here and maybe join Jerry for a little shut-eye."

"All you do in the bookstore is look through the sex novels for the seduction parts," McKay told him. "I have yet to see you buy one. Come on downtown with us."

"Okay," sighed Scott. "But don't you girls get the idea I'm a sex fiend. I'm the only flight engineer on the line who reads *Playboy* for the ads."

They grabbed an airport limo to downtown Atlanta and for the next hour wandered through a few stores. McKay picked up another blouse for Barbara, a book on horses for Nancy—she loved riding and was taking lessons—and a doll for Debbie. The stewardesses stopped in front of a jewelry-store window to examine a selection of charms. They both owned charm bracelets and were admiring one that was a tiny airplane. The quartet finally continued up the street when McKay said he forgot to pick up something Barbara wanted.

"There's a drugstore up ahead," he said. "Go in and order me a Coke—I'll be along in five minutes."

While they went ahead to the drugstore, he walked back to the jewelry store and bought two of the little airplane charms. He found Scotty and the girls sitting in a drugstore booth and, feeling almost fatherly and a little embarrassed, gave the stewardesses the charms. They were not only grateful but overwhelmed, having been told in stewardess school that the average captain made Jack Benny resemble the last of the big-time spenders.

"Let's call it a little token in honor of your first trip," McKay said.

"Captain McKay," said Norma with total sincerity, "I envy your wife."

"On my first trip," Scotty complained, "he gave me a twenty-minute lecture on why I shouldn't be satisfied to remain a flight engineer."

"Well," explained McKay, "I want you kids to get a good first impression of both Midwest and its captains. Next time you might draw Captain Snodgrass."

"Is he mean?" asked Mickey.

"No, he's just a character. You'll like him. You just have to get used to him."

He told them a couple of stories about Snorkel and it was time to return to the airport.

"I should pick up some infrared film," Scott said while they were hailing a taxi.

"Infrared film?" wondered Norma.

McKay laughed. "He's talking about those pictures some

flight engineers took in cockpits. They caught a few captains reading on flight and they got one of a stewardess sitting on a captain's lap. Raised quite a stink."

"Us Midwest flight engineers allow five minutes of lap time with no pictures—provided the captain is McKay," Scotty advised them.

"It was bad business," McKay said seriously. "By the time a Congressional committee and the press got through, it was blown up way beyond proportion. It made all pilots look bad and it gave the public the impression there was no such thing as cockpit discipline."

"I gotta agree with you, skipper. It's too bad the whole affair came out as part of a labor dispute. Those FE's were desperate."

"Guys on strike always get desperate," McKay said. "That's why I keep telling you Midwest engineers you've got to take pilot training sooner or later. United's FE's did it years ago. Most of the other carriers are doing it now. The third man in the cockpit has to be pilot-trained. Not on a DC-7 or even an Electra, but certainly on the jets. And you still can retain your own union. Someday I suppose you'll merge with ALPA but that's not an issue that has to be decided right away."

The arrival of a taxi cut short the discussion. In the cab Scotty wanted to know if McKay had heard the flight engineer's "Ballad of the Airline Captain." He hadn't.

"I'll sing it," Scott said. "It goes to the tune of 'Bless 'Em All.' "

> "Bless 'em all, bless 'em all,
> Bless the long and the short and the tall.
> Bless all our captains, so true to their wives—
> We buried the last one in nineteen-oh-five.
> We are pilots so brave and so bold,
> Of that you don't have to be told,
> We're fearless and gallant, just loaded with talent
> And nickels we clutch till they fold."

McKay roared and the stewardesses laughed.
"Any more?" the captain asked, Scotty continued.

"Bless 'em all, bless 'em all,
Bless the long and the short and the tall.
Bless all our flygirls, those angels in skirts,
The hell with the cabin, the cockpit comes first.
We face danger with nonchalant grins,
Our hero is old Errol Flynn.
We starred in some dramas, with infrared cameras,
We're sorry we sinned—bless us all!

"Bless 'em all, bless 'em all,
Bless the long and the short and the tall.
Bless airborne radar when thunderheads dance,
But better than radar is seat of the pants.
We are grateful for new DME,
And instruments shaped like a T,
But when gyros tumble, we're ever so humble,
Oh Lord we are nearer to Thee.

"Bless 'em all, bless 'em all,
Bless the long and the short and the tall,
Bless all our FE's, those wonderful chaps
Who raised so much hell 'bout the stews on our laps
The airline we love is MA,
The finest in flight all the way,
If Ben Kane is listening,
Our halos are glistening,
Just give us a big raise in pay!

"Bless 'em all, bless 'em all,
Bless the long and the short and the tall.
Bless the inspectors from dear FAA—
They don't make as much but they've got the last say.
And we honor the old CAB,
Which governs our whole industry.
It's totally chairborne, and never gets airborne,
But it's expert on what's wrong with we."

"That's great," McKay said. "How about writing that out
and letting me have a copy?"

"Sure thing, skipper. I think it's kinda cute myself. One of our flight engineers wrote it."

"What's a DME?" asked Mickey.

"Distance-measuring equipment," McKay told her. "It's a fairly new navigation aid. Didn't they teach you that in school?"

"If they did, I forgot it."

"There are times," mused the captain, "when I wonder if some of us pilots shouldn't be lecturing at stewardess school."

They sang the ballad all the way back to the airport, learning the words as they went along with Scotty's prompting. In Operations they found the conscientious Kohlmeir already had the flight plan made out for McKay's signature. McKay studied the routing, and rechecked the latest weather. It was the same as earlier, but to the Dispatch clearance had been added a NOTAM:

"IDLEWILD PAR [Precision Approach Radar] OUT OF SERVICE UNTIL 0900 3/29/63."

"Nuts," said McKay. "I always did feel a little more secure with PAR. But the weather's still holding up. Looks like a good trip."

He signed the clearance, gave it to the dispatcher, and when he turned around Helen Mitchell was standing there.

"Hi, Mac."

"Mitch! What are you doing in Atlanta?"

"Check-riding a couple of my girls. Time for some coffee?"

"About fifteen minutes. Let's go."

She looked older, subdued and sad, McKay thought. She and Barbara still were close, but he had seen comparatively little of her in recent months. She ordered coffee but hardly touched it, toying with the spoon and stirring it aimlessly.

"You act as if you have something on your mind," he said.

"Affirmative. A guy named Culver. And a guilty conscience."

"You have no reason for feeling guilty, Mitch. You warned him and he ignored it. He was just that kind of man."

"He also was my husband. And I loved him, Mac. I still

loved him when I sent him packing. I was a jealous little bitch with no tolerance for human weaknesses. And all I keep thinking is that if I had given him the second chance he begged for, he wouldn't have transferred to Chicago and he wouldn't have been killed."

"Maybe. He also might have been begging you for a third or fourth chance. And he could have been killed someplace other than Platte, Colorado."

"I've already tried that rationalization. It doesn't work."

She began to cry and McKay realized he had never seen her cry, this outwardly tough and inwardly soft woman who had so much affection to give.

"Look, Mitch, you're still young, attractive, and nobody can live in the past. Barbara told me you aren't even seeing anyone much. That's foolish."

"I just don't feel like going out. Besides, this job keeps me pretty busy and . . ."

"Baloney. Les was killed almost eight years ago. Give yourself a chance to meet other men. You might find one who has his virtues without his faults. For example, there's a United captain who lives down the street. A widower with two kids. Barbara and I met him a few weeks ago. He's a nice guy and a lonely guy. How about my inviting him over some night and we'll introduce you?"

She wiped her eyes and managed a smile. "Matchmaking, Mac?"

"I'll matchmake after I get you out of your shell. I wish I had known about the shell before this."

"You couldn't have known. I didn't even tell Barbara I was carrying around a guilt complex. Whenever she's mentioned Les, I changed the subject. I don't know why I suddenly unloaded on you."

"Feel better?"

"Somewhat. I might even take you up on that United character. Would you give me a ring?"

"Sure will. Mitch, I'd better get going. Walk me back to OPS."

He still was thinking of Mitch when he picked up Kohlmeir and Scott and went out to the plane. He had a slightly guilty feeling himself. He had left it to Barbara to comfort Mitch when Les crashed. In doing so, he had wrongly assumed that Culver's death had left few if any scars on Mitch. True, she had hidden them from Barbara, too. But he should have made some effort to crack Mitch's façade, crusted with eight years of make-believe cynicism that hid eight years of pain.

The flight had not been called yet, but some passengers were waiting at the gate when the crew walked through. McKay noticed an attractive young woman carrying a baby, and impulsively he stopped to chuck the infant under the chin.

"First flight?" he asked the mother.

"For him, yes. I've flown before."

"Well, we'll try to give him a good trip. Glad to have you aboard."

"Your attention please," blared the airport PA. "Midwest Airlines announces the departure of Flight 510, nonstop DC-7 service to New York via Idlewild International Airport. Flight 510 is boarding at Gate E."

Scotty came aboard after completing the walk-around.

"I couldn't find a damned thing wrong," he said cheerfully. "But if anybody wants to stay in Atlanta for another few hours, I'll look again."

"New York, here we come," said McKay. "Start your checklist, Jerry."

"Engine report and log," Kohlmeir said.

"Examined," responded Scott.

"Anti-icing panel."

"Checked and normal."

"DC panel."

"Checked and normal."

"AC panel."

"Checked and normal."

"Radar."

"Off and up," said McKay.

"Autopilot."

"Off, uncaged. Beacon okay."

"Fluxgate."

"Caged."

They had just completed the pretakeoff checklist when Norma Drum opened the cockpit door and handed McKay the passenger manifest.

"How many we got?" he asked.

"An even fifty, Captain."

"Keep 'em happy, Norma. And I'll take some coffee when you have a free minute. Anybody else?"

"Me," said Kohlmeir.

"No thanks," Scotty said.

"Contact Ground Control, Jerry. Norma, for your cabin PA, we'll be cruising at seventeen thousand. Flying time—make it three hours. Everything okay? Any problem children back there?"

"No sir. There's one man who's had a few drinks. But he seems quiet enough."

"If he's really drunk, he gets off," McKay snapped. "I'll take your word for it—how loaded is he?"

The young stewardess was unwilling to tackle controversy on her first trip. "I think he'll be okay, Captain. I'll watch him."

"Okay. Lemme know if he gives you any trouble."

"Yes sir." She left, thinking how accurate Scott's appraisal of the captain had been—a nice guy, but a disciplinarian. If that one passenger did give her trouble, she was in hot water with McKay. She knew all about the FAA rule requiring a stewardess to refuse boarding an obviously intoxicated passenger.

"Midwest five-ten, ready for clearance," Kohlmeir told Ground Control.

"Roger, Midwest five-ten. You're cleared IFR to Idlewild via Victor 20, Victor 39, Victor 16. Maintain seventeen thousand, maintain runway heading and three thousand for three minutes after takeoff. Contact departure control one-one-eight-point-one on release from tower. Acknowledge."

"Midwest five-ten. IFR Victor 20, Victor 39, Victor 16 to Idlewild. Maintain runway heading at three thousand after takeoff. Ready to taxi."

The tower cleared them to their assigned runway. The DC-7 rolled away from the ramp, the wing lights splitting the darkness ahead.

"Cabin check, Scotty," McKay said.

"Right." The flight engineer put his uniform coat back on and left to make the final safety inspection of the cabin, particularly the main exit door. He returned and settled himself in front of his panel.

"Midwest five-ten, cleared for takeoff."

"Midwest five-ten, rolling."

Down the runway thundered the DC-7, its wheels gulping the long ribbon of concrete.

"V_1," called Kohlmeir. "V_2 . . . rotate."

The DC-7 left the ground, an implausible violation of gravity weighing 101,000 pounds and carrying fifty-five human beings inside its aluminum hulk.

"Midwest five-ten, this is Atlanta Departure Control. We have you in radar contact one mile north. . . ."

"Roger, Departure Control. At eleven hundred and climbing. Five-ten."

The cockpit settled down to that incongruous combination of relaxation and alertness that marks every airline flight. McKay's eyes roved incessantly over his key instruments.

"What was our off time, Jerry?"

"Logging it at 1833."

"Seat belt and no smoking signs off."

"Roger."

McKay picked up the PA mike. "Good evening, ladies and gentlemen. This is Captain McKay. On behalf of my crew, First Officer Kohlmeir and Flight Engineer Scott, I'd like to welcome you aboard. Our flight tonight will take us over Charlotte, North Carolina, Washington and Baltimore and on into New York. The en-route weather is good and at seventeen thousand feet we should have a smooth trip. The weather at Idlewild is favorable, although we might encounter some traffic delay. We'll keep you advised. We appreciate your choice of Midwest, and let our girls know if there's anything they can do for you. Thank you."

Midwest 510 ambled along inside its cocoon of protected airspace, seventy miles long, ten miles wide, and two thousand feet thick. The red-lighted instruments glowed reassuringly in the dark cockpit. Scott glanced at the TV-like screen on his ignition analyzer, flashing its staccato green patterns.

"Bless 'em all, bless 'em all," he hummed peacefully, and McKay smiled.

In Atlanta operations, the weather teletype began chattering.

3/28/63 1927. AMENDED FORECAST FOR IDLEWILD VALID FROM 1940 TO 0600 3/29. FOG OBSCURATION VARIABLE TO CLEAR. VISIBILITY 1–1½ MILES GROUND FOG.

A dispatcher saw it and asked his supervisor if it should be relayed to 510.

"Naw, they're about out of our jurisdiction. Idlewild Dispatch'll pass it along."

At Idlewild a dispatcher saw the same amended forecast and wondered if he should advise 510. Then he thought he might as well wait for the flight to get closer; the way things looked outside, the forecast might be changed again anyway.

At seventeen thousand feet, somewhere over North Carolina, First Officer Jerry Kohlmeir logged a routine ATC communication: "Transmission completed, 2015." It was at that precise moment when the TEL-autograph transreceivers in the FAA control tower at Idlewild went on the blink, severing normal communications between the tower and the United States Weather Bureau office seven stories below.

Kohlmeir gave McKay the bad news a few minutes later, after talking to Midwest's Dispatch at Idlewild.

"Dispatch says the weather's fluctuating between minimums right now, Mac. We're cleared to Philadelphia if we wanna divert."

"Crud!" McKay said. "Well, it's too soon to make up our minds. But I'd better tell the customers."

Click.

"Ladies and gentlemen, this is Captain McKay. The weather at New York is getting a bit worse and there's some question whether we'll be able to land. Our alternate airport is Philadelphia and there is a possibility we'll have to divert. I'll keep you advised."

"I've got New York Center, Mac."

"Take over for a while, Jerry. I'll handle the radio. Midwest five-ten now listening one-twenty-four-point-eight."

"Midwest five-ten, we have you in radar contact. Your altitude, please."

"Eleven, one-one-thousand."

"Midwest five-ten, the altimeter at Milville is thirty-twenty-nine."

"Milville three-zero-two-nine. Roger."

"Midwest five-ten cleared to Sandy Hook via Kenton Victor 16 till you intercept the Idlewild one-ninety radial, repeat Idlewild one-ninety. Maintain one-one-thousand at Sandy Hook."

"Roger, Midwest five-ten. To Sandy Hook intersection via Kenton Victor 16 to intercept the one-nine-zero of Idlewild. Maintain one-one-thousand. How's the weather?"

"Midwest five-ten, stand by for a weather advisory. Fog right now but we're open."

"Roger. Five-ten over Kenton at forty-six. Estimate Coyle at zero-one."

McKay leaned back and shook his head wearily. "Well, we hold at Sandy Hook for God knows how long. I'll put on my decision coat when we get the latest weather. I'll take her now, Jerry."

The DC-7 grumbled her way into the vast complex that is the New York Air Traffic Control area, an incredibly complicated spider net of airways involving the hubs of Idlewild, LaGuardia, and Newark.

"Midwest five-ten, New York Center. Altitude please."

"Midwest five-ten, eleven thousand approaching Coyle. We'd like the latest Idlewild weather, please."

"Midwest five-ten, you're in radar contact. Idlewild altimeter three-zero-three-zero."

"Roger, three-zero-three-zero for Idlewild. And how about our weather?"

"Midwest five-ten, hold at Sandy Hook. Holding pattern is south on the one-ninety radial of Idlewild. Right turns. Stand by for weather."

"We've been standing by for too damned long," McKay muttered.

Kohlmeir acknowledged the holding pattern. A few minutes later the Center gave them their first encouraging news.

"Midwest five-ten, stand by for the latest weather. For your information, we had a Vanguard make a successful approach to Idlewild. They're attempting approaches."

McKay picked up the mike. "That's fine, but we'd still like the weather."

"Stand by, five-ten. All aircraft on this frequency inbound to Idlewild. The latest weather at two-one-one-zero partial obstruction a mile and a half with fog, landing runway four-right. RVR inoperative. Midwest five-ten, did you get that?"

"Midwest five-ten, roger, that's an improvement. Thank you."

"Midwest five-ten, descend to nine thousand."

"Roger, Midwest five-ten. Nine thousand we're at Sandy Hook."

McKay advised the passengers that Idlewild was open to traffic. "We still may have to hold for a while," he added, "but the weather is above minimums and our visibility is a mile and a half which is more than adequate. We'll let you know when we get our final approach clearance."

They began their circle over the Sandy Hook intersection, a radio checkpoint. Their holding pattern actually was an invisible electronic track, each side of the track transmitting a radio signal. *Beeeeeeeeep-beep* went one. *Beep-beeeeeeep* went the other. In McKay's ear the two beams merged into a steady buzz. If he strayed off course the slightest amount, the signal would pulsate unevenly. Being stacked up in a holding pattern was nerve-racking to most passengers, but pilots merely got impatient.

"Midwest five-ten, we're turning you over to Idlewild Approach Control, frequency one-one-nine-point-seven. New York Center out."

"Roger, five-ten."

Kohlmeir changed frequencies and McKay did likewise.

"Idlewild Approach Control, Midwest five-ten and nine thousand. Presently steering one-nine-zero in the Sandy Hook pattern."

"Midwest five-ten, Idlewild Approach Control. Hold Sandy Hook south of Colt's Neck one-hundred radial on the Idlewild one-nine-zero radial, right turns. Expect approach clearance twenty-one-forty. Four-right ILS in use, landing runway four-right. Idlewild weather—sky partially obscured, visibility one and one half with fog. Altimeter setting three-zero-three-one. Precision approach radar not available. Runway visual range inoperative."

"Midwest five-ten, roger, and thank you."

Approach Control for the next few minutes began letting them down the holding stack ladder, one thousand feet at a time. McKay, listening to the Approach frequency, noted that some flights were abandoning their approaches because of the ground fog. But others were landing.

"Must be intermittent," he said to Kohlmeir. "If we hit a bad patch, I'll go around. Stand by those flaps."

"Mac, I hope we get in. I'd hate to go back to Philly."

"So, I imagine, would the passengers. I wish that damned RVR was working. It's the only fog measuring device they've got."

Approach Control broke in.

"All aircraft copy. Four-right ILS still in use, landing runway four-right. Idlewild weather: sky partially obscured, visibility one mile with ground fog. Wind is northeast at six. Altimeter setting three-zero-three-one."

"Balls," said Kohlmeir. "She's socking in."

"A mile's fine. No sweat if that visibility stays up."

That was the last weather report he got. Approach Control cleared Midwest 510 for final approach. McKay did not know, nor could he have known, that as Approach Control advised them "cleared to land," the U. S. Weather Bureau observer on the ground, far below the tower, logged surface visibility on runway four-right at only one fourth of a mile. And he did not transmit this information to Approach Control. Not only were the transreceivers out, but the "hot line" to the tower had been disconnected.

Four and a half miles from runway four-right, Flight 510 passed a radio marker beacon emitting a narrow, cone-shaped electronic beam.

A purple light flashed on and off on the instrument panel.

"Outer marker," Kohlmeir called.

McKay kept his eyes glued to the ILS instrument in front of him.

Pulsating unerringly toward the sinking DC-7 were two more beams. One was the localizer, showing McKay that he was headed straight for the runway. The other was the glide slope, indicating his attitude of descent. The ILS dial in front of the captain had a vertical needle representing the localizer signal. A horizontal needle gave him the glide slope. He kept both needles in a perfect cross. They would take him toward the assigned runway, down to the last two hundred feet of altitude, at which point he had to land visually. No ILS could operate below that final two hundred feet.

On the panel flashed an amber light.

"Middle marker," sang out the copilot.

"Any approach lights yet?"

"No—wait a sec, there they are. Runway lights dead ahead."

They were two hundred feet off the ground and swept in over the threshold of runway four-right. One-fifty. One hundred. Fifty. Suddenly the lights disappeared as if a great blanket had been dropped over them. Suddenly there was no runway in front of them. Only a terrible opaqueness, reflecting the glare from the runway lights like fire flickering dimly through thick smoke.

In a split second McKay lost all visual reference.

"Scotty, props full forward!"

He rammed the throttles to maximum power.

The engines surged.

"Gear up! Flaps 20!"

Kohlmeir reacted instantly. McKay pulled back on the yoke but not too hard. His eyes were on the artificial horizon indicator to make sure they didn't rotate too sharply and stall. He started to check the rate of climb indicator but at that moment they felt the impact of the tail skid against the ground.

The DC-7 shuddered.

The fog was still wrapped around the ship in a ghostly shroud.

McKay could feel the big plane settle helplessly, surrendering with no further fight or desire to keep flying. He knew they were going to crash. His last lucid thought was, God, let me see Barbara again.

The props on the left side bit into the ground and the left wing started to crumple. Flames spurted angrily from the ruptured tanks. The right side of the cockpit seemed to explode outward as the plane ground-looped to the left and began to break up. In one sickening second, seared into his mind forever, the captain saw Kohlmeir and Scott propelled out the slashed side of the cockpit, still strapped to their seats. By some miracle McKay's seat held. When the ravaged plane came to a stop, the remains of the cockpit had been torn from the rest of the fuselage and stayed free of the devouring fire.

That was where they found McDonald McKay a full thirty

minutes later, still buckled in his seat, his eyes glazed and rivulets of tears cutting paths through the smudges of smoke on his cheeks.

Barbara had put the girls to bed and was watching television, waiting for McKay to phone from New York. She happened to glance up at the clock on the mantel. Nine forty-five. She felt an odd chill and was about to get up and see if a door was open. The domino, standing on its long edge, wavered and fell off the mantel.

She picked it up off the floor and put it back. She turned off the TV set and sat quietly, almost without feeling, and waited for the phone to ring. Only she already knew it would not be Mac.

The call came at ten forty. It was Barnwell.

"There's been a crash, Barbara. Mac's okay—just cuts and bruises. American has a flight to New York at midnight. I'll have your ticket all ready. Can you get someone to stay with the kids?"

"I'll call Marion Snodgrass," she said. "Was anyone killed, Barney?"

"I'm afraid so. The important thing is to be with Mac. I'll meet you in Operations and fly up with you."

The phone rang. It was Marion.

"I just heard and I'll be right over," she said, and hung up.

Numbly, Barbara threw some things into a small suitcase. She knew she had to tell the children and woke them up.

"I'm going to New York tonight. Daddy had a little accident and I want to be with him. Aunt Marion is coming over to stay with you while I'm gone."

"Is Daddy all right?" asked Nancy.

"Yes, he's fine."

"Honest?"

"Honest."

Debbie had a more practical thought. "Daddy won't brung me a present, then?"

"Not tonight, honey. Maybe later. Debbie, I want you to be a good girl and mind Aunt Marion."

"Aunt Marion gonna brung me present?"

"Bring, not brung. No, she's just coming to stay with you. Promise you'll be good?"

"Hokay."

Nancy followed her mother to the living room and began crying. "Is he really and truly all right? Is Daddy dead?"

"No, he's fine, Nancy. Captain Barnwell told me so. Captain Barnwell wouldn't lie to us. You go back to bed. You'll upset Debbie if you keep crying."

Marion Snodgrass arrived, almost simultaneously with Pat O'Brian.

"Paddy's on a trip," Pat said after hugging Barbara. "I just talked to him. He said he got through to Idlewild and Mac's okay. I'll drive you to the airport, a neighbor's over with my brood."

"Marion, Debbie's probably gone back to sleep but Nancy's pretty upset. Let her stay up with you for a while till she gets sleepy. I'll call you from New York as soon as I see Mac. I can't thank all of you enough. I don't know how long I'll be gone. I think there's enough food in the icebox for a couple of days."

"Don't worry about the food," Marion said firmly. "You stay with Mac as long as you have to."

"We'd better get going, Barbara," Pat said.

Barbara and she went out to the car. Before Pat could turn on the ignition, Barbara fell against her shoulder and sobbed.

"Pat, Barney wouldn't lie to me, would he? I think Mac's dead."

"He isn't dead, Barbara. Barney would have told you. Why do you think he's dead?"

"The domino. The domino fell off the fireplace. Just about the time he must have crashed."

"Pure coincidence," Pat soothed her. "Let's get started or we'll miss that flight."

The nightmare that had begun for McKay the moment he realized a crash was inevitable continued through the rest of the night. Firemen brought him to Midwest's Idlewild Operations office and he was taken from there to the pilots' lounge. A doctor gave him a quick examination.

"No bones broken, Captain. Your right thigh is bruised and you've got a few cuts. You were lucky."

McKay stared at him dully. "Yeh, lucky. How many got away? How's my crew?"

"I don't know anything about that, Captain. There were survivors, quite a few."

"How many?"

"I don't know. I suggest you just take it easy. There's plenty of time for questions."

"I want to know about my crew. Those two stewardesses. It was their first trip."

He put his hands to his throbbing temples and closed his eyes. He felt a hand on his shoulder and looked up. It was Snorkel.

"Mac, are you okay?"

"I guess so. How'd you get here, Snorkel?"

"Landed about thirty minutes ahead of you. Came in from Chicago."

"You landed okay and I didn't. Why?"

"Mac, don't think about it now. You're safe. Barbara's on her way up here with Barney."

"She shouldn't come. I'll break wide open if I see her. Snorkel, the crew. Jerry and Scotty. Did they get out?"

Snorkel hesitated. His face was a mask of pure pity. "No, they didn't, Mac. They were killed instantly. Your being alive is a miracle. The stewardesses are okay. You would have been proud of them. They kept their heads and got a lot of people out okay."

"How many?"

"About thirty. They're still taking a count. They figure some survivors might still be wandering around. It wasn't as bad as it might have been, Mac."

"That goddamned fog, Snorkel. That lousy, stinking mile visibility they told us we had. I saw the runway lights, then they weren't there any more. No lights, no runway. Nothing but fog. I started a go-around but the tail skid touched. She just quit flying, Snorkel. She just quit flying. And there wasn't a goddamned thing I could do about it."

"Mac, don't talk about it now. You're in shock."

"I gotta talk about it. I killed people."

"You can talk about it when you can think clearly. Lie down and rest. Doc, how about giving him a sedative?"

"Good idea. Captain, let me give you something to make you sleep."

"I couldn't sleep. I don't think I'll ever be able to sleep."

"Nonsense. Take this pill. Here's some water."

McKay swallowed the pill and finally consented to stretch out on a couch. But only for a minute. A burly, flat-nosed man walked up.

"Is this the captain who was flying that plane?"

McKay sat up but Snorkel motioned him to keep still.

"This is the captain. What's on your mind?"

"I'm Detective Sergeant Matson of the New York Police Department. I'd like a statement from him."

"He's in no shape to give anybody a statement."

"He's breathing, ain't he? So he can tell me what happened."

"Since when has the New York Police Department been investigating crashes? Captain McKay will talk to the CAB and his own chief pilot. Nobody else. So blow."

"You wanna get into trouble yourself, wise guy? He'll talk to the police or else."

There was something about Snorkel that commanded respect, particularly when he was mad. An angry look from Harrison Snodgrass was capable of burning holes through asbestos. Such was the look he gave the policeman. It combined disdain, disgust, and a touch of willingness to commit murder.

"Get the hell out of here, Matson. The only guy in trouble

is you. This is a Federal investigation—repeat, Federal. I'll even give you a break. I won't file charges against you. Just go. Like right now."

The detective left, still blustering but defeated. McKay fell back on the couch again. He closed his eyes but it was futile. Imprinted on his brain was that picture of the cockpit tearing open. He tried to reconstruct what he had done just before impact, what commands he had issued, what decisions he had made.

Then it struck him like a blow to the jaw.

He thought he remembered yelling at Kohlmeir: "Gear up!"

Chapter 13

His memory was a perverse, fickle betrayer. It gleefully told him, over and over again, how Kohlmeir and Scott had died. It re-created for him a hundred times the way the fog had blotted out the runway lights and every iota of forward vision, a split-second transition from routine to terror. It forced him to remember the woman passenger with her baby —and, as he had learned later, that they both died. It brought back the meeting with Mitch and made him wonder if his pity and concern for her had somehow subconsciously invaded his concentration in a moment of stress. But it dropped an insidious curtain of forgetfulness over the one thing he was straining to recall—the precise ritual he had followed for an aborted landing.

At first he was bothered only by his confusion about the gear and the vague but persistent recollection that he had called for gear up. He assumed the CAB would answer his doubts. The actuating cylinders from both the nose and main gears would be found in either the up or the down position.

A simple, unequivocal answer that would tip the delicate scales balancing pilot error against circumstances beyond a captain's control.

He was not as concerned about the failure to complete the balked-landing maneuver. He knew that a DC-7 committed to a landing was a flying brick and that a successful go-around in zero visibility involved as much luck as skill. But what haunted him was the knowledge that if the gear had been raised, the protective buffer zone was removed and blame for the fatalities could be aimed squarely at him.

It was Barnwell who demolished his assumption about the actuating cylinders. Barney had been wonderful, telling McKay to take off as much time as he wished. He even added apologetically: "If you feel up to it, we'll talk about the accident. But only if you feel up to it."

"I might as well, Barney, while it's fresh. Basically, it's simple. The RVR was inoperative on four-right. They gave us a mile visibility with ground fog. I knew some flights were having trouble—we must have heard four or five abandoned approaches—but others were getting in. We hit a patch of fog about fifty feet off the ground. I couldn't see anything so I executed a go-around. Maybe I rotated too much, I don't know. Anyway, the tail skid touched and we lost airspeed. She just settled into the ground. And that's it."

He waited for Barnwell to ask him the question he dreaded —was the gear still down, as per the revised manual? Barney didn't. But his next sentence explained why.

"Well, there's no question but that you followed the manual. Bengsten says the actuating cylinders on both the nose and main gear were almost destroyed. He never saw cylinders in worse shape. But as far as he can tell, the gear was down. You'd think it would have given you a cushion but you probably hit harder than you realized. Anything else you can remember?"

"I wish," McKay said, "there were a few things I could forget."

He knew then his reputation and probably his career had

been saved by a freak circumstance, just as his life had been saved by a one-in-a-million shot. The left side of the cockpit staying intact, and then breaking away from the fuselage to stay clear of the fire, that had been a miracle. But so was the damage to the actuating cylinders. Never, in all the crashes he had investigated or studied, had he ever heard of these components being so badly mangled that a Systems team couldn't tell for certain whether the gear was down or up at impact. The fire must have been responsible—so destructively complete that it left inconclusive evidence. Or, McKay thought grimly, it may have even falsified the evidence. He already was weighing Barnwell's confident assumption that the manual had been followed against that nagging, fuzzy suspicion about his final command.

Bengsten interviewed him, too, and was so openly sympathetic and decent that McKay was embarrassed. He insisted on coming over to McKay's house rather than talking to him in the formal atmosphere of a Midwest or CAB office.

"Just a chat between two old friends, Mac," he said. "I don't even want you to regard it as part of the investigation. I've already got Barney's report."

He came over that night, admired the children, and endeared himself to Barbara, while Mac was in the kitchen mixing drinks, by whispering: "You have nothing to worry about. He's a fine captain who ran into unbelievable bad luck. There's no pilot error in this one."

They went downstairs to the den and talked for more than an hour. Mostly, Bengsten questioned him about the weather information Flight 510 had received.

"They really loaded the dice against you," he said. "No RVR working, a misleading weather advisory just before you went into final approach. And there's more to it than that. We haven't dredged up all the dirt yet, but there was a complete breakdown of communications between the Weather Bureau and the tower. It'll all come out at the hearing."

"Which is when?" McKay asked.

"About two more weeks. Tentatively, April twentieth. Mac,

I shouldn't say this but I've got to. Speaking as director of the Bureau of Safety, the investigation still is in progress. Speaking as Alfred Bengsten, I think you can go back to the line and resume flying. For my dough, you didn't have any more to do with that accident than I did."

"There's that small matter of the tail skid touching," McKay said quietly. "That's why we impacted. I may have overrotated."

"Think that if you want, but the facts are against it. One, we found your power settings were at maximum. You couldn't have gotten any more power if you had gotten out and pushed. Two, you were committed to a landing in a DC-7, which ain't no Electra. By the time you configured to takeoff, she was already settling. Were you watching your artificial horizon indicator?"

"That's the last instrument I remember monitoring. I was starting to check rate of climb when she hit. The horizon indicator was normal."

"Even if it wasn't, I couldn't hang you for overrotating. That gyro will stick if you accelerate fast. Chances are it wasn't even giving you the right horizon. And one more thing, Mac, in case you're still feeling guilty. You had to transition from visual reference to pure instruments in about one tenth of a second. A pilot can get away with that if he's lucky. You weren't."

Bengsten left a few minutes later. He had never mentioned the gear.

McKay wanted to go back to the line and Barnwell was tempted to let him, but Shea said no when Barney suggested it.

"There's too much of a possibility that he's lost his confidence, Barney. Wait till after the CAB hearing. He'll be in the clear then."

"Why not let him fly copilot a couple of trips?"

"That smacks too much of a demotion. Almost punishment. No, leave him rest a little longer. He's been through hell. Give him a check ride if you want—that'll keep him happy until the hearing."

The check ride was uneventful, although McKay admittedly was nervous. Barney didn't let him off easy. He even threw a practice missed approach at him and nodded with satisfaction as McKay waited until a positive rate of climb had been established before calling for gear up.

"No problem, Mac," he said after they landed. "When the hearing's over, bid a regular schedule for May. I'll fly with you myself as copilot for a couple of trips the end of this month."

Only Barbara was aware something was eating at McKay's insides. She knew he was sleeping poorly and she caught him a couple of times staring vacantly off into space. At first she took it for granted he was reliving the accident, but something told her his trouble went deeper than a painful memory.

Two nights before the CAB hearing was to open, he tossed and turned, unable to sleep. She turned on the light and kissed him.

"Something bothering you, honey?"

"Things in general, Barbara. Maybe I should sleep on the couch a couple of nights. I hate to keep disturbing you."

"You're not disturbing me. I just wish I could help. I know you're thinking about the accident."

"Think about it. And dream about it. I must have seen Jerry and Scotty a thousand times the last few weeks."

"Honey, they'd tell you it wasn't your fault. You won't be able to start flying again if you keep this up. That's what you want, isn't it? You don't want to quit because of what happened?"

"No, I don't," McKay said slowly. "More than anything else, I want to go back to the line. As captain."

"And you will. Barney told you to bid trips for May. And to plan on flying before the end of this month. When the hearing's over, things'll look brighter."

"Guess I'll go get a Coke or something. Want anything?"

"No, you go ahead. Don't stay up, Mac. You need your sleep."

He went into the kitchen, opened a Coke, and took it into the living room. He sat in his favorite chair and thumbed through some already-opened mail for the want of anything better to do. One of the envelopes bore the official letterhead of the Civil Aeronautics Board. He took out the letter and re-read it for at least the fifth time.

Captain McDonald McKay
9171 Berkshire Drive
Fairfax, Virginia

Dear Captain McKay:
You are hereby requested to attend a public hearing on an accident involving an aircraft of U.S. registry, N820B, Douglas DC-7B, Midwest Airlines, on the night of March 28, 1963, at Idlewild International Airport.

The hearing will commence April 20 in the ballroom of the International Hotel, Idlewild, Jamaica, Long Island, at 10 A.M. EST. You will be called as a witness.

Very truly yours,
Jerome Simpson, Secretary
Civil Aeronautics Board

He sat in semidarkness for a long time, the letter resting in his lap, his eyes fixed on the fireplace mantel, where the little domino perched.

The ballroom of the International Hotel was jammed when McKay arrived with Tom Dayton and Snorkel. O'Brian was there, having frantically traded trips to get the time off. He came too late to sit with Barbara, who had insisted on coming, too.

The physical setup of the room was the same as McKay had seen at so many accident hearings. The hearing panel sat behind a long table, which was covered with green felt, with ashtrays and the inevitable water pitchers. There were six men on the panel, headed by CAB Chairman Charles Boyle. Two CAB hearing examiners and three men from the Bureau of Safety, including Al Bengsten, comprised the remainder.

The witness chair was in front of the panel, and off to one side was the official stenographer. The tables where the interested parties sat were about ten feet from the panel and behind them were twenty rows of seats for spectators and witnesses waiting to be called.

A buzz of muted conversation spread through the room when McKay arrived.

"That's the pilot," a fat woman in back of Barbara whispered to her companion. "I saw his picture in the paper. Wonder how he feels with all them innocent people dead."

Barbara winced. She had said nothing to her husband, but twice—when he had been at the airport conferring with Barnwell—there had been crank calls. Sick, perverted minds getting orgiastic satisfaction from cruelty. Another bit of residue from an air crash, and one that never made the papers.

A man's voice, pitched evilly low, had said, "How do you like being married to a murderer?" Then he had hung up.

And a woman: "You don't know me, Mrs. McKay, but your husband should have been the one to die. He was probably drunk when he crashed. All those pilots are godless drunkards. That's what caused the crash. He's . . ."

Barbara had hung up.

The fat woman behind her reeked of cheap perfume and Barbara felt nauseous. Maybe after the lunch break she could find a seat next to Paddy. That damned female slob. She had resurrected the memory of the crank calls. An occupational hazard of a pilot's wife, Barbara knew. It had happened to others and would always happen. There was no use rationalizing that cranks were mentally ill. Their calls still inflicted needless pain.

Her bitter meditations were interrupted by the banging of the chairman's gavel. The room stilled. Charles Boyle, a big man four inches over six feet and ruggedly handsome, officially opened the public hearing into the accident involving an aircraft of U.S. registry, N820B, a Douglas DC-7B.

"Ladies and gentlemen," he began. "We are here to determine, as far as humanly possible, the facts concerning the tragedy that occurred on March twenty-eighth.

"Let me caution all who will be called to testify that you will be taking an oath. The truth is all we seek. As in all CAB accident investigations that have preceded this one, and all those that follow, we have and will operate on a simple axiom. Find out what happened, so it will not happen again. There is no room in an accident investigation for buck-passing, whitewashing, sweeping dirt under rugs, or evasion of responsibility.

"I will ask our chief hearing examiner, Mr. Chamberlin, to call the first witness."

Irv Chamberlin, an old hand at CAB hearings, riffled through some papers, taking his sweet time. Eventually he called out: "Mr. Edward Slater of the Bureau of Safety."

Mr. Slater was duly sworn in and launched into a matter-of-fact description of the fatal flight, its logged takeoff time from Atlanta, and the routine aspects of the trip up to the accident and the fact that aircraft and crew were properly certificated in accordance with the Civil Air Regulations as formulated by the Federal Aviation Agency.

"The facts of this accident obtained thus far in the investigation indicate that weather and the means of reporting same, including communications addressed to Flight 510, were a major factor in the accident," Slater continued in a dry voice. "For the time being it is sufficient to point out that the following events transpired:

"One—there was no Precision Approach Radar, known as PAR, available on the night of the accident. This condition was made known to the crew of 510 before they left Atlanta, through a NOTAM attached to their Dispatch clearance and the same information was included in the weather advisory given them prior to departure from Atlanta.

"Two—while the flight was en route to New York, the TEL-autograph transreceivers in the FAA control tower, as well as the IFR room, became inoperative. This equipment is utilized to communicate written weather information between the Weather Bureau office, located seven stories below, to the control tower and the IFR room. The FAA will testify later as to the reasons for this malfunction.

"Three—shortly before Flight 510 was given its final approach clearance, the direct voice communication line, otherwise known as the hot line, also became inoperative. This was not a malfunction, however. The line was taken out of service by the FAA and telephone company for purposes which also will be the subject of later FAA testimony.

"Four—the Idlewild Runway Visual Range, or RVR, digital readout displays in the control tower for runway 4R, where the accident occurred, were malfunctioning and had been for some time preceding the crash. The crew of Flight 510 was advised of this inoperative aid. However, it must also be mentioned that the RVR recorder trace located in the Idlewild Weather Bureau office was operating satisfactorily.

"Five—Weather Bureau personnel who maintain the equipment were informed of the malfunction in the RVR display located in the control tower at 2015. That is, 8:15 P.M. EST, or one and a half hours before Flight 510 crashed.

"Six—the final weather advisory transmitted to Flight 510 was completed shortly before the aircraft was cleared to make its final approach. The exact wording of that advisory is contained in Exhibit A. The significant portion gave the crew a visibility of one mile with ground fog.

"And seven—at the time that final advisory was being furnished the crew of Flight 510, the RVR recorder trace in the Weather Bureau office was indicating visibility of one fourth of a mile on runway 4R. This information was not transmitted to the tower, nor to the flight."

Mr. Slater looked up expectantly.

"Mr. Slater," said Chairman Boyle, "while I don't want you to express any definite conclusions at this time, I'd appreciate having your estimate of the significance of the inoperative PAR."

"No significance, Mr. Chairman. The PAR is a very valuable landing aid and an excellent Air Traffic Control device. It is used to monitor the progress of ILS approaches, usually at the request of pilots. But the Bureau does not think it played a part, or rather that its inoperative condition played a part, in this accident. Flight 510's final approach was an ILS approach, made satisfactorily. PAR was not required for the successful conclusion of such an approach."

"I gather, Mr. Slater, the Bureau feels there was considerable significance attached to the malfunction of other equipment—such as the RVR and the communications between the Weather Bureau and the tower."

"The facts speak for themselves, Mr. Chairman. The Bureau naturally hopes that the relevance of these malfunctions, and the procedures for transmitting weather information to flights, will be brought out in the questioning of future witnesses."

"Any questions from the panel? Midwest? Douglas? Pratt & Whitney? FAA? Weather Bureau? ALPA? No questions? All right, we'll proceed."

Boyle conferred with Chamberlin. The hearing examiner nodded.

"Mr. Richard A. Brownell of the FAA."

Brownell, a stern-faced man wearing a loud sports jacket, was sworn in and began reading a prepared statement.

"My name is Richard Brownell. I am chief of the Navigation Aids Installation Division, Eastern Region, Federal Aviation Agency. My testimony this morning concerns the modernization of Air Traffic Control facilities and equipment at Idlewild International Airport. Basically, it was in the course of this modernization program that certain facilities at Idlewild were rendered temporarily inoperative. First, let me list briefly the major projects involved in this modernization process."

Brownell went on to cite the various improved installations

and the FAA's plan to shut down secondary facilities—such as PAR—during low traffic periods, while new equipment replaced old. He included the direct telephone connection between the Weather Bureau and the control tower, the hot line.

"This circuit was unavailable at the time of the accident because it was being transferred to a new and vastly more efficient telephone system that is part of the modernization program," he continued.

"Just a minute, Mr. Brownell," Chairman Boyle interrupted. "This circuit was shut down *after* the autograph transreceivers went on the blink?"

"Yes sir. The disconnect of the so-called hot line had been planned previously. It automatically was taken out of service at a prearranged time."

"For God's sake!" exploded Boyle unjudicially. "You mean you let the hot line go down, knowing that the only other means of communicating between the tower and the Weather Bureau was out of order?"

Brownell flushed. "The transreceivers were not the only means of communication," he said. "There were normal telephone lines that could have been used."

"But weren't," said Boyle.

"That's not my department," the witness said hurriedly. "May I continue?"

"Please do," Boyle said dryly.

Brownell emphasized that the "basic consideration in planning the modernization program was to avoid interference with or outage of essential services and *primary* facilities." He sucked on the word "primary" with special emphasis.

"It was concluded that the project would require some minimal outage of secondary, supplemental, or redundant facilities and that this would be acceptable if fully coordinated and confined wherever possible to periods of low traffic activity," Brownell wound up.

"Any questions from the panel?" asked Boyle.

Al Bengsten peered at the witness. "Mr. Brownell, the inoperative RVR. Was that outage part of the modernization program?"

"No sir. The RVR outage was a mechanical malfunction. The RVR display in the tower became inoperative at 8:30 P.M. and was reported to the Weather Bureau which maintains this particular equipment. The malfunction was included in the weather sequence transmitted to all flights at 9 P.M. and thereafter."

"No further questions," Bengsten said.

Boyle called the roll again. Chamberlin then summoned to the stand Warren Corley, assistant deputy administrator of the FAA's eastern region. He sat down as if the chair were wired for an execution, but his voice was firm and clear.

"The Federal Aviation Agency is anxious to help ascertain the cause of this accident and to take whatever corrective action is necessary to avoid recurrence under similar circumstances," he began. "If FAA procedures, methods, or personnel were in any way contributory, the Agency will act instantly without waiting for a formal determination of the probable cause by the CAB.

"For the record, FAA would like to disclose now that a number of corrective measures already have been taken or are in the process of being taken. If I may list these, Mr. Chairman?"

"The panel will be most interested, Mr. Corley."

"We have ordered ATC procedural changes which will require the transmission of all operationally significant weather information in terminal areas to approaching aircraft. The Agency shortly will undertake an experimental procedure of determining runway visibility when an RVR is inoperative. This will involve the utilization of observers, trained and certificated by the Weather Bureau, who will be stationed in the immediate vicinity of runways at high density airports such as Idlewild and O'Hare during fog and other restricted atmospheric conditions. They will be posted strategically the moment an RVR outage is reported. Finally, we are conducting on a priority basis conferences with the Weather

Bureau designed to prevent any future breakdown of communications between the Weather Bureau's observation posts and the ATC facility responsible for transmitting weather sequences to flights. We are confident that from these meetings will come a fail-safe procedure for advising aircraft of significant weather information up to the moment of touchdown. Now, I will be glad to answer questions."

"Thank you, Mr. Corley," smiled Boyle. "The Board appreciates and compliments the FAA for its prompt actions. Any questions from the panel? Mr. Bengsten?"

"Mr. Corley, I'd like to establish the exact role played by these various equipment malfunctions and the weather reporting procedures, insofar as this particular accident was concerned. The reforms you cited seem to indicate a major role."

"I prefer to use the phrase 'corrective action,' or possibly 'preventative action,' rather than 'reform,'" the FAA official said.

"Well, it doesn't make any difference what you call it. You've definitely ordered some moves designed to keep a similar accident from happening again. Now, I'd like to know why you ordered them."

"Why? Because there is evidence that certain deficiencies in procedures may have contributed to the accident."

"'May have' is putting it mildly," noted Bengsten. "From depositions taken prior to this hearing, and subsequent direct testimony, it is apparent that Flight 510 was not given adequate information as to the prevailing visibility on runway 4R. Is that correct?"

"It is only too apparent, I regret to say."

"So let's find out exactly why. The sequence advising the crew of one-mile visibility on runway 4R was transmitted just before the flight made its final approach. But we're also told that the Weather Bureau's own observation at this time showed only a quarter of a mile, which was below legal minimums. Mr. Corley, where did the tower get its one-mile estimate?"

"The tower was located seven stories above the Weather

Bureau. This was ground fog. As far as the tower was concerned, visibility was a mile."

"And the breakdown in communications at this point re-
sulted in the more accurate and up-to-date measurement from
the Weather Bureau not reaching the tower?"

"I've already testified that there should be no repeat performance of such a breakdown. Yes, there was a breakdown.
But I might point out that numerous other flights landed
safely immediately preceding and following Flight 510. Visibility measurements kept shifting all night long."

Bengsten could not help casting a glance at McKay. "Are
you implying that the crew of Flight 510 should have been
able to land safely, Mr. Corley? Is that the FAA's position?"

"I'm not implying anything, Mr. Bengsten. As I said before, the ground fog on runway 4R was intermittent. The
patches kept drifting. We had one TWA flight refuse a takeoff
clearance. But an American flight just ahead of it took off
without difficulty. The same was true for aircraft landing.
Some flights encountered little or no trouble at all. Others
had to abandon their approaches. Flight 510 was one of the
latter."

"Flight 510," Bengsten said crisply, "was given a one-mile
visibility estimate and therefore committed itself unknowingly
to an illegal landing—in ground fog so thick that the fire
trucks couldn't find the burning wreckage for a half hour. So
my question, Mr. Corley, is simply this: in view of fog conditions existing that night, and admitting that hindsight is only
too easy, do you think Idlewild should have been closed to
incoming traffic around the time of the accident?"

The room was fog-quiet. Corley did not answer immediately. Snorkel whispered to McKay: "If Bengsten keeps this
up, we can go home. He's hanging the FAA."

Corley, who had spent his life in both government and
aviation, had courage. His hesitation was natural. Bengsten in
effect had asked him to admit at least partial culpability.

"Mr. Bengsten," he said finally, "as you pointed out, hindsight is a very safe form of second-guessing. Based on what

we know now concerning the failures in communications, and the after-the-fact emotional knowledge that twenty-four persons died, I would have to answer yes. Idlewild should have been closed to incoming traffic. Does that answer your question, sir?"

"It does, Mr. Corley. And I compliment you on your honesty."

Again, Bengsten permitted himself a glance at McKay. A faint smile played on his lips.

The next witness was from the Weather Bureau, a nervous man who gave the impression he knew exactly how the Christians felt when they were being thrown to the lions. His testimony added nothing new nor significant, except that he explained why the quarter-mile visibility measurement available on the ground was not relayed over normal telephone lines to the tower.

"We had only two men on duty," he admitted. "The observer who took the fourth-of-a-mile reading was going to call the tower but he couldn't raise them. Line was busy. Then he got sidetracked by something else."

"Is this shortage of personnel chronic?" Boyle asked.

"Not now, sir. We've added more men since the accident. That's one of the things we agreed on in our meetings with FAA, the ones Mr. Corley mentioned. And we've changed our procedures. If the hot line's out, or if for any reasons we can't raise the tower on the regular phones or via TEL-autograph, the minute we record any drastic observation change, we'll deliver it to the tower in person and on the double."

The afternoon session featured testimony from several survivors, including the two stewardesses. The former praised the latter for their courage and coolheaded efficiency, while also reporting that the landing seemed completely normal until the moment of impact.

Norma Drum and Mickey Fletcher told the hearing that they prepared for the landing as they would have under any circumstances, checking seat belts and for still-lit cigarettes. Their first warning of trouble came when they heard the engines surge. They were in the rear lounge, and both said they felt the impact of the tail skid.

"Did the attitude of the aircraft seem abnormal in any way," Bengsten asked Norma. "Was the nose higher than usual on, say, a takeoff?"

"No sir. The engines were all I noticed. When they sounded so loud, I said to Mickey, 'I guess we're going around again,' and then the next thing I knew we had hit the ground and there was fire. We started to drop the emergency chute out of the main door but then I realized the gear must have collapsed because we were flat on the ground. We shoved most of the people out of the main door, but some left through breaks in the fuselage. The forward part of the cabin was all in flames. We tried to go up there but we started to choke from the smoke and we left ourselves."

"You girls deserve a world of credit," Chairman Boyle said. "The presence of mind and bravery you displayed under such conditions, and considering the fact that you had just graduated from stewardess school, is a tribute both to yourselves and the quality of the training Midwest gave you. If there are no further questions, Miss Drum, you and your flying partner are excused."

As Norma and Mickey left they looked in McKay's direction and smiled their encouragement. That simple little gesture of loyalty saddened the captain. For it made him think of Kohlmeir and Scott again.

At 4 p.m., the chairman recessed the hearing until 10 a.m. the next day.

For the second day Barbara made sure she had a seat next to Paddy. She was terribly worried about Mac. At supper the night before he had little to say and not even Snorkel's jokes could budge him from his depression.

"He's been that way since the crash," she told Paddy while they were waiting for Boyle to bang his gavel.

"It's understandable," O'Brian said. "He still feels guilty about the copilot and flight engineer, let alone the passengers.

He'll be okay when this is over. That's all he needs, just to be told officially he wasn't responsible. And from the way the hearing's going, there isn't any doubt about it."

There wasn't any doubt about it from the second day of testimony, either.

Barnwell was called and recited the qualifications of the flight crew. He testified at length on McKay's record. He read the chief pilot's summations of the captain's last six check rides and supplied on his own his firm conviction that "Captain McKay is not just a good pilot, but far above average in every phase—technical proficiency, attitude, relations with fellow crew members, ability to command, sense of responsibility, strict adherence to all rules, and unquestioning devotion to duty."

Bengsten asked: "Did his last check ride include a practice go-around or abandoned approach?"

"It did, sir."

"Did Captain McKay receive a satisfactory grade?"

"No sir, he received an excellent grade."

"I notice, Captain Barnwell, that in the copy of the appropriate DC-7 manual Midwest filed as part of its general deposition, page 23 is labeled 'revised.' This is the page outlining the specific steps to be taken in the event a pilot has to abandon a landing. Would you tell us, sir, what revisions were involved?"

"Only one. We had a near-accident occur under conditions very similar to this crash. A DC-7 crew encountered unexpected fog and executed a balked landing. In accordance with the manual in effect at the time, the captain advanced the throttles, ordered the gear raised, and then gave the command for 20-degree flaps. Before the aircraft climbed out, two props touched the ground. The pilot managed to retain control and continued the climb. In studying the circumstances of this incident, we decided that leaving the gear down in the initial stages of this maneuver would provide a safety margin if for any reason the aircraft failed to climb."

"The reason for raising the gear originally was to reduce drag, wasn't it?"

"Yes sir, but we ascertained in subsequent test flights that drag wasn't as great as we had assumed. Because the chances for a successful balked landing are not always in the pilot's favor, we felt that the gear should be left down to provide an impact cushion. We realized that under the type of emergency encountered in this nonfatal incident, and certainly encountered by Flight 510, it was only too possible that in the initial stage of a balked landing, a DC-7 would tend to sink before the pilot could establish a positive climb rate. Therefore, the revised procedure requires the pilot to make sure he's climbing out before he raises the gear."

"And the crew of Flight 510 was appraised of the manual revision prior to this accident?"

"Naturally."

"Thank you, Captain Barnwell. Mr. Chairman, for the record, Exhibit B, pages 3 through 23, contains the findings of the Systems, Structures, and Power Plant teams. It would seem apropos at this time to summarize their reports, for the benefit of the panel. Briefly, the teams established that at the moment of impact, N820B was developing METO or maximum power. The flaps had been moved to the required 20 degrees. There was inconclusive but reasonable evidence that both the nose gear and main gear were down. If you have no objections, Mr. Chairman, I would appreciate having Examiner Chamberlin call the witness from Douglas."

"I see no objection," Boyle replied. "Mr. Chamberlin, if you please."

Sworn in was Earl Fisher, assistant chief pilot of the Douglas Aircraft Company, a swarthy-faced man with a bristling mustache that gave him the appearance of a reincarnated pirate. Bengsten took over the bulk of the questioning.

"Mr. Fisher, would you turn to page 23 of Exhibit B?"

Fisher found the page. There was a rustle of paper throughout the room as those with copies of the prehearing exhibits and depositions also located page 23.

"Now," Bengsten continued, "you have before you a summary of the findings I have just cited regarding the configuration of aircraft N820B at time of impact. Gear down. Flaps 20. Gross weight eighty-five thousand pounds. Power application METO. Got it?"

"Yes sir."

"Would you give us, please, the performance characteristics of a DC-7B, under those power and airframe configurations, during a go-around from an altitude of about fifty feet."

The Douglas pilot consulted a chart he already had taken from a briefcase. He spoke slowly as he read from the chart.

"Using the landing configuration of gear down, flaps at 20 degrees, gross weight eighty-five thousand pounds, the aircraft should accelerate at approximately 1.7 knots per second. Even with the gross landing weight at the allowable maximum of ninety-six thousand pounds, acceleration would be at 1.52 knots per second. That would be sufficient to achieve an airspeed of 115 knots which would allow rotation into a balked-landing climb. With the lower landing weight of eighty-five thousand pounds, speed at rotation would be 135 knots."

His figures were going over the heads of most of the spectators, but Bengsten nodded. "What would be your angle of attack, or your angle of climb, at 135 knots?"

"With maximum power? And flaps at 20?"

"Yes."

The Douglas man looked at his chart again. "Seven degrees."

Bengsten tapped his forefinger on page 23 several times. "The consensus of these Structures, Power Plant, and Systems reports," he said, "is that N820B was rotating properly at seven degrees when the tail skid contacted the ground. They indicate that the aircraft had accelerated from 115 knots to 135 knots with the gear down and with 20-degree flaps. Mr. Fisher, is there any explanation why the abandoned landing maneuver was not successful?"

Fisher shook his head. "The tail skid should not have touched," he replied.

"Was it possible that the aircraft yawed or rolled?"

"Not if all engines were accelerating evenly. And from this exhibit, I take it the power output was symmetrical."

Boyle noticed that at the ALPA table Snorkel had his hand up like a schoolboy trying to get the teacher's attention.

"Captain Snodgrass, do you have a question?"

"Yes sir."

"Proceed."

"Mr. Fisher, the Douglas performance chart to which you've been referring is based on optimum operating conditions, is it not?"

Fisher smiled. "If you mean we got these specifications on a clear day with no fog to worry about, the answer's yes."

"But suppose there was fog. Wouldn't a balked-landing attempt under the conditions encountered by Flight 510 introduce some variables to your figures?"

The Douglas pilot still had a little grin on his face. He knew what Snorkel was driving at. As a Douglas employee, he wished Snorkel had kept quiet. As a fellow pilot, he was glad Snorkel hadn't.

"Under those conditions," he admitted, "I wouldn't vouch for any set of specifications. The main variable would be the pilot's reaction time when he tried to transition from visual reference to instruments. Transition would have to be accomplished in not much more time than it takes to blink your eyes."

Bengsten, who also was mentally thanking Snorkel, cut in. "In other words, Mr. Fisher, all the data you have and we have indicating that the aircraft should have climbed out safely is pretty much theory?"

"It all depends on what was happening in the cockpit," Fisher conceded. "All the pilot had to do was delay a second or two and he was in trouble. The transition to instruments in that fog would have supplied such a delay. He may have rotated a little too late. Or he might have rotated a little too soon—before he completed transition. That would have been enough to toss the book figures out the window. From then on, he was operating with luck, not skill."

Bengsten's final question broke the silence in the tense room. "As a pilot, Mr. Fisher, what chance would you have given him for getting away with this balked landing? What were his odds?"

"Forty-sixty, maybe. Or sixty-forty. It's hard to tell. I'll tell you one thing, and this is strictly a personal opinion from a guy who thinks a helluva lot of the DC-7—I'm glad I wasn't in that boy's shoes."

The next five witnesses were pilots from Eastern, TWA, United, American, and Delta testifying as to the fog conditions the night of the accident.

A few minutes later the chairman recessed the second day's session, with the announcement that testimony would be taken tomorrow from the captain of Flight 510.

Once more, the dinner the McKays had that night with Snorkel, and Paddy was a strange combination of confidence and gloom. His comrades kept telling him he had nothing to worry about. They thought his lack of response meant he still was worried about the outcome.

"What the hell are you concerned about?" Paddy scolded. "There wasn't one iota of evidence against the crew. I never saw such a cut-and-dried case."

"Maybe," McKay said. "Would you guys excuse us? I'd like to talk to Barbara for a while and I need some sleep. Tomorrow's the big day."

"It sure is," Snorkel chortled. "Tomorrow it'll all be over."

The McKays walked through the chilly streets from the restaurant to their hotel, holding hands. McKay said nothing. Wisely, neither did Barbara. She sensed the boiling crisis and the cancerous conflict inside her husband.

In their room he took off his coat and hung it in the closet. Incongruously, she thought what a carefully neat person he was—among his other virtues. She waited for him to speak, and watched him silently pace up and down the small room for a good five minutes.

"Okay," he said, "I guess I owe it to you. What's been eating me up."

"If you want to tell me, Mac, fine. If not, I'll understand."

"I've got to tell you. The question is whether I should tell anyone else. Barbara, all you've heard about no pilot error the past few weeks, particularly these past two days, could be only partially true. I think I caused the crash. I think I killed Jerry and Scotty and twenty-two innocent passengers."

She stared at him in disbelief.

"But, Mac . . ."

"Listen, honey. I'm getting off scot-free because of a freak. They found the actuating cylinders of the nose and main gear in what they thought was a down position. Nobody's really sure. But they seem to have taken it for granted right from the start that I left the gear down—down, Barbara, like the manual says. Down, like it was decided after Sam Runnion's accident. Leave it down so if you louse up a balked landing, you'll have a cushion. But I can't take it for granted. I think I told Jerry 'Gear up.' I seem to remember giving him the palm-up hand signal right after we hit the fog. If I did, that's why twenty-four people died—because I raised the goddamned gear. Only I'm the one guy who suspects it."

Barbara stood up and rushed into his arms. From that contact they both seemed to find strength.

"What do I do, Barbara? Confess and get clobbered by FAA?"

"Confess? What is there to confess, Mac? You said yourself you aren't sure. Why don't you just believe what they believe? The evidence is in your favor, not against you. Let it go at that."

"I wish I could. I can't. They're ready to hang this one on the FAA and Weather Bureau. They deserve it. They trapped me into making a mistake—if I really made one. But that's the point. If there's a doubt in my own mind, the accident hasn't been solved no matter what the evidence says. I don't deserve to be whitewashed any more than Les deserved to be crucified."

"What happens if you raise your doubts?"

"I don't know. They'll sure have second thoughts about assuming the gear was down. Then there'd be a pretty good chance of tagging me with at least partial responsibility. Or they could figure I was wrong about thinking I gave the wrong command. I only wish to hell I was positive about what happened. I could swear I goofed but those actuating cylinders say maybe I didn't. It would be so damned easy to let those cylinders do the testifying for me."

Barbara's face was pale and her eyes were filled with tears that refused to fall. "Mac, I know you've always told pilots not to lie. But this time you don't know what the truth is yourself."

He sat down on the bed and took both her hands in his.

"That's my trouble," he said. "In this case, doubt and guilt are almost synonymous. You asked me what there is to confess tomorrow. Doubt. And it hurts just as much as if I knew what happened in that cockpit. Maybe more. Sure I've told pilots to stand up like men and admit mistakes. In a way, that's easy. It's black versus white. I could keep my mouth shut—and there's a pretty good chance I'd get away with it because nobody thinks I'm guilty. And maybe I'm not, Barbara. Maybe I'm not."

"I don't think you are," she said. "But whatever happens, I love you very much."

For a long, long time that almost sleepless night, he fought with his memory so that facts, not conscience, would guide him. But when he finally dozed off into fitful sleep, he still could not be sure whether his final order had been a death sentence for those who trusted him.

"The final witness," said Chairman Boyle, "is Captain McKay."

He walked briskly to the witness chair, scarcely hearing

Snorkel's "Good luck, Mac." He took the oath, sat down, and crossed his long legs.

Hearing Examiner Chamberlin began the questioning. "You were the captain on Flight 510 the night of March twenty-eighth?"

"Yes sir."

"Would you give this panel as detailed an account as possible of the events leading up to the accident?"

McKay recounted what the panel already knew.

"And the accident itself, Captain. Exactly what transpired in the cockpit?"

"We made a normal ILS approach. First Officer Kohlmeir called out when he saw the approach lights. We . . ."

"You were flying the aircraft?"

"Yes sir. I would estimate we were about one thousand feet past the runway threshold when we flew into the fog. Because of a complete loss of visual reference, I decided on a go-around. I wish I could tell you why it failed. I can't."

Barbara's heart was pounding.

"You felt your rotation was proper?"

"As far as I know, yes, rotation was proper."

"You can offer this panel no explanation as to why the tail skid hit the ground?"

"No sir. I appreciated the remarks made by Mr. Fisher. They showed an understanding of the situation I . . . we were in."

"Do you have questions, Mr. Chairman? Any other panel members? Mr. Bengsten?"

"Captain McKay, was your decision to land based on the one-mile visibility report, the last you received?"

"Yes sir, it was."

"You would not have attempted the landing if the weather report had more accurately described the fog condition?"

Bengsten still was trying to erase the last hint of possible pilot error, McKay told himself. You're not being objective or impartial, you lovable S.O.B.

"I still would have made the approach if we had been given

three quarters of a mile. Anything lower than that, I'm not sure. Obviously we would have diverted to Philadelphia if we knew runway 4R was down to a quarter mile, which would have been below minimums."

"Thank you, Captain. So as far as you're concerned, you followed the prescribed procedures for a balked landing?" It was more of a statement than a question.

McKay let a couple of heartbeats elapse before he spoke. "No sir, I'm not sure that I did follow them."

Bengsten, already having anticipated an affirmative response, had leaned back in his chair satisfied that the hearing was over. He stared at McKay as if he thought the pilot was insane. Now he leaned forward so far that his chin almost rested on the green felt.

"You're not sure you followed the prescribed procedures?"

"In one respect, a very important respect, I think I may have violated them."

Snorkel was gripping Tom Dayton's arm. "Jesus Christ," he muttered. "He's gone off his rocker."

Barbara kept watching her husband's face. It was calm, even nonchalant. She had the crazy idea McKay was enjoying this.

"In what respect, Captain McKay?" Bengsten's voice was hoarse.

"I cannot remember whether I ordered First Officer Kohlmeir to raise the gear. But I think I did. Verbally and with a hand signal. Immediately preceding the order for flaps 20. As was prescribed in the old manual. I only wish I could testify more positively on this point but I can't."

"You were aware of the amended procedure?" Bengsten's tone was virtually a plea that McKay give a negative reply.

"Yes sir, I was. I was even present the day the new procedure was discussed with Captain Barnwell and Mr. Shea, the vice president of operations."

Bengsten desperately changed course. "Captain, you've seen the report of the Systems team. It found no evidence that the gear had been raised. In fact, the actuating cylinders—as far as could be determined—indicated that the gear was down."

"I know it, Mr. Bengsten. I would like very much to accept that evidence. But it still does not resolve the conflict in my own mind. I think there's at least a strong possibility that I did not leave the gear down until a positive rate of climb was established."

Bengsten in his emotion forgot the protocol of addressing witnesses. "Mac, you've been through a terrible experience. Your memory may be playing tricks."

McKay looked at him gratefully, and shook his head. "Perhaps, Mr. Bengsten. But I couldn't swear to it. All I know is that I definitely do not remember following the correct procedure. And I have a hazy recollection that I did just the opposite. I'm sorry I can't be more helpful."

Al Bengsten frowned unhappily.

"So am I, Captain McKay," he signed. "So am I."

McKay walked into John Shea's office a week later. Barnwell was there, wearing a cheerful smile.

"How are you, Mac?" Shea asked.

"Fine, Johnny. Just waiting for the other shoe to drop."

"Shoe? Oh, you mean what's gonna happen to you. Well, that's what I called you in for. Barney and I have been discussing it and I just got through talking to the FAA. I've got some fairly good news for you."

He waited expectantly for McKay to say something, felt disappointed that he didn't, and continued. "Mac, you drew a three-month suspension of your ATR. You'll have to fly copilot for about ninety days. But it's not an exorbitant penalty, considering . . . ah . . ."

He did not finish the sentence. McKay finished it for him. "Considering that twenty-four persons got killed, Johnny?"

Shea bobbed his head, grateful that McKay had said it.

"FAA could have been a lot tougher, Mac," Barnwell broke in. "They usually are when fatalities are involved."

"They should have been tougher," McKay said quietly,

"but I'm grateful. To them and to both of you. Anyway, it doesn't make much difference. I'm resigning from Midwest."

"You're what?" Barnwell's normally high voice rose even higher.

"You're out of your mind!" Shea said angrily. He rose out of his swivel chair. "Now look here, my fine bucko. Don't go getting noble on me."

McKay smiled, and it had the effect of tossing cold water on Shea's anger. "Sit down, Johnny, while I explain."

Shea sat down with a final flurry of protest. "Mac, you're assuming guilt when there's more than a fifty-fifty chance there was no guilt. You're ignoring the evidence of the actuating cylinders. Dammit, Mac, it's more positive than your own vague memory. So get rid of that cross you're bearing. The reason FAA's being lenient is because there's doubt you goofed."

McKay was so calm that Shea and Barnwell would have thought he actually seemed happy. Except that both suddenly noticed the pilot's eyes were bloodshot.

"I've thought this all through and I've talked it over with Barbara," McKay began. "She doesn't quite agree with me but that's another matter. Look, I don't want to quit. And I'm not trying to be noble. I'm trying to do what's best for me and for Midwest. I think I'm washed up as an airline pilot. I'm afraid I've lost my confidence and that's as bad as losing my eyesight."

"A good, stiff check ride will change your mind," Barnwell said hopefully.

"I could pass any check ride you threw at me," McKay said. "The question is how I'd react the next time I'm faced with a real emergency. Maybe I'd come through okay. But maybe I wouldn't. So why take a chance that I'm completely cured?"

"McKay," Shea said, biting off the words like a man biting off the end of a cigar and spitting out the stub, "you're not the first pilot who pulled a rock. You're not the first pilot who piled up a bunch of nightmares because he piled up an airplane. And you're not the first captain who got pushed back into the right seat. That's one purpose of the demotion—to let you get your confidence back. And our confidence in you."

"Furthermore, Mac," Barnwell interjected, "you have no reason to lose your confidence. Like Johnny said, you aren't even sure you made a mistake."

McKay shook his head. "It's not being sure that's killing me. If I were sure, I think I could live with it. I could take the demotion. I could fight my way back into the left seat. But so long as I don't know, so long as there are doubts, I think I'm a menace to every passenger and crew member who flies with me. Because I'm not sure, the memory of that flight will ride with me every mile and every hour."

"Every pilot who has a crash carries it inside him," Shea said.

"Sure. But at least he knows what happened. I don't. Put yourselves in my place, both of you. You know what kind of person I am, not only about flying but safety. Admitted guilt, the knowledge that you've done something wrong, is clean and final like surgery. The malignancy has been cut out. Mine is still inside me and always will be. I can't confess it, I can't get rid of it, and this is why I can't stay on the line. Could I speak out for ALPA, could I criticize FAA or CAB or some Congressman, when I can't be sure if I caused the deaths of twenty-four people who trusted me? Could I ever bawl out a copilot for carelessness or scold a stew who didn't know her manual? Could I preach safety from the pulpit of the left seat while I keep wondering whether I failed myself when the chips were down? I don't think I can. I'd rather draw a six-month suspension, even a year in the right seat, if I knew I was being punished for something I really did. Three months without knowing is a waste of time. When it's over, the doubts are still there. And always will be."

Shea and Barnwell sat silently, digesting McKay's reasoning. Barney started to say something but Shea interrupted him.

"Well, Mac, it's your decision. I wish you'd think it over again and stop in tomorrow."

"I will, Johnny. But I'm afraid my answer will be the same."

He walked out, leaving in his wake a stunned Barnwell and, surprisingly enough, a Shea who wore the expression of a man about to make an important decision.

"Why did you let him go, Johnny?" Barney complained. "That guilt complex of his is ninety degrees off course and you know it. He's not the kind of captain you let go that quickly. Not without trying to change his mind."

"I'm not so sure he's off course," Shea said. "He could be right. Not knowing for a guy like him could be worse than knowing."

"But are you gonna let him just walk out?"

Shea poked tobacco into a pipe, lit it, and watched the smoke curl toward the ceiling.

"Barney, did you ever stop to realize that Midwest doesn't have what every other major carrier in the United States has— namely, a full-time safety director? A man in charge of all the emergency training curriculae, for both pilots and stewardesses. Who can lecture, teach, and plan. Examine our emergency procedures and change 'em if they have to be changed. Keep up with what the rest of the industry is doing in safety work. Attend safety conferences. Represent us at accident investigations. Get the picture? Does it fit our boy?"

"It fits. Two questions. Would Kane buy a post like that and would Mac take it?"

"Kane's already bought it. He told me to find someone to fill it. As for Mac, he promised to come in tomorrow. I'll throw it at him and I've got a hunch he'll say yes. I've got Ben's okay for a salary equal to a fairly senior captain's—which for Mac would be a raise."

"Well," enthused Barnwell, "it sure as hell will make a happy ending."

Shea's homely face clouded over. "Not really, Barney. He'll miss that fourth stripe to the day he goes to his grave. What we'll be offering him is a sop to his conscience. An important job, yes, but it's too bad he couldn't choose between the job and staying in the left seat."

McKay left Shea's office and walked over to the terminal. On impulse he went out on the observation platform, conscious that he was repeating what he had done on that first day he reported to the chief pilot. That day, so very long ago, when he had been plagued with fear and uncertainty. That day he had looked down on the DC-3's and DC-4's below and had felt all doubts leave him.

Now he was looking down at a Midwest Electra and hearing the peculiar snarl of her Allison engines. It was a departing flight. The integral front cabin door tucked itself neatly into the fuselage. The ramp agent saluted the man in the left seat and the Electra turned slowly away.

So did Captain McDonald McKay.

Author's Postscript

With the exception of former Federal Aviation Administrator Elwood R. Quesada, the characters in this novel are entirely fictitious. If airline people think they can find themselves or friends portrayed therein, it will be only too natural because many of the characters are composites of real persons. Snorkel Snodgrass, for example, is drawn from the personalities of four airline captains.

Likewise, the accidents that are part of the story are based loosely on actual crashes to provide authenticity, but are imaginary in many details.

The accident involving McDonald McKay, however, had a counterpart in real life—an airliner that crashed while approaching New York International Airport. The captain of that flight had something in common with Captain McKay. He too was a crusader for air safety, an effective spokesman for all airline pilots, and a man whose own personal philosophy permitted no conflict in the search for truth. But while McKay is similar in these respects, his background, airline experiences, and personal life are totally fictitious.

And there is one other difference between the captain of real life and the captain of fiction. The real captain was killed in his crash, but failure to follow the prescribed manual was not involved. If this novel manages to capture his dedication to the cause of air safety, I would be pleased to have it regarded as an inadequate tribute to his memory.

I would like to express my gratitude to American Airlines for permission to use its Stewardess Creed (Chapter 6). It was written by Ann Flack, a former American stewardess. The Creed is displayed at American's Stewardess College in Fort Worth, and I felt that its sentiments were so representative of the stewardess profession that it deserved being a brief part of the story.

To my pilot and stewardess friends who read portions of the manuscript, supplied me with material, and offered valuable advice, my thanks. They undoubtedly will look askance at an occasional technical error—inadvertent, but sometimes deliberate for purely dramatic reasons or to simplify a highly complex situation for the lay reader.

And to my editor at Doubleday, Ellin K. Roberts, I hope this novel is worthy of her faith and encouragement throughout the project.

Robert J. Serling

Washington, D.C.
August 4, 1965